"The Sun and the Moon," Philip said, amused as he watched her. "Two fascinating jewels on one necklace."

"The Sun, a two-hundred-eighty-carat diamond of the first water, absolutely pure, brilliantly white, and according to legend a stone with a checkered past. I know about these jewels the same way I know about the Kohinoor or the Pitt—as stones I may admire, even lust after, but not as stones to risk my life for."

"When the motive is only money or acquisition, even diamonds can be resisted," Adrianne said, and started to rise, but he caught her hand. His grip was firmer than it should have been, and his eyes showed that he was no longer amused.

"When the motive is revenge, it should be resisted." Her hand flexed once in his, then lay passive. Control, he thought, could be both blessing and curse. "Revenge clouds the mind so that you can't think coolly. Passions of any kind lead to mistakes."

"I have only one passion." The candlelight flickered over her face, deepening the hollows of her cheeks. "I've had twenty years to cultivate it, channel it. Not all passions are hot and dangerous, Philip. Some are ice cold."

Bantam Books by Nora Roberts

HOT ICE
SACRED SINS
BRAZEN VIRTUE
SWEET REVENGE
GENUINE LIES
CARNAL INNOCENCE
DIVINE EVIL
PUBLIC SECRETS

SWEET REVENGE

Nora Roberts

BANTAM BOOKS
NEW YORK • TORONTO • LONDON • SYDNEY • AUCKLAND

SWEET REVENGE

A Bantam Book / January 1989
Bantam reissue / June 1997

ISBN 0-553-27859-2

Published simultaneously in the United States and Canada

Bantam Books are published by Bantam Books, a division of Bantam Doubleday Dell
Publishing Group, Inc. Its trademark, consisting of the words "Bantam Books" and the
portrayal of a rooster, is Registered in U.S. Patent and Trademark Office and in other
countries. Marca Registrada. Bantam Books, 1540 Broadway, New York, New York 10036.

PRINTED IN THE UNITED STATES OF AMERICA

OPM   32   31   30   29   28   27   26   25   24   23

*To Carolyn Nichols,
for the support and the friendship*

Part I

THE BITTER

Women are your fields.
Go, then, into your fields as you please.

THE KORAN

He was her man, but he done her wrong.

"Frankie and Johnny"

Chapter One

New York, 1989

Stuart Spencer hated his hotel room excessively. The only advantage to being in New York was that his wife was in London and couldn't hound him about sticking to his diet. He'd ordered up a club sandwich from room service and was savoring each bite.

He was a portly, balding man without the jolly disposition expected from one with his looks. A blister on his heel plagued him, as did a persistent head cold. After he'd gulped half a cup of tea, he decided with cranky British chauvinism that Americans simply couldn't brew decent tea no matter how much they tried.

He wanted a hot bath, a cup of good Earl Grey, and an hour of quiet, but, he feared, the restless man standing by the window was going to force him to postpone all of that... perhaps indefinitely.

"Well, I'm here, dammit." Scowling, he watched Philip Chamberlain twitch back the curtain.

"Lovely view." Philip gazed out at the wall of another building. "Gives such a cozy feel to this place."

"Philip, I feel compelled to remind you that I dislike flying across the Atlantic in winter. Moreover, I have a backlog of paperwork waiting for me in London, and the bulk of it is on account of you and your irregular procedures. So, if you've information for me, please pass it on. At once, if that's not too much to ask."

Philip continued to look out the window. He was edgy about the outcome of the informal meeting he'd demanded,

3

but nothing in his cool manner so much as hinted at the tension he felt.

"I really must take you to a show while you're here, Stuart. A musical. You're getting dour in your old age."

"Get on with it."

Philip let the curtain fall back into place and moved smoothly toward the man to whom he'd reported these last few years. His occupation demanded confident, athletic grace. He was thirty-five, but had a quarter of a century of professional experience behind him. He had been born in London's slums, yet even when young he'd been able to finesse invitations to society's best parties, no small accomplishment in the days before Britain's rigid class consciousness had broken down under the onslaught of the Mods and the Rockers. He knew what it was to be hungry, just as he knew what it was to have his fill of beluga. Because he preferred caviar, he had made certain he lived a life that included it. He was good, very good, at what he did, but success hadn't come easily.

"I have a hypothetical proposition for you, Stuart." Taking a seat, Philip helped himself to tea. "Let me ask you if over the last few years I've been some help to you."

Spencer took a bite of his sandwich and hoped it, and Philip, wouldn't give him indigestion. "Are you looking for a salary increase?"

"A thought, but not precisely what I have in mind." He was capable of producing a particularly charming smile which he could use to great effect when he chose. And he chose to do so now. "The question is, has having a thief on Interpol's payroll been worthwhile?"

Spencer sniffed, pulled out a handkerchief, then blew. "From time to time."

Philip noted, wondering if Stuart had, too, that this time he had not used the qualifier "retired" before "thief," and that Stuart had not corrected the omission. "You've gotten positively miserly with your compliments."

"I'm not here to flatter you, Philip, merely to learn why the devil you thought anything was important enough to demand I fly to New York in the middle of the damn winter."

"Would you care for two?"

"Two what?"

"Thieves, Stuart." He held out a triangle of the club sandwich. "You really should try this on whole wheat."

"What are you getting at?"

There was a great deal riding on the next few moments, but Philip had lived most of his life with his future, with his very neck, riding on his actions in a matter of moments. He'd been a thief, and an excellent one, leading Captain Stuart Spencer and men like him down blind alleys and dead ends from London to Paris, from Paris to Morocco, from Morocco to wherever the next prize waited. Then he'd done a complete about-face and begun to work for Spencer and Interpol instead of against them.

That had been a business decision, Philip reminded himself. It had been a matter of figuring the odds and the profit. What he was about to propose was personal.

"Let's say, hypothetically, that I knew of a particularly clever thief, one who's managed to keep Interpol jumping for a decade, one who's decided to retire from active duty, and would offer services in exchange for clemency."

"You're speaking of The Shadow."

Philip meticulously brushed crumbs from his fingertips. He was a neat man, by habit and by necessity. "Hypothetically."

The Shadow. Spencer forgot his aching heel and jet lag. Millions of dollars in jewels had been stolen by the faceless figure of the thief known only as The Shadow. For ten years Spencer had tracked him, dogged him, missed him. For the past eighteen months Interpol had intensified its investigations, going so far as to set a thief to catch a thief—Philip Chamberlain, the only man Spencer knew whose exploits exceeded those of The Shadow. The man, Spencer thought on a sudden wave of fury, he had trusted.

"You know who he is, dammit. You *have* known who he is and where we can find him." Stuart braced his hands on the table. "Ten years. Ten years we've been after this man. And, damn you, for months you've been paid to find him while stringing us along. You've known his identity and whereabouts all the time!"

"Perhaps I have." Philip spread his long, artistic fingers. "Perhaps I haven't."

"I feel like putting you in a cage and dropping the key in the Thames."

"But you won't, because I'm like the son you never had."

"I have a son, blast you."

"Not like me." Tipping back in his chair, Philip continued. "What I'm proposing is the same deal you and I made five years ago. You had the vision then to see that hiring the best had distinct advantages over pursuing the best."

"You were assigned to catch this man, not negotiate for him. If you have a name, I want a name. If you have a description, I want it. Facts, Philip, not hypothetical propositions."

"You have nothing," Philip said abruptly. "Absolutely nothing after ten years. If I walk out of this room, you'll still have nothing."

"I'll have you." Spencer's voice was flat, and final enough to have Philip narrowing his eyes. "A man with your taste would find prison very disagreeable."

"Threats?" A chill, brief but very real, ran over Philip's skin. He folded his hands and kept his eyes level, holding onto the certainty that Spencer was bluffing. Philip wasn't. "I have clemency, remember? That was the deal."

"It's you who's changed the rules. Give me the name, Philip, and let me do my job."

"You think small, Stuart. That's why you recovered only some diamonds while I took many. You put The Shadow in jail, you have only a thief in jail. Do you really think you'll recover a fraction of what was taken over the last decade?"

"It's a matter of justice."

"Yes."

Philip's tone had changed, Spencer realized, and for the first time in this conversation, he lowered his eyes. But not from shame. Spencer knew Philip too well to believe for a moment that the man was the least abashed.

"It is a matter of justice, and we'll come to that." Philip rose again, too restless to sit. "When you assigned me to the case, I took it because this particular thief interested me. That hasn't changed. In fact, you could say my interest has peaked considerably." It wouldn't do to push Spencer too far. True, they'd developed a grudging admiration for each other over the years, but Spencer had always and would always stick to the straight and narrow. "Say, hypothetically still of course, that I do know the identity of The Shadow. Say we've had conversations that lead me to believe you could use this individual's talents and that they would be given for the small consideration of a clean slate."

"*Small* consideration? The bastard's stolen more than you did."

Philip's brows shot up. With a slight frown he brushed a crumb from his sleeve. "I hardly think it's necessary to insult me. No one has stolen jewels with a greater total value than I did in my career."

"Proud of yourself, are you?" Color swept alarmingly into Spencer's face. "Living the life of a thief isn't something I'd boast about."

"Therein lies the difference between us."

"Crawling into windows, making deals in back alleys—"

"Please, you'll make me sentimental. No, better count to ten, Stuart. I don't want to be responsible for an alarming rise in your blood pressure." He picked up the teapot again. "Perhaps this is a good time to tell you that while I was lifting locks, I developed a strong respect for you. I imagine I'd still be in second-story work if it hadn't been for you edging closer with every job I pulled. I don't regret the way I lived any more than I regret changing sides."

Stuart calmed enough to gulp down the tea Philip had poured for him. "That's neither here nor there." But he could acknowledge that Philip's admission pleased him. "Fact is, you are working for me now."

"I haven't forgotten." He turned his head to gaze at the window. It was an icy, clear day that made him long for spring. "To continue then," he said, snapping around to level an intense gaze at Stuart, "as a loyal employee I feel it my obligation to recruit for you when I come upon a worthy prospect."

"Thief."

"Yes, and an excellent one." His smile bloomed once more. "Further, I'd be willing to wager that neither yours nor any other law enforcement agency is going to get a glimmer of this thief's real identity." Sobering a bit, he leaned forward. "Not now, not ever, Stuart, I promise you."

"He'll move again."

"There'll be no more moves."

"How can you be sure?"

Philip folded his hands. His wedding ring glinted dully. "I'll see to it, personally."

"What is he to you?"

"Difficult to explain. Listen to me, Stuart. For five years I've worked for you, worked beside you. More than a few of the jobs have been dirty, even more have been dirty *and* dangerous. I've never asked you for anything, but I'm asking for this: Clemency for my hypothetical thief."

"I can hardly guarantee—"

"Your word is guarantee enough," Philip said, and silenced him. "In return, I'll even retrieve the Rubens for you. And, better still, I believe I can assure you a prize that will provide political weight to cool down a particularly hot situation."

Spencer had little trouble adding two and two. "In the Middle East?"

Topping off his cup, Philip shrugged. "Hypothetically." Whatever the answer, he intended to lead Stuart to the Rubens and to Abdu. Still, he never showed his hand before the final call. "You could say that with the information I give you, England could bring pressure to bear where it might be most useful."

Spencer looked hard at Philip. They had gone so unexpectedly far beyond discussing diamonds and rubies, crime and punishment. "You're over your head, Philip."

"I appreciate the concern." He sat back again because he sensed the tide was changing. "I promise you, I know exactly what I'm doing."

"It's a delicate game you're playing."

The most delicate, Philip thought. The most important. "One we can both win, Stuart."

Wheezing a bit, Spencer rose to open a bottle of scotch. He poured a generous amount in a tumbler, hesitated, then poured a second. "Tell me what you've got, Philip. I'll do what I can."

He waited a moment, measuring. "I'm putting the only thing that matters to me into your hands. You must remember that, Stuart." He pushed his tea aside and accepted the tumbler. "I saw the Rubens when I was inside the treasure room of King Abdu of Jaquir."

Spencer's normally bland eyes widened. "And what the hell were you doing in the king's vault?"

"It's a long story." Philip saluted Stuart with his glass, then drank deeply. "It's best to start at the beginning, with Phoebe Spring."

Chapter Two

Jaquir, 1968

Curled on her side and sleepless with excitement, Adrianne watched the clock tick to midnight. Her birthday. She would be five years old. Turning on her back, she hugged her delight to herself. All around her the palace slept, but in a few hours the sun would rise and the muezzin would climb the steps of the mosque to call the faithful to prayer. The day, the most wonderful day of her life, would truly begin.

In the afternoon there would be music and presents and trays of chocolate. All of the women would wear their prettiest clothes, and there would be dancing. Everyone would come: Grandmother to tell her stories; Aunt Latifa, who always smiled and never scolded, would bring Duja; Favel, with her jolly laugh, would lead her brood. Adrianne grinned. The women's quarters would ring with laughter, and everyone would tell her how pretty she was.

Mama had promised it would be a very special day. Her special day. With her father's permission there would be a trip to the beach in the afternoon. She had a new dress, a beautiful one, of striped silk in all the colors of the rainbow. Catching her lip between her teeth, Adrianne turned her head to look at her mother.

Phoebe slept, her face like marble in the moonlight and, for once, peaceful. Adrianne loved these times when her mother allowed her to climb into the huge soft bed to sleep. It was a very special treat. She would bundle up close with Phoebe's arms around her and listen to the stories her mother told her of places like New York and Paris. Sometimes they would giggle together.

Carefully, not wanting to wake her, Adrianne reached out to stroke her mother's hair. It fascinated her. It looked like fire against the pillow, a gorgeous, hot fire. At five, Adrianne was already woman enough to envy her mother her hair. Her own was thick and black like that of the other women in Jaquir. Only Phoebe had red hair and white skin. Only Phoebe was American. Adrianne was half American, but Phoebe reminded her of it only when they were alone.

Such things made her father angry.

Adrianne was well tutored in avoiding subjects that might anger her father, though she couldn't understand why being reminded that Phoebe was American made his eyes harden and his mouth thin. She had been a movie star. That description confused Adrianne, but she liked the way it sounded. *Movie star.* The words made her think of pretty lights in a dark sky.

Her mother had been a star, now she was a queen, the first wife of Abdu ibn Faisal Rahman al-Jaquir, ruler of Jaquir, sheikh of sheikhs. Her mother was the most beautiful of women with her large blue eyes and full, soft mouth. She towered over the other women in the harem, making them seem like tiny, fussy birds. Adrianne wished only that her mother would be happy. Now that she was five, Adrianne fiercely hoped she would begin to understand why her mother so often looked sad and wept when she thought herself alone.

Women were protected in Jaquir. Those of the House of Jaquir were not supposed to work or to worry. They were given everything they needed—fine rooms, the sweetest of perfumes. Her mother had beautiful clothes and jewelry. She had The Sun and the Moon.

Adrianne closed her eyes, better to recall the dazzling vision of the necklace on her mother's neck. How the great diamond, The Sun, flashed and the priceless pearl, the Moon, gleamed. Someday, Phoebe had promised, Adrianne would wear it.

When she was grown. Comfortably, content with the sound of her mother's even breathing and the thoughts of tomorrow, Adrianne imagined. When she was grown, a woman instead of a girl, she would put on her veil. One day a husband would be chosen for her, and she would be married. On her wedding day she would wear The Sun and the Moon and become a good and fruitful wife.

She would give parties for the other women and serve them frosted cakes while servants passed trays of chocolate. Her husband would be handsome and powerful, like her father. Perhaps he would be a king, too, and he would value her above all things.

As she drifted toward sleep, Adrianne curled the ends of a lock of her long hair around her index finger. He would love her the way she wanted her father to love her. She would give him fine sons, many fine sons, so that the other women would look at her with envy and respect. Not with pity. Not with the pity they showed to her mother.

The light from the hallway roused her. It slanted in as the door opened, then fell in a harsh line across the floor. Through the gauzy netting that surrounded the bed like a cocoon, she saw the shadow.

The love came first, in a frustrated burst she recognized but was too young to understand. Then came the fear, the fear that always followed closely on the love she felt whenever she saw her father.

He would be angry to find her here, in her mother's bed. She knew, because the talk in the harem was frank, that he rarely visited here, not since the doctors had said Phoebe would bear no more children. Adrianne thought perhaps he wanted only to look at Phoebe because she was so beautiful. But when he stepped closer, fear rose up in her throat. Quickly, silently, she slid out of the bed and crouched in the shadows beside it.

Abdu, his eyes on Phoebe, pulled back the netting. He hadn't bothered to shut the door. No one would dare to disturb him.

There was moonlight over her hair, over her face. She looked like a goddess, as she had the first time he had seen her. Her face had filled the screen with its stunning beauty, its sharp sexuality. Phoebe Spring, the American actress, the woman men both desired and feared for her lush body and innocent eyes. Abdu was a man accustomed to having the best, the biggest, the costliest. He had wanted her then in a way he'd never wanted another woman. He had found her, courted her in the manner a Western woman preferred. He had made her his queen.

She had bewitched him. Because of her he had betrayed his heritage, defied tradition. He had taken for his wife a Western woman, an actress, a Christian. He had been punished. In her his seed had produced only one child, a girl child.

Still, she made him want. Her womb was barren but her beauty taunted him. Even when his fascination turned to disgust, he wanted. She shamed him, defiled his *sharaf*, his honor, with her ignorance of Islam, but his body never stopped craving her.

When he buried his manhood deep in another woman, it was Phoebe he made love to, Phoebe whose skin he smelled, Phoebe whose cries he heard. That was his secret shame. He might have hated her for that alone. But it was the public shame, the one daughter only that she had given him that caused him to despise her.

He wanted her to suffer, to pay, just as he had suffered, just as he had paid. Taking the sheet, he ripped it aside.

Phoebe awoke, confused, with her heart already pounding. She saw him standing over her in the shadowed light. At first she thought it was her dream in which he had come back to her to love her as he once had loved her. Then she saw his eyes and knew there was no dream, and no love.

"Abdu." She thought of the child and looked around quickly. The bed was empty. Adrianne was gone. Phoebe thanked God for it. "It's late," she began, but her throat was so dry the words could barely be heard. In defense, she was already sliding backward, the satin sheets whispering beneath her as she curled into herself. He said nothing, but stripped off his white *throbe*. "Please." Though she knew they were useless, the tears started. "Don't do this."

"A woman has no right to refuse her husband what he wishes." Just looking at her, at the way her ripe body quivered against the pillows, he felt powerful, in charge of his own destiny again. Whatever else she was, she was his property— as much as the jewels on his fingers, the horses in his stables. He grabbed her by the bodice of her nightgown and dragged her back.

In the shadows by the bed, Adrianne began to tremble.

Her mother was crying. They were fighting, shouting words she couldn't understand at each other. Her father stood naked in the moonlight, his dark skin gleaming with a film of sweat that sprang from lust rather than the sultry heat. She had never seen a man's body before, but wasn't upset by the sight. She knew about sex, and that her father's manhood, which looked so hard and threatening, could be used to dig into her mother and make a child. She knew there was pleasure in this, that the act was something a woman desired above all else. Indeed, she had heard this a thousand times in her young life, for the talk about sex in the harem was incessant.

But her mother could have no more children, and if there was pleasure here, why was she crying and begging him to leave her?

A woman was to welcome her husband into the marriage bed, Adrianne thought as her own eyes filled. She was to offer him whatever he desired. She was to rejoice to be desired, to be the vessel for children.

She heard the word *whore*. It wasn't a word she knew, but it sounded ugly on her father's lips, and she wouldn't forget it.

"How can you call me that?" Phoebe's voice hitched with sobs as she fought to free herself. Once she had welcomed the feel of his arms around her, delighted in the way his skin would gleam in moonlight. Now she felt only fear. "I've never been with another man. Only you. It's you who've taken another wife even after we had a child."

"You gave me nothing." He wrapped her hair around his hand, fascinated by it yet detesting its fire. "A girl. Less than nothing. I have only to look at her and feel my disgrace."

She struck him then with enough force to snap his head back. Even if she'd been faster, there would have been nowhere to run. The back of his hand smashed across her face, sending her reeling. Driven by lust and fury, he ripped the nightgown from her.

She was built like a goddess, every man's fantasy. Her lush breasts heaved as terror sent her heart racing. In the moonlight her pale skin glowed, already showing the shadow of bruises from his hands. Her hips were rounded. When passion filled her they could move like lightning, meeting a man thrust for thrust. Shameless. Desire was like a pain in him, like a devil clawing. A lamp crashed onto the table as they struggled, showering the floor with glass.

Frozen in horror, Adrianne watched as he dug his fingers into Phoebe's full white breasts. Her mother was pleading, struggling. A man had a right to beat his wife. She could not refuse him in the marital bed. That was the way. And yet... Adrianne pushed her hands hard against her ears to block out Phoebe's screams as he rose over her, as he plunged into her violently, again and again.

With her face wet with her own tears, Adrianne crawled under the bed. She pressed her hands against her ears until they hurt but still she could hear her father's grunts, her mother's desperate weeping. Above her the bed shook. She curled into a ball, trying to make herself small, so small she wouldn't hear, wouldn't even be.

She had never heard the word *rape,* but after this night she would never have to have it defined for her.

"You're so quiet, Addy." Phoebe brushed her daughter's waist-length hair with long, slow strokes. Addy. Abdu despised the nickname and only tolerated the more formal Adrianne because his first born was a female of mixed blood. Even so, out of Muslim pride, he had decreed that his daughter be given a proper Arabic name. Therefore, on all official documents "Adrianne" was recorded as Ad Riyahd An, followed by a slew of Abdu's family names. Phoebe repeated the nickname now and asked, "Don't you like your presents?"

"I like them very much." Adrianne was wearing her new dress, but it no longer pleased her. In the mirror she could see her mother's face behind her own. Phoebe had carefully covered the bruise with makeup, but Adrianne saw the shadow of it.

"You look beautiful." Phoebe turned her around to hold her. On another day Adrianne might not have noticed how tightly she was held, might not have recognized the notes of desperation in her mother's voice. "My own little princess. I love you so much, Addy. More than anything in the world."

She smelled like flowers, like the warm, rich flowers in the garden just outside. Adrianne drew in her mother's scent as she pressed her face to her breasts. She kissed them, remembering how cruelly her father had handled them the night before.

"You won't go away? You won't leave me?"

"Where would you get such an idea?" With a half laugh Phoebe pushed her an arm's length away to look at her. When she saw the tears, her laughter stopped. "Oh, baby, what's all this?"

Miserably, Adrianne dropped her head on Phoebe's shoulder. "I dreamed he sent you away. That you left and I never saw you again."

Phoebe's hand hesitated, then continued to stroke. "Just a dream, baby. I'll never leave you."

Adrianne crawled onto her mother's lap, content to be rocked and soothed. Through the latticework at the windows, fingers of scented sunlight pushed across the room and into the pattern on the rug. "If I had been a boy, he would love us."

Anger filled her so quickly, Phoebe could taste it on her tongue. Almost immediately, it turned to despair. But she was still an actress. If she could use her talent for nothing else, she could use it to protect what was hers. "What silly talk, and on your birthday. What fun is a little boy? They don't wear pretty dresses."

Adrianne giggled at that and snuggled closer. "If I put a dress on Fahid, he would look like a doll."

Phoebe pressed her lips together and tried to ignore the flash of pain. Fahid. The son Abdu's second wife had borne after she had failed. Not failed, she told herself. She was beginning to think like a Muslim woman. How could she have failed when she had a beautiful child in her arms?

You gave me nothing. A girl. Less than nothing.

Everything, Phoebe thought savagely. I gave you everything.

"Mama?"

"I was thinking." Phoebe smiled as she slid Adrianne from her lap. "I was thinking that you need one more present. A secret one."

"A secret?" Adrianne clapped her hands together, tears forgotten.

"Sit, and close your eyes."

Delighted, Adrianne obeyed, squirming in the chair as

16

she tried to be patient. Phoebe had hidden the little glass ball between layers of clothing. It hadn't been easy to smuggle it into the country, but she was learning to be inventive. The pills had been difficult as well, the small pink pills that made it possible for her to get through each day. They numbed the pain and eased the heart. Woman's best friend. God knew, in this country a woman needed any friend she could make. If the pills were found, she could face public execution. If she didn't have them, she wasn't sure she could survive.

A vicious cycle. The only thing pulling her around it was Adrianne.

"Here you are." Phoebe knelt by the chair. The child wore a chain of sapphires around her neck and glittering studs in her ears. Phoebe thought, hoped, the small gift she gave Adrianne now would mean more. "Open your eyes."

It was a simple thing, almost ridiculously simple. For a few dollars it could be bought in thousands of stores in the States during the holidays. Adrianne's eyes widened as if she were holding magic in her hands.

"It's snow." Phoebe turned the ball again, sending the white flakes dancing. "In America it snows in the winter. Well, in most places. At Christmastime, we decorate trees with pretty lights and colored balls. Pine trees, like the one you see in here. I rode with my grandfather on a sled like this one once." Resting her head against Adrianne's, she looked at the miniature horse and sleigh inside the glass ball. "One day, Addy, I'm going to take you there."

"Does it hurt?"

"Snow?" Phoebe laughed again and shook the ball. The scene came to life once more with snow swirling around the decorated pine and the little man riding in the red sleigh behind a neat brown horse. It was an illusion. All she had left were her illusions and a small child to protect. "No. It's cold and it's wet. You can build things with it. Snowmen, snowballs, forts. It looks so pretty on the trees. See? Just like in here."

Adrianne tilted the ball herself. The little brown horse had one leg lifted as the tiny white flakes danced around his head. "It is pretty, more than my new dress. I want to show Duja."

"No." Phoebe knew what would happen if Abdu learned

17

of it. The ball was a symbol of a Christian holiday. Since Adrianne's birth, he had become a fanatic about religion and tradition. "It's our secret, remember? When we're alone, you can look at it, but never, ever when anyone is about." She took the ball away and hid it in the drawer. "Now it's time for the party."

It was hot in the harem though the fans were whirling and the lattices were closed against the power of the sun. The light coming from the shaded filigree lamps was soft and flattering. The women had dressed in their brightest and finest clothes. Leaving their black *abaayas* and veils at the door, they transformed themselves from crows to peacocks in the flash of an eye.

With their veils the women also had shed their silence and begun to chatter about children, sex, fashion, and fertility. Within moments the harem with its shaded lamps and opulent cushions was filled with the heavy scent of women and incense.

Because of her rank, Adrianne greeted the guests with a kiss on each cheek as green tea and spiced coffee were served in tiny, fragile cups without handles. There were aunts and cousins and a score of minor princesses, who, like the other women, showed off with equal pride both their jewelry and their babies, the two major symbols of success in their world.

Adrianne thought them beautiful in their long, whispery dresses, color competing with color. From behind her Phoebe saw a costume parade that would have suited the eighteenth century. She accepted the pitying glances cast her way with the same stoic expression that she accepted smug ones. She recognized full well that she was the intruder here, the woman from the West who had failed to give the king an heir. It didn't matter, she told herself, whether or not they accepted her. As long as they were kind to Adrianne.

She could find no fault there. Adrianne was one of them in a way she could never be.

They fell hungrily on the buffet, sampling everything, using their fingers as often as she used the little silver spoons. If they grew too plump for their dresses, they would buy new ones. It was shopping, Phoebe thought, that got the Arab woman through the day, just as it was the pink pill that got her through. No man except husband, father, or brother

18

would see their ridiculous dresses. When they left the harem, they would cloak themselves again, veil their faces, hide their hair. Outside the walls there was *aurat*, things that cannot be shown, to remember.

What games they played! Phoebe thought wearily. With their henna and perfumes and glittering rings. Could they believe themselves happy when even she, who no longer cared, could see the boredom on their faces. She prayed to God that she would never see it on Adrianne's.

Even at the young age of five Adrianne had enough poise to see that her guests were entertained and comfortable. She was speaking Arabic now, smoothly, musically. Adrianne had never been able to tell her mother that the language came more easily to her than English. She thought in Arabic, even felt in Arabic, and both thoughts and emotions often had to be translated into English before she could communicate them to her mother.

She was happy here, in this room filled with women's voices, women's scents. The world her mother told her of from time to time was nothing more than a fairy tale to her. Snow was just something that danced inside a little glass ball.

"Duja." Adrianne raced across the room to kiss her favorite cousin's cheek. Duja was nearly ten and, to Adrianne's envy and admiration, almost a woman.

Duja returned the embrace. "Your dress is beautiful."

"I know." But Adrianne couldn't resist running a hand down the sleeve of her cousin's.

"It's velvet," Duja told her importantly. That the heavy fabric was unbearably hot was nothing compared to the reflection she had seen in her mirror. "My father bought it for me in Paris." She turned full circle, a slim, dark girl with a fine-boned face and large eyes. "When he goes next, he has promised to take me with him."

"Truly?" Adrianne stifled the envy that welled within her. It was no secret that Duja was a favorite with her father, the brother of the king. "My mother has been there."

Because she had a kind heart, and was pleased with her velvet, Duja stroked Adrianne's hair. "You will go also one day. Perhaps when we are grown, we will go together."

Adrianne felt a tug on her skirt. Glancing down, she saw her half brother, Fahid. She scooped him up to plant kisses over his face and make him squeal with laughter. "You are the most handsome baby in Jaquir." He was heavy, although only two years her junior, so that she had to brace against his weight. Staggering a bit, she carried him to the table to find him a rich dessert.

Other babies were being cooed over and coddled. Girls Adrianne's age and younger were fussing over the boys, stroking them, spoiling them. From birth, females were taught to devote their time and energies to pleasing men. Adrianne knew only that she adored her little brother and wanted to make him smile.

Phoebe couldn't bear it. She watched as her daughter served the child of the woman who had taken her place in her husband's bed and in his heart. What difference did it make if the law here said that a man could take four wives? It wasn't her law, it wasn't her world. She had lived in it for six years, and could live in it for sixty more, but it would never be her world. She hated the smells here, the thick, cloying smells that had to be tolerated day after listless day. Phoebe rubbed a hand over her temple where a headache was beginning to throb. The incense, the flowers, perfume layered over perfume.

She hated the heat, the unrelenting heat.

She wanted a drink, not the coffee or tea that was always served, but wine. Just one cool glass of wine. But there was no wine permitted in Jaquir. Rape was permitted, she thought as she touched a finger to her sore cheek. Rape, but no wine. Camel whippings and veils, prayer calls and polygamy, but not a drop of crisp Chablis or a dram of dry Sancerre.

How could she have thought the country beautiful when she had first arrived as a bride? She had looked at the desert, at the sea, at the high white walls of the palace, and she had thought it the most mysterious, the most exotic spot in the world.

She had been in love then. God help her, she was still in love.

In those early days Abdu had made her see the beauty of his country and the richness of his culture. She had given up her own land and customs to try to be what he wanted. What he wanted, it turned out, was the woman he had seen on the screen, the symbol of sex and innocence she had learned to portray. Phoebe was all too human.

Abdu had wanted a son. She had given him a daughter. He had wanted her to become a child of Allah, but she was and would always be a product of her own upbringing.

She didn't want to think of it, of him, of her life, or the pain. She needed to escape for a little while. She would take only one more pill, she told herself, just to help her get through the rest of the day.

Chapter Three

By the time he was ready to turn thirteen, Philip Chamberlain was a very accomplished thief. At the age of ten, he had graduated from picking the plump pockets of well-to-do businessmen on the way to their banks and brokers and solicitors, or nipping wallets from careless tourists bumping along in Trafalgar Square. He was a second-story man, though any looking at him would see only a handsome, neat, somewhat thin boy.

He had clever hands, shrewd eyes, and the instincts of a born cat burglar. With cunning and guile and ready fists he'd avoided being sucked into any of the street gangs that roamed London during the waning days of the sixties. Nor did he feel the urge to pass out flowers and wear love beads. Fourteen-year-old Philip was neither Mod nor Rocker. He worked for himself now and saw no reason to wear a badge of allegiance. He was a thief, not a bully, and had nothing but contempt for delinquents who terrorized old women and stole their market money. He was a businessman, and looked with amusement on those of his generation who talked of communal living or tuned second-hand guitars while their heads were stuffed with dreams of grandeur.

He had plans for himself, big plans.

At the center of them was his mother. He intended to put his hand-to-mouth existence behind him and dreamed of a big house in the country, an expensive car, elegant clothes, and parties. Over the past year he'd begun to fantasize about equally elegant women. But for now, the only woman in his life was Mary Chamberlain, the woman who had borne him, raised him single-handedly. More than anything, he wanted to give her the best life had to offer, to replace the glittery paste jewelry she wore with the real thing, to take her out of the tiny flat on the edge of what was rapidly becoming fashionable Chelsea.

It was cold in London. The wind whipped wet snow into Philip's face as he jogged toward Faraday's Cinema, where Mary worked. He dressed well. A street-corner cop rarely looked twice at a tidy boy with a clean collar. In any case, he detested mended pants and frayed cuffs. Ambitious, self-sufficient, and always with an eye to the future, Philip had found a way to have what he wanted.

He'd been born poor and fatherless. At fourteen, he wasn't mature enough to think of this as an advantage, as grit that strengthened backbones. He resented poverty—but he resented even more than he'd ever been able to express the man who had passed in and out of his mother's life and fathered him. As far as he was concerned, Mary had deserved better. And so, by God, had he. At an early age he'd begun to use his clever fingers, and his wits, to see that they both got better.

He had a pearl and diamond bracelet in his pocket, along with matching ear clips. He'd been a bit disappointed after examining them with his hand loupe. The diamonds weren't of the first water, and the biggest of them was less than half a carat. Still, the pearls had a nice sheen and he thought his fence on Broad Street would give him a fair price. Philip was every bit as good at negotiating as he was at lifting locks. He knew exactly how much he wanted for the baubles in his pocket. Enough for him to buy his mother a new coat with a fur collar for Christmas, and still have a chunk to set aside in what he called his future fund.

There was a snaking line outside the ticket booth at Faraday's. The marquee touted the holiday special as Walt Disney's *Cinderella*, so there were plenty of whiny, overexcited children and their exhausted nannies and mothers. Philip smiled as he went through the doors. He'd wager his mother had seen the movie a dozen times already. Nothing made her day more than a happy-ever-after.

"Mum." He slipped in the back of the booth to kiss her cheek. It was hardly warmer in the glass box than it was out in the wind. Philip thought of the red wool coat he'd seen in the window at Harrods. His mum would look smashing in red.

"Phil." As always, pleasure lit Mary's eyes when she looked at him. Such a handsome boy with his narrow, scholarly face and golden hair. She didn't, as many women might have, feel a pang as she saw the man she'd loved so fiercely, and so briefly, reflected in the boy's face. Philip was hers. All hers. He'd never given her a moment's trouble, not even as a baby. Not once had she ever regretted her decision to have him, though she'd been alone, without a husband, without family. Indeed, it had never occurred to Mary to seek out one of those tiny, flesh-colored rooms where a woman could rid herself of a problem before it became one.

Philip was a joy to her, and had been from the moment of conception. If she had a regret, it was that she knew he resented the father he'd never known and looked for him in the face of every man he saw.

"Your hands are cold," he told her. "You should be wearing your gloves."

"Can't make change with gloves." Mary smiled at the young woman who had a boy by the nape of the neck. She'd never had to corral her Phil that way. "There you are, dear. Enjoy the show."

She worked too hard, Philip thought. Too hard and too long for too little. Though she was coy about her age, he knew she was barely thirty. And pretty. His mother's smooth, youthful looks were a source of pride to him. Perhaps she couldn't afford Mary Quant, but she chose what little she had with care and an eye for bold colors. She loved to look through fashion and movie magazines and copy hairstyles. She might mend her stockings, but Mary Chamberlain was anything but a frump.

He kept waiting for another man to waltz into her life and change things for her. He looked around the tiny booth that smelled forever of the exhaust from the street beyond. He was going to change things first.

"You should tell Faraday to put more than that rickety old heater in here."

"Don't fuss, Phil." Mary counted out change for two giggling teenage girls who were desperately trying to flirt with her son. Mary passed the coins through the chute and muffled a laugh. She couldn't blame them, really. Why, she'd even caught her neighbor's niece—twenty-five if she was a day—making over Phil. Offering him cups of tea. Asking him to come in and fix her squeaky door. Squeaky door indeed.

Mary slapped change down hard enough to make a round-faced nanny grumble.

Well, she'd put a stop to that right enough. She knew her Phil would leave her one day and it would be a woman he left her for. But it wouldn't be some fat-breasted cow a dozen years his senior. Not as long as Mary Chamberlain drew breath.

"Something wrong, Mum?"

"What?" Catching herself, Mary nearly blushed. "No, nothing, luv. Would you like to go in and watch the movie? Mr. Faraday wouldn't mind a bit."

As long as he doesn't see me, Philip thought with a grin. He thanked God he'd long ago eliminated Faraday from his list of possible fathers. "No, thanks. I just came by to tell you I have some errands to run. Want me to pick up anything at the market?"

"We could use a nice chicken." Mary blew absently on her hands as she sat back. It was cold in the booth, and would get colder yet as winter set in. In the summer it was like one of those Turkish baths she'd read about. But it was a job. When a woman had a boy to raise and not much schooling, she had to take what she could get. She started to reach for her imitation leather purse. It would never have crossed her mind to nip a pound note or two from the till.

"I've got some money yet."

"All right, then. Be sure the chicken's fresh." She passed four tickets to a harassed woman herding two squabbling boys and a young girl with big teary eyes.

The show would start in five minutes. She'd have to stay in the booth another twenty in case there were any stragglers. "Be sure to take the price of the chicken out of the tin when you get home," she told him, knowing he wouldn't. Bless him, the boy was always putting money in instead of taking it out. "But shouldn't you be in school?"

"It's Saturday, Mum."

"Saturday. Yes, of course, it's Saturday." Trying not to sigh as she arched her back, she picked up one of her glossy magazines, already well thumbed. "Mr. Faraday's going to have a Cary Grant festival next month. He even asked me to help him choose the films."

"That's nice." The little leather bag was beginning to weigh heavy in Philip's pocket, and he was itching to be off.

"We're going to start off with my very favorite. *To Catch a Thief*. You'd love it."

"Maybe," he said, looking into his mother's guileless eyes. How much did she know, he wondered. She never asked, certainly never questioned the little extras he brought into the house. She wasn't stupid. Just optimistic, he thought, and kissed her cheek again. "Why don't I take you on your night off?"

"That would be lovely." She resisted the urge to stroke his hair, knowing it would embarrass him. "Grace Kelly's in it. Imagine, a real-life princess. I was thinking about it this very morning when I opened up this magazine to an article about Phoebe Spring."

"Who?"

"Oh, Philip." She clucked her tongue and folded the page out. "Phoebe Spring. The most beautiful woman in the world."

"My mother's the most beautiful woman in the world," he said because he knew it would make her laugh and blush.

"You've a way with you, boy." She did laugh, hugely, robustly, as he loved to hear her laugh. "But just look at her. She was an actress, a wonderful actress, then she married a king. Now she's living with the man of her dreams in his fabulous palace in Jaquir. It's all right out of a movie. That's their daughter. The princess. Not quite five years old but a regular little beauty, isn't she?"

Philip gave the picture a disinterested glance. "She's just a baby."

"I wonder. The poor mite has the saddest eyes."

"You're making up a story again." His hand closed over the pouch in his pocket. He'd leave his mother to her fantasies, her dreams of Hollywood and royalty and white limousines. But he'd see she rode in one. Hell, he'd buy her one. Maybe she could only read about queens now, but some fine day soon, he'd see she lived like one. "I'm off."

"Have a good time, dear." Mary was already engrossed in her magazine again. Such a pretty little girl, she thought again, and felt a maternal tug.

Chapter Four

Adrianne loved the suqs. By the time she was eight, she had learned to appreciate the difference between diamonds and sparkling glass, Burmese rubies and stones of lesser color and quality. From Jiddah, her grandmother, she learned to judge, as shrewdly as a master jeweler, cut, clarity, and color. With Jiddah she would wander for hours, admiring the best stones the suqs had to offer.

Jewels were the security a woman could wear, Jiddah told her. What good to a woman were gold bars and paper money stored in a bank? Diamonds, emeralds, sapphires, could be pinned on, clipped on, strung on so she could show her worth to the world.

Nothing pleased Adrianne more than watching her grandmother bargain in the suqs while the heat rose in waves to make the very air shimmer. They went often, clutches of women cloaked in black like a band of blackbirds to finger ropes of gold and silver, to push polished stones onto their fingers or simply to study the gleam of gems through dusty glass while the smells of animals and spice hung in the still air and the *matawain* roamed in their straggly henna-tipped beards ready to punish any infraction of religious law. Adrianne never feared the *matawain* when she was with Jiddah. The former queen was revered in Jaquir. She had borne twelve children. When they shopped, the air would be crowded with sound, the squawks of bargaining, the bray of a donkey, the slap of sandals on the hard ground.

When prayer call sounded, the suqs would close. Then the women would wait while men lowered their faces to the earth. Adrianne would listen to the click of prayer beads, her head bowed like those of the other women. She was not yet veiled, but no longer a child. In those last days of the Mediterranean summer, she waited, poised at the edge of change.

So did Jaquir. Though the country struggled against poverty, the House of Jaquir was wealthy. As the first daughter of the king, she was entitled to the symbols and signs of her rank. But Abdu's heart had never opened to her.

His second wife had given him two daughters after Fahid. It had been murmured in the harem that Abdu had flown into a rage after the second girl and nearly divorced Leiha. But the crown prince was strong and handsome. Speculation ran that Leiha would soon be pregnant again. To insure his line, Abdu took a third wife and planted his seed quickly.

Phoebe began to take a pill each morning. She escaped now into dreams, sleeping or waking.

In the harem, with her head comfortably nestled on her mother's knee, her eyes lazily narrowed against the smoke of the incense, Adrianne watched her cousins dance. The long, hot afternoon stretched out ahead. She had hoped to go shopping, perhaps to buy some new silk or a gold bracelet like the one Duja had shown her the day before, but her mother had seemed so listless that morning.

They would shop tomorrow. Today the fans stirred the incense-laden air while the drums beat out a slow rhythm. Latifa had smuggled in a catalog from Frederick's of Hollywood. The women were pawing over it and giggling. They talked as they always did, and the talk was of sex. Adrianne was too accustomed to the frank words and excited descriptions to be interested. She liked to watch the dancing, the long, sinuous movements, the flow of dark hair, the twists and turns of bodies.

She glanced over at Meri, the third wife of her father who, smugly content with her swollen belly, sat nearby discussing childbirth. Leiha, her face pinched as she nursed her youngest daughter, surreptitiously eyed Meri. Fahid, a sturdy five, trotted over and demanded attention and without hesitation Leiha passed the baby away. Her smile held triumph as she took her son to her breast.

"Is it any wonder they grow to abuse us?" Phoebe murmured.

"Mama?"

"Nothing." Absently, she stroked Adrianne's hair. The beat of the drum pounded in her head, monotonous, relentless, like the days she spent in the harem. "In America babies are loved whether they are boys or girls. Women aren't expected to spend their lives bearing children."

"How does a tribe stay strong?"

Phoebe sighed. There were days she no longer thought clearly. She had the pills to blame, and to thank, for that. The latest supply had cost her an emerald ring, but she'd gotten the bonus of a pint of Russian vodka. She hoarded it in the most miserly fashion, allowing herself one small glass after each time Abdu came to her room. She no longer fought him, no longer cared to; she endured by focusing her thoughts on the solace to be enjoyed from the drink she would have when he was done with her.

She could leave. If she only had the courage she could take Adrianne and run away, run back to the real world, where women weren't forced to cover their bodies in shame and submit themselves to the cruel whims of men. She could go back to America, where she was loved, where people crowded into theaters to watch her. She could still act. Wasn't she acting every day? In America she could give Adrianne a good life.

She couldn't leave. Phoebe shut her eyes and tried to block out the sound of drums. To leave Jaquir a woman needed written permission from a man of her family. Abdu would never give it to her, for as much as he hated her, he wanted her.

She had already begged him to let her go, but he had refused. To escape would take thousands of dollars, and a risk she was nearly ready to take. But she would never make it out of the country with Adrianne. No bribe was large enough to tempt a smuggler to give illegal passage to the daughter of the king.

And she was afraid. Afraid of what he might do to Adrianne. He would take her away, Phoebe thought. There would be nothing she could do to stop him, no court to plead to but his court, no police to go to but his police. She would never risk Adrianne.

More than once she had thought of suicide. The ultimate escape. She thought of it the way she had once thought of lovemaking, as something to be desired, treasured, lingered over. Sometimes on hot, endless afternoons she stared at the bottle of pills and wondered how it would feel to take all of them, to drift finally, completely, into the fuzzy world of dreams. Glorious. She had even gone so far as to pour them into her hand, to count them, to fondle them.

But there was Adrianne. Always Adrianne.

So she would stay. She would drug herself until reality was bearable, and she would stay. But she would give Adrianne something of herself.

"I want the sun," Phoebe said abruptly. "Let's walk in the gardens."

Adrianne wanted to stay where she was, lulled by the scents and the sounds, but she rose dutifully and went with her mother.

The dry heat surrounded them. As always, it hurt Phoebe's eyes and made her long for a Pacific breeze. Once she'd owned a house in Malibu and had loved sitting by the big, wide window and watching the water swell with waves.

Here there were flowers, lush, exotic, and dripping with perfume. The walls rose high, to prevent a woman who walked there from tempting any passing man. Such was the way of Islam. A woman was a weak sexual creature without the strength or intellect to guard her virtue. Men guarded it for her.

The air in the garden oasis was alive with birdsong. The first time Phoebe had seen this garden, with its tangle of rich blossoms and heady scents, she had thought it straight out of a movie. All around the desert sands shifted, but here there were jasmine, oleander, hibiscus. Miniature orange and lemon trees thrived. She knew their fruit, like her husband's eyes, was bitter.

Irresistibly, she was drawn to the fountain. It had been Abdu's gift to her when he had brought her to his country as his queen. A symbol of the constant flow of his love. The love had long since dried up, but the fountain continued to play.

She was still his wife, the first of the four his laws

entitled him to. But in Jaquir her marriage had become her prison. Twisting the diamond circle on her finger, she watched the water tumble into the little pond. Adrianne began to toss in pebbles to make the bright carp swim.

"I do not like Meri," Adrianne began. In a world as restricted as a harem, there was little to talk about except the other women and children. "She pokes out her belly and smiles like this." She screwed up her face and made Phoebe laugh.

"Oh, you're good for me." She kissed the top of her head. "My little actress." She had her father's eyes, Phoebe thought as she brushed the hair back from Adrianne's face. They helped her remember the time when he had looked at her with love and warmth. "In America they'd line up for miles to see you."

Pleased with the idea, Adrianne smiled. "The way they did for you?"

"Yes." She looked back at the water. It was sometimes hard to remember the other person she had been. "They did. I always wanted to make people happy, Addy."

"When the reporter came, she said you were missed."

"Reporter?" That had been two or three years before. No, longer ago than that. Perhaps four years. Strange how time was blurring. Abdu had agreed to the interview to silence any gossip about their marriage. She hadn't expected the child to remember it. Why, Addy couldn't have been more than four or five then. "What did you think of her?"

"Her talk was strange and sometimes too fast. Her hair was cut very short, like a little boy's, and it was the color of straw. She was angry because her camera was allowed only for a few pictures, then taken away from her." When Phoebe sat on a marble bench, Adrianne continued to throw pebbles. "She said you were the most beautiful and most envied woman in the world. She asked if you wore a veil."

"You don't forget anything, do you?" Phoebe remembered as well, and remembered spinning a tale about the heat and dust and using the veil to protect her complexion.

"I liked when she talked about you." Adrianne remembered, too, that her mother had cried after the reporter had gone. "Will she come back?"

"Maybe, someday." But Phoebe knew that people forgot.

31

There were new faces, new names in Hollywood, and she even knew a few of them for Abdu allowed some letters to be delivered to her. Faye Dunaway, Jane Fonda, Ann-Margret. Beautiful young actresses making their marks, taking the place that had once been hers.

She touched her own face, knowing there were lines around her eyes now. Once it had been on every magazine cover. Women had dyed their hair to match hers. She had been compared to Monroe, to Gardner, to Loren. Later she had not been compared to anyone; she had set a standard.

"Once I almost won an Oscar. That's the very biggest prize for an actress. Even though I didn't, there was a wonderful party. Everyone was laughing and talking and making plans. It was all so different from Nebraska. That's where I lived when I was the age you are now, darling."

"Where there was snow?"

"Yes." Phoebe smiled and held out her arms. "Where there was snow. I lived there with my grandparents because my mother and father had died. I was very happy, but I didn't always know it. I wanted to be an actress, to wear beautiful clothes, and to have lots of people love me."

"So you became a movie star."

"I did." Phoebe rubbed her cheek against Adrianne's hair. "It seems like hundreds of years ago. It didn't snow in California, but I had the ocean. To me it was a fairy tale, and I was the princess I'd read of in all the storybooks. It was very hard work, but I loved being there, being a part of it. I had a house on the water all to myself."

"You would be lonely."

"No, I had friends and people to talk to. I went places I'd never imagined going—Paris, New York, London . . . I met your father in London."

"Where is London?"

"England, Europe. You're forgetting your lessons."

"I don't like lessons. I like stories." But she thought hard because she knew the lessons were important to Phoebe, and another secret between them. "A queen lives in London whose husband is only a prince." Adrianne waited, certain her mother would correct her this time. It was such a ridiculous idea—a woman ruling a country. But Phoebe merely

32

smiled and nodded. "It gets cold in London, and it rains. In Jaquir the sun always shines."

"London's beautiful." One of her greatest skills was the ability to put herself in a place, real or imagined, and see it clearly. "I thought it was the most beautiful place I'd ever seen. We were filming there and people would line up at the barricades to watch. They would call for me, and sometimes I would sign autographs or pose for pictures. Then I met your father. He was so handsome. So elegant."

"Elegant?"

A dreamy smile on her face, Phoebe closed her eyes. "Never mind. I was very nervous because he was a king, and there was protocol to remember and photographers everywhere. But then, after we talked, it didn't seem to matter. He took me to dinner, he took me dancing."

"You danced for him?"

"With him." Phoebe set Adrianne on the bench beside her. Nearby a bee droned lazily, drunk on nectar. The sound buzzed pleasantly in Phoebe's ears, made musical by the drug. "In Europe and America men and women dance together."

Adrianne's eyes narrowed. "This is permitted?"

"Yes, it's permitted to dance with a man, to talk to a man, to take drives or go to the theater. So many things. People go on dates together."

"Go on?" Adrianne struggled with her English. "Dates are to eat."

Phoebe laughed again, sleepy in the sun. She could remember dancing in Abdu's arms, and his smiling down at her. How strong his face had been. How gentle his hands. "These dates are different. A man invites a woman out. He comes to her house to pick her up. Sometimes he'll bring her flowers." Roses, she remembered dreamily. Abdu had sent her dozens of white roses. "Then they might go to dinner, or to a show and a late supper. They might go dancing in some crowded little club."

"You danced with my father because you were married?"

"No. We danced, we fell in love, then we were married. It's different, Adrianne, and so hard to explain. Most parts of the world aren't like Jaquir."

The niggling fear she had lived with since the night she

had witnessed her mother's rape took hold. "You want to go back."

Phoebe didn't hear the fear, only her own regrets. "It's a long way back, Addy. Too far. When I married Abdu I left it all behind. More than I understood then. I loved him, and he wanted me. The day we were married was the happiest day of my life. He gave me The Sun and the Moon." She touched a hand to her bodice, almost feeling the weight and the power of the necklace. "When I wore it, I felt like a queen, and it seemed that all those dreams I'd had as a young girl in Nebraska were coming true. He gave me part of himself then, part of his country. It meant everything to me when he fastened the gems around my neck."

"That is the most precious treasure in Jaquir. It showed that he valued you above all else."

"Yes, he did once. He doesn't love me anymore, Addy."

She knew it, had known it, but wanted to deny it. "You are his wife."

She looked down at her wedding ring, a symbol that had once meant so much. "One of three."

"No, he takes others only because he needs sons. A man must have sons."

Phoebe cupped Adrianne's face in her hands. She saw the tears, and the pain. Perhaps she had said too much, but it was too late to take the words back. "I know he ignores you, and it hurts you. Try to understand that it isn't you, but me."

"He hates me."

"No." But he did hate his daughter, Phoebe thought as she gathered her close. And it frightened her, the cold hate she saw in Abdu's eyes whenever he looked at Adrianne. "No, he doesn't hate you. He resents me, what I am, what I'm not. You're mine. He sees only that when he looks at you; he does not see the part of himself, maybe the best part of himself, that is in you."

"I hate him."

The fear grew sharper as she looked quickly around. They were alone in the garden, but voices carried and there were always ears to listen. "You mustn't say that. You mustn't even think that. You can't understand what's between Abdu and me, Addy. You aren't meant to."

"He strikes you." She drew back, and now her eyes were

dry and suddenly old. "For that I hate him. He looks at me and doesn't see. For that I hate him."

"Shh." Not knowing what else to do, Phoebe pulled Adrianne back in her arms and rocked.

She said nothing else. It had never been her intention to upset her mother. Until the words had been spoken, she hadn't even been aware she'd held them in her heart. Now that they had been voiced, she accepted them. The hate had been rooted even before the night she had seen her father abuse her mother. Since then it had grown, nurtured by his neglect and disinterest in her, the subtle insults that set her apart from his other children.

She hated, but the hate shamed her. A child was meant to revere her parents. So she no longer spoke of it.

Over the next weeks she spent more time than ever with her mother, walking in the garden, listening to the stories of other worlds. They continued to seem unreal to her, but she enjoyed them in much the same way she enjoyed her grandmother's tales of pirates and dragons.

When Meri gave birth to a girl and was summarily divorced, Adrianne was glad.

"I'm happy she's gone." Adrianne played a game of jacks with Duja. The toy had been allowed in the harem after much discussion and debate.

"Where will they send her?" Though Duja was older, it was understood that Adrianne had a way of ferreting out information.

"She is to have a house in the city. A small one." Adrianne chuckled and scooped up three jacks with nimble fingers. She might have pitied Meri her fate, but the ex-wife of the king had made herself disliked among the women.

"I'm glad she won't live here." Duja flipped back her hair as she waited her turn. "Now we won't have to listen to her brag about how often the king visited her and how many ways he plants his seed."

Adrianne missed the ball. She glanced quickly around for her mother, but since they were speaking Arabic, she decided Phoebe wouldn't have understood. "Do you want sex?"

"Of course." Duja let the jacks fall, then studied the outcome. "When I marry, my husband will visit me every

night. I will give him so much pleasure he will never need
another wife. I will keep my skin soft, my breasts firm. And
my legs open." She laughed and plucked up jacks.

Adrianne noticed one of the jacks shivered, but let the
infraction pass. Her hands were quicker and more clever than
Duja's, and it was her cousin's turn to win. "I don't want sex."

"Don't be stupid. All women want sex. The law keeps us
separate from men because we're too weak to resist it. We
stop only when we are as old as Grandmother."

"Then I am as old as Grandmother."

They both laughed at that and went back to the game.

Duja wouldn't understand, Adrianne thought as they
continued to play. Mama didn't want sex, and she was young
and beautiful. Leiha was afraid of it because it had given her
two daughters. Adrianne didn't want it because she had seen
that it was cruel and ugly.

Still, there was no other way to get babies, and she liked
babies very much. Perhaps she would get a kind husband
who already had wives and children. Then he wouldn't want
sex from her and she could care for the babies of the house.

When they tired of the game, Adrianne found her grandmother and climbed into her lap. Jiddah was a widow, and
had been a queen. Her love of sweets was costing her her
teeth, but her eyes were dark and clear.

"Here's my pretty Adrianne." Jiddah opened her hand
and offered the foil-wrapped chocolate. With a giggle Adrianne
took it. Because she loved the pretty paper as much as the
candy, she worked slowly. In a habit that never failed to
soothe, Jiddah picked up a brush and began to draw it
through Adrianne's hair.

"Will you visit the new baby, Grandmother?"

"Of course. I love all my grandchildren. Even ones who
steal my chocolate. Why does my Adrianne look so sad?"

"Do you think the king will divorce my mother?"

Jiddah had noticed, and worried, that Adrianne no longer
called Abdu her father. "I cannot say. He has not in nine
years."

"If he divorced her, we would go away. I would miss you
very much."

"And I would miss you." The child was not a child in too
many ways, Jiddah thought as she set the brush aside. "This

is not for you to worry about, Adrianne. You are growing up. One day soon I will watch you marry. Then I will have great-grandchildren."

"And you will give them chocolate and tell them stories."

"Yes. *Inshallah*." She pressed a kiss to Adrianne's hair. It was lightly scented and dark as night. "And I will love them as I love you."

Turning, Adrianne circled Jiddah's neck with her arms. The fragrance of poppies and spice on her skin was as comforting as the press of her thin body. "I will always love you, Grandmother."

"Adrianne. *Yellah*." Fahid tugged at her skirt. His mouth was already smeared from an earlier visit to his grandmother. The silk *throbe* his mother had had designed for him was streaked with dirt. "Come on," he repeated in Arabic, tugging again.

"Come where?" Because she was always ready to entertain him, Adrianne slid down and tickled his ribs.

"I want the top." He squealed and squirmed, then gave her a smacking kiss. "I want to see the top."

She pocketed another handful of chocolate before she let him drag her along. They were laughing as they raced down the corridors with Adrianne making exaggerated moans and pants as Fahid pulled on her hand. Her room was smaller than most of the others, one of the subtle insults dealt by her father. Its single window faced the very edge of the garden. Still, it was beautiful, decorated in the pink and white she had chosen herself. In one corner were shelves. On them were toys, many of which had been sent from America by a woman named Celeste, her mother's best friend.

The top had come years before. It was a simple toy, but very brightly colored. When the handle was pumped, it made a satisfying whirling sound as it spun fast, blurring the red and blue and green. It had quickly become Fahid's favorite—such a favorite that Adrianne had recently taken it from the shelves and hidden it.

"I want the top."

"I know. The last time you wanted it you bumped your head trying to climb up and get it when I wasn't here." And when the king had heard of it, Adrianne had been confined to her room for a week. "Close your eyes."

He grinned, and shook his head.

Grinning right back at him, Adrianne bent down until they were nose to nose. "Close your eyes, my brother, or no top." His eyes snapped shut. "If you are very good, I will let you keep it all day." As she spoke she backed away from him, then she wiggled under the bed, where she kept the best of her treasures. Even as she reached for the top, Fahid wiggled under beside her. "Fahid!" With the exasperation mothers show to their favored children, she pinched his cheek. "You are very bad."

"I love Adrianne."

As always, her heart softened. She stroked his untidy hair back from his face and nuzzled his cheek. "I love Fahid. Even when he is bad." She took the top and started back out, but his sharp eyes had landed on the Christmas ball.

"Pretty." Delighted, he grabbed it with hands that were sticky with candy. "Mine."

"It's not yours." She took his ankles to pull him out from under the bed. "And it's a secret." As they snuggled together on the rug, Adrianne put her hands on either side of Fahid's and shook. The top was forgotten as they watched the snow fall. "It's my most precious treasure." She held it up so that the light shot through the glass. "A magic ball."

"Magic." His mouth hung slack as Adrianne tilted it again. "Let me, let me!" Taking it from her, he scrambled to his feet. "Magic. I want to show Mother."

"No. Fahid, no." Adrianne was up and after him as he raced to the door.

Thrilled by the new game, he set his short, husky legs pumping. His laughter rang off the walls as he raced, brandishing the glass ball like a trophy. To keep the game alive, he swerved into the tunnel that connected the women's quarters with the king's apartments.

Adrianne felt her first true concern then, and it made her hesitate. As a daughter of the house, the tunnel was forbidden to her. She stepped forward with the idea of luring Fahid back with a promise of some new treat. But when his laughter shut off abruptly, she hurried inside. He was sprawled, lips quivering, at Abdu's feet.

Abdu looked so tall and so powerful as he stood, legs spread, staring down at his son. His white *throbe* skimmed the floor where Fahid had fallen. The lights in the tunnel were dim, but Adrianne could see the glint of anger in his eyes.

"Where is your mother?"

"Please, sir." Adrianne rushed forward. She kept her head bowed in submission while her heartbeat thundered. "I was caring for my brother."

He looked at her, the tumbled hair, the dust on her dress, her damp, nervous hands. He could have knocked her aside with one sweep of his arm. His pride told him she was worth not even that. "You do a poor job of caring for the prince."

She said nothing, knowing no response was expected. She kept her head lowered so that he couldn't see the flash of fury in her eyes.

"Tears are not for men, and never for kings," he said, but he bent with some gentleness to set Fahid on his feet. It was then he noticed the ball his son still gripped tightly. "Where did you get this?" The anger was back, slicing like a sword. "This is forbidden." He snatched the ball from Fahid and made him wail. "Would you disgrace me, disgrace our house?"

Because she knew her father's hand could strike quickly and with force, Adrianne stepped between him and her brother. "It belongs to me. I gave it to him."

She braced for the blow, but it never came. Rather than fury, she confronted ice. Adrianne learned that cold disinterest could be the most painful of punishments. Her eyes had filled, but facing her father, she fought back the tears. He wanted her to cry, she felt it. If dry eyes were her only defense, then hers would remain dry.

"So you would corrupt my son? Give him Christian symbols in the guise of a toy? I should have expected treachery from such as you." He flung the ball against the wall, shattering it. Terrified, Fahid clung to Adrianne's legs. "Go back to the women, where you belong. From this moment you are forbidden to care for Fahid."

He snatched up his son and turned away. Fahid, his face wet and swollen, reached out for her and called her name.

Chapter Five

Disgrace made her strong. It made her silent. It made her proud. Over the months that followed, Phoebe worried about Adrianne. For years Phoebe had lived with her own unhappiness, using it like a crutch because she saw no choice. Her American way of life had ended when she had stepped onto the soil of her husband's country. From the beginning, the laws and traditions of Jaquir had been against her. She was a woman, and as such, despite her own beliefs, despite her own desires, she was forced to conform.

Over the years Phoebe had found one comfort to ease her imprisonment. In her eyes Adrianne had been content, even suited to the life in Jaquir. She had a heritage, a title, a position even the king's disfavor couldn't take from her. She had family, playmates. She had security.

Phoebe knew that Westerners were beginning to come in droves to Jaquir and the Middle East, lured by oil. And because of this new state of affairs she saw reporters again and played the role of the fairy-tale desert queen. Abdu wanted the money and technology the West would bring, even while he detested Westerners for providing them. With Westerners pouring into Jaquir, there would be progress. In time there even might be liberation. She was clinging to that—not for herself any longer, but for Adrianne. As the months went by, she began to see that if new freedoms did come to Jaquir, they would arrive too late to benefit her daughter.

Adrianne was quietly obedient but no longer happy. She played games with the other girls and listened to her grand-mother's stories, but she was no longer young. Phoebe began to long for home more fiercely than ever before. She began to dream of going back, taking Adrianne, of showing her daughter a world beyond the laws and limitations of Jaquir.

But even as she dreamed, she didn't believe it possible. So she took her escape where she could find it, in tranquilizers and forbidden liquor.

She was not a sophisticated woman. In spite of her rise in the glittery world of entertainment, she had remained very much the naive girl from the small farm in Nebraska. In her days in movie making, she had seen drinking and drug use. But in a way that was innate to her, she passed over what was unpleasant and believed in illusions.

In Jaquir she became an addict, though she was ignorant of it. Drugs made the days bearable and blurred the nights. She had lived in the Middle East almost as long as she had lived in California, but with drugs she blissfully lost track of time and of the fact that she had become as much of an illusion here as the women she had played on the screen.

To be called to Abdu's apartments filled Phoebe with fear. They never spoke privately now. In public, when he wished it, they portrayed themselves as a couple from a romance. The breathtaking movie star and the elegant king. Though Abdu detested cameras, he allowed the press to photograph them together. He trod a delicate line between the traditional leader of his culture and the symbol of progress. But dollars, deutsche marks, and yen were flowing into his country as oil flowed out.

He was a man who had been educated in the West and who could dine with presidents and prime ministers, leaving them with the impression of a brilliant and open mind. He had been raised in Jaquir, bred on Islam. In his youth he had believed there could be a merging. Now he saw the West only as a threat, even an abomination to Allah. Those beliefs had crystallized because of Phoebe. She was his symbol of the corruption and the dishonor.

He looked at her now as she stood before him in a black dress that covered her from neck to ankle. Her hair was bound in a scarf so that not a hint of fire showed. Her skin was pale, not as creamy as it once had been, and her eyes were dull.

Drugs, Abdu thought with disgust. He knew about them but chose to ignore them.

41

He tapped a finger on the edge of his ebony desk, knowing every moment he made her wait her fear increased. "You have been invited to Paris to participate in a charity ball."

"Paris?"

"It appears that there has been a revival of your films. Perhaps people find it amusing to watch the wife of the King of Jaquir expose herself."

Her head snapped up. He was smiling at her, waiting for her to protest so that he could crush even that small defiance. But she spoke quietly. "There was a time the King of Jaquir was also pleased to watch Phoebe Spring."

His smile faded. He remembered with self-loathing the hours he had spent watching her, desiring her. "It is thought that your presence would be of interest to those who attend this charity affair."

Phoebe fought to keep calm, to keep her voice level. "You will permit me to go to Paris?"

"I have business there. It will be convenient for my American wife to accompany me and show Jaquir's link with the West. You understand what is expected of you."

"Yes, yes, of course." It wouldn't do to appear too pleased, but she couldn't prevent a smile. "A ball. In Paris?"

"A dress is being designed. You will wear The Sun and the Moon and present yourself as expected of the wife of the King of Jaquir. If you cause me shame, you will 'develop an indisposition' and be sent back at once."

"I understand perfectly." The idea of Paris, just the idea, made her stronger. "Adrianne—"

"Arrangements have been made for her," Abdu interrupted.

"Arrangements?" She felt the lick of fear at the base of her neck. She should have remembered that whenever Abdu gave with one hand, he took with the other. "What kind of arrangements?"

"They do not concern you."

"Please." She had to be careful, very careful. "I only want to prepare her, to be certain she is an asset to the House of Jaquir." Phoebe bowed her head but couldn't stop her fingers from twisting and knotting together. "I am only a woman, and she is my one child."

Abdu lowered himself into the chair behind his desk but

didn't gesture for Phoebe to sit. "She is to go to Germany, to school. We have found this a good arrangement for females of rank before their marriages."

"No! Dear God, Abdu, don't send her to school so far away." Forgetting pride, forgetting caution, she charged around the desk to drop at his feet. "You can't take her. She's all I have. You don't care what happens to her. It can't matter to you if she stays with me."

He took her hands at the wrists and removed them from where she clutched at his *throbe*. "She is a member of the House of Jaquir. The fact that your blood runs through her veins is only more reason for her to be separated and properly trained before her betrothal to Kadeem al-Misha."

"Betrothal?" Wild with fear, Phoebe clutched at him again. "She's only a child. Even in Jaquir you don't marry off children."

"She will be married on her fifteenth birthday. The arrangements are nearly complete. Then she will at last be of some use to me as the wife of an ally." He took Phoebe's hands again, but this time hauled her against him. "Be grateful that I do not give her to an enemy."

She was breathing heavily, her face close to his. For one blinding instant she wanted to kill him with her bare hands, to drag her fingers down his face and watch the blood run. If it would have saved Adrianne, she would have done it. Force would never work, nor would reason. She still had guile.

"Forgive me." She let herself go limp. She let her eyes fill now, let them shimmer. "I'm weak and selfish. I was thinking only of losing my child, not of how generous you are to make a good marriage for her." She dropped back down to a kneeling position, careful to keep her pose subservient in the extreme, then she wiped her eyes as if coming to her senses. "I am a foolish woman, Abdu, but not so foolish that I cannot be grateful. She will learn to be a proper wife in Germany. I hope you will be proud of her."

"I will do my duty by her." He gestured impatiently for her to stand.

"Perhaps you would consider allowing her to accompany us to Paris." Her heart was pounding against her ribs as she folded her hands. "Many men prefer a wife who has traveled, who is able to accompany them on business or pleasure trips and be a help rather than a hindrance. Because of her rank, a great deal will be expected of Adrianne. I wouldn't want her to cause you embarrassment. The education you received in Europe and the experiences you had there have certainly given you a better understanding of the world and Jaquir's place in it."

His first thought had been to dismiss the idea out of hand, but her last words hit home. He believed strongly that his time in cities like Paris, London, and New York had made him a better king and a more pure child of Allah.

"I will consider it."

She bit back the urge to beg and bowed her head. "Thank you."

Phoebe's heart was still pounding when she returned to her room. She wanted a drink, a pill, oblivion. Instead, she lay on the bed and forced herself to think.

All the years wasted, waiting for Abdu to return to the man he had once been, for her life to return. She had remained in Jaquir because he had demanded it, because even if she had somehow managed to escape, he would have taken Adrianne.

Because she'd been weak, confused, afraid, she had lived almost ten years of her life in bondage. Not Adrianne. Never Adrianne. No matter what she had to do, she wasn't going to see Adrianne taken away, given to some stranger to live her life out as a virtual prisoner.

The first step was Paris, she told herself as she wiped a film of sweat from her brow. She would get Adrianne to Paris, and they would never come back.

"When I go to Paris, I will buy trunkfuls of beautiful clothes." Duja watched Adrianne slip on a gold bracelet and tried not to be jealous. "My father says we will eat at a place called Maxim's and that I will have anything I want."

Adrianne turned. Her palms were continually damp from nerves, but she was afraid to wipe them on her dress. "I will bring you a present."

Jealousy forgotten, Duja grinned. "Only one?"

"A special one. We are going to go to the top of the Eiffel Tower and to a place where they have thousands of paintings. And then—" She pressed a hand to her stomach. "I am sick."

"If you are sick, you will not go, so you will not be sick. Leiha is sulking." She said it only in hopes to make Adrianne feel better. Servants had already taken the bags, so Duja put her arm around Adrianne's shoulder to lead her out. "Sh wants to go, but the king takes only you and your mother. Leiha has to be content that she is pregnant again."

"If I can buy presents for Fahid and my sisters, you will give them?"

"I will." She kissed Adrianne's cheek. "I will miss you."

"We will be back soon."

"But you have never gone away before."

The harem was filled with women and the excitement of the journey only two would take. There were embraces to be exchanged, and laughter. Phoebe stood in her veil and *abaaya*, her hands knotted together at her waist, her face impassive. The scents, the dark, smoky scents of the harem weighed down on her until she thought she could almost see them. If there were a God, she would never see these people or this place again. For once she was grateful for the scarves and the veil. It meant she had to control only her eyes.

The wave of regret surprised her as she kissed her sisters-in-law, her mother-in-law, the cousins by marriage. All the women she had lived with for almost a decade.

"Adrianne must sit by the window," Jiddah told Phoebe as she kissed and embraced them both. "So she can look down at Jaquir as the plane rises." She smiled, pleased that her son was at last showing an interest in the child who was secretly her favorite. "Do not eat too much French cream, my sweet girl."

Adrianne grinned and rose on her toes to kiss Jiddah one last time. "I will eat so much that I will get fat. You will not know me when I return."

Jiddah laughed, patting Adrianne's cheek with a hand lavishly decorated with henna. "I will always know you. Go, go now. Come back safe. *Inshallah*."

They walked out of the harem, through the garden and beyond the wall, where a car was waiting. Adrianne's nerves were too tightly strung for her to notice her mother's silence. She chattered about the plane ride, Paris, what they would see, what they would buy. She asked a question, then hurried on to another without expecting an answer.

By the time they reached the airport, Adrianne was sick with excitement. Phoebe was sick with fear.

Thus far, the coming of Western businessmen had only complicated airport procedure. Planes landed and departed more often, and ground transportation was limited to a smattering of cabs whose drivers spoke no English. The small terminal was already packed; women shuffled to one end, men to the other. Confused Americans and Europeans fought to guard their luggage from overenthusiastic porters while searching desperately for connections often delayed for days. Those czars of capitalism more often than not were stalled, victims of a culture gap that had widened to a chasm over the centuries.

The air roared with the noise of planes, the cacophony of voices in different languages that rose and fell often without understanding. Adrianne saw a woman sitting by a pile of baggage, her face wet with tears and pale with exhaustion. Another rode herd on three young children who stared and pointed at the Arabic women in their black cloaks and veils.

"There are so many of them," Adrianne murmured as they were led through the crowd by their bodyguards. "Why do they come?"

"Money." Phoebe shifted her eyes right and left. It was hot, so hot she feared she might faint. But her hands were like ice. "Hurry."

Taking Adrianne's hand, she pulled her outside again. Abdu's gleaming new private plane, recently purchased with oil money, waited.

Adrianne's mouth dried up at the sight of it. "It's very small."

"Don't worry. I'm with you."

Inside, the cabin was very plush despite its size. The seats were upholstered in a rich fabric the color of pewter; the carpet was bloodred. The tiny lights bolted near each seat had crystal shades. Wonderfully cool, the air smelled of sandalwood, the king's preferred scent. Servants, bowing silently, waited to serve from the store of food and drink.

Abdu was already on board, bent with his secretary over a file of papers. His *throbe* had been discarded for a suit tailored in London, but he wore it with the headdress of the East. He never glanced up as they climbed in and took their seats. Instead, he gave a careless signal to one of his men. Within moments the engine caught. Adrianne's stomach did a quick flip when the nose rose into the air.

"Mama."

"We'll be over the clouds soon." Phoebe kept her voice low, grateful that Abdu ignored them. "Just like birds, Addy. Watch." She rested her cheek against Adrianne's. "Jaquir is going away."

Adrianne wanted to be sick, but was afraid to because her father was with them. Determined, she clenched her teeth, swallowed hard, and watched the world drop away. After a while the churning in her stomach eased. It was Phoebe's turn to chatter. She did so in a low voice that ultimately lulled Adrianne to sleep. While her daughter dozed on her shoulder, Phoebe stared down at the blue waters of the Mediterranean and prayed.

Paris was a feast for the senses. Adrianne clung to her mother's hand and stared at everything as they hurried through the airport. She had always believed that her mother's stories about other places were no more than fairy tales. She had loved them as such, dreamed of them as such. Now she had stepped through a door into a world that had existed only in her imagination.

Even her mother was different. She had shed the *abaaya* and veil. Beneath she wore a trim Western suit the same shade as her eyes. Her hair was loose and free, gloriously red over her shoulders. She had even spoken to a man, a stranger, when they had passed through customs. Adrianne had glanced fearfully up at her father, waiting for punishment. But he had done nothing.

Women walked here, sometimes alone, sometimes arm in arm with men. They wore skirts and tight pants that showed their legs. They walked with their heads up, their hips swinging, but no one stared at them. To her astonishment, she saw a couple embrace and kiss while others elbowed around them. There were no *matawain*, with their camel whips and henna-tipped beards, to arrest them.

The sun was setting when they exited the terminal. Adrianne waited to hear the prayer call sound, but there was nothing. There was confusion here, but it was faster and somehow more organized than the confusion at the airport in Jaquir. People bundled into cabs, men and women together without shame or secrecy. Phoebe had to pull her into the limo as she craned to see more.

To see Paris at sunset for the first time. Whenever Adrianne thought of the city again, she would remember the magic of that first view, when the light was caught between day and night. The old buildings rose, fussy, somehow feminine, glowing pink and gold and soft white in the dying sun. The big car swooped down the boulevard, driving fast into the heart of the city. But it wasn't the speed that made her giddy and breathless.

She thought there would be music. In such a place there had to be music. But she didn't risk asking permission to lower the window. Instead, she let it play inside her head, grandly, gloriously, as they cruised along the Seine.

There were couples walking, hand in hand, their hair and the little short skirts of the women fluttering in a breeze that smelled of water and flowers. That smelled of Paris. She saw cafés where people huddled around small round tables and drank from glasses that glinted red and gold like the sunlight.

If she had been told that the plane had taken them to another planet and another time, she would have believed it.

When the car stopped at the hotel, Adrianne waited until her father had stepped out. "Can we see more later?"

"Tomorrow." Phoebe squeezed her hand so tightly she winced. "Tomorrow." She fought not to shiver in the balmy evening air. The hotel looked like a palace, and she was through with palaces.

With the entourage of servants and bodyguards and secretaries, they took an entire floor of the Crillion. To Adrianne's disappointment, she and her mother were ushered to their suite and left alone.

"Can't we go and have dinner at this place called Maxim's?"

"Not tonight, darling." Phoebe peered out through the peephole in the door. A guard was already in place outside the door. There was to be a harem even in Paris. Her face was pale when she turned back, but she smiled and struggled to keep her voice light. "We'll have something sent up. Anything you want."

"Being here is no different from being in Jaquir." She looked around the elegant suite. Like the women's quarters, it was plush and secluded. Unlike them, there were windows open to the evening. She crossed the room and looked out at Paris. Lights had twinkled on, giving the city a festive, fairy-tale look. She was in Paris but was not permitted to be a part of it. It was as if she'd been given the most glorious jewel in the world and allowed to look at it for a few moments before it was snatched back and locked away in a vault.

"Addy, you must be patient." Like her daughter, Phoebe was drawn to the window, to the lights, to the life in the streets. Her yearnings were only the stronger because she had once been free. "Tomorrow . . . tomorrow is going to be the most exciting day in your life." She gathered Adrianne close to kiss her. "You trust me, don't you?"

"Yes, Mama."

"I'm going to do what's best for you, I swear it." Her grip tightened, then abruptly she released Adrianne and laughed. "Now, you enjoy the view. I'll be back in a moment."

"Where are you going?"

"Just into the next room. I promise." She smiled, hoping to reassure them both. "Look out the window, baby. Paris is beautiful this time of day."

Phoebe closed the door between the parlor and her bedroom. It was risky to use the phone. For days she had tried to think of a better, of a safer way. Though she had needed relief, she hadn't touched a tranquilizer or a drink since Abdu had announced the trip. Her mind was clearer than it had been in years. So clear it hurt. Still, she could think of no way except the phone. Her only hope was that Abdu wouldn't suspect betrayal from a woman who had tolerated his abuse for so long.

She picked up the receiver. It felt foreign in her hand, like something from another century. She nearly laughed. She was a grown woman, living in the twentieth century, yet it had been almost a decade since she had touched a telephone. Her fingers shook as she dialed. The voice spoke in quick French.

"Do you speak English?"

"Yes, madame. May I help you?"

There was a God, she thought as she lowered herself to

sit on the bed. "I want to send a cablegram. An urgent one. To the United States. To New York."

Adrianne stood at the windows, her hands pressed against the glass as if by will alone she could dissolve it and become a part of the world that hurried by outside. Something was wrong with her mother. Her deepest fear was that Phoebe was ill and they would both be sent back to Jaquir. She knew if they were taken back now, she would never see a place such as Paris again. She would not see the women with their bare legs and painted faces or the high buildings with their hundreds of lights. She thought her father would be glad, glad that she had seen but not touched, smelled but not tasted. It would be another way to punish her for being female and of mixed blood.

As if her thoughts had conjured him, he strode through the door and into the suite. Adrianne turned. She was small for her age, as delicate as a doll. Already there were hints of the dark, sultry beauty from her bedouin blood. Abdu saw only a thin girl with wide eyes and a stubborn mouth. As always, his eyes frosted over when he looked at her.

"Where is your mother?"

"She is through there." When he started for the door, Adrianne took a quick step forward. "May we go out tonight?"

He spared her a brief, disinterested glance. "You will remain here."

Because she was young, she persisted when others would have bowed away. "It is not late. The sun has only just set. Grandmother told me there was much to do in Paris at night."

He stopped fully now. It was rare for her to dare to speak to him, rarer still for him to bother to listen. "You will remain inside. You are here only because I permitted it."

"Why did you?"

That she had the temerity to ask had his eyes narrowing. "My reasons are of no concern to you. Be warned that if you remind me of your presence too often, I will rid myself of it."

Adrianne's eyes glistened with a combination of grief and anger she couldn't understand. "I am blood of your blood," she said softly. "What reason is there for you to hate me?"

"You are blood of her blood." And he turned to open the

door. Phoebe stepped out quickly. Her color was high, her eyes round and wide, like a doe's when she scents the hunter.

"Abdu. Did you want to see me? I needed to wash after the trip."

He saw the nerves. He smelled the fear. It pleased him that she did not consider herself secure even outside the walls of the harem. "An interview has been arranged. We will have breakfast here at nine o'clock with the reporter. You will dress accordingly, and see that she is prepared."

Phoebe glanced toward Adrianne. "Of course. After the interview I'd like to do some shopping, perhaps take Adrianne to a museum."

"You will do what you wish between ten o'clock and four. Then I will require you."

"Thank you. We're grateful for the chance to visit Paris."

"See that the girl holds her tongue, or she will see Paris only through that window."

When he left, Phoebe let her shaking legs buckle. "Addy, please, don't anger him."

"I have only to *be* to anger him."

When she saw the first tears, Phoebe opened her arms. "You're so young," she said as she rocked Adrianne in her lap. "Too young for all of this. I promise I'll make it up to you." Over Adrianne's head her eyes focused and hardened. "I swear I'll make it all up to you."

She had never taken a meal with her father. Because she had the resilience of an eight-year-old, Adrianne found it easy to skip over the words that had been spoken the night before and look forward to her first day in Paris.

If she was disappointed that they would take their meal in the suite, she said nothing. She liked her new blue dress and matching coat too well to complain. In an hour she would truly begin her week in Paris.

"I can't tell you how much I appreciate this interview, Your Highness." The reporter, already charmed by Abdu, took her seat at the table. Adrianne kept her hands folded in her lap and tried not to stare.

The reporter had very long, very straight hair the color of ripe peaches. Her fingernails were painted red, as was her mouth. Her dress was of the same shade, cut snug, and its skirt skimmed her thighs as she crossed her legs. She spoke English with a rolling French accent. To Adrianne, she was as exotic as a jungle bird and just as fascinating.

"It is our pleasure, Mademoiselle Grandeau." Abdu signaled for coffee. A servant jumped to obey.

"I hope you enjoy your stay in Paris."

"I always enjoy Paris." Abdu smiled in a way Adrianne had never seen. He suddenly looked approachable. Then his eyes passed over her as though her chair were empty. "My wife and I are looking forward to participating in the ball this evening."

"Parisian society is looking forward to greeting you and your beautiful wife." Mademoiselle Grandeau turned to Phoebe. "Your fans are thrilled, Your Highness. They've felt you deserted them for love."

The coffee burned bitter in Phoebe's throat as she smiled. She would have traded every jewel she owned for a whiskey. "Anyone who has ever been in love would understand that there is no sacrifice and no risk too great."

"Might I ask you if you have any regrets about giving up your thriving career in films?"

Phoebe looked at Adrianne and her eyes softened. "How can I have regrets when I have so much?"

"It is like a fairy tale, is it not? The beautiful woman swept off by the desert sheikh to a mysterious and exotic land. A land," Mademoiselle Grandeau added, "which becomes wealthier every day because of oil. How do you feel," she asked Abdu, "about the Westerners pouring into your country?"

"Jaquir is a small country which welcomes the advances that oil brings. However, as king, it is my responsibility to preserve our culture while opening doors for progress."

"Obviously you have an affection for the West, as you fell in love and married an American. Is it true, Your Highness, that you have another wife?"

He lifted a crystal glass of juice. His expression seemed blandly amused, but his fingers gripped tightly. He despised being questioned by a woman. "In my religion, a man is permitted four wives as long as he can treat each of them equally."

"With the women's movement growing stronger in the

United States and Europe, do you believe this clash of cultures will cause problems for the countries which come to the Middle East to build?"

"We are different, mademoiselle, in dress, in beliefs. The people of Jaquir would be equally shocked that a woman in your country is permitted to become intimate with a man before marriage. This difference will not deter financial interest on either side."

"No." Mademoiselle Grandeau wasn't there to argue politics. Her readers wanted to know if Phoebe Spring was still beautiful. If her marriage was still romantic. She cut into her crepe and smiled at Adrianne. The child was striking, with the king's sultry black eyes and Phoebe's full, sculpted mouth. Though the coloring spoke of her bedouin ancestors, she had the stamp of her mother. The features were smaller, finer, than those of the woman who had once been called the Amazon queen of films. The purity of bone structure, the stunning profile, and the clear-eyed vulnerability were there.

"Princess Adrianne, how do you feel knowing your mother was considered the most beautiful woman to grace the screen?"

She fumbled. The hard, brief glance from her father had her straightening. "I am proud of her. My mother is the most beautiful woman in the world."

Mademoiselle Grandeau laughed and took another bite of crepe. "It would be hard to find anyone to disagree with you. Perhaps one day you'll follow her footsteps to Hollywood. Is there any chance that you'll make another movie, Your Highness?"

Phoebe swallowed more coffee and prayed that it would stay down. "My priority is my family." She touched Adrianne's hand under the table. "Of course I'm thrilled to have been asked to come here, to see old friends. But the choice I made, as you said, was made for love." Over the table her eyes met Abdu's and held. "Where there is love, there is very little a woman won't do."

"Hollywood's loss is obviously Jaquir's gain. There is a great deal of speculation that you'll wear The Sun and the Moon tonight. It's considered one of the world's greatest treasures. Like all the great jewels, The Sun and the Moon has legends and mystery and romance attached to it and people are eager to see the fabled necklace. Will you wear it?"

"The Sun and the Moon was a gift from my husband on our marriage. In Jaquir this is considered the bride price, a kind of reverse dowry. It is, second only to Adrianne, the most precious gift Abdu has given me." She looked at him again with a hint of challenge. "I'm proud to wear it."

"There won't be a woman in the world who won't envy you tonight, Your Highness."

With Adrianne's hand still caught in hers, Phoebe smiled. "I can say only that I look forward to this evening more than any other in years. It will be glorious." Her eyes met Abdu's again. *"Inshallah."*

As Phoebe had suspected, they were joined by two guards and a driver when they left the hotel. She was ecstatic over her first victory. She had stopped at the desk and requested her passport on which Adrianne traveled as her minor child. The guards were chattering, apparently believing she was inquiring about the performance of some trivial service, and never even noticed when the clerk returned from the rear office and slipped the leather-encased document into her hand. She could have wept with joy . . . and the first glow of pride she'd felt in years, but she disciplined herself to betray nothing. Now she had no real plan, only a fierce and edgy determination. Beside her in the limo, Adrianne all but bounced with excitement. They were truly in Paris now, with hours to spare before she would have to go back to the hotel. She wanted to ride to the top of the Eiffel Tower, to sit in a café, to walk and walk and walk and hear the music of the city she had only imagined.

"We'll shop a little." Phoebe's mouth was so dry she had to force her tongue from the roof of her mouth. "There's Chanel, Dior. Wait until you see all the beautiful clothes, Addy. The colors, the materials. But you have to stay close to me, very close. I don't want to lose you. Don't wander. Promise."

"I won't." Adrianne felt her own nerves begin to rise. At the times when her mother talked like this—very fast, with the words jumping out on top of each other—she soon and always fell into depression. Then she would grow so quiet, so removed, so closed in upon herself and unmindful of others that it terrified Adrianne. Frightened about what she knew was about to happen, Adrianne kept up her own chatter, staying glued to Phoebe's side as they were escorted into the most exclusive shops in Europe.

It was like another dream, different from the vision of Paris at dusk. The salons were bright with gilt tables and velvet chairs. In each one they were ushered in with a deference Adrianne had never received in her own country. She was cooed over by women with glossy faces, served lemonade or tea and tiny sweet cookies while models with thin limbs and frail-looking bodies glided out draped in the latest fashions.

Phoebe ordered with abandon, dozens of cocktail dresses with skinny straps and layers of beads, slim suits in raw silk and linen. If her plan succeeded, she would never wear a stitch of what she recklessly purchased. It seemed a kind of justice to her, the smallest and sweetest of revenges. She swept from salon to salon, ladening the silent guards with boxes and bags.

"We'll go to the Louvre before lunch," she told Adrianne as they settled in the limo again. She checked her watch, then sat back and shut her eyes.

"Can we eat in a café?"

"We'll see." She groped for Adrianne's hand. "I want you to be happy, darling. Happy and safe. That's all that matters."

"I like being here with you." Despite all the cookies and tea and lemonade at the couturier's she was hungry, but she didn't want to say so. "There is so much to see. When you told me about places like this, I thought you were making up stories. It's better than a story."

Phoebe opened her eyes to stare out the window. They were driving along the river in the most romantic city in the world. Recklessly, she lowered the glass and drew in a deep breath. "There, Addy, do you smell it?"

Laughing, Adrianne leaned closer, like a puppy, to let the breeze race against her face. "The water?"

"The freedom," Phoebe murmured. "I want you to remember this moment."

When the car stopped, Phoebe alighted slowly, regally, not sparing a glance at the guards. With Adrianne's hand in hers, she entered the Louvre. There were throngs of people—students, tourists, lovers. Adrianne found them as fascinating as the art her mother pointed out as they strolled through the galleries. Voices echoed off the high ceilings, a variety of tones and accents. She saw a man with hair as long as a woman's, wearing jeans torn off at the knee and carrying a battered knapsack. When he caught her staring, he grinned and winked, then held up two fingers in a V. Embarrassed, Adrianne looked down at her shoes.

"So much has changed," Phoebe said. "It seems like a different world. The way people dress, the way they talk. I feel like Rip Van Winkle."

"Who?"

With a sound perilously close to a sob, Phoebe bent to hug her. "It's just a story." As she straightened, she glanced toward the guards. They were a few paces behind, bored. "I want you to do exactly what I say," Phoebe whispered. "Don't ask questions. Hold tight to me." Before Adrianne could agree, Phoebe pulled her into a group of students. Moving fast, elbowing and shoving when necessary, she worked her way through, then sprinted down a long corridor.

There were shouts behind her. Without breaking rhythm, she scooped Adrianne up and raced down a flight of stairs. She needed a door, any door that led to the outside. If she could get to the street, somehow get out and into a cab, she had a chance. Whenever a corridor snaked off, she took it, barreling her way past visitors and staff. It didn't matter whether she was heading out of the building or deeper into it. She had to lose the guards. She heard footsteps pounding behind her and ran blindly, like a hare trying desperately to outrun a fox.

Paintings flashed by as she ran. Her labored breathing grew loud as she streaked by the most treasured art in the world. People stared. Her hair had fallen from its neat twist to tumble wild and red around her shoulders. She saw the door and nearly stumbled. Gripping Adrianne, her heart about to burst, she broke free of the building. But she did not stop running.

She could smell the river again, and the freedom. She stopped, gasping for breath, a beautiful, terrified woman clinging to a child. She had only to lift a hand and a cab swerved to the curb. "Orly airport," she managed to say, looking right and left as she bundled Adrianne inside. "Hurry, please, hurry."

"*Oui*, madame." The driver tipped his cap, then pushed down the accelerator.

"Mama. What is it? Why did we run? Where are we going?"

Phoebe covered her face with her hands. There was no going back now. "Trust me, Addy. I can't explain yet."

When Phoebe began to shake, Adrianne cuddled close. Clinging to each other, they drove out of Paris.

Adrianne's lip trembled as she heard the roar of planes. "Are we going back to Jaquir?"

Phoebe fumbled with her wallet, recklessly giving the driver double his fare. The fear was still with her, a metallic, ugly taste on her tongue. He would kill her if he caught her now. Kill her, then wreak the rest of his vengeance on Adrianne.

"No." She crouched down on the sidewalk so that her face was even with Adrianne's. "We're never going back to Jaquir." She looked over her shoulder, certain Abdu would leap out of the next car and make her words a lie. "I'm taking you to America, to New York. Believe me, Addy, it's because I love you. Now, hurry."

She pulled Adrianne inside. For a moment the noise and rush confused her. It had been years since she had gone anywhere alone. Even before her marriage she had traveled with an entourage of publicists, secretaries, and dressers. The panic nearly overwhelmed her until she felt Adrianne's small, tense fingers link with hers.

Pan American. She had asked for Celeste to have the tickets waiting at the Pan American counter. As she hurried across the terminal, Phoebe prayed that her friend had come through. At the ticket counter she pulled her passport out of her bag and offered it and her most brilliant smile to the clerk.

"Good afternoon. I have two tickets, prepaid, for New York."

The smile dazzled him so that he blinked. "*Oui*, madame." Star struck, he lingered over the paperwork. "I have seen your movies. You are magnificent."

"Thank you." She felt some of her courage return. She hadn't been forgotten. "Are the tickets in order?"

"Pardon?" Oh, yes, yes." He stamped and scribbled. "Your flight number," he said, pointing at the ticket jacket. "Your gate. You have forty-five minutes."

Her palms were clammy with sweat when she took the tickets and slipped them into her purse. "Thank you."

"Wait, please."

She froze, poised to run as her hand locked on Adrianne's.

"You would give your autograph?"

She pressed her fingers to her eyes, giving way enough for one quick laugh. "Of course. I'd be delighted. What's your name?"

"It is Henri, madame." He handed her a scrap of paper. "I will never forget you."

She signed, as she had always, in a generous, looping hand. "Believe me, Henri. I will never forget you." She gave him the autograph and a smile. "Come along, Adrianne. We don't want to miss our plane. God bless Celeste," she said as they walked. "She's going to meet us in New York, Addy. She's my closest friend."

"Like Duja?"

"Yes." Fighting for calm, she looked down and managed another smile. "Yes, like Duja is to you. She's going to help us."

The terminal no longer interested Adrianne. She was afraid because her mother's face was very white and her hand shook. "He is going to be angry."

"He's not going to hurt you." Phoebe stopped again and took Adrianne by the shoulders. "I promise you that no matter what I have to do, he'll never hurt you." Then the tension of all the days and nights she had waited broke. With one hand pressed to her heaving stomach, she raced with Adrianne into the ladies' room and was violently sick.

"Mama, please." Terrified, Adrianne clung to Phoebe's waist as she bent over the bowl. "We must go back before he knows. We will say we were lost, separated. He will be only a little angry. It will be my fault. I will say it was my fault."

"Can't." Phoebe leaned against the stall door and waited for the nausea to pass. "We can't ever go back. He was going to send you away, baby."

"Away?"

"To Germany." With an unsteady hand Phoebe found a handkerchief and dried her damp face. "I won't let him send you away, to marry you off to a man who could be like him." Steadier, Phoebe knelt and wrapped her arms around her daughter. "I won't see you live your life the way I've had to live mine. It would kill me."

Slowly, the fear in Adrianne's eyes faded. In the narrow stall that still reeked of sickness, they crossed a new threshold in their lives. Gently, Adrianne helped Phoebe to her feet. "You are better? Lean on me."

Phoebe was only more pale when they boarded, when at last they sat on the plane with their seat belts in place and listened to the whine of engines. Her heart had stopped beating too fast. Now it was only a drumming in her head, one that reminded her of the harem and the oppressive heat. The taste of sickness was still in her mouth as she closed her eyes.

"Madame? May I serve you and the mademoiselle a drink after we have taken off?"

"Yes." She didn't bother to open her eyes. "Bring my daughter something cool and sweet."

"And for you?"

"Scotch," she said dully. "A double."

Chapter Six

Celeste Michaels loved a good drama. As a young child she had made up her mind to be an actress—not just an actress, but a star. She had begged, wheedled, sulked, and cajoled acting lessons out of her parents, who indulgently believed their little girl was going through a phase. They continued to think so even when they drove Celeste to auditions, rehearsals, and performances in community theater. Andrew Michaels was an accountant who preferred to look at life as a balance sheet of profit and loss. Nancy Michaels was a pretty housewife who enjoyed making fancy desserts for church socials. Both of them believed, even after theater began to dictate their lives, that little Celeste would outgrow her love of greasepaint and curtain calls.

At fifteen Celeste decided she was born to be blond and had tinted her tame brown hair to a golden halo that would become her trademark. Her mother had shrieked, her father had lectured. Celeste's hair had stayed blond. And she had won the part of Marion in her high school's production of *The Music Man*.

Once Nancy had complained to Andrew that she might have been able to handle it better if Celeste had been involved with boys and liquor rather than Shakespeare and Tennessee Williams.

The day after she received her high school diploma, Celeste moved from the cozy New Jersey suburb of her childhood to Manhattan. Her parents saw her off on the train with a mixture of relief and bafflement.

She auditioned, scrounging up enough to pay for her acting lessons and the rent on her fourth-floor walkup by flipping hamburgers and frying eggs at a greasy spoon. She married at twenty, a relationship that began with a bang and ended with a whimper a year later. By then Celeste had stopped looking back.

Just over ten years later she was the reigning lady of theater with a trail of hits behind her, a trio of Tonys, and a penthouse on Central Park West. She'd sent her parents a Lincoln for their last anniversary, but they still believed she'd come back to New Jersey when acting was out of her system and settle down with some nice Methodist boy.

Just now, pacing the airport lounge, she welcomed the relative anonymity of the theater actress. If people noticed her, they saw an attractive blonde, sturdily built and of average height. They didn't see the sultry Maggie the Cat or the ambitious Lady Macbeth. Not unless Celeste wanted them to.

She checked her watch and wondered again if Phoebe would be on the plane.

Nearly ten years, she thought as she took a seat and searched through her bag for a cigarette. They had become close friends quickly when Phoebe had come to New York to film on location for her first movie. Celeste had just ended her marriage and had been feeling a bit rough around the edges. Phoebe had been like a breath of fresh air, so funny and sweet. Each had become the sister to the other that neither had been born with, visiting coast to coast when possible, piling up huge long distance phone bills when it wasn't.

No one had been more thrilled when Phoebe had been nominated for an Oscar. No one had cheered more loudly when Celeste had won her first Tony.

They were opposites in many ways. Celeste was tough and driven, Phoebe malleable and trusting. Without realizing it, they had given each other a balance, and a friendship each would always cherish.

Then Phoebe had married and flown off to her desert kingdom. Correspondence had become sporadic after the first year, then almost nonexistent. It had hurt. Celeste would never have admitted it to anyone, but Phoebe's gradual termination of their friendship had hurt very much. On the surface she'd taken it philosophically. Her life was full and rich and progressing along the route she had mapped out as a girl in New Jersey. But there was a place in her heart that had grieved. Over the years Celeste had continued to send gifts to the girl she considered her godchild, and had been amused by the quaint and formal notes of acknowledgment Adrianne had sent back to her.

She was ready to love the child. In part because she was married to the theater, and that love affair would never produce children. And in part because Adrianne was Phoebe's.

Celeste tapped out her cigarette before reaching into a shopping bag and taking out a red-haired china doll. It was dressed in blue velvet trimmed in white. Celeste had chosen it because she thought the little girl would enjoy having a doll with the same color hair as her mother. And she didn't have any idea of what to say to the child, or to Phoebe.

When she heard the flight announced, she was up and pacing again. It wouldn't be long now. The deplaning, the trip through customs. There was no reason for the nagging worry at the base of her skull.

Except that the cablegram had said so little.

Celeste remembered each word, and, like a good actress, put her own inflection on them.

> CELESTE. I NEED YOUR HELP. PLEASE HAVE TWO
> TICKETS FOR NEW YORK AT THE PAN AMERICAN COUNT-
> ER AT ORLY. THE TWO O'CLOCK FLIGHT TOMORROW.
> MEET ME IF YOU CAN. I HAVE NO ONE ELSE. PHOEBE.

She saw them the moment they passed through the doors, the tall, striking redhead and the doll-like girl. They huddled close together, hands joined, bodies brushing. Celeste found it odd that for a moment she couldn't be certain who was reassuring whom.

Then Phoebe looked up. A range of emotions raced across her face, relief dominant. Before the relief, Celeste had recognized terror. Moving quickly, Celeste crossed to her.

"Phoebe." Putting everything but friendship on hold, Celeste hugged her close. "It's so good to see you again."

"Celeste, thank God. Oh, thank God you're here."

The desperation concerned her much more than the fact that the words were slurred from drinking. Careful to keep her smile in place, she looked down at Adrianne.

"So this is your Addy." Celeste touched a hand lightly to

the child's hair, noting the shadowed eyes and signs of exhaustion. She was reminded of pictures of survivors of disasters, the same flat, vulnerable look of shock. "You've had a long trip, but it's nearly over now. I have a car right outside."

"I'll never be able to repay you," Phoebe began.

"Don't be ridiculous." She gave Phoebe a last quick squeeze, then handed the shopping bag to Adrianne. "I brought you a present to celebrate your visit to America."

Adrianne looked at the doll, stirring enough energy to trace a finger down the sleeve of the gown. The velvet reminded her of Duja, but she was too tired to cry. "She is pretty. Thank you."

Celeste lifted a brow in surprise. The child sounded as exotic and as foreign as she looked. "Let's get your bags and go home, where you can relax."

"We don't have any bags." Phoebe nearly swayed, then steadied herself with a hand on Celeste's shoulder. "We don't have anything."

"All right." Questions could wait, Celeste decided as she slipped an arm around Phoebe's waist. A look told her the child could stand on her own. "Let's go home."

Unlike her experience in Paris, Adrianne noticed little of her drive from the airport into Manhattan. The limo was quiet and warm, but she couldn't relax. As she had during the long flight across the Atlantic, she carefully watched her mother. She tucked the doll Celeste had given her under her arm and kept Phoebe's hand firmly in her own. She was too weary to ask questions, but was ready to run.

"It's been so long." Phoebe looked around as if coming out of a trance. A little pulse beside her mouth kept jumping as her eyes darted from window to window. "It's changed. But it hasn't changed."

"You can always count on New York." Celeste blew out a stream of smoke, noting that Adrianne watched her cigarette with dark, fascinated eyes. "Maybe tomorrow Addy would like to walk in the park or do some shopping. Have you ever ridden on a merry-go-round, Adrianne?"

"What is it?"

"It's wooden horses you can ride around in a circle to music. There's one in the park across from where I live." She smiled at Adrianne, noting that Phoebe jumped every time the car stopped. If the mother was a mass of nerves, the child seemed a tower of control. What in God's name was she going to say to a kid who didn't know what a merry-go-round was? "You couldn't have picked a better time to come to New York. All the shops are decorated for Christmas."

Adrianne thought of the little glass ball and her brother. All at once she wanted to lay her head in her mother's lap and weep. She wanted to go home, to see her grandmother and her aunts, to smell the smells of the harem. But there was no going back.

"Will it snow?" she asked.

"Sooner or later." The urge to gather the child up and comfort her surprised Celeste. She'd never considered herself particularly maternal. There was something so sad yet strong about the way Adrianne stroked Phoebe's hand. "We've been having a warm spell. I doubt if it'll last much longer." Good Lord, she was talking about the weather. With some relief she leaned forward as the car slowed. "Here we are," Celeste said briskly when the limo cruised to the curb. "I moved here about five years ago, Phoebe. It suits me so well, they'll have to blast me out."

She led them past the security guard into the lobby of the elegant old building on Central Park West. She moved quickly, sweeping both Phoebe and Adrianne into the paneled elevator. To Adrianne it was like a slow ride to nowhere as fatigue weighed down her limbs. On the plane she'd fought off sleep, dragging herself out of fitful dozes to be certain no one separated her from Phoebe. Now, enervated, she walked mechanically between the two women into Celeste's penthouse.

"I'll give you the grand tour when you're not so exhausted." Celeste tossed her coat over the back of a chair and wondered what in the hell to do next. "You must be starving. Shall I send out or whip up an omelette?"

"I couldn't." With care Phoebe sat on a sofa. She felt as if every bone in her body would break if she moved too quickly. "Addy, are you hungry?"

"No." Even the thought of food had her stomach roiling.

"Poor thing's dead on her feet." Celeste moved over to wrap an arm around Adrianne's shoulders. "How about a nap?"

"Go with Celeste," Phoebe said before Adrianne could protest. "She'll take care of you."

"You won't go away?"

"No, I'll be right here when you wake up." Phoebe kissed both of her cheeks. "I promise."

"Come along, love." Celeste half carried the exhausted child up a long sweep of stairs. Talking nonsense, she stripped off Adrianne's coat and shoes and tucked her into bed. "You've had a long day."

"If he comes, you will wake me up so I can take care of Mama?"

Celeste's hand hesitated as she started to stroke Adrianne's hair. The skin beneath her eyes was bruised with fatigue, but the eyes themselves were awake and demanding.

"Yes, don't worry." Not knowing what else to do, she kissed Adrianne's brow. "I love her too, honey. We'll take care of her."

Content with that, Adrianne closed her eyes.

Celeste drew the drapes and left the door ajar. By the time she left the room, Adrianne was already asleep, as was Phoebe when Celeste came quietly downstairs.

The nightmare woke Adrianne. She had had the same dream sporadically since her fifth birthday: the dream of her father coming into her mother's room, of the crying, the shouting, of glass shattering. Of herself crawling under the bed with her hands over her ears.

She woke with her face wet with tears, biting back a cry because she was afraid to disturb the other women in the harem. But she wasn't in the harem. Her sense of time and place was so jumbled that she had to sit very still for several minutes before events fell into an ordered progression in her mind.

They had gone to Paris on the little plane and she had been frightened. The city had looked like a storybook with its oddly dressed people and its banks of flowers. Then there had been the shops, all the colors, the silks, the satins. Mama had bought her a pink dress with a white collar. But they had left it behind. They hadn't gone to the top of the Eiffel Tower. But they had gone to the Louvre. And they had run. Mama had been frightened, and sick.

Now they were in New York with the blond lady who had the beautiful voice.

She didn't want to be in New York. She wanted to be in Jaquir with Jiddah and Aunt Latifa and her cousins. Sniffling, Adrianne rubbed at her eyes as she crawled out of bed. She wanted to go home, where the smells were smells she recognized, where the voices spoke in a language she understood. Taking the doll Celeste had given her for comfort, she went to find her mother.

She heard the voices as she reached the top of the curving stairs. Adrianne walked down halfway to where she could see her mother and Celeste sitting in a big white room with black windows. Hugging the doll, she sat and listened.

"I'll never be able to repay you."

"Don't be silly." With one theatrical gesture Celeste dismissed everything. "We're friends."

"You can't imagine how much I've needed a friend these past years." Too wired up to sit, Phoebe rose, drink in hand, to circle the room.

"No, I can't," Celeste said slowly, concerned with the nerves she saw in every jerky movement. "But I'd like to."

"I don't know where to begin."

"The last time I saw you, you were looking radiant, in miles of white silk and tulle, wearing a necklace straight out of the Arabian Nights."

"The Sun and the Moon." Phoebe closed her eyes, then took a long drink. "It was the most beautiful thing I'd ever seen. I thought it was a gift—the most exquisite symbol of love any woman could ever dream of. What I didn't know was that he'd bought me with it."

"What are you talking about?"

"I could never make you understand life in Jaquir." She turned. Her brilliant blue eyes were bloodshot. Though she'd been drinking since she'd woken from her restless sleep, the liquor wasn't relaxing her.

"Try."

"At first it was really lovely. At least I wanted to believe it was. Abdu was kind, attentive. And there I was, the kid from Nebraska, queen. Because it seemed important to Abdu, I tried to live by the local customs—dress, attitude, that kind of thing. The first time I put on a veil I felt, well, sexy and exotic."

"Like *I Dream of Jeannie*?" Celeste asked with a smile, but Phoebe only sent her a blank look. "Never mind. Bad joke."

"I didn't mind the veil, really. It seemed like such a little thing, and Abdu insisted on it only when we were in Jaquir. We traveled a lot that first year, so it all seemed like an adventure. While I was pregnant, I was treated like some kind of precious jewel. There were complications and Abdu couldn't have been more loving and concerned. Then I had Adrianne." She looked down at her glass. "I need another drink."

"Help yourself."

Phoebe walked to the bar and filled the short glass to within a millimeter of the rim. "I was surprised when Abdu was upset. She was such a pretty, healthy baby, and like a miracle because I'd nearly miscarried twice. I know he'd talked incessantly about a son, but I had never expected him to be actually angry to have a daughter. I was hurt. I'd had a very long and difficult labor and his feelings about the baby set me off. We had a terrible fight right there in the hospital. Then it got worse; it got so much worse when the doctors told us I couldn't have any more children."

Phoebe took another drink, shuddering as the liquor punched into her system. "He changed, Celeste. He blamed me, not just for giving him a daughter he didn't want, but for somehow seducing him away from his duty and tradition."

"Seducing him? What a crock." Celeste kicked off her shoes. "The man never gave you a chance, sweeping you off your feet with hundreds of white roses, buying out restaurants so you could have intimate dinners. He wanted you, and he made damn sure he got you."

"None of that mattered. He saw me as a test, some kind of test that he failed, and he hated me for it. He saw Adrianne as a punishment instead of a gift, a punishment for his marrying a Western woman, a Christian, an actress. He wouldn't have anything to do with her, and as little as possible to do with me. I was shuffled off into the harem and supposed to be grateful he didn't divorce me."

"Harem? You mean like women only? Veils and pomegranates?"

Phoebe sat again, cupping the glass in both hands. "There's nothing romantic about it. The women's quarters.

You sit endlessly day after day while they talk about sex and childbirth and fashion. Your status depends on how many male children you've given birth to. A woman who's unable to have children is set apart to be pitied."

"Obviously none of them have read Gloria Steinem," Celeste interjected.

"Women don't read at all. They don't work, they don't drive. There's nothing to do but sit and drink tea and wait for the day to be over. Or you go out in groups to shop, covered from head to foot in black so you won't tempt a man."

"Give me a break, Phoebe."

"It's true. There are religious police everywhere. You can be whipped for saying the wrong thing, doing the wrong thing, wearing the wrong thing. You can't even speak to a man who isn't a member of your family. Not a word."

"Phoebe, this is 1971."

"Not in Jaquir." With a half laugh she pressed a hand to her eyes. "There's no time in Jaquir. Celeste, I tell you, I lost nearly ten years of my life. Sometimes it seems like a hundred, other times it seems like months. That's the way it is there. When I couldn't have any more children, Abdu took a second wife. The law allows it. The man's law."

Celeste plucked a cigarette out of the porcelain holder on the low table. She studied it as she tried to understand what Phoebe was describing. "I've read some articles. There've been a number of them in the last couple of years about you and Abdu. You never spoke of any of this."

"I couldn't. I was permitted to speak to the press only because he wanted publicity for the oil boom in the Middle East."

"I've heard," Celeste said dryly.

"You'd have to be there to understand it. Even the press isn't allowed to tell the full story. If they tried, the connection would be broken. Billions of dollars are at stake. Abdu's an ambitious man, and a smart one. As long as I was of some use, I was kept."

Celeste lit the cigarette, then let out smoke slowly. She wasn't convinced that half of what Phoebe was saying wasn't a product of her friend's abundant imagination. If any of it were true, even part of it, there was one point that couldn't be resolved.

"Why did you stay? If you were treated like that, if you were so unhappy, why the hell didn't you pack your bags and leave?"

"I threatened to leave. At that point, right after Addy was born, I still believed I could salvage something if I stood my ground. He beat me up."

"My God, Phoebe." Shaken, Celeste went to her.

"In all my nightmares, nothing was as horrible. I screamed and screamed, but no one helped." She shook her head, rubbing away the tears as quickly as they fell. "No one dared help. He kept hitting me and hitting me, until I didn't even feel it anymore. Then he raped me."

"That's insane." With her arms around Phoebe, Celeste led her to the couch. "There must have been something you could have done to protect yourself. Did you go to the police?"

With a humorless laugh, Phoebe sipped at her drink. "It's legal for a man to beat his wife in Jaquir. If he has cause. The women took care of me. They were really very kind."

"Phoebe, why didn't you write me, let me know what was happening? I might have been able to help. I would have helped."

"Even if I could have smuggled a letter out, there would have been nothing you could have done. Abdu is absolute power in Jaquir, religiously, politically, legally. You have never experienced anything like it. I know it must be almost impossible for you to imagine my way of life there. I started to dream of getting out. I would have needed Abdu's permission to leave legally, but I fantasized about escaping. But there was Adrianne. I couldn't have gotten out with her, I couldn't leave without her. She's the most precious thing in my life, Celeste. I think I would have ended it a dozen times if it hadn't been for Addy."

"How much does she know?"

"I can't be sure. Very little, I hope. She knows her father's feelings for her, but I've tried to explain that they're just a reflection of his feelings for me. The women loved her, and I think she was happy enough the way things were. After all, she'd never known anything else. He was going to send her away."

"Away? Where?"

"To school, in Germany. That's when I knew I *had* to make a move. He was making arrangements to have her married on her fifteenth birthday."

"Jesus. Poor little girl."

"I couldn't bear it, couldn't bear to think that she would go through what I was going through. The trip to Paris was like a sign. Now or never. Without you it would have been never."

"I only wish I could do more. I'd like to find the bastard and castrate him with a butter knife."

"I can't ever go back, Celeste."

Celeste glanced up in some surprise. "Of course not."

"No, I mean never." Phoebe poured another drink, spilling liquor over the sides of the glass. "If he comes, I'll kill myself before I go back."

"Don't talk like that. You're in New York, you're safe."

"But there's Addy."

"She's safe too." Celeste thought of the dark, intense eyes with the bruises of fatigue beneath. "He'll have to get through me. First thing we do is go to the press, maybe the State Department."

"No, no, I don't want the publicity. I don't dare risk it, for Addy's sake. She already knows more than she should."

Celeste opened her mouth to protest, then shut it again. "You have a point."

"I need to put it behind me, behind both of us. I want to go back to work, start living again."

"Why don't you start the living first? When you're a little steadier on your feet, you can think about going back to work."

"I've got to get Addy a place to live, school, clothes."

"There's time for all that. Right now you can stay here, catch your breath, give both yourself and Addy time to adjust."

Phoebe nodded as the tears began to fall. "You know the worst of it, Celeste? I still love him."

Silently, Adrianne climbed back up the stairs.

Chapter Seven

The sun was streaming through the chink of the drapes when Adrianne woke again. Her eyes were gritty from crying, her head light. Still, she was eight, and her first thought was of food. She shrugged back into the dress she had worn in Paris and started downstairs.

The apartment was much bigger than it had seemed to her the night before. Arching doorways led off the hallway. She was too hungry to explore, so went quietly downstairs, hoping to find fruit and bread.

She heard people talking. A man and a woman. Then there was laughter, a great deal of it. The people were talking again, arguing, the woman in a high-pitched, nagging voice, the man in a strange sort of English. The more they talked, the more laughter Adrianne heard. Cautious, she crept toward the sound and found herself in Celeste's kitchen.

The room was empty, but there were still voices. Adrianne saw they were coming from a small box and in the box were little people. Enchanted, she walked over to touch the box. The people didn't notice her, but went on arguing.

Not people, Adrianne realized with a grin. Pictures of people, moving, talking pictures. That meant the people in the box were movie stars, like her mother. Forgetting food, she put her elbows on the counter and stared.

"Just put everything over there. Oh, Adrianne, you're up."

Adrianne straightened quickly, waiting to be scolded.

"Good." Celeste waited until the delivery boy set the bags on the counter. "Now I'll have more company than *I Love Lucy*." She handed the boy some bills. "Thanks."

"Thank you, Miss Michaels." He sent Adrianne a wink, and left.

"Your mother's still asleep, but I thought your stomach might wake you up. I'm afraid I had no idea what kind of things little girls like to eat, so I left it up to the grocer." She pulled out a box of Rice Krispies. "Looks like a good start."

The television switched to a commercial with a blast of sound and color. Adrianne's mouth fell open. The White Tornado whirled in to save a housewife from waxy yellow buildup.

"Pretty amazing, huh?" Celeste dropped a hand on Adrianne's shoulder. "You don't have television in Jaquir?"

Too impressed to speak, Adrianne merely shook her head.

"Well, you can watch all you want for the next few days. There's a bigger television in the other room. I keep this one in here to make my housekeeper happy. How about some breakfast?"

"Please."

"Rice Krispies?"

Adrianne eyed the box. There were funny little people on it in big white hats. "I like rice."

"This is a little different. I'll show you." At Celeste's gesture Adrianne took a chair. From the table she could watch the television and Celeste at the same time. "First you pour it into a bowl. Then . . ." Enjoying herself, Celeste made a business out of pouring milk. "Now listen to it." She wiggled her fingers at Adrianne. "Go ahead, put your ear down close."

"It hisses."

"Snaps, crackles, and pops," Celeste corrected the child as she sprinkled on some sugar. "Hissing cereal wouldn't go over very well. Give it a try."

Hesitantly, Adrianne dipped the spoon in. She couldn't understand why anyone would want to eat food that made noise, but she was too well bred to be rude. She took a bite, then two, then rewarded Celeste with her first genuine smile. "It is good. Thank you. I like American rice."

"Rice Krispies." Celeste ruffled her hair. "I think I might just have a bowl myself."

Of all her memories of her first days in America, that

hour she spent with Celeste remained a favorite. It wasn't so different from the harem. Celeste was a woman, and they spoke of women's things. Shopping, the food she helped Celeste put away. There were things like butter made from peanuts and soup made out of letters. To her relief, there was also chocolate.

Celeste was different, with her short golden hair and the pants she wore. Adrianne liked the way her voice rose and fell so gracefully, the way she used her hands and arms, and even her body, with the words.

When Phoebe joined them, Adrianne was sitting primly on Celeste's couch watching her first soap opera.

"Lord, I don't know when I've slept so long. Hello, baby."

"Mama." Adrianne sprang up immediately to wrap her arms around Phoebe.

Despite a pounding hangover, Phoebe gathered Adrianne close for a hug. "The best way to start a day." Smiling, she drew back. "How did you start yours?"

"I had Rice Krispies and watched television."

Celeste breezed in, trailing cigarette smoke behind her. "As you can see, Addy's becoming Americanized already. How's the head?"

"It's been worse."

"If anyone had a right to tie one on, you did." She glanced at the TV, wondering if the program was suitable for an eight-year-old. Then again, from what Phoebe had told her, Adrianne would be more shocked by *Sesame Street* than the passions of *General Hospital*. "Well, now that you're up, I'd suggest a cup of coffee and some breakfast before we go out."

The light through the window hurt Phoebe's eyes, so she turned her back to it. "We're going out?"

"Darling, you know I'd share anything in my closet with you, but nothing I have is going to fit you anymore than it's going to fit Adrianne. I know you have a lot to deal with, so I thought we'd take up first things first."

Phoebe pressed her fingers to her eyes and fought the urge to run back to bed and toss the covers over her head. "You're right. Addy, why don't you go up and brush your hair, tidy up? Then we'll go see New York."

"You would like to?"

"Yes." Phoebe kissed the tip of her nose. "Go on. I'll call you when we're ready to go."

Celeste waited until Adrianne started upstairs. "The kid adores you."

"I know." Giving into her throbbing head, Phoebe sat. "Sometimes I'd think she was the reward for everything I went through."

"Honey, if you don't feel like going out—"

"No." Phoebe cut Celeste off with a shake of her head. "No, you're right, we've got to start with the basics. Besides, I don't want to keep Addy cooped up in here. She's been cooped up all her life. It's money."

"Oh, if that's all."

"Celeste, I've already taken enough from you. I don't have much pride left, so I need to hang on to what I have."

"Okay. I'll make you a loan."

"When I left, you and I were pretty much on equal terms." On a sigh she looked around the penthouse. "You've gone up, and I've gone nowhere."

Celeste sat on the arm of the sofa. "Phoebe, you took a wrong turn. People do."

"Yeah." She found she wanted a drink badly. To fight it off, she thought of Adrianne and the life she wanted to give her. "I have some jewelry. I had to leave most of it behind, but I did get some out. I'm going to sell it, then after I begin divorce proceedings, the settlement Abdu makes on me and on Addy will keep us well enough. Of course, I'm going back to work, so money won't be a problem for long." She turned to the window again to stare at the blank sky. "I'm going to give her everything, the best of everything. I have to."

"Let's worry about that later. Right now I think Addy could use a couple of pairs of jeans and some sneakers."

Adrianne stood on the corner of Fifth and Fifty-second with one hand gripping her mother's and the other fiddling restlessly with the buttons of her new fur-collared coat. If her brief glimpse of Paris had made that city seem like another world, then New York was another universe. And she was part of it.

There were people everywhere, millions of them, it

seemed to her, and none of them looked the same. There was no unity of dress here as there was in Jaquir. At a glance it was often difficult to tell men from women. Both sexes tended to wear their hair long. Some of the women chose to wear pants. New York had no law against it, nor against the other costume women wore—the tiny skirts that rose high above the knee. She saw men in beads and headbands, men in business suits and overcoats. There were women wrapped in mink and women in tight denim.

No matter what they wore, they moved fast. Adrianne crossed the street between her mother and Celeste and tried to see it all at once. They filled the city, every inch, every corner, and the noise of their existence rose off the pavement like a celebration. They traveled in packs, or they traveled alone. They dressed like beggars and like kings. Thousands of words in thousands of voices rang in her ears.

Then there were the buildings. They rose right into the sky, taller than any mosque, grander than any palace. She wondered if they had been built to honor Allah, but she had yet to hear a prayer call. People hurried into them, and out of them, yet she saw none that were restricted to women.

Some shopkeepers spread their goods on the pavement, but when Adrianne stopped to look at the wares, her mother pulled her away.

She went patiently into the shops, but for once buying didn't interest her. She wanted to be outside, absorbing. There were smells to remember. The stink of exhaust from the hundreds of cars, trucks, and buses that crept along the streets, horns blaring. There was the smoky tang she learned was roasting chestnuts. And there was the rich fleshy scent of so much humanity.

It was a dirty, often unforgiving city, but Adrianne didn't see the layers of grime or the jagged edges. She saw life, in a variety and with an excitement she'd never known existed. And she wanted more.

"Sneakers." Pleasantly exhausted, Celeste dropped into a chair in the shoe department of Lord & Taylor. She grinned at Adrianne. The child's face, she thought, told a thousand stories. All of wonder. She was glad they'd dismissed the driver and opted to walk, even though her feet were killing her. "What do you think of our big, bad city so far, Addy?"

"We can see more?"

"Yes." Already in love, Celeste tucked Adrianne's hair behind her ear. "We can see all you like. How are you holding up, Phoebe?"

"Fine." Phoebe forced a smile and unbuttoned her coat. Her nerves were raw. All the noise, the people, after so many years of silence and solitude. The decisions. There seemed to be hundreds of decisions to make when for so long she had none. She wanted a drink. God, she would kill for just one drink. Or a pill.

"Phoebe?"

"Yes, what?" On a long breath she brought herself back and smiled calmly at Celeste. "I'm sorry. My mind was wandering."

"I was saying you look tired. Do you want to call it a day?"

She started to agree, gratefully, then caught the quick look of disappointment on Adrianne's face. "No. I just need to catch my second wind." She bent down to kiss Adrianne's cheek. "Are you having fun?"

"It is better than a party."

Celeste laughed and flexed her toes. "Honey, New York's the biggest party this country has got." Then she crossed her legs and smiled flirtatiously up at the salesman. "We want to see some sneakers suitable for a little girl. I noticed those pink ones over there, with the flowers? And maybe a pair in plain white."

"Of course." He crouched down to smile in Adrianne's face. He smelled like the peppermint cream Jiddah sometimes ate, and had only a thin fringe of gray hair. "What size do you wear, young lady?"

He was speaking to her. Directly to her. Adrianne stared at him without the least idea what to do. He was not a member of her family. She looked helplessly toward her mother, but Phoebe was staring off at nothing.

"Why don't you measure her?" Celeste suggested, reaching over to give Adrianne's hand a quick squeeze. She saw, with a combination of amusement and distress, the way Adrianne's eyes widened when he took her foot in his hand to remove her shoe. "He's going to measure your foot to see what size you wear."

"That's right." Cheerful, he slid Adrianne's foot onto the measuring board. "Stand up, sweetheart."

Swallowing, Adrianne did so, looking straight over his head as her face filled with color. She wondered if the shoe person was like a doctor.

"Uh-huh. Well, I'll go see what I have in stock."

"Why don't you take off your other shoe, Addy? Then you can walk around in the new ones and see if you like them."

Adrianne bent to unfasten the buckle. "It is permitted for the shoe person to touch?"

Celeste bit her lip to prevent a smile. "Yes. It's his job to sell you shoes that fit well. To make sure, he has to measure your foot. As part of the service, he takes off your old shoes and puts on the new ones."

"A ritual?"

At a loss, Celeste sat back. "In a way."

Satisfied, Adrianne folded her hands and sat meekly when the clerk returned with boxes. She watched solemnly as he laced up the pink flowered sneakers and slipped them on her feet, tying them in a bow.

"There you go, sweetheart." The clerk patted her foot. "Try them out."

At Celeste's gesture, Adrianne stood and took a few steps. "They are different."

"Different good," Celeste asked, "or different bad?"

"Different good." She grinned at the idea of wearing flowers on her feet. She didn't mind when the clerk pressed his thumb against her toe.

"It's a good fit."

Adrianne took a deep breath and smiled at him. "I like them very much. Thank you." She let the breath out on a giggle. For the first time in her life, she had spoken to a man not of her family.

The three weeks Adrianne spent in New York were some of the happiest and the saddest days of her life. There was so much to learn, so much to see. Part of her, the part that had been raised with the strict, unwavering rules of behavior, disapproved of the brashness of the city. Another part, the part that was opening, was thrilled by it. New York was America to Adrianne. It would remain America always, at its best and at its worst.

The rules had changed. She had a room of her own, but it was bigger and brighter than the room she had been given in her father's palace. She wasn't a princess here, but she was cherished. Still, she often slipped into her mother's bed at night to comfort if Phoebe wept, to lay awake if Phoebe slept. She understood there were demons inside her mother, and it frightened her. Some days Phoebe seemed full of life and energy, of joy and optimism. There would be talk about past glories, and the glories of the future. Plans and promises were made in a whirl of laughing words. Then a day or two later the animation would be gone. Phoebe would complain of headaches or fatigue and spend hours alone in her room.

On those days Celeste would take Adrianne out to walk in the park or to go to the theater.

Even the food was different, and she was allowed to take what she wanted when she wanted. She became addicted quickly to the sharp, sparkling taste of Pepsi straight out of a cold bottle. She ate her first hot dog without any idea it was made of pork, forbidden to Muslims.

Television became both teacher and entertainment. She was both embarrassed and fascinated when she saw women embrace men—openly, even aggressively. The stories often had fairy-tale endings about falling in love or losing your heart. In the stories women chose what man they wanted to marry, and sometimes chose not to marry at all. She watched, silent and astonished. Bette Davis in *Jezebel*, Katharine Hepburn's *Philadelphia Story*, and, wonderingly, Phoebe Spring in *Nights of Passion*. From that point grew an admiration for strong women who could win in a man's world.

Yet it was the commercials, where the people dressed oddly and solved their problems in seconds, that delighted her more than the comedies and drama. Through them her American-style English was refined, fleshed out.

In those three weeks she learned more than she might have in three years of school. Her mind was like a willing sponge eager to absorb.

It was her spirit, so in tune with Phoebe's, that suffered the highs and lows.

Then the letter came. Adrianne knew about the divorce. It was still her habit to creep down the stairs at night and listen to her mother and Celeste talk of the things neither would tell her. So she understood that her mother was going to divorce Abdu. And she was glad. If there was divorce, there would be no more beatings, no more rapes.

When the letter had come, the letter from Jaquir, Phoebe had gone to her room. She had stayed there all day, not coming out to eat, asking to be left alone whenever Celeste knocked on the door.

Now, as it neared midnight, Adrianne was awakened from a restless sleep by her mother's laughter. Moving quickly, she climbed out of bed and ran on tiptoe to Phoebe's door.

"I've been worried sick about you." Celeste paced the room, her silk lounging pajamas whispering around her.

"I'm sorry, darling, really. I needed some time." Adrianne pressed against the crack in the door. She could see Phoebe sprawled in a chair, her hair tumbled, her eyes bright, and her fingers drumming to some rapid inner tune. "Hearing from Abdu hit me hard. I knew it was going to happen, but I still wasn't ready. Congratulate me, Celeste, I'm a free woman."

"What are you talking about?"

Her movements jerky, Phoebe rose to refill her glass from a decanter. She smiled, toasted, then drank deeply. "Abdu has divorced me."

"In three weeks?"

"He could do it in three seconds, and he has. Of course, I'm still going to go through the formalities on this end, but it's as good as done."

Celeste noted the level of whiskey in the decanter. "Why don't we go down and have some coffee?"

"This is a celebration." She pressed the glass against her brow and began to weep. "The bastard didn't even give me the chance to end it in my own way. Not once in all these years have I had a choice, not even in this."

"Let's sit down." Celeste reached out for her, but Phoebe shook her head and went back to the decanter.

"No, I'm all right. I needed to get drunk. The coward's way."

"No one who's done what you've done could ever be called a coward, Phoebe." Celeste took the glass from her hand, then drew Phoebe to the bed to sit. "I know it's rough. Divorce makes you feel as though you've put your foot down, knowing just where you're going only to find out there's nothing there. Sooner or later you come to solid ground again, believe me."

"There's no one else for me."

"That's foolish. You're young, you're beautiful. This divorce is a beginning for you, not an ending."

"He took something from me, Celeste. I can't seem to get it back." She covered her face with her hands. "It doesn't matter. Only Addy matters now."

"Addy's fine."

"She needs things, she deserves things." Phoebe fumbled for a tissue. "I need to know she's well taken care of."

"She will be."

Phoebe wiped her eyes and drew a deep breath. "There's not going to be a settlement."

"What do you mean?"

"I mean he's not going to make any financial arrangements for Addy. Nothing. No trust fund, no child support, nothing. All she has is a worthless title that even he can't strip her of. He's keeping it all, what I had when we married, what he gave me. Even The Sun and the Moon, the necklace he bought me with."

"He can't. Phoebe, you have a good lawyer. It might take some time and effort, but Abdu has a responsibility to you and to Adrianne."

"No, his terms were very clear. If I try to fight him on this, he'll take Adrianne." The whiskey had thickened her tongue. She drank more to loosen it. "He can do it, Celeste, believe me. He doesn't want her, and God knows what he would put her through if he got her, but he would take her away from me. Nothing's worth that, not The Sun and the Moon, not anything."

For the second time Celeste took Phoebe's glass and set it aside. "All right, I agree with you that Addy's welfare comes first. What are you going to do?"

"I've already done it." She was up, pacing, her long

white robe billowing. "I got drunk, then I got sick, then I called Larry Curtis."

"Your agent?"

"That's right." She swung around. Her face was alive again, still pale, but gorgeous. "He's flying right out."

Gorgeous, Celeste thought—the way a fire was when it burned too brightly. "Darling, are you sure you're ready?"

"I've got to be ready."

"Okay." Celeste held up a hand. "But Larry Curtis? There's talk about him, not very nice talk."

"There's always talk in Hollywood."

"I know, but... listen, he's a good-looking bastard and very slick, but I remember you were toying with dropping him before you retired."

"That's behind me." Phoebe picked up her glass again. She felt on top of the world. And sick to the bone. "Larry was good for me once; he's going to be good for me again. I'm making a comeback, Celeste. I'm going to be somebody again."

Adrianne couldn't say why her first glimpse of Larry Curtis made her uneasy any more than she could say why he reminded her of her father. There was certainly no physical resemblance. Curtis was stocky and a fraction shorter than Phoebe's five ten. He had a mass of curling blond hair that reached his collar and framed a smooth, boxy, tanned face. And he had smiled constantly, showing big white teeth, uniformly straight.

Adrianne had liked his costume. She still thought of Western clothing as costumes. He'd worn a lavender shirt with big sleeves, the collar opened low to show off a thick gold chain. His pants with a tiny checked pattern flared at the ankle and were cinched at the waist with a wide black belt.

Her mother had been glad to see him, embracing him openly when he walked in. Adrianne squirmed and looked away when Larry casually patted Phoebe's bottom.

"Welcome back, sweetheart."

"Oh, Larry, I'm so glad to see you." She laughed and kept her tone light, but he was sharp enough to recognize the desperation beneath. And to play on it.

"Good to see you too, baby. Let's have a look." He held

her at arm's length, scanning her up and down in a way that made Adrianne's cheeks warm. "Looking pretty good. Lost a little weight, but thin's in fashion now." He thought it was too bad about the lines around her eyes and mouth, but figured a tuck here and there and some soft focus would take care of them.

Phoebe Spring had been a gold mine when she'd left Hollywood. With a little effort and a lot of savvy she would be one again.

"So, Celeste." With his arm still around Phoebe's shoulders, he swung around. "Nice place."

"Thanks." Celeste reminded herself that Phoebe wanted him, perhaps needed him. He did have a reputation for making the right moves. And gossip, particularly the sleazy kind, was often just gossip. "How was your flight?"

"Smooth as silk." He grinned, moving his fingers up and down Phoebe's arm. "But I could use a drink."

"I'll get it." Phoebe jumped to serve in a way that made Celeste wince. "It's bourbon, right, Larry?"

"That's right, sweetheart." He made himself at home on Celeste's long white sofa. "Now, who's this pretty little thing?" He flashed a smile at Adrianne as she sat stiffly in a chair by the window.

"That's my daughter." Phoebe offered the glass, then sat beside him. "Adrianne, come meet Mr. Curtis. He's a very dear, old friend of mine."

Reluctant, and unconsciously regal, Adrianne rose and crossed to him. "I am pleased to meet you, Mr. Curtis."

He laughed and took her hand before she could avoid it. "None of that Mr. Curtis stuff, honeybunch. We're practically family. I'm just Uncle Larry."

Adrianne's eyes narrowed. She didn't like his touch. It wasn't like the shoe person, but hot and grasping. "You are the brother of my mother?"

Larry sat back and roared as if she'd executed a clever trick. "She's a pistol."

"Addy's very literal minded," Phoebe explained, sending Adrianne a nervous smile.

"We're going to get along fine." He sipped, sizing Adrianne up over the rim of the glass as he might a new car or an expensive suit. Potential, he decided. A few more years, a few curves, and it might be a very interesting arrangement.

"Adrianne and I thought we'd finish up our Christmas shopping." Celeste held out a hand. Adrianne clasped it gratefully. "We'll leave you two alone to talk business."

"Thank you, Celeste. Have a good time, baby."

"Bundle up, honeybunch." Larry winked at Adrianne. "It's cold out there." He waited until the door shut behind them, then leaned back against the cushions. "Like I said, sweetheart, it's good to have you back, but you're on the wrong coast."

"I needed some time." Phoebe twisted her fingers together. "Celeste has been wonderful to us. I don't know what I would have done without her."

"That's what friends are for." He patted her thigh, satisfied that she didn't object when his hand lingered. Generally, he preferred the less voluptuous type, but there was nothing like sex to put a man in the driver's seat. "So tell me, baby, how long are you staying?"

"I'm here for good." The moment he finished his last swallow of bourbon, Phoebe was up to refill his glass. This time she poured a glass for herself. Larry only lifted a brow. The Phoebe he remembered had never sipped at anything harder than wine.

"What about the sheikh?"

"I've filed for divorce." She wet her lips, glancing around as though someone might strike her down for the statement. "I can't live with him anymore." She drank, afraid she wouldn't be able to live without him either. "He changed, Larry. I can't begin to tell you how much. If he comes after me—"

"You're in the U. S. of A. now, sweetheart." He drew her close, once more skimming his glance down her body. She was well into her thirties, he calculated. Older than his usual choice. But she was vulnerable. He preferred his women, and his clients, vulnerable. "Haven't I always taken care of you?"

"Yes." She held on, ready to weep with relief. She knew her looks had begun to fade. It didn't matter, she told herself as Larry stroked her back. He was going to take care of her.

"I want a part, Larry. Anything to start. I have Adrianne to think of. She needs things, deserves things."

"Leave it all to me. We'll start off with an interview before you go to the West Coast. 'The queen' is back, that kind of thing." He gave her breast a quick, casual squeeze before reaching for his drink. "Make sure they get a picture of you with the little princess. Kids make great copy. I'll start paving the way, do some talking, some dealing. Trust me. We'll have them in the palm of our hand inside of six weeks."

"I hope so." She squeezed her eyes tight. "I've been away for so long, so much has changed."

"Pack your bags and head out by the end of the week. I'll take it from there." Her name alone would make the deals, he decided. If she bombed, he'd still make a bundle. Then, there was the kid. He had a feeling the kid was going to come in handy.

"I don't have a lot of money." She set her jaw, determined to brazen out the shame. "I've sold some jewelry, and it's enough to keep us for a while, but I need most of it to pay for a good school for Adrianne. I know how expensive it is to live in L.A."

Yeah, the kid was going to come in handy. As long as she was in the picture, Phoebe would be willing to do anything. "Didn't I say I'd take care of you?" He drew down the zipper at the back of her dress.

"Larry—"

"Come on, sweetheart. Show me you trust me. I'll get you a part, a house, a nice school for the kid. The best. That's what you want, isn't it?"

"Yes. I want Addy to have the best."

"And you too. I'll put you right back in the spotlight. As long as you cooperate."

What difference did it make, she asked herself as he stripped her. Abdu had taken her body whenever he had liked and given nothing back, not to her, not to Adrianne. With Larry there was a promise of protection, and maybe a little affection.

"You've still got great tits, honey."

Phoebe closed her eyes and let him do what he wanted.

Chapter Eight

Philip Chamberlain listened to the swish and thud of tennis balls and sipped his long gin and tonic. He looked especially good in tennis whites since he'd developed a smooth tan in the three weeks he'd been in California. Crossing his ankles, he looked onto the courts through mirrored sunglasses.

Making friends with Eddie Treewalter, III, hadn't been all that pleasant for Philip, but it had paid off with invitations to Eddie's country club. Philip had come to Beverly Hills on business, but it never hurt to enjoy a little sun. Because he had let Eddie trounce him in the last two games of their match, the young American was in a very expansive mood.

"Sure you won't have lunch, old man?"

To Philip's credit, he didn't wince at the "old man," which clearly Eddie believed to be the height of camaraderie among the English.

"Wish I could. But I'm going to have to run in a moment if I'm to make my appointment."

"Hell of a day to think of business." Eddie pushed up his amber-tinted sunglasses, a thick gold watch glinting on his wrist. Teeth that had given up their braces only two years before flashed as he smiled. He had a nickel bag of prime Colombian pot in his monogrammed leather tennis bag.

As the son of one of the most successful plastic surgeons in California, he hadn't had to work a day in his life. Treewalter, II, nipped and tucked the stars while his son yawned his way through college, dealt drugs as a hobby, and scored at the country club.

"You'll be at the party tonight at Stoneway's?"

"Wouldn't miss it."

Eddie downed his vodka on the rocks and signaled for another. "The man makes lousy pictures but knows how to throw a party. There'll be enough snow and grass for an army." He grinned. "I forgot. You don't indulge, do you?"

"I prefer to indulge in other things."

"Suit yourself, but Stoneway serves coke on silver platters. Very chic." His glance passed over a thin blonde in tight tennis shorts. "You could always indulge in that. Give little Marci some nose candy and she'll fuck anything."

"She's a teenager." Philip used the gin to wash the taste of disgust at Eddie's youthful arrogance and stupidity out of his mouth.

"No one in this town's a teenager. And speaking of easy lays." He nodded toward a lush redhead in a sundress. "Old reliable Phoebe." He snickered. "The name's not Spring for nothing. I think even my old man's bounced on her. A little shopworn, but great tits."

Perhaps, Philip thought, exploiting Eddie's companionship wasn't worth the price. "I'd better be off."

"Sure. Hey, she's got her daughter with her." Eddie ran his tongue over his lips. "Now, there's a kid who's going to be a prime piece of ass, old man. Pure and sweet. She'll be ready for plowing soon. Mama won't let her come to the party tonight, but she can't keep her locked up forever."

Concealing annoyance, Philip glanced over. And felt the punch. He caught only a glimpse of the young, fine-boned face. But there was a mass of straight, glorious black hair. And legs. Despite himself, Philip stared at them. Truly gorgeous legs. He snorted in self-disgust. The girl was so young, she made Marci look middle-aged. He stood abruptly and turned his back.

"A bit young for my taste... old man. See you tonight."

Bastard, Philip thought of Eddie as he moved away from the tables. In a day or two he wouldn't have to be his "pal" any longer and could go home. Back to London. It would be cool and green in London, and he could wash the smog of Los Angeles out of his eyes. He'd have to pick up some souvenirs for his mother. He knew Mary would adore a map of the stars' homes.

Let her have her romance with Hollywood. There was

no need to tell her that under the glitter was an ugly layer of scum. Drugs, sex, and betrayal. Not all of it, certainly, but enough to make him glad his mother had never pursued her dream of being an actress. Still, he should bring her here one day. Take her to lunch at Grauman's Chinese Theater, let her slip her feet into Marilyn Monroe's footprints. He'd get a bang out of the town if his mother were along to be awed and excited.

A tennis ball rolled in front of him and he bent down to retrieve it. The girl with great legs had put on huge concealing sunglasses. She smiled beneath them and he felt the same punch as he tossed the ball back to her.

"Thanks."

"Sure." Dipping his hands in his pockets, Philip relegated Phoebe Spring's very young daughter to the back of his mind. He had a job to do.

Twenty minutes later he was cruising into Bel Air in a white paneled van. The legend on the side boasted KARPETS KLEANED. Eddie's mother was going to be very unhappy when she discovered her jewelry was going to be cleaned as well. For free.

A brown wig covering his now sunstreaked hair, a natty mustache above his thin lips, Philip hopped out of the van. He still wore white, but it was overalls now, padded a bit to give the illusion of bulk. It had taken him two weeks to case the Treewalters' house and learn the routines of family and servants. He had twenty-five minutes to get in and out before the housekeeper returned from her weekly trip to the market.

It was almost too easy. A week before, he'd taken an impression of Eddie's keys when Eddie had been too stoned to walk through his own front door. Once in, Philip turned off the alarm, then broke a window in the patio door to give the job the look of forced entry.

Moving quickly, he went up to the master bedroom to go to work on the safe. It pleased him that it was the same model as the Mezzenis' in Venice. It had taken him only twelve minutes to crack that and relieve the amorous Italian matron of one of the hottest suites of emeralds in Europe. But that had been six months before. Philip wasn't a man to rest on his laurels.

Concentration was everything. Though Philip was just

shy of twenty-one, he knew how to concentrate fully, on a safe, on an alarm, on a woman. Each held its own fascination for cracking.

He heard the first tumblers fall into place.

He was as smooth here as he was over cocktails or between the sheets. He'd taught himself well. How to dress, how to speak, how to seduce a woman. His talents had opened doors for him, society's as well as vaults'. He'd managed to move his mother into a spacious flat. She spent her afternoons now shopping or playing bridge rather than shivering or sweating in the ticket booth at Faraday's. He was going to see that she continued to do so. There were other women in his life, but she was still his first love.

He heard the tumblers fall into place through the stethoscope.

He'd done just as well for himself, and intended to do even better. He had a small, elegant town house in London. Soon, very soon, he was going to start scouting the outlying districts for that home in the country. With a garden. He had a weakness for small, beautiful things that needed to be nurtured.

He stood, one hand moving delicately on the dial, eyes half closed, like a man listening to soothing music, or appreciating the touch of a clever woman.

The safe opened, smooth as butter.

He unrolled the velvet pouch he found inside and took the time to examine the gems with his loupe. All that glittered, he knew, was not gold. Or diamonds. These were the real thing. Grade D, undoubtedly Russian. He studied the largest sapphire. Its center drop was slightly flawed as expected in a gem that size. It was a pretty, and valuable, cornflower blue. Like a patient doctor giving an exam, he studied each bracelet, each ring and bauble. He found the ruby earrings particularly ugly—and as a man who considered himself an artist, he judged it a crime to create something so aesthetically displeasing out of such a passionate stone. Judging the jewels to be worth about thirty-five thousand American, he took them out. Artist or not, he was a businessman first.

Satisfied, he set everything in the center of the Aubusson carpet and rolled up the rug.

Twenty minutes after entering, Philip shouldered the rug into the van. Whistling between his teeth, he got behind the wheel and cruised off, passing the Treewalters' housekeeper as she rounded the corner.

Eddie was right, Phil thought as he turned up the radio. It was a hell of a day for business.

Nothing was exactly as it seemed in Hollywood. Adrianne's first impression had been of wonder. This America was far different from the America of New York. The people were sleeker, in less of a hurry, and everyone seemed to know everyone else. Adrianne thought it was like a small village, yet the natives weren't as friendly as they pretended to be.

By the time she was fourteen she had learned that attitudes were often as false as the storefronts on a movie lot. She also knew that Phoebe's comeback was a failure.

They had a house, she had school, but Phoebe's career had moved steadily in reverse. More than her looks had begun to fade in Jaquir; her talent had eroded as rapidly as her self-esteem.

"Aren't you ready yet?" Phoebe hurried into Adrianne's room. The overbright eyes and overexcited voice told Adrianne that her mother had gotten a new supply of amphetamines. She struggled to subdue a feeling of helplessness and managed to smile. She couldn't bear another fight tonight, or her mother's tears and useless promises.

"Nearly." Adrianne fastened the cummerbund on her tuxedo-style suit. She wanted to tell her mother that she looked beautiful, but Phoebe's evening dress made her cringe. It was cut embarrassingly low and fit like a skin of gold sequins. Larry's doing, Adrianne thought. Larry Curtis was still her mother's agent, her sometime lover, and constant manipulator.

"We still have plenty of time," she said instead.

"Oh, I know." Phoebe moved around the room, glittering, fueled by the manic energy of the pills and her own unpredictable mood swings. "But premieres are so exciting. The people, the cameras." She stopped by Adrianne's mirror and saw herself as she once had been, without the marks of her illness and her disappointments. "Everyone's going to be there. It'll be just like the old days."

Faced with her reflection, she fell to dreaming, as she

too often did. She saw herself in the center spotlight, surrounded by admiring fans and associates. They all loved her, all wanted to be near her, to talk to her, to listen, to touch.

"Mama." Uneasy with Phoebe's abrupt silence, Adrianne laid a hand on her shoulder. There were days when she lost touch like this and didn't come out again for hours. "Mama," she repeated, tightening her grip, afraid that Phoebe was traveling down that long tunnel into her own fantasies.

"What?" Phoebe surfaced, blinking, then smiled as she focused on Adrianne's face. "My own little princess. You're so grown-up."

"I love you, Mama." Fighting back tears, Adrianne wrapped her arms tight around her mother. In the past year Phoebe's moods had become more and more like the roller coaster they had once ridden in Disneyland. A confusion of streaking highs and bottomless lows. She could never be sure whether Phoebe would be full of laughter and wild promises or tears and regrets.

"I love you, Addy." She stroked her daughter's hair, wishing the color and texture didn't remind her of Abdu. "We're making something of ourselves, aren't we?" She drew away and began circling the room, pacing, prowling, but never making progress. "In a few months we'll be going to my premiere. Oh, I know it's not as big a movie as this one, but these low-budget films are very popular. It's like Larry says, I have to keep myself available. And with the publicity he's planning . . ." She thought of the nude layout she'd posed for the week before. It wasn't the time to tell Adrianne about it. It was business, she reminded herself as she twisted her fingers together. Just business.

"I'm sure it's going to be a wonderful movie." But the others hadn't been, Adrianne reflected. The reviews had been insulting. She'd hated watching her mother embarrass herself on the screen, using her body instead of talent. Even now, after five years in California, Adrianne was aware that Phoebe had traded one kind of bondage for another.

"When the picture is a success, a big success, we'll have that house on the beach I promised you."

"We have a nice house."

"This little place . . ." Phoebe glanced out the window at the struggling garden separating them from the street. There was no grand stone wall, no pretty gates, no lush lawn. They were on the fringes of Beverly Hills, on the fringes of success. Phoebe's name had dropped to the B list of Hollywood's important hostesses. Major producers no longer sent her scripts.

She thought of the palace she had whisked Adrianne away from and all its luxuries. It became easier as time went by to forget the limitations of Jaquir and remember the opulence.

"It's not what I want for you, not nearly what you deserve, but rebuilding a career takes time."

"I know." They'd had this talk too many times before. "School's out in a couple of weeks. I thought we might go to New York to visit Celeste. You could relax."

"Hmm? Oh, we'll have to see. Larry's negotiating for a part for me."

Adrianne felt her spirits sink. She didn't have to be told that the part would be mediocre, or that her mother would spend hours away from home being manipulated by the men who'd chosen to exploit her body. The harder Phoebe tried to prove she could climb back on top, the faster she slipped toward the very bottom.

Phoebe wanted her house on the ocean and her name up in lights. Adrianne could have resented Phoebe's ambition, maybe even have fought it if the motives had been selfish. But what she did, she did out of love and a need to give. There was no way for Adrianne to make her see that she was building a cage as strong as the one she had escaped from.

"Mama, you haven't had any real time off in months. We could see Celeste's new play, visit some museums. It would do you good."

"It'll do me more good to watch everyone fuss over Princess Adrianne tonight. You look beautiful, sweetheart." She put an arm around Adrianne's shoulders as the two started for the door. "I bet the boys just break their hearts over you."

Adrianne shrugged. She wasn't interested in boys or their hearts.

"Well, tonight's our night. It's a shame Larry's out of town so we don't have a handsome man to escort us."

"We don't need anyone but each other."

*   *   *

Adrianne was used to the crowds, the flash of lights, and the cameras. Phoebe often worried that her daughter was too serious, but she never had cause to worry about Adrianne's poise. Young as she was, she handled the press like royalty, smiling when a smile was required, answering questions without ever giving too much away, and fading into the background when she had reached the limit of her tolerance. As a result, the press adored her. It was common knowledge that the columns were kinder to Phoebe Spring than they had to be because they had a love affair going with her daughter. Adrianne knew it, and with the skill of someone twice her age, used it.

She made certain that Phoebe stepped out of the car they had hired first, and that they stood arm in arm when the lights flashed. Any picture printed would be of both of them.

Phoebe came alive. Adrianne had seen it happen before. Whenever it did, the fervor of her wish that her mother would divorce herself from the movie business diminished. There was happiness on Phoebe's face, the kind of simple joy Adrianne saw there so rarely. She didn't need pills now, or a bottle, or her daydreams.

The crowd roared around her, the lights and music swelled. For an instant she was a star again.

Pressed against the barricades, onlookers waited for a glimpse of their favorite celebrities and settled for lesser lights. Good-humored, they cheered for everyone while a few pockets were picked and a large number of packets of drugs casually changed hands.

Seeing only the smiles, Phoebe stopped to wave, then bask in the sound of applause as she glided toward the theater. Unobtrusively, Adrianne guided her inside to the lobby that was already sprinkled with men and women of the film world. There was plenty of sparkle, plenty of cleavage, and plenty of gossip.

"Darling, how delightful to see you." Althea Gray, a streamlined actress who had made her mark in series television, strolled over to kiss the air an inch from Phoebe's cheek. She gave Adrianne a neutral smile and an annoying pat on the head. "Just as pretty as ever, aren't you? A tuxedo—what a cute idea." She wondered how quickly she could have one designed for herself.

Phoebe blinked at the friendly greeting. The last time she had seen the actress, Althea had given her the most pointed of snubs. "You look wonderful, Althea."

"Why, thank you, dear." She waited until one of the cameramen who'd been allowed inside focused, then gave Phoebe's cheek a chummy pat. "I'm so glad to see a couple of friendly faces at this circus." She flicked a lighter at the end of a long cigarette so that the emerald on her finger glinted in the overhead lights. "I was going to skip tonight, but my publicist had a fit. What are you doing these days, sweetheart? I haven't seen you for ages."

"I've just finished a movie." Grateful for the interest, Phoebe smiled and ignored the smoke burning her eyes. "A thriller," she said, elevating the low-budget slash and gash. "It should be released this winter."

"Wonderful. I'm about to make a film, now that I'm free of the mire of television. It's a Dan Bitterman screenplay. You might have heard about it. *Torment?*" She gave Phoebe a lazy, knowing look. "I just signed to play Melanie." Pausing only long enough to be sure she'd hit home, Althea smiled again. "I must go back to my date before he gets restless. Wonderful seeing you, darling. Let's have lunch soon."

"Mama, what's wrong?" Adrianne asked.

"Nothing." Phoebe fixed a smile to her face as someone called her name. *Melanie.* Larry had promised the part was hers. It had been only a matter of tying up a few loose ends in the negotiations, he'd said, promising that the movie would finally bring her back to where she had been.

"Do you want to go home?"

"Home?" Phoebe turned up the voltage of her smile until it crackled. "Of course not, but I'd love a drink before we go in. Oh, there's Michael."

She waved and caught the attention of the actor who'd been her first leading man, Michael Adams. There was a little gray at his temples that he didn't bother to touch up, a few lines in his face he didn't choose to have pulled taut or plumped up. He'd often thought his success had come as much from knowing who he was as from any acting skill. He was still playing leading men even as he cruised toward fifty with an expanded waistline.

"Phoebe." With affection, and a trace of pity, he bent down to kiss her. "And who is this beautiful young lady?" He smiled at Adrianne, apparently without recognition.

"Hello, Michael." Adrianne rose to her toes to kiss his cheek, a gesture she usually performed with reluctance. With Michael, it was done with pleasure. He was the only man she knew with whom she felt truly comfortable.

"This can't be our little Addy. You put all our fledgling starlets to shame." Then he laughed and pinched her chin, making her smile again. "The best work you ever did is right here, Phoebe."

"I know." She caught her lip between her teeth before it trembled, and managed another smile.

Problems, he thought, sharp enough to interpret Phoebe's overbright eyes. Then again, there were always problems with Phoebe. "Don't tell me you two are unescorted."

"Larry's out of town."

"Uh-huh." It wasn't the time to lecture Phoebe again about Larry Curtis. "I don't suppose I could talk you into keeping a lonely man company through this."

"You're never lonely," Adrianne said. "I read just last week where you were romancing Ginger Frye in Aspen."

"Precocious child. Actually, it was a skiing weekend and I was lucky to get away without broken bones. Ginger was along in case I needed medical attention."

Adrianne grinned. "Did you?"

"Here." Michael pulled a bill from his money clip. "Go buy yourself a soda like a good girl."

Chuckling, she wandered off.

Michael watched her, admiring the way she maneuvered through the crowd. In a year or two she would have the men of this town, of any town, falling at her feet. "She's a treasure, Phoebe. My daughter Marjorie's seventeen. I haven't seen her in anything but ripped blue jeans in three years, and she does whatever she can to make my life miserable. I envy you."

"Addy's never given me a moment's trouble. I honestly don't know what I'd do without her."

"She's devoted to you." He lowered his voice. "Have you thought any more about seeing the doctor I suggested?"

"I haven't had time," she hedged, wishing he'd leave her alone long enough for her to slip into the ladies' room and swallow another pill. "And to tell you the truth, I've been feeling a lot better. Analysis is overrated, Michael. At times I think the movie industry was formed to support psychiatrists and plastic surgeons."

He bit back a sigh. She was high on something and falling fast. "It never hurts to talk to someone."

"I'll think about it."

Adrianne took her time, knowing that if he had the opportunity, Michael would speak to her mother about therapy. He'd already discussed it with Adrianne when he had found her nearly hysterical at not being able to get Phoebe to respond one afternoon after school. Phoebe had simply sat there, mute, staring out the window of her room.

There had been excuses when she had come around. Fatigue, overwork, tranquilizers. Michael had talked to them both about getting help, but Phoebe was dragging her feet. It was for that reason Adrianne desperately wanted to get her mother back to New York, away from Larry Curtis and his abundantly supplied drugs.

She didn't have to be an adult to know it was snowing in southern California. Cocaine had become the drug of choice in the movie industry. Too often it was served as casually as a catered lunch on the sets. So far Phoebe had refused it, preferring the hell of her pills to the hell of the powder, but Adrianne knew sooner or later the day would come. She had to get Phoebe away before that last line was crossed.

Adrianne sipped her Pepsi and took a slow circle around the room. She couldn't say she disliked all the people in the world her mother had chosen. Many of them were like Michael Adams, genuinely talented, loyal to friends, dedicated to a business that often called for grinding schedules with only flickers of glamour.

And she enjoyed the glamour, the meals in elegant restaurants, the wonderful clothes. She understood herself well enough to know she would find it hard to be satisfied with the ordinary. But she didn't want the extraordinary at the cost of her mother's sanity.

"God, did you see the dress?" Althea Gray took a drag on a cigarette and nodded in Phoebe's direction. Adrianne stopped behind her. "You'd think she needed to let everyone know she still has those breasts."

"After her last couple of movies," her companion commented, "no one should have any doubt. They should have gotten twin billing."

Althea laughed. "Looks like an Amazon beyond her prime. You know, she actually believed she was going to be offered the part of Melanie. Everyone knows she'll never get a decent part again. If it wasn't so pathetic, it might be funny."

"She had something once," the man beside Althea said softly. "There's never been anyone quite like her."

"Really, darling." Althea crushed out her cigarette. "Cruises down memory lane are so frigging boring."

"Not as boring as hearing a second-rate actress whine." Adrianne spoke clearly, and didn't flinch when heads turned in her direction.

"Oh, dear." Althea tapped her bottom lip with a fingertip. "Little pitchers have big ears."

Adrianne faced her, woman to woman. "Small talents have large egos."

When her companion chuckled, Althea sent him a fulminating look, then tossed back her hair. "Run along, dear. This is an adult conversation."

"Really?" Adrianne controlled the urge to toss her soda in Althea's face, and sipped from it instead. "It sounded remarkably immature to me. Dear."

"Rude little brat." Althea shrugged off her companion's restraining arm and took a step forward. "Someone ought to teach you some manners."

"I don't need lessons in manners from a woman like you." She flicked her glance over Althea, then scanned the group surrounding her. It was a long, steady look, cold enough and adult enough to make them squirm. "I don't see anyone here who can teach me anything except hypocrisy."

"Little bitch," Althea muttered when Adrianne turned and left them.

"Shut up, Althea," her escort advised. "You've been outclassed."

* * *

"Baby, I wish you'd tell me if something's wrong."

Adrianne pushed open the side door that led to their tiny garden. There was very little that had endeared her to California, but she'd learned to appreciate the sun. "Nothing's wrong. I've had a lot of homework." It was the best way to keep to herself and think through the things she had heard since the night of the premiere. She'd already dealt with the rumor that Phoebe had posed for a nude layout for a men's magazine. Two hundred thousand dollars had been the price tag on her mother's self-respect.

It was hard, so very hard to justify the shame through love. Adrianne had spent years struggling to learn a new way of life. She had come to embrace wholeheartedly a woman's equality, her freedom to choose, her right to be her own person rather than a mere symbol of fragility or desire. She wanted to believe, needed to believe. Yet her mother had stripped, selling her body so that any man could open the pages of a magazine and own her.

The school was too expensive. Adrianne watched the overblown roses drop their petals and thought of the tuition her mother paid to keep her in the exclusive private school. Phoebe was selling her pride for her daughter's education.

Then there were the clothes, the clothes her mother insisted Adrianne needed. And the driver—the combination driver and bodyguard Phoebe felt was necessary to keep her daughter safe from terrorism . . . and Abdu. The Middle East was perpetually plagued now by ugly violence, and whether Abdu acknowledged her or not, Adrianne was still the daughter of Jaquir's king.

"Mama, I was wondering about going to a public high school next year."

"Public school?" Phoebe checked her purse to be certain she'd included her credit card. Until Larry came back, she was a little short of cash. "Don't be ridiculous, Addy. I want you to have the *best* education." She paused, at a loss for a moment. What had she been looking for in her purse? She stared at the plastic credit card, shook her head, then slipped it back into her wallet. "Aren't you happy there? Your instructors are always telling me how bright you are, but if the other girls are a problem, we can look for another school."

"No, the other girls aren't a problem." Adrianne privately thought most of them snotty and self-absorbed, but harmless. "It just seems like a waste of money when I could learn the same things somewhere else."

"Is that all?" Laughing, Phoebe crossed the room to kiss her. "Money's the last thing you have to worry about. It's important to me, so important, Addy, that I give you the best. Without that . . . well, it doesn't matter." She kissed her again. "You are going to have the best, and next year you're going to be looking out the window at the ocean."

"I already have the best," Adrianne told her. "I have you."

"You're good for me. Now, are you sure you don't want to come with me, get a manicure?"

"No, I have a Spanish test on Monday. I need to study."

"You work too hard."

This time Adrianne smiled. "So does my mother."

"Then we both deserve a treat." Phoebe opened her bag again. Did she have her credit card? "We'll go to the Italian place you like so much and eat spaghetti until they have to roll us out the door."

"With extra garlic?"

"Enough so no one will come near us. We'll go to the movies after. See that *Star Wars* everyone's talking about. I'll be back around five."

"I'll be ready."

It was going to be all right, Adrianne decided when she was alone. Phoebe was fine—they were both fine as long as they had each other. She turned on the radio, fiddling with the dial until she found a rock station. American music. Adrianne grinned and sang a few lines along with Linda Ronstadt.

She liked American music, American cars, American clothes. Phoebe had seen to it that Adrianne was given citizenship, but Adrianne couldn't see herself as an American teenager.

She was wary of boys, while the girls her age pursued them relentlessly. They giggled and talked about open-mouth kissing and petting. It was doubtful any one of those girls had ever seen her mother raped. Even her closest friends seemed to make rebellion their highest priority. How could Adrianne rebel against the woman who had risked her life to keep her safe?

Some of them smuggled pot into school, smoking it in the bathroom. They accepted drugs so casually while she was terrified of them.

There was the title that separated her from her companions. More than a word, it was in her blood, a tie with the world she had lived in for the first eight years of her life. A world none of the privileged American girls would understand.

She shared their culture with them, grateful for many things they took for granted. But there were still moments, private moments, when she missed the harem and the comfort of family.

She thought of Duja, who had married a rich American oilman, but was as far removed from her life as Jiddah or Fahid or the brother and sister who had been born since she had left Jaquir.

Then she pushed the past behind and opened her books at a table near the garden window.

She passed the afternoon pleasantly enough, with the music louder than Phoebe liked, and the bag of barbecued potato chips for lunch. School was a joy to her, another thing that baffled her friends. But they thought of education as a right, even a boring necessity, not a privilege. Nine years of Adrianne's life had passed before she had learned to read, but she had made up for lost time, pleasing and astonishing Phoebe by becoming an honor student. Learning was as much a fascination to Adrianne as the bouncy rock and roll pouring out of the radio.

She had dreams. At fourteen they focused on becoming an engineer. Math was like a language to her, and she was already fluent in algebra. With the help of an interested teacher, she was tackling calculus. She was also intrigued by computers and by electronics.

Adrianne was trying to solve a difficult equation when she heard the door open.

"You're back early." Her smile of greeting faded when she looked up at Larry Curtis.

"Did you miss me, honeybunch?" He tossed his flight bag aside and grinned at her. He'd done a line of coke in the lavatory of the plane just before touchdown. He was feeling fine. "How about a kiss for Uncle Larry?"

"My mother isn't here." Adrianne stopped swinging her legs and straightened in her seat. He made her conscious of her brief shorts and the small breasts under her T-shirt. With him, she wished for the protection of the *abaaya* and veil.

"She leave you all alone?" It was a rare thing for him to come across Adrianne unattended. Making himself at home, he went to a cabinet and took out a bottle of bourbon. Adrianne watched in disapproving silence.

"She wasn't expecting you."

"Tied things up early." He drank, then turned to study her slim brown legs under the table. He'd wanted to get his hands between those pretty thighs for months. "Congratulate me, sweetie. I just made a deal that's going to keep me on top for the next five years."

"Congratulations," she said politely, then began to stack her books. She would escape to her room, locking the door behind her.

"Is this what you do on a great Saturday afternoon?" Larry put a hand over hers on her Spanish book. Adrianne went still, waiting for the hammering at the base of her skull to slow. She knew when a man wanted. She'd been raised on it. Her stomach turned sour as she looked up at him.

He had changed little since the first time she'd seen him. His hair was trimmed a bit shorter, and the pastel shirts and chains had given way to Izod sportswear and jogging shoes. But underneath he was exactly what he had always been. Celeste had once called him slick. As she looked at him, the word made Adrianne think of slime.

"I want to put my books away." She kept her eyes steady, but nerves jumped in her voice. Hearing them, Larry smiled.

"You look pretty with all your books stacked around. Studious." He finished off his drink but kept his hand over hers. She was excited, he thought as he felt her pulse bounce under his fingers. Scared and excited. Just the way he liked them. "You've grown up on me, honeybunch." Definitely, he thought. Her hair fell to her waist, black and straight as an arrow. Her skin was fresh, dewy, the color of gold dust, and her eyes, as dark as her hair, were wide with fear. She knew just what he was thinking. It aroused him, the same way her firm, underripe body aroused him.

"I've been keeping my eye on you over the years, baby. You and I could make quite a team." He wet his lips, then deliberately rubbed his free hand over his crotch. "I could teach you more than you'll find in these books."

"You have sex with my mother."

His teeth flashed. He liked the way she called a spade a spade. "That's right. We'll just keep it in the family."

"You're disgusting." She yanked her hand away and lifted the books like a shield. "When I tell my mother—"

"You won't tell your old lady a thing." He kept smiling. The drug made him feel tall and strong and sexy; the alcohol made him feel confident and tough and determined. "I'm the meal ticket, remember."

"You work for my mother; she doesn't work for you."

"Get real. Without me Phoebe Spring couldn't get a job peddling garbage bags in a thirty-second commercial. She's washed up, and you and I both know it. I put a roof over your head, honeybunch. Get her a job now and again and keep the fact that she's a pill junkie and a booze hound out of the press. You should show a little gratitude."

He lunged, so quickly that Adrianne's scream caught in her throat. The books flew as he dragged her across the table. She bucked, kicking out, raking with her hands, but managed only a glancing scrape down his face before he pinned her arms.

"You're going to thank me for this," he told her before he closed his mouth over hers.

She felt the sickness rise up, hot and bitter in her throat. It clogged there so that she had to gasp to draw in even a breath of air. He bent over her on the table. When she kept her lips locked, he moved on, sucking at her breast through her shirt. There was pain, sharp pain, but deeper was the shame.

She began to scream, over and over, squirming, twisting, desperate to free herself. The glass he'd set on the table went shattering to the floor. The sound of it tossed her back to Jaquir, her mother's room.

Through her terrified eyes she saw her father looming over her, felt his hands violate her as they ripped at her shirt.

Her screams turned to sobs as his hand slid up her leg and under her shorts to probe and penetrate.

Her struggles were driving him into a sexual frenzy. To him she was like young fruit, firm, smooth, moist. Her body was as slim as a boy's but soft as butter. He felt hard and heavy as stone. There was nothing like a virgin, he thought as he dragged her to the floor. Nothing quite like a virgin. Panting, he squeezed her small breasts in his hands and watched the tears stream down her face. The fight was going out of her. He pulled her back under him easily as she tried to crawl away.

She hardly felt him now. Body and mind had separated. She heard weeping, but it seemed to come from someone else. There was pain, but it was dull, cushioned by shock.

A woman was weaker than a man, bound to a man, made to be guided by a man.

Then he was gone. She heard screaming, crashing. It didn't concern her. Rolling to her side, Adrianne curled into a ball.

"You bastard." Phoebe had him by the throat. Eyes wild, teeth bared, she squeezed the breath out of him. Caught off guard, Larry stumbled back. He managed to pry her off and draw in air just before her freshly manicured nails sliced down his face.

"Crazy fucking bitch." On a howl of pain he knocked her back. "She asked for it. She wanted it."

Phoebe was on him like a tiger, fists pounding, sinking in teeth and nails. She ripped at him, tearing clothes and flesh. They were nearly even when it came to height and weight, but she was driven by a rage so hot, so deep, only murder would quench it.

"I'll kill you. I'll kill you for putting your filthy hands on my baby." She bit deep into his shoulder and tasted his blood.

Cursing, he struck out and through more luck than skill caught her on the jaw hard enough to stun her. "Useless cunt." He was crying himself, deep, gulping sobs, amazed that a woman could have hurt him. His face was bleeding and his chest and arms felt like putty. A shooting pain ran up his leg as he struggled to his feet. "Jealous 'cause I wanted a little taste of the kid." He swiped a hand under his nose, then fumbled for a handkerchief to staunch the blood. "You broke my fucking nose."

Panting, Phoebe stumbled to her feet. She saw the bourbon open on the counter. Taking the bottle, she smashed it down, then held out the broken shard. Her glorious face was twisted with fury, and a smear of blood, his blood, was on her lip. "Get out. Get out before I cut you into little pieces."

"I'm going." He limped to the door, holding the dripping handkerchief to his face. "We're through, baby. And if you think another agent's going to take you on, you're in for a surprise. You're washed up, sweetheart. You're nothing but a fucking joke in this town." He pulled open the door when Phoebe advanced. "Don't call me when you run out of pills and money."

When the door slammed, she heaved the bottle against it. She wanted to scream, to stand in the middle of the room, lift up her face, and scream. But there was Adrianne. Phoebe crouched beside her and gently gathered her close.

"There, baby, don't be afraid. Mama's here." Shivering, Adrianne curled against her. "I'm right here, Addy, right here. He's gone. He's gone and he's never coming back. Nobody's going to hurt you again."

Her shirt was in tatters. Phoebe wrapped her arms tightly around her daughter and rocked. There was no blood. She held on to that. He hadn't raped her. God knew what he'd done to Adrianne before she found them, but he hadn't raped her little girl.

When Adrianne began to cry, Phoebe closed her eyes and continued to rock. The tears would help. No one knew better. "Everything's going to be all right, Addy. I promise. I'm going to do what's best for you."

Chapter Nine

She was eighteen years old. Adrianne stood in the quiet, pastel-toned office of Dr. Horace Schroeder, one of the leading authorities on abnormal behavior in the country. It was her birthday, but she didn't feel any sweep of joy, any tingle of excitement.

Outside the window was a long blanket of lawn, criss-crossed by bricked paths where people walked or were wheeled by white-coated orderlies and nurses. There was a weeping cherry in full bloom and an ornamental hedge of azaleas. She could see honeybees hovering over the blossoms, then streaking off, plump with nectar. Sun struck the water in a marble birdbath, but the robins and swallows that nested in the nearby grove of oak weren't tempted today.

Through the window she could see beyond the lawn and the trees to the shadows of the Catskills to the north. They gave the view a sense of openness, of freedom. Adrianne wondered if it was the same when the window was barred.

"Oh, Mama." She rested her forehead against the glass a moment, letting her eyes close and her shoulders droop. "How did we come to this?"

When she heard the door open, she straightened quickly. Dr. Schroeder walked in to see a calm young woman, slightly too thin, in a pale blue suit. She'd pinned her hair up to add height and maturity.

"Princess Adrianne." He crossed to her, accepting the hand she offered. "Forgive me for keeping you waiting."

"It wasn't long." For Adrianne, five minutes in this place was too long. "You wanted to see me before I take my mother home."

"Yes. Please sit down." He offered one of the wing chairs that helped his office look like a cozy parlor. There was an antique piecrust table beside it. On it was a discreet box of white tissues. Adrianne remembered having had need of them on her first visit two years before. Now she folded her hands in her lap and gave Dr. Schroeder a small smile. With his long-jawed face and sagging brown eyes, he made her think of a big, sad dog. "Can I get you some coffee or tea?"

"No, thank you. I want you to know how much I appreciate everything you've done for my mother—and for me." When he started to brush this aside, she held up a hand. "No, I mean it. She feels very comfortable with you, and that means a great deal to me. I also know that you've done more than you had to do to keep details of her illness out of the press."

"All my patients have a right to their privacy." He took a seat, choosing the chair beside her rather than the one behind his desk. "My dear, I know how much your mother means to you, and how concerned you are about her well-being. I'd like you to reconsider taking her home."

Adrianne braced herself. Though her eyes never wavered, her fingers tightened in her lap. "Are you telling me she's had a relapse?"

"No, no, not at all. Phoebe's progress is satisfactory. The medication and treatment have done a great deal to stabilize her condition." He paused, then let out a long breath. "I don't want to crowd this conversation with technical terms. You've heard them all before. Neither do I want to downplay her condition or the prognosis."

"I understand that." She resisted the urge to pull herself out of the chair and pace. "Dr. Schroeder, I know what's wrong with my mother, I know why and I know what needs to be done for her."

"My dear, manic depression is a very difficult and heart-breaking illness—for the patient and the patient's family. You're well aware by now that the depressions and the hyperactivity can have abrupt onsets and recoveries. Phoebe's response over the last two months has been good, but it has been only two months."

"This time," Adrianne reminded him. "In the past two years she's been in this sanitarium as much as she's been

105

home. There's been nothing I could do to change that until now. I turned eighteen today, Doctor. In the eyes of the law, I'm an adult. I can take responsibility for my mother, and I intend to."

"We both know that you took responsibility for your mother a long time ago. I admire you for it more than I can say."

"There's nothing to admire." This time she did rise. She needed to see the sun, the mountains. The freedom. "She's my mother. Nothing and no one means more to me. No one knows as much about her life and mine as you do. Tell me, Dr. Schroeder, in my place could you do less?"

He studied her when she faced him. Her eyes were very dark, very adult, very determined. "I would hope not. You're quite young, Princess Adrianne. The fact is, your mother may need constant and intense care for the rest of her life."

"She'll get it. I hired a nurse from the list of candidates you gave me. I've arranged my schedule to be certain my mother is never left alone. Our apartment is in a very quiet neighborhood near my mother's oldest and closest friend."

"Love and friendship will certainly play an important part in your mother's emotional and mental health."

Adrianne smiled. "That's the easy part."

"She'll have to be brought in for therapy weekly at this point."

"I'll arrange it."

"I can't insist that you leave Phoebe with us for another month or two. But I am going to recommend it strongly. As much for your sake as hers."

"I can't." Because she respected him, she wanted him to understand. "I promised her. When I brought her in this time, I swore to her that I'd take her home again by spring."

"My dear, I needn't remind you that Phoebe was comatose when she arrived. She won't remember that promise."

"I remember it." She crossed to him, offering her hand again. "Thank you for all you've done, and all that I'm sure you'll continue to do. I'm going to take Mama home now."

He'd known he'd been wasting his time. Dr. Schroeder held her hand a moment longer. "Call, even if you need only to talk."

"I will." She was afraid she would cry again, as she had

the first time she'd met him. "I'm going to take very good care of her."

Who's going to take care of you, he wondered, but led her out into the corridor.

She walked beside him in silence. It was too easy to remember other visits, other walks down the wide hallways. It wasn't always quiet. Sometimes there had been weeping. Or worse, much worse, laughing. The first time her mother had been hospitalized she had been brought in looking like a broken doll with eyes opened and fixed, body limp. Adrianne had been sixteen, but had managed to rent a room at a motel twenty miles away so that she could visit daily. It had been three weeks before her mother had spoken a word.

Panic. Adrianne felt a little bubble of it skip through her body, echoing the panic she'd felt the first time. She'd been so certain that Phoebe had been going to die in that narrow white bed in chronic care, surrounded by strangers. Then she had spoken. Just one word. *Adrianne.*

From that point their life had entered a new phase. Adrianne had done everything she could to see that Phoebe would receive the best treatment. Everything, including writing Abdu and begging for help. When he'd refused, she'd found another way. She drew a deep breath as they turned a corner. She was still finding another way.

At the Richardson Institute, nonviolent patients were given spacious rooms furnished as elegantly as a suite in a five-star hotel. Security was unobtrusive, unlike the east wing with its bars and locks and reinforced glass, where Phoebe had spent two miserable weeks the year before.

Adrianne found her now, sitting by the window of her room, her red hair freshly washed and pinned back from her face. She was wearing a bright blue dress with a gold butterfly pinned to the collar.

"Mama."

Phoebe turned her head quickly. The face she'd carefully composed in case a nurse should look brightened. She managed, with what acting skill she had left, to hide the desperation she felt as she rose, arms open wide. "Addy."

"You look wonderful." Adrianne held on tight, drawing in the scent Phoebe wore. For a moment she wanted to wallow in her mother's embrace, be a child again. She pulled back, smiling to disguise her careful study of her mother's face. "Rested," she said with some relief.

"I feel wonderful, especially now that you're here. I'm all packed." It was hard to keep the edge out of her voice. "We are going home, aren't we?"

"Yes." It was the right decision, Adrianne thought as she stroked her mother's cheek. It had to be. "Do you want to see anyone before we go?"

"No, I've said good-bye." She held out a hand. She wanted out, and quickly. But she knew a good actress made her exit as beautifully as she timed her entrance. "Dr. Schroeder, it's good of you to come. I want to thank you for everything."

"Take care of yourself, and that's thanks enough." He cupped her hand between his. "You're a very special woman, Phoebe. And you have a very special daughter. I'll see you next week."

"Next week?" Phoebe tightened her arm around Adrianne.

"You're going to come in for therapy," Adrianne explained, soothing. "On an outpatient basis."

"But I'll live at home, with you."

"Yes. I'll drive up with you for your sessions. It's a lovely drive. Then you'll talk with Dr. Schroeder about anything you like."

"All right." She relaxed enough to smile. "Are we ready?"

"Just let me get your bag." Adrianne lifted the small case, then because she felt Phoebe needed it, took her hand once more. "Thank you again, Doctor. It's a beautiful day," she began when they started down the corridor again. "It was wonderful to see all the trees in bud on the way up, and the flowers." They walked outside into the sunshine and delicately scented air. "Every time I drive upstate I think how nice it might be to have a house in the country. Thank you, Robert," she said to the driver as he took the bag. She slid into the back of the limousine with her mother. "Then I get back to New York, and I don't see how anyone lives anywhere else."

"You're happy there." Phoebe swallowed hard as the car pulled away from the institute. Escape. They were escaping again.

"I've always liked it, since the first time. Remember the

first afternoon, when you and Celeste and I walked all over midtown? I thought it was the most fabulous place on earth."

"Will Celeste be there?" Celeste had had the tickets waiting. She'd met them at the airport.

"She said she'd come over later today. She's about to start a new play."

Phoebe blinked as she focused on Adrianne's face. Her little girl was grown-up. They were only driving home, not running away from Abdu. No one was going to hurt Adrianne ever again. "I'm so glad you've had her while—while I haven't been well." She glanced out the window. Adrianne had been right. It was a beautiful day. Perhaps the most beautiful day she'd ever seen. "But I'm better now." She gave Adrianne a quick, laughing kiss. "In fact, I've never felt better in my life. I can't wait to go back to work."

"Mama—"

She felt the adrenaline rise like champagne bubbles, fast and frothy. "Now, don't start telling me I should rest. I've rested enough. I just need a good script." She linked her hands together, certain there was one waiting. "It's time I got back to taking care of my little girl. As soon as word gets out that I'm available, the offers will come in. Don't worry."

She seemed unable to stem the flow of optimistic words about the parts awaiting her, the producers she should lunch with, the trips she and Adrianne should take together. Adrianne said little. She knew the excitement, the utterly unrealistic planning was as symptomatic of her mother's illness as the deep depressions. But after seeing Phoebe's misery, it was impossible to even try to crush her illusions.

"I've hated to think of you living here on your own," Phoebe began as they walked into the apartment.

"I've hardly been alone." After setting down the bag, Adrianne peeled off the jacket of her suit. "Celeste has been staying here more than she stayed at home. She took the fact that you made her my guardian very seriously."

Worry flicked back into Phoebe's eyes. Without the suit jacket, Adrianne looked like a child again. Vulnerable. "I knew she would. I counted on it."

"Well, we don't have to worry about it anymore. Celeste can go back to just being my friend. Oh, Mama." Adrianne hugged her, swaying with the embrace. "It's so good to have you home."

"Baby." Cupping her face, Phoebe drew away. "Not a baby anymore. You're eighteen today. I hadn't forgotten. I haven't been able to get you anything yet but—"

"Yes, you did, and I love it. Would you like to see it?"

Pleased by the laughter in Adrianne's eyes, Phoebe said lightly, "Oh, dear, I hope it was in good taste."

"The very best." She pulled Phoebe through the foyer and into the living area. Over a small fireplace was a portrait.

Phoebe had been twenty-two when the photograph it was painted from had been taken. She'd been at the zenith of her beauty, with a face that made men quiver, eyes that made them believe. She was a goddess wearing the jewels of a queen. Around her neck The Sun and the Moon glinted. Fire and ice.

"Oh, Addy."

"Lieberitz painted it. He's the best, a little eccentric and definitely on the dramatic side, but a master. He didn't want to give it up once it was done."

"Thank you."

"It's my present," Adrianne reminded her teasingly. "The only thing I wanted more was to have the real thing back with me."

"The necklace." She ran a hand over her neck, down her breasts. "I still remember what it was like to wear it, to feel the weight of it. It had magic, Addy."

"It still belongs to you." Adrianne looked up at the portrait and remembered. Everything. "One day you'll have it back."

"One day." She smiled, enjoying the moment. "I'm going to do better this time. I promise. No drinking, no pills, no dwelling on past mistakes."

"That's what I want to hear." She stepped aside to answer the phone. "Hello. Yes. Please send her up." Adrianne replaced the receiver and kept her smile in place. "That's the nurse. I explained to you that Dr. Schroeder recommended having her, at least temporarily."

"Yes." Phoebe turned her back on the portrait and sat. "Mama, please, don't feel that way."

"Don't feel what way?" Phoebe hunched her shoulders. "I don't want her to wear one of those damn white uniforms."

"All right. I'll arrange it."

"And she isn't to stare at me when I sleep."

"No one's going to stare at you, Mama."

"Might as well be back at the sanitarium."

"No." Adrianne reached out, but Phoebe yanked her hand out of reach. "This is a step forward, not a step back. She's a very nice woman, and I think you'll like her. Please don't—don't pull away," she ended helplessly.

"I'll try."

She did. Over the next two and a half years Phoebe struggled against an illness that seemed constantly to outpace her. She wanted to be well and strong, but it was easier, so much easier, to close her eyes and drift back to the way things had been. Or more, into the illusion of the way things could have been.

When she let the reins slip, she imagined she was between jobs, a movie being edited, a new script being considered. She could float for days on the euphoria of the reality she created within her own mind. She liked to think of Adrianne as a blissful young socialite without a care in the world, gliding through life on the wealth and prestige she'd been born to.

Then the world would turn upside down, dance fitfully over the middle ground until she was mired in a depression so deep, so dark, she lost days at a time. She would imagine herself back in the harem with the same smells, the same dim light, the same endless hours of heat and frustration. Trapped, she would hear Adrianne call to her, plead with her, but she couldn't find the energy to answer.

Again and again she fought her way back, and each time it was more difficult, more painful.

"Merry Christmas Eve." Celeste glided in, a Russian lynx over her shoulders and her arms full of boxes wrapped in silver paper.

Adrianne sprang up to take the boxes while eyeing the coat with a mixture of envy and amusement. "Did Santa come early this year?"

"Just a little gift to myself for a successful eight-month

run in *Windows*." She touched the collar before taking off the coat and tossing it over a chair. "Phoebe, you look wonderful." It was a lie, but a kind one. Still, Celeste thought her friend looked better than she had a few weeks before. The sallowness was less pronounced. Adrianne had brought in a hairdresser just that afternoon to color and style Phoebe's hair. It looked nearly as rich and full as it once had.

"It's so sweet of you to come. I know you must have been invited to a dozen parties."

"Ranging from obnoxious to boring." On a sigh Celeste dropped down on the sofa and stretched out her firm, still shapely legs. "You know very well there's no one I'd rather spend Christmas Eve with than you and Addy."

"Not even Kenneth Twee?" Phoebe asked, managing a smile.

"Old news, darling." Grinning, she tossed both arms over the back of the couch. "I decided Kenneth was entirely too staid." Sensing Adrianne behind her, she lifted a hand. "You've outdone yourself with the tree this year."

"I wanted something special." She took the offered hand. Celeste felt the nerves like thin little wires.

"You've succeeded." Celeste scanned the spruce. On each branch was a different hand-painted ornament. Elves danced on the limbs, reindeer flew, angels glittered. "Those are the decorations you had commissioned for the battered children fund drive?"

"Yes. I think they came out really well."

"It looks like you bought them all up yourself."

"Not quite." Laughing, Adrianne walked over to fuss with the positioning of a teardrop ball. "The project exceeded the goals. In fact, it did so well I'm thinking of making it an annual event." Satisfied, she turned back. Behind her the tree tossed out glittering light. "Well, how about some eggnog?"

"My dear, you read my mind." Celeste slipped off her shoes. "I don't suppose your Mrs. Grange has any of those holiday cookies left?"

"Baked a fresh batch this morning."

"Bring them on." Celeste patted her flat stomach. "I renewed my membership at the gym."

"I'll be just a minute." She cast one worried look at her mother, then hurried off.

"Adrianne's hoping for snow." Phoebe stared at the window, letting the colored lights Adrianne had strung around the frame blur in her vision. "Do you remember that first Christmas, right before we left for Hollywood? I'll never forget Adrianne's face when we lit the tree."

"Neither will I."

"I gave her a ball once, one of those little glass balls that you turn over to make a snowfall. I wonder what became of it." Absently, she rubbed at a headache behind her eyes. She seemed to get them constantly. "I wanted her to go out tonight, be with young people."

"Christmas is best when you spend it with family."

"You're right." Phoebe shook her hair back and determined to be gay. "She's so busy these days, with all her charity work and socializing. Then she spends hours with her computer. I have no idea what she does with it, but it makes her happy."

"Now if we could only put our heads together and match her up with some wonderful, wildly handsome man."

With a laugh Phoebe stretched out both hands. "That would be great, wouldn't it? Before you know it, we'd be grandmothers."

"Speak for yourself." Celeste lifted a brow as she patted the back of her hand under her chin. "I'm years too young to be a grandmother."

"Christmas cheer, anyone?" Adrianne carried in a large tray. "What are you two giggling about?"

"Giggling's undignified," Celeste pointed out. "Your mother and I were sharing a sophisticated chuckle. Oh, God, are those snickerdoodles?"

"Just the cookie for the sophisticated palate." Adrianne handed her one, then poured the eggnog. It was spiced with nothing more than nutmeg. "To another Christmas with my two favorite people."

"And to dozens more," Celeste added before she sipped.

Dozens more. The words screamed in Phoebe's mind, taunting. She forced a smile and held the cup to her lips. How could she celebrate the thought of years when each day was a torment to live through? But Adrianne wasn't to know. Shifting her eyes, Phoebe saw that her daughter was watching her, the beginnings of worry on her face. She managed to make her smile brighter, but her hand shook a little as she set down her cup.

"We should have some music." Phoebe linked her trembling fingers. Even when Adrianne rose to turn on the stereo she didn't relax. It felt as if there were hundreds of eyes watching her, waiting for her to make a mistake. If she had a drink, just one, then the pounding in her head would stop and she could think clearly.

"Phoebe?"

"What?" She jolted, terrified Celeste had read her thoughts. Celeste always saw too much, wanted too much. Why did everyone want so much?

"I asked what you thought of Adrianne's plans for the New Year's Eve charity ball." Concerned, she reached over to squeeze her friend's hand. "It's wonderful, isn't it, the reputation Addy's building as an organizer?"

"Yes." "Silent Night"? Wasn't that "Silent Night" on the radio? Phoebe remembered teaching the carol to Adrianne long ago in the hot, silent rooms in Jaquir. It had been a secret between them. They'd had so many secrets. Just as she had secrets now.

All is calm, all is bright. She had to be calm because everyone was watching.

"I'm sure it's going to be a terrific success." Celeste glanced over at Adrianne, and the message passed silently between them.

"I'm counting on it." In an old habit she sat close to Phoebe and took her hand. On a good day that small contact was all her mother needed. "We hope to raise about two hundred thousand for the homeless. I've worried that a gala dinner dance with champagne and truffles isn't really appropriate for a benefit for New York's homeless."

"Anything that raises money for a good cause is appropriate," Celeste corrected her.

Adrianne sent her a quick, humorless smile, then looked at Phoebe. "Yes, I believe that. I believe that very strongly. When the end's important enough, it more than justifies the means."

"I'm tired." If her voice sounded petulant, Phoebe didn't care. She wanted to get away from the watchful eyes, the unspoken expectations. "I think I'll go up to bed."

"I'll take you up."

"Don't be silly." Phoebe fought off annoyance. It faded completely when she looked at Adrianne's face. "You stay down here with Celeste and enjoy the tree." She wrapped her arms tight around her daughter. "I'll see you in the morning, baby. We'll get up early and open presents just like we did when you were a little girl."

"All right." Adrianne turned her face up for a kiss and tried to ignore the fact that Phoebe's once sturdy body seemed so brittle. "I love you, Mama."

"I love you, Addy. Merry Christmas." She turned, holding out both hands for Celeste. "Merry Christmas, Celeste."

"Merry Christmas, Phoebe." Celeste brushed her lips over both of Phoebe's cheeks, then on a sudden impulse hugged her. "Sleep well."

Phoebe walked to the stairs, pausing once to look back. Adrianne was standing beneath the portrait, the portrait of Phoebe Spring in the prime of her youth and beauty, beneath the power and glamour of The Sun and the Moon. With a last smile Phoebe turned and walked up alone.

"How about some more eggnog?" Adrianne asked quickly. Celeste caught her hand before she reached the punch bowl.

"Sit down, honey. You don't have to be strong for me."

It was heartbreaking to watch. Layer by layer, degree by degree, Adrianne's control crumbled. At first it was a trembling of the lips, a blurring of the eyes. Strength melted into hopelessness until she sat, weeping into her hands.

Saying nothing, Celeste sat beside her. The child didn't cry enough, she thought. There were times tears helped more than bolstering words or comforting arms.

"I don't know why I'm doing this."

"Because it's better than screaming." There wasn't a drop of liquor in the house, not even a dram of medicinal brandy. "Let me make you some tea."

Adrianne dragged her fingers over her eyes. "No, I'm all right. Really." She sat back, deliberately relaxing. She'd taught herself how to ease the tension out of her limbs, her mind, her heart. It was a matter of survival. "I guess I'm not feeling very festive."

"Feel like talking to a friend?"

With her eyes closed Adrianne reached out and found Celeste's hand. "What would we do without you?"

"I haven't been too much help lately. The last few months the play's taken most of my time and energy. But I'm here now."

"It's just so hard to watch." Adrianne kept her head back. The tears had been an indulgence she hadn't realized she'd needed. It felt good, so good to be empty. "I know the signs. She's drifting away again. She tries. It almost makes it worse to know how much effort she makes. For weeks now she's been fighting the depression, and losing."

"Is she still seeing Dr. Schroeder?"

"He wants to hospitalize her again." Impatient, Adrianne pushed herself off the couch. She'd had enough self-pity. "We agreed to wait until after the first of the year because the holidays have always been so important to Mama. But this time . . ." Trailing off, she looked up at the portrait. "I'm going to drive her up the day after tomorrow."

"I'm so sorry, Addy."

"She's been talking about him." By the way Adrianne's voice tightened, Celeste understood she was referring to her father. "Twice last week I found her sitting and crying. Over him. The day nurse told me Mama had asked her when he was coming. She'd wanted her hair fixed so she'd look nice for him."

Celeste bit back an oath. "She's so confused."

With a laugh Adrianne looked over her shoulder. "Confused? Yes, she's confused. For years she's been given drugs to keep her emotions from falling too low or reaching too high. She's been strapped down and fed through tubes. She's been through stages when she can't even dress herself and others when she's ready to dance on the ceiling. Why? Why is she *confused*, Celeste? Because of him. All because of him. One day, I swear it, he'll pay for what he did to her."

The cold hate in Adrianne's eyes had Celeste rising. "I know how you feel. Yes, I do," she said when Adrianne shook her head. "I love her too, and I hate what she's been through. But concentrating on Abdu, and on some kind of revenge, isn't good for you. And it won't help her."

"When the end is important enough," Adrianne repeated, "it more than justifies the means."

116

"Honey, you worry me when you talk that way." Though she detested taking Abdu's side, Celeste felt it best for all of them. "I know he's the cause of many of Phoebe's problems, but he has given back something over the past few years, making sure there was enough money for her treatment and her living expenses."

Silent, Adrianne turned back to the portrait. It wasn't yet the time to tell Celeste that was all a lie. Her lie. There had never been a cent from Abdu. Sooner or later she'd have to tell her, but for now she wasn't certain if Celeste could handle the truth about where the money had come from.

"There's only one payment he can make that will satisfy me." Adrianne folded her arms to ward off a sudden chill. "I promised her that one day she'd have it back. When I have The Sun and the Moon, when he knows how much I detest him, I may wipe the slate clean."

Part II

THE SHADOW

Himself a shadow, hunting shadows.
—HOMER

Always set a thief to catch a thief.
—THOMAS FULLER

Chapter Ten

Black gloves clung to the knotted rope, going hand over hand, supple wrists taut but flexible. The rope itself was thin, yet strong as steel. It had to be. The streets of Manhattan were fifty stories below, shiny from the early morning rain.

It was all a matter of timing. The security system was good, very good, but not impenetrable. Nothing was impenetrable. The preliminary work had already been done in a few hours at a drawing board at a computer with a set of calculations. The alarm had been disengaged, really the most elementary part of the job. It had been the cameras scanning the hallways that had determined the method of break-in. Entrance from inside would be inconvenient at best. But there were other ways, always other ways.

There was only a drizzle now, and the chill that went with it, but the wind had died. If it had still kicked, the figure hanging on to the rope would have been bashed into the brick face of the building. Streetlamps made greasy rainbows in the puddles so very far below; the clouds masked the stars overhead. But the black-clad figure looked neither up nor down. There was a light film of sweat on the brow below a snug stocking cap; it sprang not from fear, but concentration. The figure slipped down another foot, focusing on the rope while strong legs bent and pressed against the bricks for support and balance. Even ankles had to be well tuned, flexible like a runner's or a dancer's.

The body and mind of a thief were as important, often

121

more so, than the bag of tools required to open a lock or foil an alarm.

There was little activity on the streets, an occasional gypsy cab scouting for a fare, a lone drunk who had wandered over from a less affluent neighborhood. Even New York could be subtle at four A.M. If there had been a parade with marching bands and floats, it would have made no difference. For the figure in black there was only the reality of the rope. A missed grip, an instant of carelessness, would have meant a nasty death.

But success would mean . . . everything.

Inch by cautious inch, the narrow terrace with its abundance of potted plants and sturdy railings came closer. The pores and cracks of the bricks, the tiny flaws in the mortar, could be seen clearly. If the drunk had looked up and been able to focus, the black figure would have appeared tiny, an insect crawling along the face of the building.

No one would have believed him. In the fuzzy-headed morning after, he wouldn't have believed himself.

It was tempting to hurry, to give in to cramping shoulders and aching arms and just take the last few feet in a leap. Steady, patient, the figure hung in the air, letting instinct guide the final descent.

Black sneakers skimmed the railing, swung back, and found purchase, stood poised there, slim and dramatic. No one heard the laugh, but it came, quick and satisfied.

There was time, now that feet were firmly planted on the terrace floor, to look out at New York, and the odds that had been beaten. It was a great city, a favored city, almost a home for one who had never really found a home. It had grit and glitter, and what it lacked in compassion, it made up for in possibilities.

Central Park was a patchwork of color, majestically rural from this height and in this season. Trees were gold and bronze and scarlet, triumphant in their final burst of color before the cold and the wind swirled down from Canada to sweep the leaves aside.

This stretch of Central Park West was quiet. It was a street for doormen and dog walkers, for doctors and old money. Though it was part of the city, the true frenzy, the rush of reality, was a cab ride, and a world, away.

Beyond the trees, beyond the reservoir, buildings sprang

up, taller and sleeker than this elegant old apartment house. They were the future, perhaps. They were certainly the present. In the dark they were shadows looming, or perhaps promising. Anything that could be bought, sold, traded, or desired could be found within those buildings or, a bit grimier, on the streets. There was a price to any facet of luxury or lust. New York understood that and wasn't coy about it.

The city was dozing now, resting up for the day only a few hours away, but its energy was still in the air, pulsing. There could be great victory here, or miserable failure, or every sensation in between. Some, like the thief, had experienced it all.

Turning from the rail, the figure walked quietly across the terrace and knelt by the doors. There was only the lock to deal with now, and locks were only an illusion of safety. From a dark leather bag came a small tool kit.

It was a very good lock, one the thief approved of. It took just under two minutes to pick it. There were some who could have done it in less, but they were few.

As the latch clicked open, the tools were carefully replaced. Organization, control, and caution were what kept thieves out of jail. This one had no intention of going behind bars. There was still too much to be done.

But tonight the future would have to wait. Tonight there were ice cold diamonds and red hot rubies for the taking. Jewels were the only booty worth stealing. They had life and magic and history. They had, perhaps most important, a kind of honor. Even in the dark a gem would flirt and flash and tease, like a lover. A painting, however beautiful, could only be stared at, admired from a distance. Cash was cold, lifeless, and practical. Jewels were personal.

For this thief every heist was personal.

The sneakers were silent on the gleaming floor. There was a light, homey scent of paste wax that lingered from the morning's polishing and competed against some spicy autumnal bouquet. Because it appealed, the thief smiled and took a moment to draw it in. But only a moment. In the generous shoulder bag was a high-powered flashlight, but it wasn't necessary here. Every inch of the room had been memorized. Three steps, then a turn to the right. Seven steps, then left. A staircase wound there up to the second floor with a balustrade hand-fashioned with brass leaves and cherubs. In the alcove below was a high marble pedestal. There was a sculpture on it, pre-Columbian and priceless. The thief ignored it and moved silently into the library.

The safe was behind the collected works of Shakespeare. The thief laid a finger on *Othello*, tipped it back, then spun around as the lights flooded on.

"As they say," came a calm, beautifully modulated voice, "you're busted."

The woman in the doorway was dressed in a glimmering pink negligee, her pale, angular face gleaming with night creams and her silvery-blond hair swept back from her brow. At first glance she would have been taken for a youthful forty. She admitted to forty-five, which was still five years shy of the mark.

She was small, and unarmed, unless the banana in her hand counted. With her head thrown back dramatically, she pointed the banana at the thief. "Bang."

The thief let out a sound of disgust and dropped into a deep leather chair. "Dammit, Celeste, what are you doing up?"

"Eating." To prove a point, she nipped off a bite of banana. "What are you doing skulking around the library?"

"Practicing." The voice was husky, low, but definitely feminine. She began to peel off her gloves. "I nearly robbed you blind."

"Thank goodness I raided the refrigerator." Celeste swept across the room as she had swept across so many stages. Pieces of her roles remained with her, from Lady Macbeth to Blanche DuBois. It was the toughness of her own character, the one-time New Jersey native who had stormed her way to Broadway, that allowed Celeste Michaels to dominate the sum of her strongest parts.

"Adrianne dear, not that I like to criticize, but it isn't really cricket to burgle when you have a key."

"I didn't use it." Pouting, Adrianne pulled off the cap. Her hair, nearly as black, fell past her shoulders. "I came down from the roof."

"You—" Celeste took a deep breath, knowing it would do no good to shout. Instead, she sat in the chair facing Adrianne. "Are you crazy?"

She merely shrugged. It was, after all, a question she'd

heard before. "It nearly worked. If you had any willpower, it would have worked."

"So it's my fault."

"Well, it doesn't matter now, Celeste." Adrianne leaned forward, gripping the older woman's hands which were studded with a sapphire on the left ring finger and a diamond on the right. Adrianne's were bare. Any rings she owned had been sold long before she'd begun her career. "You wouldn't believe how it feels, to hang over the city that way. It's so quiet, so solitary."

"So birdbrained."

"Darling, you know I can take care of myself." Adrianne touched her tongue to her top lip. Her mouth was wide and generous, as her mother's had been. "Aren't you wondering why your alarm didn't sound?"

Celeste adjusted the hem of her negligee. "I'm sure I don't want to know."

"Celeste."

"All right, why?"

"I turned it off this afternoon when we had lunch."

"Thank you very much. You left me unprotected against the underworld."

"I knew I'd be back." Because the energy was still flowing, Adrianne rose to pace the room. She was a small, delicately built woman who moved like a dancer, or like a thief. Her hair skimmed down her shoulder blades, straight as an arrow, lifting and falling as she turned. "It was so easy once I thought it through. I doctored the alarm, so that when you turned it on, it short-circuited the terrace doors. I waltzed in a couple of hours ago and chatted with the security guard. His wife's arthritis is acting up again."

"I'm sorry to hear that."

"So I told him you weren't feeling terribly well and left some flowers for you. When he got involved with answering a tenant's summons, I sneaked up the staircase."

Celeste raised one pale blond brow, a handy little gesture she'd cultivated decades before. "I was feeling quite well until a few minutes ago."

"I took the elevator from the fifth floor up to the roof," Adrianne continued. "I had the rope in my bag. Then it was over and down and through."

"Fifty stories, Adrianne." It wasn't easy to block out the fear, but Celeste used anger to smother it. "Dammit, how would I have explained that Princess Adrianne was just practicing when she fell off the roof of my building and smashed herself on Central Park West?"

"I didn't fall off," Adrianne pointed out. "And if you hadn't been foraging in the kitchen, I would have cleaned out the safe, gone back up to the roof, and made my getaway."

"Most inconsiderate of me."

"Never mind, Celeste." Adrianne patted her hand before she sat on the arm of the chair. "Though I did want to see your face when I dumped your ruby necklace into your lap. I'll have to settle for this." Adrianne drew a chamois pouch from her shoulder bag, opened it, and poured out diamonds.

"Oh my God."

"Gorgeous, aren't they?" Adrianne held the necklace up to the light. It was a single tier of brilliant cuts dipping down to a huge center stone that would nest cozily in a woman's cleavage. The gems seemed to drip with cold, arrogant life. Experimentally, Adrianne turned it in her hands.

"About sixty carats all told, just a touch of pink in the color. Excellent workmanship, well balanced. It even managed to make the old crow's neck interesting."

Celeste told herself she should be used to it by now, but had the sudden urge for a drink. Rising, she walked over to a French rococo cabinet and chose a decanter of brandy. "Which old crow was that, Addy?"

"Dorothea Barnsworth." Dipping into her bag again, Adrianne plucked out matching earrings. "Now, these are nice, don't you think?"

Celeste merely glanced over at several thousand dollars worth of ice. "Dorothea, yes. I thought it looked familiar." Celeste offered a snifter of brandy. "She lives in a fortress on Long Island."

"Her security system has some major flaws." Adrianne sipped. After her cold trip down from the roof, the brandy slipped into her system like a warm hug. "Would you like to see the bracelet?"

"I've already seen it, last week at the Autumn Ball."

"That was a pleasant evening." Adrianne jingled the earrings in her free hand. She judged them to be about ten carats apiece. There was a jeweler's loupe in her bag as well, which she had made use of in the Barnsworths' study. Just to make certain she didn't leave Long Island with a bagful of pretty paste. "Once they're fenced, these little baubles should bring about two hundred thousand."

"She has dogs," Celeste said into her brandy. "Dobermans. Five of them."

"Three," Adrianne corrected Celeste before she checked her watch. "They should be awake by now. Celeste dear, I'm starving. Have you got another banana?"

"We have to talk."

"You talk, I'll eat." Celeste managed only a frustrated oath when Adrianne started out of the library toward the kitchen. "Must have something to do with all the fresh air I've had tonight. Christ, it was cold out on Long Island. The wind cut right through me. Oh, by the way, don't let me forget that I left my mink on your roof."

Covering her face with her hands, Celeste sank into the ice cream parlor chair by the kitchen window while Adrianne rummaged through the refrigerator. "Addy, how long is this going to go on?"

"What's that? Ah, pâté forestier. This should hit the spot." She heard the drawn-out sigh behind her and fought back a smile. "I love you, Celeste."

"And I you. Darling, I'm getting older. Think of my heart."

Adrianne balanced a plate filled with pâté, green grapes, and thin butter crackers. "You've got the strongest and biggest heart of anyone I know." She brushed a kiss on Celeste's cheek and caught the comforting scent of her night cream. "Don't worry about me, Celeste. I'm very good at what I do."

"I know." Who would have believed it? Celeste took a deep breath as she studied the woman who sat across from her. The Princess Adrianne of Jaquir—daughter of King Abdu ibn Faisal Rahman al-Jaquir and Phoebe Spring, movie star— at twenty-five years of age was a socialite, benefactress of numerous charities, the darling of gossip columnists . . . and a cat burglar.

Who would suspect? Celeste had comforted herself with that thought over the years, though there was something of the Gypsy in Adrianne's looks. The stunning little girl had become a stunning woman. She had the golden skin and dark

eyes and hair of her father's heritage, and her mother's strong
bone structure, refined to suit her small stature. She was a
combination of the delicate and the exotic with her slim,
almost waiflike build and strong features. The mouth was
Phoebe's and always gave Celeste a pang when she looked at
it. The eyes, the eyes, no matter how Adrianne might have
wished to have nothing of her father's, were Abdu's. Black,
almond-shaped, and shrewd.

From her mother she'd inherited her heart, her warmth,
and generous spirit. From her father she'd taken a thirst for
power and a taste for revenge.

"Adrianne, there's no need for you to continue this way."

"There's every need." Adrianne popped a cracker into
her mouth.

"Phoebe's gone, dear. We can't bring her back."

For a moment, just a moment, Adrianne's expression
was young and achingly vulnerable. Then her eyes hardened.
Deliberately, she spread pâté on another cracker. "I know
that, Celeste. No one knows better."

"My love." Gently, Celeste laid a hand on hers. "She was
my closest and dearest friend, as you are now. I know how
you suffered with her, for her, and how hard you tried to help
her. But there's no need for you to take these risks now.
There was no need before. I've always been there."

"Yes." Adrianne turned her hand over so that their palms
met. "You have. And I know that if I'd allowed it, you would
have taken care of everything—the bills, the doctors, the
medicine. I'll never forget what you tried to do for Mama,
and for me. Without you she wouldn't have held on so long."

"She held on for you."

"Yes, that's true. And what I did, what I do, and what I
plan to do, I do for her."

"Addy..." The fear came, not from the words, but from
the cold, matter-of-fact way they were spoken. "Addy, it's
been more than sixteen years since you left Jaquir. And it's
been five since Phoebe died."

"And with each day the debt increases. Celeste, don't
look like that." Adrianne grinned, trying to lighten the mood.
"What would I be without this... this hobby of mine? I'd be
exactly what the press makes me out to be, a rich, titled

social butterfly who dabbles in charitable causes and floats from party to party."

Adrianne made a face at the description and went back to her pâté. "According to the gossip columns, I'm just another bored jet-setter with too little to do and too much money to do it with. Let them think it here, and in Jaquir. Let *him* think it." Celeste needed no more than the look in Adrianne's eyes to know she spoke of her father. "It only makes it easier to relieve the genuinely frivolous of their baubles."

"You don't need the money now, Addy."

"No." She looked down into the brandy. "I've invested well and could live off what I have quite comfortably. But it's not the money, Celeste. Maybe it never was." She lifted her gaze again. It was there, the heat, the chilling almost frightening heat of the diamonds she stole. "I was eight when we landed in America. And I knew even then I'd go back one day and take what was hers. What was mine."

"He might regret; by now he might regret."

"Did he come to her funeral?" The question ripped out as she sprang up to pace. "Did he even acknowledge that she was gone? All those years, those terrible years, he didn't so much as acknowledge that she was alive." Struggling for control, she leaned against the counter. When she spoke again, her voice was calm and certain. "In a very real sense she wasn't. He killed her, Celeste, all those years ago, when I was too young to stop him. Soon, very soon, he's going to pay for it."

Celeste felt the shiver run down her back. She remembered Adrianne at eight. The eyes had already been dark and haunted and much too old. "Do you think Phoebe would want this?"

"I think she'd appreciate the irony of it. I'm going to take The Sun and the Moon, Celeste. Just as I promised her, as I promised myself. And he'll pay dearly to get them back." Turning around, she smiled and lifted her snifter to salute her friend. "In the meantime I can't afford to get rusty. Did you know Lady Fume is having a gala next month in London?"

"Addy—"

"Lord Fume, the old goat, paid over a quarter of a million for her emeralds. Lady Fume really shouldn't wear emeralds. They make her look pallid." With a laugh Adrianne leaned over and kissed Celeste's cheek. "Go get some more beauty sleep, darling. I'll just let myself out."

"The front door?"

"Naturally. Don't forget we have brunch at the Palm Court on Sunday. My treat."

Adrianne swept out, reminding herself to make a quick stop on the roof to get her mink.

It had been at her mother's knee that Adrianne had learned the art of makeup. Phoebe had always been fascinated that a few dabs of paint, a few strokes with a grease pencil, could add beauty or years or take both away.

Being in the theater, Celeste had taught her even more. After a quarter of a century on the boards, Celeste still did her own makeup and knew every trick. Adrianne combined the arts of her two teachers as she transformed herself into Rose Sparrow, girlfriend of The Shadow.

The process took forty-five minutes, but Adrianne was pleased with the results. Contacts turned her eyes into a muddy gray, and a little plumping added sleepy sacks under them. She added a half inch to her nose and filled out her cheeks. Heavy Pan-Cake turned her golden complexion sallow. The red wig was handmade and expensive and teased high. Cheap glass balls dangled at her ears. She slipped a wad of strawberry-flavored Bubble Yum into her mouth as she stood back from the full-length mirror to look for flaws.

Too tawdry, she thought with a quick grin. Couldn't be better. Black spandex molded the hips she'd padded, and skinny spiked heels added three inches. A cheap fake fur was slung over her shoulders. Satisfied, Adrianne slipped on rhinestone-studded cat's-eye sunglasses and headed out.

She took the service elevator. A small precaution; no one looking at her would see Princess Adrianne. Just as no one looking at Princess Adrianne would see The Shadow. Still, she didn't want Rose to be seen leaving Princess Adrianne's penthouse apartment.

On the street she ignored the cab she would have preferred and strode off toward the subway. She had a fistful of diamonds in her imitation leather bag. She smelled as though she'd bathed in dime-store perfume. Which indeed she had.

She enjoyed these subway rides as Rose. No one who knew her would walk beneath the streets. Here she was just a body among other bodies. Anonymous, as she had never been from the day she had been born. Her heels clicked on the concrete steps as she descended, and she remembered the first time she had left the streets to go underground. She'd been sixteen and desperate. Desperately afraid, desperately excited.

Then, she'd been certain a hand would fall on her shoulder, and a voice, the cold, deep voice of the police, would demand she open her bag. It had been pearls then, a single twenty-one-inch strand of milky Japanese pearls. The five thousand dollars she'd exchanged them for had paid for medicine and a month's therapy at the Richardson Institute.

Now she walked through the turnstile with the ease of long practice. No one looked at her. Adrianne had come to understand that people rarely really looked at one another down here. In New York, people went about their business while keeping up the stubborn hope, or defense, that everyone else would do the same.

There was a rush of sound and wind from an incoming train. There was a smell, faint but somehow comforting, of old liquor and damp. Adrianne avoided a wad of gum stuck to the ground and joined the smattering of people waiting for the train that would take them downtown.

Beside her, two women hunched against the chill and complained about their husbands.

"So I says to him, you got a wife, not a goddamn maid, Harry. I promised to love, honor, and cherish, but I didn't say nothing about picking up your slop. I tell him the next time I find your smelly socks on the rug, I'm stuffing them in your big mouth."

"Good for you, Lorraine."

Adrianne wanted to second that. Good for you, Lorraine. Let the bastard pick up his own socks. That's what she loved about American women. They didn't cower and cringe when the almighty man walked through the door. They handed him a bag of garbage and told him to dump it.

The train rumbled to a halt in front of them. People filed

off, people filed on. She stepped on behind the two women. One quick glance had Adrianne crossing the car and taking a seat near a man wearing chains on his leather jacket. She always felt it wiser to choose a seatmate who looked as though he might be carrying a concealed weapon.

The train swayed, then picked up speed. Adrianne skimmed the graffiti and the ads, then the people. A man in a suit and tie with a briefcase tucked under his arm read the latest Ludlum novel. A young woman in a suede skirt looked dreamily out the black window while she listened to music through earphones. Down the car a man lay stretched along three seats with his coat over his head and slept like the dead. The two women were still discussing Harry. Beside her, the man shifted, rattling his chains.

At the next station the briefcase got off and three young girls who should have been in school piled on, giggling. Adrianne listened to them argue about what movie they would see, and envied them. She'd never been that young, or that free.

At her station she rose, shifted her bag more securely, then stepped out. It was foolish to regret what she'd never been.

Outside, the wind was brisk, cutting through the thin spandex of her pants and making a joke out of her fake fur. But this was the diamond district. There was enough heat radiating through the display glass to warm the coldest blood.

Princess Adrianne might stroll here now and then, window-shopping, making the merchants' hearts patter with the hope that she would take a few baubles off their hands. But Rose came to do business.

A great deal of business was done on the streets from Forty-eighth to Forty-sixth between Fifth and Sixth avenues. The swifts, trying to look nonchalant, hawked last night's takes. Stones, hot enough to burn their pockets, were waiting to be sold, popped from their settings and sold again. Groups of Hasidic Jews in their hats and long black coats scurried from shop to shop with attaché cases full of gems. Fortunes were carried along the narrow sidewalk by men who took care against even a casual brush with a pedestrian.

Adrianne took the same care; she had never, even at

sixteen, dealt on the street. She preferred to take her business indoors.

Every window beckoned for attention. Tiffany's or Cartier would dress them with more subtlety and class, but without the carnival flair that could draw in everyman. Shiny stones against black velvet, armies of rings, legions of necklaces. Earrings, brooches, bracelets by the armful were all polished and positioned to catch the sun and the eye. Twenty-five percent off. What a deal.

She turned down Forty-eighth and slipped into a shop.

The lights were always a little dim, the ambiance a little seedy. At first glance it looked as if it were a business on the edge of bankruptcy. At second glance it looked the same. Jack Cohen had always believed it a waste to put money into appearances. If the customer didn't like a little dust, let him go to Tiffany's. But Tiffany's wouldn't take twenty down and twenty a month. A clerk glanced over as Adrianne entered but continued his spiel to the stoop-shouldered customer with a trace of acne on his chin.

"A ring like this'll bowl her over, and it won't put you in hock for the next ten years. It's tasteful, you know, but flashy enough so she'll want to show it off to her girlfriends."

As he spoke, his eyes shifted to the door at the rear of the shop. With barely a nod of acknowledgment, Adrianne crossed to it. The low buzz told her that the salesman had released the lock. On the other side of the door was what passed as an office. Files were piled high on a metal army surplus desk. Crates and boxes lined the walls and the scent of garlic and pastrami hung in the air.

Jack Cohen was a short, barrel-chested man who wore a thick mustache as defense against the thinning hair on the top of his head. He'd come into the jewelry trade through the front door of a business his father had built up. His father had also taught him how to handle backroom negotiations. He prided himself on being able to spot a cop posing as a client as easily as he spotted a cubic zircon posing as a diamond. He knew what businesses were feeling the pinch, what dealers would be interested in a quick deal, and how to cool a handful of hot rocks.

When Adrianne stepped in, he was holding a briefke, a paper folded to form pockets for carrying loose stones. He nodded at her, then poured perhaps a dozen small, polished diamonds on the desk. With tweezers he began to separate and examine them.

"Russian," he said. "Good quality. D to F." Taking out a hand loupe, he studied each one in turn. "Ah, beautiful, just beautiful. V.S.I.," he said, meaning very slight imperfections. "Such scintillation." Then he mumbled, clucked his tongue and brushed two stones aside. "Well, well, an interesting package all in all." Satisfied, he scooped the diamonds back into the briefke and slipped it into his pocket as casually as an Avon lady might pack up her samples. "What can I do for you today, Rose?"

For an answer, she reached in her bag and drew out a large chamois sack. Turning it over, she emptied the glistening contents onto his desk. Cohen's little blue eyes lit up like sapphires.

"Rose, Rose, Rose, the day is always brighter when you're in it."

She grinned, pulled off her sunglasses, and inched a hip onto the corner of the desk. "Real pretty, huh?" The flavor of the Bronx was in her voice now. "I nearly died when I saw them. I said, 'Honey, those are the prettiest things I ever saw.'" Her full mouth moved into a pout. "I wish he'd let me keep them."

"I imagine they're hot enough to burn your skin, Rose." Making use of the loupe again, he began examining the necklace stone by stone. "How long has he had them?"

"You know he don't tell me stuff like that. But not long. They're real, ain't they, Mr. Cohen? I swear, those rocks are so big they don't look real."

"They're real, Rose." He might have tried to play games with her, but not with the man who fed him a steady amount of merchandise. "V.V.S.I., fancy stones with just a touch of pink. Excellent workmanship in this." Gently, he set the necklace down and picked up the bracelet. "Of course, that's neither here nor there. It's only the diamonds that interest us."

She poked at the necklace with the tip of a hot pink press-on nail. "I like pretty things."

"Don't we all? That's what keeps us both in business." Breathing through his teeth, Cohen studied the earrings. "A magnificent set." He turned aside to push at a file and unearth his adding machine. Mumbling figures to himself, he clicked buttons. "A hundred and twenty-five, Rose."

She pushed her chin forward. "He said I should get two fifty."

"Rose." Cohen folded his hands on his chest. With his calm blue eyes and thinning hair, he looked like a patient uncle. There was a .38 automatic under his rumpled jacket. "We both know I have to sit on these, warehouse them, so to speak, before I pass them along."

"He said two fifty." There was a whine in her voice now. "If I go home with half that, he's going to be real unhappy."

Cohen shifted back to the adding machine. He could pay two hundred and still make the standard commission, but he liked playing with Rose. If it hadn't been for the reputation of the man she represented, he would have liked making the play more personal. "Every time you come in here, I lose money. I don't know what it is about you, Rose, but I like you."

She brightened instantly. It was an old game. "I like you too, Mr. Cohen."

"How about a hundred and seventy-five, and a couple of those pretty little stones I was looking at when you came in? It'd be our secret."

She allowed herself to look tempted, then regretful. "He'd find out. He always finds out, and he don't like it when I take presents from other guys."

"All right, Rose, I'm cutting my own throat, but we'll make it two hundred. You tell him a set like that brings extra heat, and extra heat costs. I'll have the cash in a couple of hours."

"Okay." She stood and tugged at her coat. "I can calm him down if he gets mad. He won't stay mad for long. Can I leave the stuff here with you, Mr. Cohen? I don't like carrying it around on the street."

"Naturally." They both knew he wouldn't have the bad sense to steal from his best supplier. In his careful handwriting he wrote out a memo and passed it to her. This would serve as a receipt in any deal, legal or otherwise. "Go do a little shopping, Rose. I'll take care of everything."

* * *

Three hours later Adrianne dumped her bag, her coat, and her wig on the huge brass bed in her room. The contacts came out first, were cleaned and stored before she pried off the fake nails. Dragging her hand through her freed hair, she picked up the phone.

"Kendal and Kendal."

"George, Jr., please. Princess Adrianne calling."

"Yes, Your Highness, right away."

With a sigh of relief, Adrianne kicked off Rose's shoes before she sat on the bed.

"Addy, nice to hear from you."

"Hello, George, I won't keep you, I know how busy you lawyers are."

"Never too busy for you."

"That's sweet."

"And true. In fact, I was hoping we could have lunch one day this week. Social for a change."

"I'll see what I can do." Since he was a nice man and only half in love with her, she meant it.

"I read where you were getting engaged to some German baroness. Von Weisburg."

"Really? Well, I believe we had a five-minute conversation at a political fund-raiser last month. I don't recall marriage coming up."

Dipping into her bag, she drew out a wrapped wad of hundreds. They weren't new, nor were the serial numbers consecutive. The bills had the soft feel and sweaty scent of well-used money.

"George, I want to make a little contribution to Women in Need."

"The women's shelter?"

"That's right. I'll want the contribution to be made anonymously, of course, through your office. I'm going to transfer a hundred and seventy-five thousand into my special account today. You'll take care of it?"

"Of course, Addy. You're very generous."

Adrianne riffled a finger over the edge of the bills. She remembered other women in need. "It's the least I can do."

Chapter Eleven

Behind him a lion roared more out of boredom than ferocity. Philip bit into a peanut and didn't glance back. It always depressed him a little to see cats in captivity. He had an empathy for them, and more, for anything that found itself caged. Still, he enjoyed strolling through the London zoo. Perhaps it did him good to see the bars and cages and remind himself that he'd avoided looking through them from the inside throughout his career.

He didn't particularly miss stealing. At least not very much. It had been a good, steady profession while it had lasted, and had certainly provided him with the means to live well. That had always been Philip's main ambition. Comfort was always preferable to discomfort, but it was luxury that soothed a man's soul.

From time to time he considered writing a thriller based on one of his more elegant heists. The Trafalgi sapphires perhaps. He had such fond memories of that particular job. It would be taken as fiction, of course. Truth was most often odder and more harrowing than make-believe. The pity was he didn't think his present employer would see the humor or the irony of it. It was a project he could save for his retirement, when he was snuggled nicely in Oxfordshire raising hounds and hunting pheasant.

He could see himself as a country squire with muddy boots and a faithful staff—as long as it was a couple of decades off.

Popping another peanut into his mouth, he walked over to look at the panthers. Restless, angry, they stalked back and forth over the length of their enclosure, never quite able to take their captivity as philosophically as other cats. He sympathized. He was fond of their sleek lines and dangerous eyes. He'd been compared to one, by associates, by police, by women. In build and moves only, he supposed, because he was fair in coloring.

He continued to nibble on peanuts and told himself that when a man was nearing thirty-five he had to think about his health. Cigarettes were a filthy habit and one he had done well to give up. He felt positively self-righteous about it. It was a shame he was so fond of tobacco.

Taking a bench, he watched people walk by. Since it was remarkably warm for October, nannies and prams were in full attendance. He caught the eye of a young, pretty brunette strolling with a short-coated toddler. She smiled, gave him a quick flirtatious sweep of her lashes, and was more than a little disappointed when he didn't follow her.

As he might have, Philip thought, if he didn't have a meeting. Women had always been of interest to him, not only because they wore, and owned, the bulk of the baubles, but because they were—women. They were one more of life's luxuries with their soft skin and fragrant hair. He glanced at his watch just as the second hand swept up to the twelve. It was one exactly. Philip wasn't surprised when a portly, balding man dropped onto the bench beside him.

"Don't see why we couldn't meet at Whites."

Philip offered the bag of peanuts. "Too stuffy. You could use the fresh air, old man. You're looking pale."

Captain Stuart Spencer grumbled, but took a nut. The diet his wife had him on was murder. If the truth were known, he was glad to be away from the office, from the paperwork, from the phone. There were days he missed fieldwork, though fortunately they were few and far between. It was more true, though he would never admit it, that the captain had an affection for the trim man beside him. Regardless of, or perhaps due to the fact that Spencer had tried for almost a decade to put Philip behind bars. There was something unceasingly annoying, and therefore satisfying, in working with a man who had skillfully eluded justice.

When Philip had made the decision to work *with* rather than *against* the law, Spencer hadn't been fooled into thinking that the thief had suddenly repented his crimes. With Philip it was business, first and last. It was hard not to admire a man who made his decisions with such exquisite timing and with personal advancement uppermost.

Despite the warmth of the afternoon sun, Spencer huddled inside his overcoat. He had a blister on his left heel, the beginnings of a head cold, and was approaching his fifty-sixth birthday. It was difficult not to envy Philip Chamberlain his youth, health, and smooth good looks.

"Damned silly place to meet," Spencer muttered only because it made him feel better to complain.

"Have another peanut, Captain." Philip was too used to Spencer's black moods to be bothered. "You can look around and think of all the hardened criminals you put behind bars."

"We've more important things to do than eat peanuts and look at monkeys." He dipped into the bag again anyway. The taste, and the scent of animals reminded him of Sunday trips to the zoo as a child. He harrumphed away the sentimentality. "There was another robbery last week."

Intrigued, Philip leaned back and imagined smoking a leisurely cigarette. "Our same friend?"

"From the looks of it. An estate on Long Island in New York. Barnsworth—wealthy, upper crust. Owns department stores or some such thing."

"If you're speaking of Frederick and Dorothea Barnsworth, they do have a rather pricey chain of department stores in the States. What did they get taken for?"

"Diamonds."

"Always my first choice," Philip said, reminiscing.

"Necklace, bracelet. Insured for half a million."

Philip crossed his ankles. "Well done."

"It's damned annoying." Spencer sucked another nut into his mouth, then slapped his worn leather gloves against his palm. "If I didn't know for certain where you were last week, you'd have some questions of your own to answer."

"Flattery, Stuart, after all these years."

Spencer drew out a pipe, more because he knew Philip had quit smoking than because he desired it. Taking his time, and puffing clouds of smoke, he settled back. "The fellow's slick. In and out without a trace, drugged the dogs. Dobermans—nasty, vicious beasts. Brother had one once—detested it. Security system's top-notch, but he slipped right through.

Took only the set of diamonds. Left bonds, securities, a ruby brooch, and a particularly ugly ruby necklace."

"He's not greedy," Philip mused. He knew how tempting it was, and how foolhardy, to be a greedy thief. Over the past six months he'd developed a fine and very personal admiration for this particular thief. Class, he thought. Class, style, and brains. He grinned. They had a great deal in common. "He wouldn't interest me so much if he were greedy. How long have you fellows at Interpol been after him now?"

"Almost ten years." He didn't like to admit it. Though it wasn't true he always got his man, his record was excellent. "The man doesn't have any pattern. Five hits one month, then nothing for half a year. But we'll get him. One mistake, he'll make one mistake, and then we'll have him."

Philip brushed some dust from the lapel of his coat. "Is that what you used to say about me?"

Spencer deliberately puffed smoke in Philip's direction. "You'd have made one—we both know it."

"Perhaps." Which was precisely why he'd quit while he'd been ahead. "So, do you think he's in America?" Philip thought he'd enjoy a trip to the States.

"I think not. I'm inclined to think he'll put some distance between himself and the heat. We've got a man in New York, in any case."

Pity. "What do you want from me?"

"He seems to prefer hitting the very rich, and doesn't mind lifting well-known pieces. In fact, if there's any pattern at all, it's that he prefers to take well-publicized jewelry. The Stradford pearls, the Lady Caroline sapphire."

"The Lady Caroline," Philip said with a sigh. "I have to envy him that."

"We're keeping an eye on the more posh parties and dos around Europe. Having an agent who's accepted as part of the inner circle is helpful."

Philip only smiled and examined his manicure.

"It appears Lady Fume is planning a gala."

"Yes, I've been invited."

"And accepted?"

"Not yet. I didn't know if I'd be in town."

"You'll be here," Spencer told him, sucking on his pipe.

140

"Place will be full of baubles. We'd like to have you inside, keeping your eyes on and your hands off."

"Captain, you know you can trust me." He grinned. It was a particularly engaging grin that caused women to think reckless thoughts. "How is that sweet daughter of yours?"

"There's something else you're to keep your hands off."

"A purely platonic question, I promise you."

"You've never had a platonic thought about a female in your life."

"Caught." Philip balled up the empty bag and tossed it in a trash can. "I'd like the report on this last incident."

Rogue, Spencer thought, sticking his pipe in his mouth to hide a smile. "You'll have it tomorrow."

"Good. You know, I begin to see how you might have felt a few years back. It's like an itch. . . ." His eyes, smoke-gray, looked out over the bars. "I find myself thinking about him at the oddest time, his next move, where he lives, what he eats, when he makes love. I've been where he is, and yet . . . well." With a shake of his head, Philip rose. "I'm looking forward to the day we meet."

"It may not be a meeting of the minds, Philip." Favoring his heel, Spencer rose as well. "He could be a very dangerous man."

"So could we all, under the right circumstances. Good afternoon, Captain."

Adrianne checked into the Ritz in London several days before Lady Fume's gala. She preferred the Ritz because it was unashamedly grandiose and because it had been her mother's choice during the one happy trip they'd taken there. The Connaught was more distinguished, the Savoy more grand, but there was something wonderfully extravagant about gilt angels climbing the walls.

The staff members knew her well, and because she tipped generously and treated them with warmth, they didn't have to pretend a pleasure in serving her. She took a suite overlooking Green Park and spoke casually to the bellman about spending a few days shopping and relaxing.

The minute she was alone she did not saunter to the plush bath to soak in salts and bubbles. Nor did she change to see and be seen at tea. All she unpacked was a silver

141

Valentino gown with a plunging neckline. Folded with the
tissue paper protecting it were blueprints, floor plans, and
the specs for a security system. They'd cost her more than
the gown. Taking them into the sitting room, Adrianne
spread them on the table and prepared to see if she'd spent
her money as well as she believed she had.

The Fumes' town house was elegant and Edwardian,
tucked quietly in Grosvenor Square with a pretty view of the
green. Adrianne thought it was a pity the Fumes weren't
having their gala in their country house in Kent, but beggars,
and thieves, couldn't be choosers. She'd spent a particularly
boring weekend in Kent with the Fumes and could have
drawn detailed floor plans herself. The house in London was
relatively unknown, and therefore she would have to depend
on the information she'd purchased and her own observations
on the evening of the gala.

Lady Fume's emeralds would bring in a pretty penny,
she mused. The stingy and snobbish Fumes would, indirectly,
contribute to widows' and orphans' funds in several cities.
And the emeralds really were wasted against Lady Fume's
sallow skin.

The beauty was the Fumes were so tightfisted they had
spent only the minimum on security. They had nothing more
than a standard wire system running on the doors and
windows. Scanning the specs, Adrianne decided even an
average thief could bypass the alarm and gain entrance. And
she was much better than average.

The first order of business was the neighborhood, the
proximity of other houses, and the habits of the residents.
Adrianne replaced her papers in the tissue, unearthed a black
cape, and went out to take a first-hand look at the layout.

She knew London well, the streets, the traffic, the clubs.
If she'd chosen to dip into Annabel's or the clandestine La
Cage, she would have been recognized and welcomed. Another night she would have enjoyed it—the music, the gossip. But this trip to London was business. It would be
necessary to put in a few appearances before she left the city.
Such things were expected of Princess Adrianne. Just as it
was expected that she cause enough of a stir to be talked
about. But tonight she had a job to case.

She drove by first, noting the traffic, both pedestrian and

automobile, the proximity of the house to its neighbors, and to the street, which lights were on. Since only the foyer was lit, she imagined they were out—at the theater probably. It took her only one trip around to decide her best approach would be across the lawn. After parking her car on Bond Street, she began to walk.

The warm snap London had been enjoying was at an end. It was chill and damp, as Adrianne liked it best. Most Londoners were settled in their homes or crowded in clubs so that the walk was lonely, with the sound of leaves skimming across the ground and the evening wind moving through the rapidly molting trees.

There were fingers of fog at her feet, thin and gray. If she was lucky, it would be thicker and more concealing when she took this trip again. Now it was clear enough to show her the gates and gardens of the houses, and the pretty paned windows she might climb through. The leisurely walk had taken her three and a half minutes. In a dash she could make it in less than two. Moving closer, she checked for annoyances such as dogs or nosy neighbors. It was then she noticed the man loitering on the street watching her.

It had been impulse as much as instinct that had brought Philip out. There was no guarantee that the Fume house would be a target. But if it were, and if he were targeting it himself, he would certainly have wanted to stroll around the neighborhood, familiarize himself with its habits before the hit.

In any case, he'd been restless, unwilling to go out in company, and dissatisfied with his own. There were times like these when he missed the excitement, the anticipation of planning a job. The work itself was tense and concentrated and left no room for nervy pleasure. But before, and after, brought the thrill. He envied the man he was seeking to catch those thrills.

And yet, he'd made the decision to retire from second-story work coolheadedly, practically. He couldn't regret it. Except on a damp, cool night when he could almost feel the heat from jewels nestled in velvet boxes in airless vaults.

Then he saw the woman. She was small, and draped in black so that he couldn't see her face or figure. Still, he sensed youth in the easy swing of her gait, confidence in the casual way her hands disappeared into the folds of the cape. She made an intriguing picture with the fog winding around her feet and leaves racing toward the gutters at her back. But his senses sharpened because he saw that her head was turned toward the house in Grosvenor Square. The same house he'd been watching.

When she saw him, her hesitation was brief, so brief that he wouldn't have noticed if he hadn't been waiting for it. He stood where he was, his thumbs tucked into the pockets of a leather bomber jacket, curious to see what she would do. She continued toward him, no faster, no slower. As she drew nearer, her face turned up to his.

Her features were exotic, and faintly familiar. Not British, Philip thought.

"Good evening," he said, wanting to hear her voice return his greeting.

Her eyes, as dark as her cape, met his levelly. Stunning eyes, he thought, almond-shaped, thickly lashed and shadowed by the night. She only nodded and continued on.

Adrianne didn't glance back, though it worried her that she wanted to. He could have been standing there for a dozen plausible reasons, but she didn't discount the tension at the back of her neck. His eyes had been like the fog, gray and secretive. His stance, though casual, had seemed too alert to her, too ready.

Silly, Adrianne told herself as she drew the cloak closer at her throat. He was just a man taking in the night or waiting for a woman. British from the accent, extremely attractive with gray eyes and fair hair. There was no reason that the encounter should unnerve her. Except . . . except that it had.

Blaming it on jet lag, she decided to make it an early evening.

Perhaps it had been a mistake to go to bed with only a glass of wine on her stomach. It might have been better if she'd gone to Annabel's and socialized, eaten, worn herself out before she tried to sleep. She could have filled her mind with other memories, with old faces and with new, with idle conversation, flirtations, and simple laughter. She might not have dreamed then, but once the dream began, it was too late.

Scents stay with us the longest, a whiff of fragrance bringing back memories long buried, feelings long forgotten. This scent was of coffee laced with cardamom, competing with the heavy, opulent scents of perfume. The scent, even the dream scent, took her unerringly back to that night on the eve of her fifth birthday.

Her own sobbing woke her. Sitting up, Adrianne pressed the heels of her hands against her eyes and tried to break out of the dream. When it came strongly, as it had tonight, it tended to linger. While her breathing was shallow, and sweat pooled at the base of her spine, she fought to regain awareness of who she was now.

She wasn't a child anymore, curled under the bed praying for her father to stop and leave her mother in peace. That had been a lifetime ago.

She rose, fumbling for the light and then her robe. She was never able to bear the dark after one of her dreams. In the bathroom she splashed cold water on her face, knowing that the trembling had to run its course. It was a blessing that this time the nausea didn't accompany it.

She had hung from a rope fifty stories above Manhattan, had sprinted down alleyways in Paris, and had waded through a swamp in Louisiana. Nothing, nothing frightened her more than the memories that came back in dreams.

As long as her hands continued to shake, she leaned against the sink. Once they were steady, she lifted her head to study her own face. She was still pale, but the fear was no longer in her eyes. That was the first thing that had to be controlled.

The streets of London were quiet. In the sitting room she leaned her forehead against the window, grateful that it was cool. The time was coming, Adrianne thought, and the knowledge both thrilled and terrified her. The date had been chosen, though she hadn't even confided in Celeste. She would be going back to Jaquir soon, to get revenge on the man who had abused and humiliated her mother. She would take what was hers. The Sun and the Moon.

Chapter Twelve

"Darling." Adrianne brushed the baby soft cheek of Helen Fume. "So sorry to be late."

"Nonsense. You're not late at all." Lady Fume wore green silk cut low and snug to show off not only her emeralds but the ten-pounds-lighter figure she'd acquired in the last month in a spa in Switzerland. "But I do have a bone to pick with you."

"Oh?" Adrianne unhooked the clasp of her cape.

"I've heard you've been in London for days and you haven't rung me once."

"I've been hiding out." Adrianne smiled as she swirled off her cape and handed it to a waiting servant. "Not fit company."

"Oh, dear, a tiff with Roger?"

"Roger?" Adrianne linked arms with her hostess and started down the wide checkerboard-tiled hallway. Like most women, Helen would assume that a woman's moods depended on a man. "You're behind, Helen. That's been dead for weeks. I'm a free agent these days."

"We should be able to fix that. Tony Fitzwalter has separated from his wife."

"Spare me. There's nothing worse than a man newly released from holy wedlock."

The ballroom, with its polished floors and ivory-papered walls, was already filled with people and music. There was the glint of wine in crystal, the scents of perfume, male and female, and the shimmer of jewels. Millions of pounds, Adrianne thought, in stones and metal. She was going to take only the tiniest percentage.

Most of the faces were familiar. That was one of the problems with these parties. The same people, the same conversations, the same underlying boredom.

She spotted an earl whom she'd relieved of a diamond and ruby ring six months earlier, and Madeline Moreau, the French ex-wife of a film star she hoped to hit next spring. With a smile for both, she slipped a glass of champagne from the tray of a passing waiter.

"Everything looks lovely, as always, Helen."

"Such a dreadful amount of work for such a short time," she complained, though she'd done nothing more strenuous than try on the dress she was wearing. "But I do so love to entertain."

"One should enjoy what one does well," Adrianne said before she sipped. "By the way, you're looking smashing. What have you done to yourself?"

"A little trip to Switzerland." Helen ran a hand over one whittled-down hip. "There's the most marvelous spa there, if you ever feel the need. They starve you to death, then exhaust you until you're grateful for the few leaves and berries they toss your way. Then, when you're about to chuck it all, they pamper you with facials and massages and the most exquisite Roman bath. An experience, my dear, I'll never forget. And I'll kill myself if I ever have to go back."

Adrianne had to laugh. Helen's light, nonsensical conversation was always delightful. It was a pity she and her husband worshiped the British pound above all else. "I'll do my best to avoid your spa."

"While you're here, you must get a glimpse of the Countess Tegari's bracelet. It's from the Duchess of Windsor's collection. She outbid me."

The glint of avarice in Helen's eyes helped soothe away a twinge of guilt Adrianne had felt. "Really?"

"She's much too old for it, of course, but that's neither here nor there. You know almost everyone, darling, so do mingle and perk things up while I play hostess."

"Of course." She'd need only fifteen minutes to scout out the safe in the master bedroom. Thinking ahead, Adrianne moved toward Madeline Moreau. It wouldn't hurt to find out if she had any plans for spring trips.

Philip saw her the moment she walked in. She was the

kind of woman a man was compelled to notice. She fit well into a room filled with the beautiful and the glamourous. Yet, as a man trained through necessity and desire to observe, she seemed just a few degrees too detached and aloof.

She wore a black tunic with a high, jeweled neck. It fit low and snug over her hips before it flared out in a gold-flecked illusion skirt that showed off her sheerly clad legs. Only the best legs could risk it. As Philip sipped from his glass, he decided hers did nicely.

Her hair was held back from her face by diamond pins that matched the starbursts at her ears. Even as he approved he recognized her, and wondered.

Why had this beauty been walking alone on a damp London night, away from the clubs and restaurants and night spots? And where had he seen her face before?

At least one puzzle could be solved easily. Philip tapped the arm of the man beside him and nodded in Adrianne's direction. "The small woman with the gorgeous legs. Who is she?"

The man whose biggest claim to fame was being a cousin twice removed of the Princess of Wales zeroed in. "Princess Adrianne of Jaquir. Gorgeous from head to foot and a heart-breaker. She doesn't give a man more than the time of day until he's groveled for several years."

Of course. The tabloids, which his mother read religiously, always carried some juicy little bit about Adrianne of Jaquir. She was the daughter of an Arab tyrant and an American film star of some note. Had the mother committed suicide? There was some scandal there, but Philip couldn't pin it down. Now that he knew who she was, he found it even odder that he'd seen her walking late at night near the house of their hostess.

Philip's informant picked at a brochette from the banquet of tidbits that had already been ravaged. "Want an introduction?" He made the offer without enthusiasm. He'd made a play for the elusive Adrianne himself, and had been brushed away like a mosquito.

"No, I'll handle it."

Philip watched her awhile longer, his suspicion growing that she wasn't truly a part of this scene, but, like he, an observer. Intrigued, he wound his way through the crowd until he was at her side.

"Hello again."

Adrianne turned. The recognition was instant. His weren't eyes she would forget. In a matter of seconds she calculated, then smiled. Better to acknowledge, her instincts told her, than to rebuff with a blank stare.

"Hello." She drained her champagne, then handed him the empty glass with just enough of an imperial quality to the gesture to distance him. "Do you often walk at night?"

"Not often enough or I would have seen you." Smoothly, Philip signaled a waiter. He replaced the empty glass and selected two fresh ones. "Were you visiting here?"

She considered the lie, then rejected it in the same instant. If he chose, though God knew why he should, he could find her out. "No, just walking. I wasn't looking for company that evening."

Nor had he been, but he'd found her. "You made a picture that stayed with me—all wrapped in black with fog at your feet. Very mysterious and romantic."

She should have been amused, but she wasn't. It was the way he looked at her, as though she could have all the secrets she wanted, but he would find them out, one by one. "Nothing romantic about jet lag. I'm often restless the first night after a long flight."

"From?"

She studied him over the rim of her glass. "New York."

"How long will you be in London?"

It was small talk, nothing more, nothing less. Adrianne wished she knew why it made her uneasy. "Another few days."

"Good. Then we can start out with a dance and work our way up to dinner."

When he took the glass out of her hand, she didn't protest. She knew how to handle men. With a neutral smile she pushed her hair behind her back. "We can dance."

She allowed him to lead her through the fringes of the crowd in front of the orchestra. His hand surprised her. He looked to be a man who was well suited to formal dinner jackets and cummerbunds, yet the palm of his hand was hard

149

with a ridge of callus running under the fingers and along the tips.

Workingman's hands, an aristocratic face, and a suave manner. It added up to a dangerous combination. Adrianne forced herself not to stiffen when he drew her into his arms. Something had clicked when their bodies brushed, something she didn't want to feel or acknowledge. Sexuality was part of her image, but the image was only skin deep. No man had had her, and she had decided years before that no man would.

She felt his hand firm at her back, felt the slope of muscle in his shoulder where she rested her palm. She had felt muscle before, and the hard line of a man, but she hadn't been disturbed by it. Until now. The band was playing a low and intense tune. Despite the champagne, her mouth was dry. Because it was, she lifted her face and kept her eyes on his.

"Are you good friends with Lord and Lady Fume?"

"Acquainted," Philip told her. She had a unique scent. Something that brought pictures of dimly lit, hushed rooms redolent with incense and female secrets. "We were introduced through a mutual friend. Carlotta Bundy."

"Yes, Carlotta." Adrianne matched her steps to his. He danced as he spoke, smoothly, without a ripple. Another time, another place, she would have enjoyed it. But like everything else about him, his way of moving made her uneasy. "I don't believe I've seen her here tonight."

"No, she's in the Caribbean, I think. On her newest honeymoon." Testing only, he moved her an inch closer. She complied, but he didn't miss the wariness in her eyes. "Are you free tomorrow?"

"I make it a habit to be free."

"Have dinner with me."

"Why?"

It wasn't a coy question, but a direct one. He found himself drawing her closer this time for no reason other than to enjoy her scent. "Because I prefer having dinner with a beautiful woman, particularly one who takes lonely walks."

She felt his fingers tangle lightly with the tips of her hair. She could have ended that subtle flirtation with a look. But she let it pass. "Are you a romantic?" He had the face for it, she thought, poetic, lean, with eyes that could be quiet or intense.

"Yes, I suppose I am. You?"

"No. And I don't have dinner with men I don't know."

"Chamberlain, Philip Chamberlain. Shall I arrange for Helen to give us a more formal introduction?"

The name meant something, stirred some memory that nagged, then slipped away. She decided to dig it out later, but for now it might be more interesting to play the game. The slow song blended into one with a quicker tempo. He ignored it and continued to move in the same slow rhythm. Why that should have made her pulse throb she didn't know. Intrigued, she continued to sway with him.

"What would she tell me about you?"

"That I'm unmarried and discreet about my affairs, business and otherwise. That I travel extensively and have a mysterious past. That I live most of the year in London and have a country home in Oxfordshire. I like to gamble, and prefer winning to losing. That when I'm attracted to a woman, I like to let her know immediately." He brought their joined hands to his lips, brushing her knuckles.

It wasn't easy to ignore the heat that raced up her arm. "Is that because you're honest or in a hurry?"

He smiled, and nearly coaxed her lips to curve in response. "I'd say that would depend on the woman."

It was a challenge. A challenge from a man had always been difficult for Adrianne to refuse. She made the decision on impulse, knowing she'd regret it.

"I'm at the Ritz," she told him as she drew away. "I'll be ready at eight."

Philip found himself reaching for a nonexistent cigarette as she walked away. If she jangled his nerves after one dance, it would be more than interesting to see what she did to him during an entire evening. He signaled the waiter for another glass of champagne.

It took Adrianne over an hour to slip away. She'd been in the Fumes' London house only once before, but she had a very good memory, which had been refreshed by the floor plans she'd bought. The first problem was to avoid Lady Fume, the ever-anxious hostess, and the staff of efficient servants. In the end, she decided on the bold tack. Experience had taught her that often subterfuge was effective under a mask of brazen action. She took the main stairs as though she had every right to wander the second floor.

The music was muted here and the hallways smelled more of lemon oil than the mums and hothouse roses that crowded the tables in the rooms below. All the doors were painted Wedgwood blue against the white walls, and all were closed. Adrianne counted down four on the right, then as a precaution, knocked. If anyone answered, she had the ready excuse of a raging headache and the search for an aspirin. When no one answered, she took a quick look left, then right, before pushing the door open. Once it was closed again, she took a slim flashlight out of her evening bag and scanned the room by its narrow beam.

She wanted to know the placement of every stick of furniture. If she entered the room while her host and hostess were sleeping, it wouldn't do to bash into a Louis Quinze table or a Queen Anne chair.

Carefully, she made mental notes of the layout while privately deciding that Lady Fume could use a more creative decorator. Fortunately, the security was no more imaginative. The safe was hidden behind a rather bland seascape on the wall opposite the bed. The safe itself was a simple combination affair that she estimated would take no more than twenty minutes to crack.

Moving quietly, she checked the windows. They were the same style as those on the main floor, and could be jimmied easily enough if it became necessary. There was a trace of dust on the sill. Adrianne clucked her tongue. Lady Fume's housekeeper should be more conscientious.

Satisfied, she took a step back just as she heard the doorknob turn behind her. Swearing under her breath, Adrianne took a dive into the closet and found herself surrounded by Lord Fume's peer-of-the-realm suits.

She held her breath. Her eyes, accustomed to the dark, made out the movement of the door through the louvers of the closet. As it opened, some of the dim light from the hallway spilled in. Enough light, as it happened, to allow her to see Philip clearly.

Adrianne set her teeth and cursed him even as she

racked her brain for some reason for his being there. He simply stood in the doorway while his gaze moved from one end of the room to the other. Alert, she thought again. Too alert, and too ready. And he looked dangerous. It must have been the way the light behind his back haloed his head while condemning his face to the shadows.

A dangerous man, Adrianne thought as she peered through the slats. No matter how sophisticated his manners or cultured his speech, he would handle himself well on the street.

Adrianne damned him to hell and back as he stared at the closet door. The fact that he didn't belong in there any more than she did wouldn't offset being discovered in Lord Fume's closet. She damned him again and held her breath. A chance encounter on a deserted street, a one-in-a-million coincidence, and he'd ruined a job she'd planned for weeks.

Then he smiled, and the smile worried her even more. It was as though he smiled at her directly, personally, through the panel of wood that separated them. She almost expected him to speak, and felt as if she should be searching for some plausible response when he turned and left the room, closing the door firmly behind him.

She waited a full two minutes before stepping out of the closet. Always cautious, she fluffed out her skirts and smoothed her hair. Perhaps she'd been right to agree to have dinner with him. Something told her she'd be better off keeping an eye on him rather than trying to avoid him.

Philip Chamberlain was forcing her to change her plans. She took a last glance around the darkened bedroom. Lady Fume was going to keep her emeralds, at least for a while. But she'd be damned if the trip and her time would be wasted. She cast one regretful look at the seascape.

She would keep Philip Chamberlain occupied for a few hours at dinner, return to her suite, and change into her working clothes. Madeline Moreau was going to lose her sapphire pendant a little ahead of schedule.

Chapter Thirteen

Refocusing her plans on Madeline Moreau kept Adrianne up late, and had her up and on the job early. Figuring in the factor of Philip Chamberlain might have tilted the odds on the Fume job, but it didn't mean The Shadow had to leave London emptyhanded.

As a thief, Adrianne was very successful. Part of the reason was caution. Another part, perhaps a larger part, was flexibility. The blueprints and specs she'd carried over from New York would wait. The Widows' and Orphans' Fund wouldn't.

At eight forty-five, Madeline's day maid, Lucille, opened the door to an attractive, bearded young man in gray overalls.

"May I help you?"

"Pest control." Adrianne grinned through a sandy-colored beard and sent Lucille a broad wink. Under a battered cap she wore a straggly blond wig, a bit on the dirty side, that skimmed over her ears. "Got six flats to do this morning, luv, and you're number one."

"Pests?" Lucille hesitated, blushing as the exterminator gave her a long, interested study. "The mademoiselle said nothing about pests."

"Building superintendent ordered it." Adrianne held out a pink sheet. She wore workingman's gloves, frayed, that reached past her wrists. "Got some complaints. Mice."

"Mice?" On a muffled squeal, Lucille snatched her hand back. "But my mistress is asleep."

"No skin off my nose. You don't want Jimmy to kill the little buggers, I'll just toddle along to the next on my list." She offered the sheet again. "You want to sign this? It just says you didn't want the service. Gets the super off the hook if any rodents crawl up your leg."

"But no." Lucille lifted a hand to her mouth and chewed on her nails. Mice. Even the thought of them made her shudder. "You will wait here. I will wake up the mistress."

"Take your time, luv. I get paid by the hour."

Adrianne watched Lucille scurry off. Setting down her tank, she moved quickly around the room, lifting paintings, shifting books. She smiled a little when she heard Madeline's voice rise from a room down the hallway, apparently unhappy to have her beauty sleep interrupted. When Lucille came back out, Adrianne was leaning aginst the door, whistling between her teeth.

"Please, you will start in the kitchen. Mademoiselle wishes to leave before you go through the bedrooms."

"At your service, luv." Adrianne hefted the tank. "Want to keep me company?"

Lucille swept up her lashes. He was small, and skinny, she thought. But very pretty in the face. "Perhaps. After mademoiselle is gone."

"I'll be around." Whistling again, Adrianne followed Lucille's direction into the kitchen. Working fast, she slipped into the utility room. The alarm system was hardly more than a toy, making her sigh at the lack of challenge. Quickly, one ear turned for noise, she unscrewed the plate. From the deep pockets of her coveralls she took a pocket computer the size of a credit card and two spring clamps. Forcing herself not to hurry, she clamped the wires, cutting off the power.

She heard the click of heels, and dashed back through the door to pump a fog of organic rose dust into the air.

"Better give me another minute, luv," she advised when Lucille poked a head into the kitchen. "This stuff needs to settle. Wouldn't want to make those pretty eyes red."

Coughing, Lucille waved a hand in front of her face. "Mademoiselle wants to know how long you will be."

"An hour, tops." She pumped more, hastening Lucille's retreat. Counting five, Adrianne slipped back into the utility room and pulled out her wire cutters. It took under two minutes to feed the wires into her computer and change the security code. Getting in would be no problem, she thought as she replaced the face plate. Now all she had to do was find the safe. With the tank on her shoulder, Adrianne strolled back out to Lucille.

"Where next?"

"The guest room." Lucille indicated the way, then was interrupted by a stream of French curses.

"Lucille. Goddammit, where did you put my red bag? Do I have to do everything myself?"

"Sounds like a real sweetheart," Adrianne commented. Lucille only rolled her eyes and hurried off. If she threw a temper tantrum over a bag, Adrianne imagined Madeline would have apoplexy over the loss of her sapphire. Never pays to be greedy, she thought, then went off to search the guest room.

Twenty minutes later she heard the front door slam. It took her less than ten more to locate the safe in Madeline's fussy red and black bedroom. It stood behind a false front in a vanity covered with pots and jars.

Standard combination, Adrianne mused with a cluck of her tongue. One would have thought Madeline would have spent as much on her security as she had on her wardrobe. Hefting the tank once more, Adrianne went out to find Lucille waiting for her.

The maid had spritzed herself with her best perfume.

"You have finished?"

"Any mouse that tries to sneak in here is dead meat." This was going to take some delicate footwork, Adrianne decided as Lucille smiled at her. "The mademoiselle is gone?"

"She won't be back for at least an hour." The invitation was obvious as Lucille took a step closer. Adrianne felt a giggle well up and had to remind herself this was no laughing matter.

"Wish I had a little free time now. But I've got some later. What time does she let you off?"

"She has moods." Pouting, Lucille toyed with the collar of Adrianne's coveralls. She'd never been kissed by a man with a beard. "Sometimes she keeps me all evening."

"She's got to go to bed sometime." Since Adrianne had plans for Madeline that evening, she thought it best to make some for Lucille as well. "Can you get out, say, midnight? You could meet me at Bester's in Soho. We'll have a drink."

"Only a drink?"

"That depends." Adrianne grinned. "I live right around the corner from the club. You could come by and give me . . . a French lesson. Midnight." She ran a quick finger down Lucille's cheek, then headed for the door.

"Maybe."

Adrianne turned and winked.

An hour later, in a blond wig and pink sweater set, Adrianne paid cash for two dozen red roses and an elegant champagne dinner for two in a private dining room of a country inn an hour's drive from London.

"My boss wants only the best," Adrianne explained in a stern British accent as she handed a fistful of five-pound notes to the manager. "And, of course, discretion."

"Of course." The manager bowed, careful not to show too much enthusiasm. "And the name?"

Adrianne lifted a brow, à la Celeste. "Mr. Smythe. You will see that the champagne is properly chilled by midnight." As she spoke, she added a twenty-pound note.

"Personally."

Stiff-backed, head erect, Adrianne walked out to the car she'd rented for the trip out of London. She couldn't prevent the briefest of smiles. By now Madeline would have received the first delivery of roses, and the romantic, mysterious invitation to a midnight supper in the country with a secret admirer.

Human nature was as important a tool as limber fingers. Madeline Moreau was very French, and very vain. Adrianne didn't doubt for a minute that the Frenchwoman would step out of her flat and into the limousine Adrianne had arranged, leaving her flat empty. Madeline would be disappointed, naturally, when her anonymous admirer proved a no-show. But the Dom Pérignon and her own curiosity should occupy her for a while. Adrianne doubted if Madeline would return to London before two. By then Adrianne would have the sapphire, and Madeline a brilliant French temper tantrum.

It took her very little time once she was back in her rooms to go over notes and recheck her timing. The second delivery of roses, with a foolish, lovesick poem and another plea for an intimate evening would be arriving on Madeline's doorstep within the hour.

She'd never resist it. Adrianne lit a match to her notes

and watched the paper catch flame. Her instincts were right about this, she assured herself. Philip Chamberlain's intrusion might have been simple coincidence, but The Shadow preferred tidy calculations. She smiled to herself. At this point Philip was giving her the best possible cover. She'd be seen going to dinner with him, then coming home again. She would make certain no one saw her leave her suite at midnight.

Adrianne was in the best of moods when she dressed for dinner. The basic black she chose was very slim, interest added by an explosion of multicolored mosaic beading along one shoulder. She clipped on royal blue glass earrings trimmed in gold that would be taken for sapphires by anyone but an expert. She stole the best, the most precious of jewels, but rarely bought them for herself. Only The Sun and the Moon interested her.

Standing back, she took a long hard look at herself. This image, like the image of Rose Sparrow, was important to her. She decided she was pleased she'd gone with the impulse to have her hair crimped, but changed her mind about her lipstick and applied a darker shade. Yes, she thought, that added just a hint more power. Philip Chamberlain might be a dangerous man, but he wouldn't find her easy prey.

When the desk clerk phoned, she was ready, even looking forward to the evening. She insisted on coming down to the lobby to meet Philip.

He wasn't dressed so formally tonight. The gray suit was Italian casual and only shades lighter than his eyes. Rather than a shirt and tie, he wore a black turtleneck, which set off his hair well. Too well, Adrianne thought. Her smile was very cool.

"You're prompt."

"You're lovely." He offered her a single red rose.

She knew men too well to be seduced by a flower, but couldn't prevent her smile from softening.

She had a sable over her arm. He took it. As he slid the coat slowly over her shoulders, he let his fingers linger to free her hair from the collar. It was as rich and thick as the fur.

The warmth spread unexpectedly. Determined to ignore it, Adrianne looked over her shoulder. Her face was teasingly close to his. She let her lips curve as their gazes held.

She knew how to unnerve a man with a look, with a movement, he realized. He wondered how she'd earned a reputation as unattainable with eyes like that.

"There's an inn about forty kilometers east of London. It's quiet, atmospheric, and the food's delightful."

She'd expected a slick, sophisticated restaurant in the heart of the city. Could it be they would dine in the very spot where Madeline would be waiting for her mystery lover at midnight? Philip caught the sudden humor in her eyes, and wondered at it.

"You are a romantic." Carefully, she stepped out of his arms. "But I'd like a drive. On the way you can tell me all about Philip Chamberlain."

With a smile he took her arm. "We'll need more than forty kilometers for that."

When Adrianne settled in the Rolls, she let her fur slide down her shoulders. The brisk autumn air couldn't compete with the warmth. The moment the driver pulled away from the curb, Philip took a bottle of Dom Pérignon from an ice bucket.

It was too perfect, she thought, and battled back another smile. Red roses, champagne, the plush car, and an evening at a country inn. Poor Madeline, she thought, greatly amused as she studied Philip's profile.

"Have you been enjoying your time in London?" The cork came out with a muffled pop. In the quiet interior she could hear the excited fizz of air and wine rise in the neck of the bottle.

"Yes, I always enjoy it here."

"Doing?"

"Doing?" She accepted the glass he offered. "Shopping, seeing friends. Walking." She allowed him to spoon caviar onto a cracker for her. "What do you do?"

He watched her nip into the caviar before he sipped. "About what?"

Crossing her legs, she settled comfortably in the corner. It was the image she chose to project, lush furs, silk-clad legs, glittering jewels. "Work, pleasure, whatever."

"What appeals most at the moment."

She found it odd he didn't elaborate. Most of the men she knew needed only the slightest opening to expound on their businesses, their hobbies, and their egos. "You mentioned gambling."

"Did I?"

He was watching her, in the steady, disconcerting way he had before. It was as if he knew the Rolls was a stage and they were only playing parts. "Yes. What sort do you prefer?"

He smiled. It was the same smile she'd seen through the louvers in the Fumes' closet door. "Long shots. More caviar?"

"Thank you." They were playing a game, Adrianne thought. She wasn't sure what the rules were, or what form the prize at the end would take, but a game was on. She took the caviar, beluga, the best, as was the wine and the car that was driving smoothly out of London. She trailed a finger along the swatch of upholstery that separated them. "Your long shots must pay off."

"Usually." With her he was counting on it. "What do you do when you're not walking in London?"

"I walk someplace else, shop someplace else. When one city becomes tedious, there's always another."

He might have believed it if he hadn't seen those flickers of passion in her eyes. This was no bored former debutante with too much money and too much time. "Are you going back to New York when you're done with London?"

"I haven't decided." How dreary life would be, she thought, if she lived as she pretended. "I thought I might try somewhere hot for the holidays."

There was a joke here, he thought. It was just behind her eyes, just edging the tone of her voice. Philip wondered if he'd find it amusing when he heard the punch line.

"Jaquir is hot."

It wasn't a joke he saw in her eyes now, but the passion, swift, vital, and quickly concealed. "Yes." Her voice was flat and disinterested. "But I prefer the tropics to the desert."

He knew he could prod, and had decided to when the phone interrupted him. "Sorry," he said, then lifted the receiver. "Chamberlain." There was only the briefest sigh. "Hello, Mum."

Adrianne lifted a brow. If it hadn't been for the slightly sheepish expression in the word, she wouldn't have believed he had a mother, much less one who would call him on his car phone. Amused, she topped off his glass, then her own.

"No, I haven't forgotten. It's on for tomorrow. Anything at all, I'm sure you'll look wonderful. Of course I'm not annoyed. On my way to dinner." He glanced at Adrianne. "Yes, I do. No, you haven't. Mum . . ." The sigh came again. "I really don't think it's—yes, of course." He lowered the receiver to his knee. "My mother. She'd like to say hello to you."

"Oh." Nonplussed, Adrianne stared at the phone.

"She's harmless."

Feeling foolish, she took the receiver. "Hello."

"Hello, dearie. That's a lovely car, isn't it?"

The voice had none of Philip's smoothness, and the accent veered toward cockney. Adrianne automatically glanced around the Rolls and smiled. "Yes, it is."

"Always makes me feel like a queen. What's your name, dear?"

"Adrianne, Adrianne Spring." She didn't notice that she'd dropped her title and used her mother's maiden name as she did with those she felt comfortable with. But Philip did.

"Pretty name. You have a lovely time now. He's a good boy, my Phil. Handsome, too, isn't he?"

Eyes bright with humor, Adrianne grinned at Philip. It was the first time the full warmth of her was offered to him. "Yes, he is. Very."

"Don't let him charm you too quick, dearie. He can be a rogue."

"Really?" Adrianne eyed Philip over the rim of her glass. "I'll remember that. It was nice talking to you, Mrs. Chamberlain."

"You just call me Mary. Everyone does. Have Phil bring you by anytime. We'll have some tea and a nice chat."

"Thank you. Good night." Still grinning, she handed the phone back to Philip.

"I'll see you tomorrow, Mum. No, she's not pretty. Her eyes are crossed, she has a harelip, and warts. Go watch the telly. I love you too." He hung up, then took a long sip of wine. "Sorry."

"Don't be." The phone call had changed her feelings for him. It would be difficult for her to be cool to a man who had both love and affection for his mother. "She sounds delightful."

"She is. She's the love of my life."

161

She paused a moment, studying. "I believe you mean it."

"I do."

"And your father? Is he as delightful?"

"I wouldn't know."

If she understood anything, it was the need to draw a shade over private family business. "Why did you tell her my eyes were crossed?"

With a laugh he took her hand and brought it to his lips. "For your own good, Adrianne." His lips lingered there while his gaze held hers. "She's desperate for a daughter-in-law."

"I see."

"And grandchildren."

"I see," she repeated, and drew her hand away.

The inn was all he had promised. But then, she'd chosen it for Madeline because it was quiet, out of the way, and unabashedly romantic. The manager she'd met just that afternoon greeted her with a bow and not a flicker of recognition.

There was a huge, ox-roasting fireplace where logs as thick as a man's trunk blazed behind a gilt-edged screen. They kept up a hot, humming roar. Mullioned windows held out the blast of autumn wind that came from the sea. Huge Victorian furniture, the sideboards groaning with silver and crystal, seemed cozy in the enormous room.

They dined on the house specialty of beef Wellington while candles in heavy pewter holders flickered around them and music came from an old man and his gleaming violin.

She'd never expected to be relaxed with Philip. Not like this, not so she could laugh and listen and linger over brandy. He knew old movies, which were still her passion, though for now he skirted around her mother and her tragedy. They skipped back another generation to Hepburn, Bacall, Gable, and Tracy.

It disarmed her that he could remember dialogue, and could mimic it amazingly well. Both her English and her talent for accents had come from the screen, small and large. Since her love of fantasy had come naturally enough through Phoebe, she couldn't help feeling kindred with him.

She discovered he had an interest in gardening, which

he indulged both at his country home and in the greenhouse attached to his home in London.

"It's difficult to imagine you puttering around and scouting out weeds. But it explains the calluses."

"Calluses?"

"On your hands," she said, and immediately regretted her slip. What should have been a casual observation seemed too personal, too intimate with candlelight and violins. "They don't suit the rest of you."

"Better than you think," he murmured. "We all have our images and illusions, don't we?"

She thought she felt the sting of a double entendre and neatly sidestepped with a comment about the gardens of Buckingham Palace.

They'd traveled to many of the same places. Over brandy they learned they both had stayed at the Excelsior in Rome during the same week five years before. What wasn't mentioned was that Adrianne had been there to relieve a contessa of a suite of diamonds and rubies. Philip had been on one of his last jobs, acquiring a pouch of unset gems from a movie mogul. Both of them smiled reminiscently at their separate memories.

"I had a particularly lovely time in Rome that summer," Adrianne remembered as they started back out to the car. A lovely time that had amounted to roughly three hundred and fifty million lire.

"And I." Philip's take had been nearly half again that amount when he'd bartered the stones in Zurich. "It's a pity we didn't run into each other."

Adrianne slid across the plush seat. "Yes." She would have enjoyed drinking heavy red wine and walking down the steamy streets of Rome with him. But she was glad she hadn't met him then. He would have distracted her as, unfortunately, he was distracting her now. His leg brushed casually against hers as the car began to roll. It was a good thing her work at Madeline's would be so straightforward.

"There's a café there with the most incredible ice cream."

"San Filippo," Adrianne said with a laugh. "I gain five pounds whenever I sit down at that café."

"Perhaps one day we'll find ourselves there together."

His finger grazed her cheek, just enough to remind her

163

of the game to be played, and it wouldn't pay to enjoy it too much. With some regret she drew back. "Perhaps."

She'd moved only slightly, but he'd felt the distance grow. A strange woman, he mused. The exotic looks, that come-hither mouth, the quick flashes of passion he saw from time to time in her eyes. All real enough, but deceiving. She wasn't the kind of woman to settle comfortably, pliably, in a man's arms, but one who would freeze that man with a word or a look. He'd always preferred a woman who enjoyed an open physicality, an easy sexual relationship. And yet he found himself not only intrigued but drawn to the contrasts in Adrianne.

Philip knew as well as she the value of timing. He waited until they drove into London.

"What were you doing in the Fumes' bedroom last night?"

She nearly jumped, nearly swore. The evening, the company, the warmth of brandy, had relaxed her enough to take her off guard. It was only the years of self-training that enabled her to look at him with vague curiosity. "I beg your pardon?"

"I asked what you were doing in the Fumes' bedroom during the party." Idly, he curled the tips of her hair around his finger. A man could get lost in hair like that, he thought. Drown in it.

"What makes you think I was?"

"Not think, know. Your scent's very individual, Adrianne. Unmistakable. I smelled you the moment I opened the door."

"Really?" She shifted the sable back on her shoulders while her mind scrambled for the right answer. "One might ask what you were doing poking about."

"One might."

As the silence grew, she decided it would only make it more of a mystery if she did not answer. "As it happens, I'd gone up to fix a loose hem. Should I be flattered that I impressed you enough that you recognized my perfume?"

"You should be flattered that I don't call you a liar," he said lightly. "But then, beautiful women are apt to lie about most anything."

He touched her face, not teasingly, not flirtatiously as he had before, but possessively. His palm curved over her chin, his fingers spread over her cheek so that between them and his thumb her mouth was framed. Incredibly soft, incredibly desirable was his first thought. Then he saw what surprised him. It wasn't anger in her eyes, nor was it humor or aloofness. It was fear, just a flicker, just an instant, but very clear.

"I choose my lies more discriminately, Philip." God, a touch shouldn't make her feel this way, shaky, unsure, needy. Her back went rigid against the seat. She couldn't control that. She barely managed to force her lips to curve into a cool smile. "It seems we've arrived."

"Why should you be afraid for me to kiss you, Adrianne?"

Why should he see so clearly what she'd managed to hide from dozens of others? "You're mistaken," she said evenly. "I simply don't want you to."

"Now I will call you a liar."

She let out her breath very slowly, very carefully. No one knew better than she how destructive her temper could be. "As you like. It was a lovely evening, Philip. Good night."

"I'll see you to your suite."

"Don't bother."

The driver was already holding her door open. Without glancing back, she slid out, then hurried into the hotel, the fur swirling around her.

Adrianne waited until the stroke of midnight before she sneaked out of the service entrance of the hotel. She was still dressed in black, but now it was a wool turtleneck and snug leggings under a leather jacket. The stocking cap was pulled low, with her hair tucked beneath it. On her feet were soft-soled leather boots, and slung over her arm was an oversize shoulder bag.

A half mile from the hotel she hailed a cab. She took three of them, by winding routes, to within a mile of Madeline's flat. She was grateful for the fog, knee-high now. It was like wading through a shallow river so that even as the mist parted and swirled at her steps, it dampened her boots. Her steps were silent on the pavement. As she approached the building, she could see the streetlights beam down, then disappear as the fog swallowed them.

The street was silent; the houses dark.

With one quick look Adrianne scaled the low wall at the back of the building and crossed the postage-stamp lawn to the side facing west. There was ivy here, dark and smelling of damp. Melting against it, she scanned right, then left.

She could be seen if a neighbor with insomnia happened to glance her way, but she'd be hidden from any cars passing on the street. Competently, even mechanically, she uncoiled her rope.

It took only a few minutes to scale the wall to the second level, and Madeline's bedroom window. There was a low light burning on the dresser, allowing Adrianne to see the room clearly. From the mess, it appeared that Madeline had had trouble deciding on the proper dress for the evening.

Poor Lucille, she thought as she took out her glass cutter. There was little doubt that the maid would bear the brunt of her mistress's temper in the morning.

She needed only a small hole. Her hand was narrow. She used the adhesive to draw the circle of glass out. With her gloves as protection, she reached inside to trip the lock. Eight minutes after her arrival, Adrianne was crawling through the window.

She waited, listening. Around her the building settled, murmuring and creaking as old buildings do in the night. Her feet were silent over the antique Persian carpet at the foot of the bed.

She crossed to the vanity and pushed the spring that controlled the false front. Making herself comfortable, Adrianne took out her stethoscope and went to work.

It could be tedious work, and like most aspects of the job, it couldn't be rushed. The first time she'd burgled a house it had been occupied, and her palms had grown sweaty, her hands had shaken so badly that it had taken her twice as long as it should have to crack the safe. Now her hands were dry and steady.

The first tumbler clicked into place.

She stopped, patient, cautious, when a car passed on the street below. She let out a slow breath, checked her watch. Five seconds, ten, then she focused her concentration on the safe.

She thought of the prime sapphire in the necklace. In its present setting it was a bit overdone. A stone of that caliber was wasted in the outrageously extravagant filigree work. Just as it was wasted on someone as selfish and self-serving as Madeline Moreau. Popped, it would be a different story. She'd already estimated that the stone along with its companion sapphires were worth at least two hundred thousand punds, perhaps two fifty. She'd be pleased to take half that on delivery.

The second tumbler clicked.

Adrianne didn't look at her watch, but she thought, felt, she was well within schedule—just as the tingling in her fingers told her she was very close to finishing. In the jacket she was overly warm, but she ignored the discomfort. In moments she would be holding a cool quarter of a million pounds in sapphires.

The third and final tumbler clicked.

She was too skilled to rush. The stethoscope was replaced before Adrianne eased the safe door outward. Making use of her flashlight, she scanned the contents. Papers and manila envelopes were ignored, as were the first three jewelry cases she opened. The amethysts were rather sweet, and the pearl and diamond earrings elegant, but it was the sapphire she'd come for. It glinted out at her from a blanket of buff-colored velvet, intensely blue, as the best Siamese stones were. The main stone was perhaps twenty carats, circled by smaller stars of diamonds and sapphires.

It wasn't the time or the place to use her loupe. That would have to wait until she was back in her room. Lucille's patience might have worn thin by now. Adrianne would prefer to be out of the flat before the maid returned. If it was paste, she'd have wasted her time. Again, Adrianne held the pendant up to the light. She didn't think so.

After sliding the box in her pouch, she closed the safe and spinned the dial. She didn't want Madeline to have a shock before she'd drunk her morning coffee.

Moving through the dark of the flat, she went back into the utility room. With care she disengaged the wires from her computer, and left them dangling.

As silently as she'd entered, she exited.

Outside, she drew deep breaths of cold, damp air but forced herself not to laugh. It felt good, so damn good. The accomplishment was everything. She'd never been able to explain to Celeste the thrill, part sexual, part intellectual, that came the moment a job was successfully completed. It was then that tensed muscles could relax, that the heart could be allowed to beat recklessly. For those few seconds, a minute at the most, she felt invulnerable. Nothing else in her life had ever compared.

Adrianne allowed herself thirty seconds of self-indulgence, then cut across the lawn, scaled the wall, and moved through the shifting fog.

Philip didn't know why he'd come out. A hunch, an itch. Unable to sleep, he'd wandered toward the place where he'd first seen Adrianne. Not because of her, he assured himself, but because he had a feeling about the Fumes. And it was a good night to steal.

That was true, but it wasn't accurate. He'd also come because of Adrianne. Alone in his house, restless, dissatisfied, he hadn't been able to stop thinking about her. A walk in the cool night through the streets he knew so well would clear his head. So he thought.

He was what he supposed his mother would call smitten. It wasn't that unusual. She was elusive, exotic, and mysterious. She was also a liar. Such qualities in a woman were hard to resist, he thought, and wished desperately for a cigarette.

Perhaps that was why he'd found himself walking toward her hotel. As he rounded the corner he saw her. She stepped off the curb and walked across the deserted street. She wore black again, not the romance of the cape, but slim pants and a leather jacket with her hair hidden by a cap. Still, he had only to see her move to know it was Adrianne. He nearly called out to her, but some instinct held him back. Even as he watched, she slipped into the service doors and out of sight.

Philip found himself staring up at her windows. It was ridiculous, he thought. Absurd. Yet he stood for a long time, rocking back on his heels, speculating.

Chapter Fourteen

Adrianne had a leisurely breakfast in her room. While she scanned the headlines, she nibbled at a poached egg and enjoyed a second cup of coffee. The only problem Adrianne had with her double life was that it wasn't possible to share the best of it with anyone. There was no one to talk to, to brainstorm with when she was working out a complicated heist, no one who could understand the excitement, the rush of adrenaline that came from rappeling down a building or outwitting a sophisticated alarm. No one in her circle of friends would have felt that sharp-edged concentration that came from thinking on your feet when a security guard changed his pattern. There was no one to celebrate with, no one to share that whippy, exhilarating high that came from holding a fortune in your hands and knowing you'd succeeded.

Instead, there were solitary meals in endless hotel rooms.

She saw the irony of it, even the humor. She could hardly announce at lunch while her companions spoke of their latest hobbies or lovers that she'd spent an enjoyable weekend in London stealing a sapphire as big as a robin's egg.

It was like being Clark Kent, she'd once told Celeste. Adrianne imagined the dogged reporter had felt more than a little frustration trapped behind horn rims and a mild manner.

Too little sleep, Adrianne decided. When she started comparing herself to comic book characters, it was time to get a grip on herself. She might be lonely, but she was accomplished.

It was time to dress, in any case. She wondered if Madeline was up, or if anyone had noticed the damaged window. Adrianne had carefully replaced the circle of glass to prevent a draft. If Lucille neglected to dust the windowsills, it might go unnoticed for days.

Either way, it didn't matter. Rose Sparrow had work to do this morning, and Princess Adrianne had a plane to catch at six this evening.

When Adrianne, in her red wig, leather miniskirt, and pink tights walked out of the Ritz, Philip walked in. They passed through the double doors shoulder to shoulder. Philip even murmured an apology for the slight brush as Adrianne's mouth fell open. If he'd looked at her, really looked, she would never have pulled it off. Stifling a giggle, she managed a "No problem, guv," in a broad cockney.

The doorman gave her a sniff of disapproval. Undoubtedly, he took her for a working girl who'd spent the night entertaining some wealthy and totally tasteless businessman. Pleased with herself, Adrianne let her hips roll as she strode off to the Underground. She'd take the tube to the West End, where a man named Freddie ran a discreet passageway for the hottest rocks.

By two she was back in her suite with a thick stack of twenty-pound notes. Freddie had been generous, which told Adrianne he probably had a client with an affection for sapphires. All that was left was to deposit the funds in her Swiss account and have her London solicitors make an anonymous donation to the Widows' and Orphans' Fund.

Minus her commission, Adrianne thought as she tossed Rose's wig in her suitcase. Ten thousand pounds seemed fair. She was standing in her underwear, removing the last traces of Rose from her face, when her buzzer sounded. She tugged the belt of her robe secure before she answered.

"Philip." She was astonished.

"I was hoping I'd catch you in." He stepped through the doorway because he didn't want her to have the chance to close the door in his face. "I dropped by earlier, but you were out."

"I had business to attend to. Was there something you wanted?"

He stared at her. It was a ridiculous question for a woman to ask a man when she was dressed only in thin ivory silk. "I thought you might be free for lunch."

"Oh. That's sweet of you, but I'm leaving in a few hours."

"Back to New York?"

"Briefly. I'm chairing a charity ball and have dozens of details to tie up."

"I see." She wasn't wearing any makeup. The lack of it made her seem younger but no less alluring. "And then?"

"Then?"

"You said briefly."

"I'm booked to Mexico, Cozumel. A charity fashion show for Christmas." The moment she'd told him, she regretted it. She didn't like telling anyone of her plans. "I'm sorry, Philip, but you caught me in the middle of packing."

"Go ahead. Mind if I have a drink?"

"Help yourself." She bit the words off, then turned to stride into the bedroom. The wig was already hidden in a bag at the bottom of her suitcase. The money was tucked safely in her oversize shoulder bag. When a quick glance showed her nothing incriminating, Adrianne continued to pack.

"It's a pity you're leaving so soon," Philip said from the doorway. "You'll miss all the excitement."

"Oh?" She folded a sweater with quick, competent movements that told him she was used to doing such things for herself and doing them often.

"Perhaps you haven't heard, there was a burglary last night."

She picked up another sweater without missing a beat. "No, really? Where?"

"Madeline Moreau."

"Oh, God." Properly shocked, Adrianne turned around. He was leaning against the doorjamb, a glass of what she assumed was whiskey in his hand. And he was watching her just a bit too closely. "Poor Madeline. What was taken?"

"Her sapphire pendant," he murmured. "Just the pendant."

"Just?" As if weak at the knees, she sank onto the bed. "Why, this is dreadful. To think we were all there at the Fumes' a couple of days ago. And she was wearing it, too, wasn't she?"

"Yes." He sipped again. She was good, he thought. She was damn good. "She was."

"She must be devastated. Should I call her, I wonder. Perhaps not. She may not want to speak to anyone."

"It's kind of you to be concerned."

"Well, we have to stick together at times like this. I'm sure they were insured, but a woman's jewelry is personal. I think I'll get a drink myself, then you can tell me what you know."

When she moved by him into the sitting room, he took her seat on the bed. He wrinkled his nose as he sipped. The maid must have appalling taste in cologne, he thought as he caught a whiff of Rose. He noticed the leather miniskirt waiting to be packed. Not exactly Adrianne's style, he mused, and wondered why he thought he'd seen it before.

"Have the police any clues?" Adrianne asked as she came back in with a glass of iced vermouth.

"I couldn't say. Apparently, someone came in through the second-story window and cracked the safe in the master bedroom. It seems Madeline was off in the country. Coincidentally, at the same inn where we dined last night."

"You're joking. Odd we didn't see her."

"She'd come out later. On a wild goose chase, you might say. It seems the thief was clever enough to lure her out of the house with the promise of a romantic midnight supper with a secret admirer."

"Now I know you're joking." She smiled, then let her eyes sober when he didn't respond. "How dreadful for her."

"And her ego."

"That too." She shuddered delicately. "At least she wasn't there when he broke in. She might have been murdered."

Philip sipped at his whiskey. It was smooth. Every bit as smooth as The Shadow. He couldn't help admiring both. "I don't think so."

She didn't care for the way he said it, or the way he looked at her as he did. Adrianne set down her glass to continue her packing. "Did you say he took only one necklace? That's strange, don't you think? Certainly there'd be many valuables in Madeline's safe."

"One has to assume the pendant was the only thing of interest."

"An eccentric thief?" She smiled and moved to the

closet. "Well, I'm terribly sorry for Madeline, but I'm sure the police will have him in a matter of days."

"Sooner or later, in any case." He drained the whiskey. "They're looking for a young man with a beard. It seems he talked his way into the flat with some business about exterminating mice. The Yard thinks he cased the place from inside, probably tampered with the alarm system so that either he or his accomplice could break in later."

"Complicated." Adrianne tilted her head. "You seem to know a great deal about it."

"Connections." He passed his empty glass from hand to hand. "One has to admire him."

"A thief? Why?"

"Skill. Style. The ruse to get Madeline out of London showed creativity. Flair. I admire both." He set the glass aside. "Did you sleep well last night, Adrianne?"

She glanced over her shoulder. There was something in the question—rather, something under it. "Shouldn't I have?"

He held up the miniskirt, studying it with a frown. "I didn't. Oddly enough, I took a walk, ended up strolling along near here, as a matter of fact. It must have been about one, one-fifteen."

She felt a need for the vermouth again. "Did you? Too much champagne perhaps. Personally, it makes me sleep like the dead."

His eyes met hers, and held. "I'd wondered. This isn't your usual style, is it?"

She took the leather skirt from him and laid it in her suitcase. "A whim. It was nice of you to bring me the news."

"Just part of the service."

"I hate to rush you along, Philip, but I really must organize myself. My plane leaves at six."

"I'll see you again."

She lifted a brow in a gesture she'd learned from Celeste. "It's hard to tell about these things."

"I'll see you again," he repeated as he rose. He knew how to move quickly and without warning. She had time to toss her chin up when his hand slid around her neck. But she didn't have time to brace before his mouth came down to hers.

It might have made a difference. She needed to believe

173

it would have made a difference. If she had had even an instant to prepare, she wouldn't have responded. Still, she wouldn't have known his mouth would be so warm or so clever.

His fingers tightened at the back of her neck. It should have been enough to have her pulling away. Instead, she leaned toward him. It was only a hint of acceptance, but more than she'd ever given anyone else.

It had been impulse, unplanned, with the consequences uncalculated. He'd simply wanted to taste her, to leave her with something of him. Other women would have responded easily or pulled back in refusal. Adrianne merely stood, as if stunned by the most basic contact of man to woman. The hesitation, the confusion he sensed in her, contrasted sharply with the heat of her mouth. Her lips were soft, smooth, and open, and a low, reluctant moan of passion slipped through them and into him. He was rocked more by that than by any sexual experience he'd ever encountered.

She'd paled, and he saw that glimmer of fear in her eyes again when she stepped back. The urge to take her then, to roll madly with her over the clothes neatly folded on the bed, was banked. Her secrets were still secrets, and his desire to unravel them was stronger than ever.

"I want you to go."

"All right." To satisfy himself, he took her hand. It trembled lightly in his. No act this, he thought. No game or pretense. "But we haven't finished." Though her fingers were stiff, he brought them to his lips. "No, we haven't finished. I think we both know it. Have a pleasant flight, Adrianne."

She waited until she was alone before she sat again. She didn't want to feel this way, to need this way. Not now, not ever.

"You're not telling me everything, Adrianne. I can feel it."

"Everything about what?" Adrianne scanned the ballroom at the Plaza. The orchestra was tuning up, the flowers were fresh and abundant. Along one wall the staff was lined up, uniforms sharply pressed, shoulders back as if they were marines receiving a final inspection by the manager.

In a few moments the doors would be opened to the

cream of society. They would come to dance, to drink, and to be photographed. That was fine with Adrianne. The cool thousand a head they paid for the privilege would go a long way toward paying for a new pediatric wing she was sponsoring in an upstate hospital.

"Perhaps I should have gone with poinsettias," she mused. "They're so festive, and Christmas is only a few weeks off."

"Adrianne."

The impatience in Celeste's voice had her smiling as she turned. "Yes, darling?"

"What exactly went on in London?"

"I told you." She glided around the tables. No, she'd been right to go with the asters. The lavender shade was striking against the pastel green cloths. And festive or not, poinsettias were everywhere this time of year.

"What did you leave out, Addy?"

"Celeste, really, you're distracting me and I don't have much time."

"Everything's perfect, as usual." Taking matters into her own hands, Celeste gripped Adrianne's arm and drew her farther away from the tuxedoed band members. "Did something go wrong?"

"No, nothing."

"You've been edgy since you've been back."

"I've been busy since I've been back," Adrianne retorted, brushing Celeste's cheek with her lips. "You know how important this function is to me."

"I know." Relenting, Celeste took her hand. "No one does it better, and I'd swear no one cares more. You know, Addy, if you concentrated on this kind of work, gave it all the energy and talent you do the other, there wouldn't be a need—"

"Not tonight." The easiest way to end the conversation was to signal for the doors to be opened. "Curtain up, darling."

"Addy. You'd tell me if you were in trouble."

"You'd be the first." With a brilliant smile Adrianne swept forward to greet the early arrivals.

It wasn't difficult to keep the partygoers happy. It required only seeing that the food was first class, the music loud, and the wine free-flowing. As the evening progressed,

Adrianne drifted from table to table and group to group. She wound her way through the silks and taffetas and velvets, the Saint Laurents, the Diors, and de la Rentas.

Though she didn't settle long enough to eat, she danced when pressed, and she flirted and flattered. She noticed Lauren St. John, the deplorable second wife of a hotel tycoon, wearing a new suite of diamonds and rubies. Adrianne waited her chance. When Lauren walked toward the ladies' lounge, Adrianne followed her.

Inside, two actresses were having a low-toned and bitter fight. Over a man, Adrianne realized as she chose a stall. Typical. They were lucky *People* had sent a male reporter who couldn't be privy to women's room gossip. Of course if the lounge attendant had a good memory, she could make herself an extra fifty by passing the story along. Adrianne heard Lauren swear in the next stall and guessed she was struggling to pull the snug skirt over her hips. On cue, Adrianne walked to the sinks to wait. When Lauren joined her, the actresses slammed out, one then the other.

"Were they haggling over who I think they were haggling over?" Lauren asked as she washed her hands.

"Sounded like it."

"He is a sexy son of a bitch. Do you think he's going to divorce her?" She picked up a bottle of scent, sniffed it, then sprayed with abandon.

"Odds are." Adrianne crossed to the lighted vanity and took out her compact. "The question is, why does she want to hold on to him?"

"Because he's the best fuck around...I hear." Lauren sat on one of the cushy white stools and fussed with her lipstick. "We got to see a great deal of his—talent—in his last movie. I wouldn't mind a trial run myself." She took out a monogrammed silver brush and smoothed her sleekly cut blond hair.

"A woman can get sex without humiliation." Adrianne spoke with casual conviction, though it was something she'd never been quite sure of.

"Of course, but with some a little humiliation is worth it." Lauren leaned forward to peer into her own eyes, satisfying herself that the need for a lift was still years off. "Whose heart are you breaking this week, darling?"

"I'm taking a rest." Adrianne used her fingers to fluff out the hair around her face before she took a vial of perfume out of her bag. "Lauren, that necklace is simply stunning. Is it new?" She already knew when it had been bought and for how much. She'd almost finished calculating just how long Lauren would own it.

"Yes." She turned, right then left, so the stones caught the light and shimmered. "Charlie gave it to me for our anniversary. One year last week."

"And they said it wouldn't last," Adrianne murmured, shifting to admire it. "Exquisite, really."

"Seventy carats in diamonds, fifty-eight in rubies. Burmese."

"Of course." That was how Lauren's mind worked. Adrianne both disdained and appreciated it.

"Not counting the earrings." Lauren turned her head to be certain they showed to the best advantage. "Luckily, I'm tall enough to carry them. Nothing tackier than seeing some of these little women so loaded down with jewelry they can hardly totter about. The older they get, the more they pile it on—so you don't notice how many chins they have. Now, you . . ." Lauren glanced over at Adrianne's filigree necklace studded with brilliant-cut sapphires and diamonds. "You always know exactly what to wear and how to wear it. That's a very sweet necklace."

Adrianne only smiled. If the stones had been real, it would have been worth a cool hundred thousand. As it was, the pretty colored stones could be had for less than one percent of that. "Thanks." Rising, Adrianne brushed at her skirt. The full silver skirt contrasted nicely with the snug bustier of royal blue velvet. "I must go out and do my duty. We'll have to have lunch soon, Lauren, and discuss the fashion show."

"Love to." Lauren glanced at the dollar Adrianne had left for the attendant. It was enough to cover both of them, she decided, then tucked the bottle of scent into her bag.

Charles and Lauren St. John, Adrianne mused. The gala star-studded fashion show would take place in their new hotel in Cozumel. Wasn't that handy? Everyone who was anyone would be there. Even handier. It was always an advantage to steal in a crowd. Smiling, she thought about Lauren's anniversary gift. She'd have to arrange that lunch very soon.

"Is that smile for me?"

When Adrianne found herself caught in Philip's arms, the smile not only disappeared, her mouth fell open. Before she could react, he was kissing her, just a bit too hard and too long for a casual greeting. Then he drew back, but kept her hands firmly in his.

"Miss me?"

"No."

"Lucky I know you're a habitual liar." He let his gaze skim over her bare shoulders, the blue stones at her throat, then back to her face. "You look gorgeous."

She had to do something, and quickly. It was bad enough that people were watching them, but it was worse, much worse, that her heart was hammering. "I'm sorry, Philip, but this isn't an open party. I'm quite sure you didn't buy a ticket."

"But I'm a gate crasher bearing gifts." He took a check out of the inside pocket of his dinner jacket. "For your very worthy cause, Adrianne."

It was twice the price of a ticket. Even if she hated him for disrupting her routine, she had to admire his generosity. "Thank you." She dropped the folded check into her bag.

He was glad she'd left her hair down so that he could let his fingers loose in it. "Dance with me."

"No."

"Afraid to let me get my hands on you again?"

Her eyes narrowed as temper spit out of them. He was laughing at her. That was something she took from no one. "Again?" But her voice wasn't as icy as she'd hoped.

This time he did laugh, out loud. "Adrianne, you're delightful. Do you know I haven't been able to get you out of my mind?"

"Obviously, you haven't enough to occupy your time. Now, if you'll excuse me, I do."

"Addy." With the instinctive timing of a veteran, Celeste glided to her side. "You haven't introduced me to your friend."

"Philip Chamberlain," she said between her teeth. "Celeste Michaels."

178

"I've seen Ms. Michaels dozens of times." Taking Celeste's hand, Philip kissed it. "She's been breaking my heart for years."

"A pity I didn't know it until now." A quick study, Celeste summed up both Philip and the situation. If ever there was a man to make a woman edgy, this was he. "Did you meet Addy in London?"

"Yes. Unfortunately, she couldn't stay." In a smooth move he ran a hand along Adrianne's shoulder and the back of her neck. "She also refuses to dance with me. Perhaps you will."

"Certainly." Taking Philip's arm, Celeste sent one quick and mischievous grin over her shoulder. "You've infuriated her."

"I certainly hope so."

Celeste settled a hand on his shoulder. "Addy's not easily rattled."

"So I gather. You're fond of her."

"I love her above all others. Which is why I intend to keep a very close eye on you, Mr. Chamberlain."

"Philip." He turned Celeste so that he could watch Adrianne lean over a prune-faced grande dame. "She's a fascinating woman, both less and more than what she seems."

Celeste heard the jingle of warning bells as she studied his face. "You're very astute. The point is, Adrianne is a woman, a very sensitive, very vulnerable one. If I were to find out that someone hurt her, I'd be very unhappy. And I'm not sensitive at all, Philip. Just mean."

He smiled down at her. "Have you ever considered having an affair with a younger man?"

She laughed, taking the compliment as it was meant. "You're a charmer. Since you amuse me, I'll give you a little advice. Charm doesn't work on Addy. Patience might."

"I appreciate it," Philip said. He was watching Adrianne when she lifted a hand to her throat and found it bare. He saw her instant of surprise and confusion, then the tightly controlled temper as she zeroed in on him. With a smile he sent her a nod of acknowledgment. Her necklace of faux diamonds and sapphires was resting comfortably in his pocket.

The bastard. The low, slimy bastard. He'd stolen from her. He'd lifted the necklace right off her throat without her feeling a thing but the pumping of her pulse. Then he'd taunted her. He'd looked right at her and grinned.

He was going to pay for it, Adrianne thought as she tossed her gloves into her shoulder bag. And he was going to pay for it tonight.

She knew it was reckless. There hadn't been time to work out a plan coolheadedly. All she knew was that he'd taken from her, laughed at her, challenged her. Celeste, innocently enough, had passed on the information that Philip was staying at the Carlyle. That was all Adrianne needed.

She'd had an hour to change out of her gown and into her working clothes. She'd rejected the notion of bribing the night clerk. The staff at the Carlyle was well known for their honesty. She'd simply break into his room.

Adrianne walked into the lobby. There was only one clerk at the desk, male and young. Blessing her luck, Adrianne staggered over.

"Please," she began, choosing a shaky French accent. "Two men, outside. They tried to..." With a hand to her head she shuddered and swayed. "I must call a cab, so foolish to think I could walk. Water, *s'il vous plaît*. May I have some water?"

He was already rounding the desk to lead her to a chair. "Were you hurt?"

She turned her face up to his, making certain her eyes were liquid and helpless. "No, just frightened. They tried to get me into a car, and there was no one, no one to..."

"It's all right. You're safe now."

He was so young, Adrianne thought as she leaned against him. And playing on his sympathy was too easy. "Thank you. You're so kind, so good. If you would please call me a cab. But first the water, or perhaps some brandy."

"Of course. Just try to relax. I'll be only a minute."

And a minute was all she needed. As soon as he was out of sight, she leapt up, vaulted the counter, and hit the computer. He was on the twentieth floor, she saw with a grim smile. Smugly asleep, she was sure, and waiting for her next move. She doubted he expected one so quickly.

When the clerk returned with a snifter of brandy, she was sprawled in the chair, her eyes closed and a hand to her heart.

"So kind of you." She made sure her hand shook ever so slightly as she drank. "I must get home." She brushed a tear from her lashes. "I'll feel so much better behind my own doors."

"Should I call the police?"

"No," she said with a brave smile. "I didn't see them. It was dark. Thank God I was able to get away and run in here." After handing the snifter back to him, she managed to stand. "I'll never forget how kind you've been."

"It was nothing." Pleased, he puffed out with masculine pride.

"It was everything to me." Adrianne leaned against him as they walked outside. The cab she'd already paid to be waiting a half a block away glided to the curb. *"Merci bien."* Adrianne kissed him on the cheek before she slid inside. The moment they were out of sight, she straightened in her seat. "Let me off around the corner."

"Want me to wait again?"

"No." She handed him a twenty. "Thanks."

"Anytime, lady."

Fifteen minutes later Adrianne was standing outside Philip's door. The entry through the service entrance and elevator had been routine. Now it was just a matter of getting through the lock and security chain. She blamed her own impatience and temper for the amount of time it took her.

Inside, the suite was silent. Because he hadn't drawn the drapes in the sitting room, there was enough light to guide her. It took her less than five minutes to determine that he'd left nothing of value in there.

The bedroom was dark. She opted for her penlight and kept the beam away from the bed, though she would have enjoyed shining it in his face and scaring the life out of him. There would be satisfaction enough in retrieving her necklace, and the diamond cuff links he'd worn that evening.

Adrianne began a silent and thorough search of the room. It would be a damn shame if he'd put everything in the hotel safe. Somehow she didn't think he had. It would have been late, nearly three, by the time he'd gotten in. Odds were that he'd been suffering from jet lag. As Adrianne saw it, he'd probably come in, dumped everything in a drawer, then crawled into bed.

Underneath his neatly folded shirts from Turnbull, she discovered she'd been right. The light shone on her necklace. Beside it was a man's jewel case in monogrammed alligator. More than the diamond cuff links rested inside. She found other links in heavy gold, a stick pin with a particularly fine topaz, and other assorted pieces of man's vanity, all tasteful and expensive.

Delighted, Adrianne slipped the case and her necklace into her bag. She thought it was a pity she wouldn't see his face in the morning. Then she turned and collided with him.

She barely had time to suck in her breath before he tossed her over his shoulder. Even as she kicked out, she found herself tumbling through the air. This time the breath was knocked out of her as she hit the mattress. Adrianne could only swear as her arms were pinned to her sides and Philip's body spread over hers.

"Good morning, darling," he said, then pressed his mouth to hers. He felt her arms strain against him, her body arch and buck even as her mouth softened, heated, opened. Aroused by the contrast, he took the kiss deeper than he'd intended.

Pulling himself back, he braceleted her wrists with one hand and reached for the light. The moment it came on, he decided he liked the way she looked in his bed.

She was well aware of her position. Her own fault, Adrianne thought in disgust as she struggled between temper and bitterness. For nearly ten years she'd stolen the best, and she'd stolen with a cool head and logic. Now, because of a worthless necklace—and her own pride—she was caught. The only choice left was to brazen it out.

"Let go of me."

"Not a chance." Holding her arms above her head, he used his free hand to brush the hair from her cheek. "You must admit it was a clever way to get you into bed."

"I came for my necklace, not to go to bed with you."

"You could do both." He grinned. Because he was unprepared for the sudden violence of her struggle, he lost his grip. The next thirty seconds were a heated and silent bid for supremacy. She was agile, and one hell of a lot stronger than she looked. Philip discovered that when she landed a solid blow in his solar plexus. This time he pinned her hands between their bodies and kept his face an inch from hers. "All right, we'll discuss it later."

It wasn't the cool Princess Adrianne who glared up at him, but the woman he'd suspected lay beneath, passionate, volatile... and involved. "You set me up, you bastard."

"Guilty on both counts. I'm surprised you'd risk so much to get the necklace back. It's worth only a few hundred pounds. Sentimental value, Addy?"

Panting, she pulled her thoughts together. He either had an excellent eye or a jeweler's loupe. "Why did you take it?"

"Curiosity. Why does Princess Adrianne wear colored glass?"

"I've better things to spend my money on." His chest was bare. She could feel each beat of his heart against her fingers. "If you let me go, I'll take it back and we can forget this happened. I won't turn you over to the police."

"Do better."

She had her wind back and, she hoped, her control. "What do you want?"

His brow lifted at that, and he took a long, leisurely study of her face. "I'll let that pass," he decided. "It's too easy."

"I won't apologize for breaking into your room to take back my own property."

"What about my jewelry case?"

"That was revenge." The flash of passion, quick and intense, came into her eyes. "I believe strongly in revenge."

"Fair enough. Would you like a drink?"

"Yes."

He smiled at her again. "Then I'll have your word that you'll stay where you are." He could almost see her thoughts shifting and taking shape. "You could run, Adrianne, and as I'm hardly dressed to chase you, you'd get away. Today. There'd still be tomorrow."

"My word," she agreed. "I could use a drink."

He rose, giving her a chance to slip off the bed and into a chair. He was bare-chested and the drawstring pants hung precariously low on his hips. Steadying herself, Adrianne drew off her gloves as she listened to the sound of liquid hitting glass.

"Scotch all right?"

"Fine." She took the glass, then sipped calmly as he sat on the edge of the bed.

"I'm hoping for an explanation."

"Then you'll be disappointed. I don't owe you one."

"You've prodded my curiosity." He reached beside the bed for a pack of cigarettes. "You know, I'd given these up until I met you."

"Sorry." She smiled. "It's just a matter of willpower, after all."

"Oh, I have it." His gaze skimmed down her, then up. "I'm using it up elsewhere. Now, my question is, why does a woman like you steal?"

"It's not stealing to take back what belongs to you."

"Madeline Moreau's pendant didn't belong to you."

If her control hadn't been so well tuned, she'd have choked on the scotch. "What does one have to do with the other?"

He blew smoke out thoughtfully as he watched her. She was no amateur, he thought, and a long way from being a novice. "Oh, you took them, Addy. Or you know who did. Does the name Rose Sparrow ring a bell?"

She continued to sip, though her palms had broken into a sweat. "Should it?"

"It was the skirt," Philip mused. "It took me quite a while to put it together. You're a distraction. But when I visited our mutual friend, Freddie, he mentioned Rose, described her. And I remembered that little blue leather skirt you were packing. The one that was so unlike your usual style."

"If you're going to talk in circles, I really have to go. I haven't had any sleep."

"Sit down."

She wouldn't have obeyed, but the sharp snap of his voice warned her it would be less complicated if she did. "If I read you correctly, you've somehow gotten it into your head that I had something to do with Madeline's burglary." Setting the scotch aside, she ordered her shoulders to relax. "I can only ask you, why would I? I hardly need the money."

"It's not a matter of need, but of motive."

The pulse in her throat was beating uncomfortably. She

ignored it and kept her eyes steadily in contact with his. "What are you, a Scotland Yard man?"

With a laugh he tapped his cigarette out. "Not precisely. You've heard the adage it takes a thief to catch a thief?"

When the bell rang, it rang loud and clear. She'd heard talk of the legendary thief known only as P.C. He was reputed to be charming, ruthless, and the master of second-story work. He specialized in jewels. Some said he'd stolen the Wellingford diamond, a seventy-five-carat stone of the first water. Then he'd retired. Adrianne had always pictured an older man, a cunning veteran. She picked up the scotch again.

It was ironic that she was at last in the company of one of her own, and the best, yet she wasn't free to talk shop.

"Is that your way of telling me you're a thief?"

"Was."

"Fascinating. Then I suppose you might have taken Madeline's pendant."

"A few years ago I would have. The point is, you had a hand in it, Addy, and I want to know why."

She rose, swirling the inch of scotch left in the glass. "Philip, if for some insane reason I had a part in taking it, it wouldn't be any of your business."

"Your title doesn't mean a damn here, between the two of us, nor do social graces. Either you tell me, or you tell my superiors."

"Who are?"

"I work for Interpol." He watched her lift the scotch to her lips and drain it. "They've tied several burglaries during almost a decade to one man, one very elusive man. The Moreau sapphire is just the last of a very long list."

"Interesting. But what does it have to do with me?"

"We can set up a meeting. I might be able to work a deal and keep you out of it."

"That's very gallant," she said as she set the glass aside. "Or would be if you were right." Though she knew how close the edge was, still she smiled confidently. "Can you imagine how amused my friends would be if I told them I'd been accused of being involved with a thief? I could dine off it for weeks."

"Dammit, can't you see I'm trying to help you?" He was

up quickly, his hands on her arms, shaking her. "There's no reason for the act with me. There's no one else here, no need for pretense. I saw you outside of your hotel on the night of the robbery, dressed all in black, sneaking in the service entrance. I know you had something to do with seeing the jewels were fenced. You're involved in this, Addy. I was in the business, for Christ's sake. I know how it works."

"You have nothing solid to take to your superiors."

"Not yet. It's only a matter of time. No one knows better how high the odds become after a few years. If you're in trouble, if you've had to sell a few baubles to save face, I've got no reason to embarrass you by making it public. Talk to me, Addy. I want to help you."

It was ridiculous, but he sounded as though he meant it. A part of her she'd strapped down for years wanted to believe him. "Why?"

"Don't be an idiot," he muttered, and brought his lips to hers.

Her initial struggle died on a moan. The passion she tasted was no less volatile than the passion she felt. His hands were in her hair, rough, possessive, as he dragged her head back for more freedom. For the first time she let her hands roam, search, linger over a man's flesh. The need started out as a warmth in her stomach, then spread to a heat, then an ache, then a fire.

He knew it was madness to want her this way, to forget his priorities and sink into her. But she was all softness and strength, all trembles and demands. The scent radiating from the skin of her neck made his head spin as they tumbled onto the bed.

He forgot finesse and style in an explosion of desire. Whoever she was, whatever her secrets, he wanted her now more than he'd ever wanted before. He'd coveted diamonds for their inner fire, rubies for their arrogant flame, sapphires for their flash of blue heat. In Adrianne he found all the qualities he'd found before only in the gems he'd stolen.

She was small, agile. Her hair wound around him as they rolled on the bed, wrapping him in scent and texture. The taste of scotch lingered on her tongue, intoxicating. There was a desperation in her response that stripped his control layer by layer.

When he slipped his hand under her sweater to find her breast, full and soft, he felt her heart thundering under his palm.

It had never been like this. Year after year, time after time, she'd convinced herself it could never be like this. Not for her. For the first time she wanted completely, as a woman. To use and be used. As her body responded, struggling toward pleasure, arching toward release, the fear stabbed through.

She could see her mother's face, wet with tears. And she could hear, muffled through her childish hands, her father's groans of satisfaction.

"No!" The word ripped out of her as she shoved Philip away. "Don't touch me. Don't."

In reflex he grabbed her wrists as she swung out at him. "Goddammit, Adrianne." Fury had him dragging her against him, bitter accusations on his tongue. They died before they could be spoken. The tears trembling in her eyes were real, as was the terror behind them.

"All right, steady." He gentled his grip and fought to keep his voice low. She was a roller coaster he still wasn't certain he wanted to ride. "Stop," he ordered when she continued to fight him. "I'm not going to hurt you."

"Just let me go." Her throat was so tight even the whisper hurt. "Keep your hands off me."

Temper rose again and had to be battled back. "I don't attack women," he said evenly. "I'd apologize if I'd read you wrong, but we both know I didn't."

"I've already told you I didn't come here to sleep with you." She jerked one hand free, then the other. "If you expect me to fall on my back just because you want to be entertained, you're going to be disappointed."

He drew away from her slowly. That was a measure of his own control. "Someone's given you a bad time."

"The simple fact is I'm not interested." Before he could touch her again, she pushed herself off the bed and grabbed her bag.

"The simple fact is you're afraid." He, too, rose from the bed. He wouldn't know until later that the sheets would smell of her and she would haunt him for the rest of the night. "Of me, I wonder, or yourself."

Her hands weren't steady when she lifted the strap to her shoulder. "A man's ego is an unending fascination. Goodbye, Philip."

"One more question, Adrianne." She was at the door, but she stopped, tilting her head. "We're alone here, no recorders. I'd like the truth for once, for myself. Personally. Are you involved in all this because of a man?"

She should have ignored him. She should have given him her coolest smile and walked out, leaving his question unanswered. She would ask herself a dozen times why she didn't. "Yes." She saw her father as he'd looked striding down the wide, sunwashed halls, ignoring her mother's tears and her own silent cries. "Yes, because of a man."

The disappointment was deep and as ripe as his anger. "Is he threatening you? Blackmailing you?"

"That's a total of three questions." She found the strength to smile. "But I'll tell you this, which is nothing but the truth. I've done what I've done by choice." Remembering, she reached into her bag and drew out his jewelry case. On impulse she tossed it to him. "Honor among thieves, Philip. At least for today."

Chapter Fifteen

"Darling, isn't this glorious?" Lauren St. John swirled around the edge of the pool to kiss Adrianne's cheek. She made certain the cameraman got her best side and used Adrianne's body to block the fact that she'd put on five pounds since Thanksgiving. "Everything's going so well, isn't it?"

Adrianne lifted her iced margarita. "Right on schedule." There were a hundred people, by invitation only, mingling on the pool terrace. Inside the ballroom were another fifty, who preferred air-conditioning to sea-swept breezes. She allowed herself one quick, wistful look at the beach before smiling back at Lauren. "It's a lovely hotel, Lauren, and I'm sure this fashion show is going to be a huge success."

"It already is. Why, the press alone's worth a million. *People*'s here, of course. We're getting a three-page spread. We have a good shot at the cover. Of course you know I did *Good Morning America* last week."

"You looked wonderful."

"So sweet of you." Lauren pivoted toward a camera crew. "Are you sure you wouldn't rather have champagne, dear? We're serving the margaritas mostly for atmosphere."

She imagined Lauren's five-thousand-dollar Mexican peasant outfit was equally atmospheric. "This is fine."

She scanned the crowd. There were dozens of people she knew, dozens more she recognized. The rich, the powerful, the famous. Members of the press were circling, documenting every pair of designer sunglasses. Guests had donned their best resort wear, from skimpy bikinis with gorgeous coverups to billowing silk skirts. No one had left her gems at home. Diamonds flashed, gold gleamed in the tropical sun. For two days the little island of Cozumel had become a thief's paradise. If she'd been looking for the big score, Adrianne could have moved among them, plucking stones.

Not quite like picking wildflowers in a meadow, she mused. But close, close enough when one was an accepted member of their very exclusive club. Interpol undoubtedly had agents on the island. But she hadn't spotted Philip. Thank God.

"I've heard the clothes are marvelous." Playing her role, Adrianne tilted her head and smiled for a photographer.

"You shouldn't have heard anything. The clothes are under tighter security than the crown jewels. The bigger the secret, the bigger the anticipation. What do you think of the idea of putting the runway right over the pool?"

"Marvelous."

"Wait until you see the finale." She leaned closer, whispering. "The swimsuit models are going to dive in."

"I can't wait."

"I'd wanted to fill the pool with champagne, but Charlie wouldn't hear of it. I did get a champagne fountain in the ballroom, though. And you must try the piñata later. Such a quaint custom. You." She turned on a waitress. The charming smile flattened into a hard line. "You're supposed to serve the drinks, not just stroll around with them." Lauren turned back, smoothing her features into a smile. "Where was I? Oh, the piñata. When Charlie and I were down here last year, we went to a fiesta. All these sticky-fingered little brats were swinging a bat at a papier-mâché donkey. After it breaks—"

"I know the game, Lauren."

"Oh, well then. I thought I'd adapt the custom more to our tastes. I had this gorgeous parrot designed. It's filled with some charming little pieces of faux jewelry. Should make a marvelous feature on *Entertainment Tonight*."

Adrianne had to bite her lip at the image of the attending luminaries scrambling on the ground to scoop up glass baubles and beads. "Sounds like great fun."

"That's what we're here for. I'm determined everyone remembers this benefit. I can recommend the buffet, though I've had nothing but trouble with the staff." She waved cheerily to a group on the other side of the pool. "But, of course, they're Mexican."

Adrianne drank slowly and cooled her temper. "We're in Mexico."

"Yes, well, I can't understand why they can't make more of an effort to learn the language. Always muttering among themselves. Lazy too. You've no idea how difficult it is to keep them in line. But they will work cheap. Do let me know if you have any problem at all with the service. Christie darling, you look heavenly." She sniffed as the leggy blonde strolled past. "What I could tell you about *her*," Lauren added.

"I'm sure you must have a lot on your mind at the moment." And if I don't get away from you, Adrianne decided, I'm going to scream.

"Oh, you've no idea. No idea at all. How I envy you your quiet life. Still, I'm certain this is going to be the biggest and splashiest hotel opening of the year."

Well aware that Lauren wouldn't have understood her own pun, Adrianne nearly smiled.

"I hope I didn't make a mistake by planning this as an afternoon event rather than an evening. Afternoons are so . . . casual."

"Island life is casual."

"Mmmm." Lauren watched a hot young film star stroll past, wearing brief trunks and a sheen of suntan oil. "There's something to be said for casual wear. I've heard he's got tremendous endurance."

"How's Charlie?"

"What?" Lauren kept her eye on the young stud. "Fine, just fine. I confess, I'm nervous as a cat. It's so important that this event be a smash."

"It will be. You're going to raise thousands of dollars for leukemia."

"Hmm? Oh, that too." Lauren shrugged one slim bare shoulder. "But naturally people aren't here to think about some nasty disease. Too damn depressing. The important thing is just *being* here. Did I mention that the Duchess of York sent her personal regrets?"

"No."

"It was a pity she couldn't make it, but we have you for

royalty." She gave Adrianne's arm an intimate squeeze. "Oh, I see Elizabeth. I must say hello. Enjoy, darling."

"I will," Adrianne murmured. "More than you know."

People like the St. Johns didn't change. Adrianne wandered behind a trumpet vine to sit in the sun and enjoy the music. A resort like El Grande certainly brought jobs to a troubled Mexican economy, just as the star-studded fashion show would earn funds for charity. For Lauren, and others like her, those benefits were accidental. Or worse, a springboard for their own ambitions.

The St. Johns were concerned first with the St. Johns—money, status, fame. Adrianne sipped her drink and watched Lauren flutter around poolside.

She'd get her press, all right. More than she bargained for. Adrianne imagined the theft of Lauren's diamond and ruby jewelry would make excellent copy.

"Are you playing Greta Garbo, or would you like some company?"

"Marjorie!" Flooded with genuine pleasure, Adrianne sprang up. The daughter of actor Michael Adams who'd been such a friend to her and Phoebe in Hollywood, Marjorie had become her friend after they had both broken away from the film world. "I had no idea you were coming."

"Impulse." The slender California-style blonde returned Adrianne's embrace.

"Did Michael come with you? I haven't seen him in over a year."

"I'm sorry. Daddy couldn't make it. He's on location in Ontario of all places." She glanced around and grinned. "Give me palm trees any day."

"He never stops, does he? Give him my love when you see him."

"Day after tomorrow. I'm going up to spend Christmas with him." Marjorie shook her hair back as she settled onto a chaise. "Fruit juice," she told a passing waiter. "A double." She let out a long sigh. "Quite a zoo, isn't it?"

"Don't start." But Adrianne grinned too. "So what are you doing here? You've never been one for haute couture."

"A yen for the tropics—and for Keith Dixon."

"Keith Dixon?"

"I know he's an actor." Marjorie lifted a hand. "That's why I've been dragging my feet, but..."

"Is it serious?"

She turned the hand over to reveal a marquise-cut diamond. "You could say so."

"Engaged." When Marjorie put a finger to her lips, Adrianne lifted a brow but lowered her voice. "A secret? Does Michael know?"

"Knows and approves. The two of them get along so well, they hardly need me. It's weird."

"Weird that they get along?"

"Weird when I spent most of my life looking for friends and lovers Daddy wouldn't approve of."

Adrianne settled back. "Must have been exhausting."

"It was. With Keith it's been the easiest thing I've ever done."

"So why the secret?"

"To avoid the gossip columns for a while. Anyway, it's a secret for only a few more days. We're going to be married on Christmas. I'd love it if you could be there. But I know how you feel about the holidays. Can you have dinner with us tonight, in the village?"

"I'd like that. He must make you happy," she added. "You look wonderful, Marjorie."

"I am better." She pulled a cigarette out of the pocket of her linen skirt. They were the one vice she still allowed herself. "Sometimes I look back and I can't believe what I put Daddy through, what I put myself through. I weigh a hundred twenty these days."

"I'm happy for you."

"I've kept a picture of myself, one of the newspaper shots from when I got out of the hospital three years ago. Eighty-two pounds. I looked like a ghoul." She crossed long, shapely legs. "It reminds me I'm lucky to be alive."

"I know Michael's proud of you. The last time I saw him you were all he could talk about."

"I wouldn't have made it without him—once I got it through my head he wasn't the enemy." She took the glass of juice and passed the waiter an American five. "You helped too. To second generation Hollywood brats." She tapped her glass against Adrianne's. "Your coming to the hospital to see me that time, talking to me even when I didn't want to listen, telling me how difficult it had been to watch your mother lose herself. Addy, I've never been able to tell you, really tell you what that did for me."

"You don't have to. Michael was one of the few people who really cared about my mother. He wasn't able to help her, but he tried."

"I always thought he was a little in love with her. With both of you. I really hated you when we were kids." Marjorie laughed and tapped her cigarette out. "Daddy used to talk about you all the time, what a model student you were, how well-bred and polite."

"How revolting," Adrianne added, and made Marjorie laugh again.

"So I inhaled, smoked, swallowed any drug I could get my hands on, married a creep I knew would abuse me, made a spectacle of myself in public whenever possible. In general, I did everything I could to make Daddy's life miserable—and it nearly killed me. The anorexia was the last."

"The key word is last."

"Yes." Marjorie smiled, the same quick, self-deprecating smile that had made her father famous. "Well, enough of all that. Did you know Althea was here?"

"Althea Gray? No."

"Yes, indeed. Right—" Marjorie scanned the crowd, then honed in. "There."

Deliberately, Adrianne tipped on her sunglasses before she looked. The actress was indeed present, wearing a snug tank and mini in hot pink.

"That outfit might be suitable for her teenage daughter, if she had one."

"Althea always liked to show her talent," Adrianne said.

"Her last two movies were bombs—I mean nuclear."

"So I heard." It didn't interest her. She'd had her revenge on Althea years before. A particularly fine set of opals with diamond baguettes had translated into an anonymous contribution to the Retired Actors' Fund.

"She had her thighs sucked a few months ago."

"Meow." But she couldn't help taking a harder look at Althea's legs.

"I gave up drinking and drugs and studs, Addy, let me

have something. Oh, I heard another tidbit from tinsel town—about your mother's former agent. Larry Curtis."

Adrianne's smile froze.

"It seems the rumors about his preference for young girls were fact. He was caught last week *auditioning* a new client. She was fifteen."

Nausea churned in her stomach. With deliberate care she set her drink aside. She heard her own voice, glassy, distant. "You said he was caught?"

"In the act and by the kid's father. The scumbag came out of it with a broken jaw. Too bad somebody didn't tie those balls he's so proud of around his neck, but it doesn't look like he'll be working again. Hey." Alarmed, Marjorie sat up. "You're white as a sheet."

She wasn't going to remember. Adrianne swallowed, battling the hard knot in her stomach. "Too much sun."

"Let's get you into the shade before this production starts. Can you stand up? I hate to use a cliché, but you look as if you'd seen a ghost."

"I'm fine, really." She had to be. Larry Curtis was in the past. All of that was. She rose and walked with Marjorie to the chairs set under a bright red canopy. "I wouldn't miss this for the world."

"It promises to be quite a show."

It did indeed. She watched as Lauren went up to a podium decked with tropical flowers. Tomorrow, she had a production of her own.

Adrianne's suite at the El Grande was decorated in pastels with wraparound windows that opened up onto a flower-strewn balcony. It had a fully stocked refrigerator and wet bar, a mirrored bath with a whirlpool tub, and its own key-lock safe. It had its points, but she preferred the rooms she'd engaged at the El Presidente under the name of Lara O'Conner.

With some regret Adrianne had retired Rose Sparrow.

In her second suite of rooms, Adrianne kept her supplies. A few hours after the fashion show she was seated at the small table near the window, nibbling on kiwi as she studied the blueprints of the El Grande. She wasn't yet certain which of the two methods of entry she would use. A perfectionist, she worked out the finer details of both.

The phone beside her rang. *"Hola. Sí."* Adrianne tipped back in her chair. Her contact was anxious. In her experience, messengers tried to sound their toughest when they were nervous. "I'll be there, exactly as agreed. If you don't trust me, amigo, now's the time to pull out. There's always another buyer." She waited, sipping from her warming glass of Perrier. "You know his reputation. When The Shadow makes a deal, he delivers. You wouldn't want me to tell him you doubt his ability to complete this transaction? I thought not. Mañana."

She replaced the receiver and stood, working out the kinks in her back and neck. Nerves. Annoyed, she closed her eyes, rolling her head slowly from side to side. She couldn't remember having nerves like this in years.

The job was routine—almost too simple. And yet...

Philip, she thought. He'd thrown her a curve and she hadn't quite fielded it. It worried her that he wasn't on the island. It would have infuriated her if he had been.

He could prove nothing, she assured herself as she pushed the balcony doors open. And soon, very soon, she'd be finished with what she'd set out to do.

The sun hung in the western sky, brilliantly gold over the water. In a few hours the moon would rise, cool and white.

The Sun and the Moon. Adrianne rested her palms on the rail and leaned out. Symbols of night and day, of continuity, of eternity. I'll take it back soon, Mama, she vowed silently. Once I do, maybe we both can have some peace.

The breeze fluttered over her face, warm fingers, caressing. There was a scent, hot, floral, that rose everywhere, inescapable. She could hear the waves hitting the sand, then sucking back. Over that was the sound of people laughing, shouting as they walked along the beach or snorkeled among the reefs.

Loneliness. Adrianne squeezed her eyes tight but couldn't ward it off. The season—she could blame it on the holiday season and the memories it brought back. She could even blame it on seeing Marjorie, and envying her hold on life after so many years of floundering. But it was more, so much more than that. She wasn't just a woman standing alone on a balcony. No matter how many people she knew, or how involved she kept herself, she was alone everywhere.

No one knew her. Not even Celeste fully understood the wars and questions that raced inside her. She was a princess from a land that was no longer her own. She was a visitor in a country that remained foreign. She was a woman who was afraid to be a woman. A thief who wanted justice.

Just now, with the late afternoon breeze on her face and the smell of the sea and the flowers surrounding her, she wanted someone to hold on to.

Turning, she went back inside. She might not have had someone, but she had something. Revenge.

Chapter Sixteen

Business wasn't on the agenda this morning. Adrianne wanted to bake in the tropical sun, snorkel along the reef in the diamond-pure waters. She wanted to sleep under a palm tree and do as little thinking as possible.

It was Christmas Eve. Some of the guests had already returned home—Chicago, Los Angeles, Paris, New York, London. Most remained at El Grande to celebrate the holidays with piña coladas instead of hot rum punch, with palm trees rather than pines.

Adrianne never spent the holidays in New York. She couldn't bear the sight of snow or the view through the windows at Macy's or Saks. Christmas was an event in New York, one that had thrilled her as a child.

She could still remember her first sight of the elegant Victorian dolls twirling and spinning in Lord & Taylor's window display while the bitter wind had blown through her fur-collared coat and the smell of hot chestnuts had drifted around her. In New York there would be bells ringing on every corner, music piped into every store. Cartier would be wrapped in its bright bow. Along Fifth Avenue the sea of people would be so thick that you could get caught in the current and be swept along for blocks.

Exhilarating. There was no other place in the world that was more exhilarating than New York at Christmas. And for Adrianne, there was no place more depressing.

Christmas had been forbidden in Jaquir, even public celebrations for the tourists and Western workers. There could be no ornaments, no carols, not even a branch of pine.

No little glass balls with snow dancing inside. The law forbade it.

There were memories of Christmas, some happy, some sad. She knew they had to be faced, but not in New York, where she had decorated her last tree, trying desperately to involve her mother in the festivities. It was in New York that she had wrapped her last bright packages, boxes Phoebe had never opened.

It was in New York five years before that she had found her mother dead on the bathroom floor in the predawn hours of Christmas morning. That last Christmas, where she and Phoebe and Celeste had sat together, drinking eggnog and listening to carols on the stereo. And her mother had gone to bed early.

Where Phoebe had gotten the scotch or the bright blue pills Adrianne had never learned. Wherever they had come from, they had done their work.

So she ran at Christmas, though she knew it was weak. Monte Carlo, Aruba, Maui—wherever the sun was hot. Sometimes she worked when she ran, sometimes she did nothing. On this trip she would do both, and tomorrow morning, when the bells rang for Christmas, she would have completed the job.

It hadn't been nerves that had made her decide to spend the day away from the St. Johns' resort. She'd simply wanted to be alone, anonymous. After two days she'd had enough of cocktail parties and chummy chats by the pool. She chose the beach bordering the El Presidente, not as Princess Adrianne or as Lara O'Conner, but as Adrianne Spring.

Thirsty, with her legs beginning to ache, she paddled toward the beach. Carrying her mask and flippers, she crossed the sand to the thatched umbrellalike hut that shaded the rest of her gear. Easily, she ignored two men who lay sunning nearby, sipping Dos Equis and hoping for a score.

"Adrianne."

Still rubbing her hair dry, Adrianne turned toward a woman approaching her. Her body was lush and golden, set off by two narrow strings that made Adrianne's bikini look like a suit of armor. Her hair was dark, cut short and swingy at the chin. For a moment there was only annoyance at being disturbed. Then there was recognition.

"Duja?" With a laugh Adrianne dropped the towel and opened her arms to her cousin. "It is you." They exchanged kisses on both cheeks then drew back, one to study the other.

"This is wonderful." Duja's low musical voice brought back memories both sweet and sad. Long, stifling afternoons in the harem, a cool arbor in the garden where two young girls had listened to stories told by an old woman. "How long has it been?"

"Seven years, eight. What are you doing here?"

"Pouting, until now. We were in Cancún, and J.T. decided to sail over because he thinks the diving's best here. I can't believe I nearly stayed back at the hotel pool. Are you alone?"

"Yes."

"Then I'll buy you a drink and we'll catch up." She linked her arm through Adrianne's and started toward the bar. "I read about you all the time, Princess Adrianne attending the opening of the ballet, Princess Adrianne arriving at the Spring Ball. I suppose that you've been too busy to come to Houston for a visit."

"I couldn't. While Mama was alive it wasn't easy to travel. After..." She watched as Duja lit up a slim brown cigarette. "I didn't think I could bear seeing you, or anyone from Jaquir."

"I grieved for you." Duja touched on the subject of Phoebe's death as lightly as she touched Adrianne's hand. "Your mother was always kind to me. I have warm memories. *Dos margaritas, por favor,*" she told the bartender, then glanced at Adrianne. "All right?"

"Yes, thanks. So much time gone. It doesn't seem real."

She blew out a stream of smoke. "A long way from the harem."

Not long enough, Adrianne thought. "Are you happy?"

"Yes." Duja crossed long brown legs and flirted automatically with a man across the circular bar. She was thirty, lushly built, and secure in her own power. "I'm liberated." Laughing, she lifted her glass. "J.T. is a wonderful man, very kind, very American. I have my own credit cards."

"Is that all it takes?"

"It helps. He also loves me, and I love him. I know how frightened I was when my father agreed to give me to him.

Everything we'd heard or been taught about Americans." She sighed and turned on the stool so that she could watch the sunbathers at the edge of the pool. "When I think I could be sitting in the harem, pregnant with my sixth or seventh child and wondering if my husband would be pleased or displeased with me." She licked salt from the rim of her glass. "Yes, I'm happy. The world's different from the one we knew as children. American men don't expect their women to sit quietly in the corner and have baby after baby. I love my son, but I'm also content to have only him."

"Where is he?"

"With his father. Johnny is as much a fanatic about diving as J.T. He's also very much the American. Baseball, pizza, arcade games. Sometimes I look back and wonder what my life would have been like if oil hadn't brought J.T. to Jaquir... and me to J.T." She shrugged it off as she blew out fragrant smoke that reminded Adrianne of afternoons in the harem and the sound of drums. "But I don't look back often."

"I'm happy for you. When we were children I used to look up to you. You were always so poised and well-behaved, so beautiful. I thought it was because you were a few years older and that I'd be like you when I caught up."

"Things were more difficult for you. You wanted to please your father, but your loyalties were always with your mother. I realize now how miserable she must have been when the king took a second wife."

"It was the beginning of the end for her." The bitterness came through. She sipped to wash it away. "Do you ever go back?"

"I go once a year to see my mother. I sneak her movies for her VCR and red silk underwear. It hasn't changed," she said, answering Adrianne's unspoken question. "When I go back, I'm a proper, obedient daughter, with my hair bound and my face veiled. I wear my *abaaya* and sit in the harem drinking green tea. Strange, while I'm there it doesn't feel odd, it feels right."

"How?"

"It's hard to explain. When I go to Jaquir, when I put on the veil, I begin to think like a woman of Jaquir, feel like a woman of Jaquir. What seems right, even natural in America

201

becomes totally foreign. When I leave, the veil comes off and so do all those feelings, along with the restrictions."

"I don't understand that. It's like being two people."

"Aren't we? The way we were raised and the way we live. Have you never been back?"

"No. But I am considering it."

"We won't go this year. J.T. is uneasy about the trouble in the Persian Gulf. Jaquir has been successful in avoiding a confrontation, but it can't last."

"Abdu knows how to pick his fights, and his friends."

Duja lifted a brow. Even after all these years she would never have called the king by his first name. "J.T. said the same just a little while ago." Unsure of her ground, Duja skirted the edge. "You know your father has divorced Risa? She was barren."

"I heard." She felt a faint tug of pity for her father's latest wife.

"He's taken another, only a few months ago."

"So soon?" Adrianne drank again, more deeply. "I didn't know. Leiha gave him seven healthy children."

"Five of which were girls." Duja shrugged again. It seemed Adrianne was cool enough discussing her half siblings. "The two oldest have already been married."

"Yes, I know. I get news."

"The king bartered wisely with each, sending one to Iran and one to Iraq. The next is only fourteen. It's said she'll go to Egypt or perhaps Saudi Arabia."

"He shows more affection to his horses than his daughters."

"In Jaquir, horses are of more use." Duja signaled for another round.

From his window five flights up, Philip had an excellent view of the pool, the gardens, and the sea. He'd been watching Adrianne since she'd come out of the water. With his field glasses he'd been able to see the drops of water glistening as they clung to her skin.

He could only speculate about the woman she was with. Not a contact; of that he was all but sure. There had been too much surprise, then pleasure on Adrianne's face when they'd met.

An old friend or perhaps a relative. Adrianne hadn't

come to the beach to meet her. Unless Philip missed his guess, she'd come to be alone, as she had once or twice before when he'd followed her from the El Grande.

He thought it a pity he'd had to miss the festivities there over the last couple of days. But it had been wiser all around to keep a low profile.

He blew out a lazy stream of smoke and waited for Spencer to come on the line.

"Spencer here."

"Hello, Captain."

"All right, Chamberlain, what the devil's going on?"

"You got the report I gave to the contact in New York?"

"And a fat lot it tells me."

"These things take time." He studied the way Adrianne's damp hair fell down her back. "Often more than we'd like."

"I don't need any bloody philosophy, I need information."

"Of course." Lifting his binoculars, Philip focused on Adrianne's face. She was laughing. There was nothing cool or aloof about the way her lips curved now. With reluctance he shifted the glasses to her companion. A relative, he decided now. Slightly older, very Americanized. He caught the glint of the diamond circle on her finger. And married.

"Well." The impatience in Spencer's voice was as clear as the sound of him sucking on his pipe.

"There isn't much to add to my earlier report." For his own pleasure, he tilted the glasses back to Adrianne. She had the most incredible skin—like the color of gold in an old painting. It was foolish, but for now Philip was going to take a few steps to save it for her. "If our man was in New York, he slipped out again. The only lead I scrounged up pointed to Paris. You might want to put your men there on alert." Sorry old fellow, he added silently, but I need to buy some time.

"Why Paris?"

"The Countess Tegari. She's spending the holidays there with her daughter. The old dear plucked a few prized pieces from the Duchess of Windsor collection. If I were still in the business, I'd find them very appealing."

"Is that the best you can do?"

"At the moment."

"Where the hell are you and when will you be back?"

"I'm taking the holidays off, Stuart. Expect me in the

new year. My best to your family," he said over the first bluster of protest. "Happy Christmas."

Yes, she did have incredible skin, Philip thought again. Everywhere a man was lucky enough to see it.

Because Adrianne could find no gracious way to refuse her cousin's invitation for dinner aboard the yacht, she pushed up her plans. Part of her looked forward to the evening, to the chance to sit back and observe, to see if the mix of culture and tradition could indeed work. It would also be an iron-clad alibi, if indeed an alibi were ever required.

Adrianne used her rooms at the El Presidente to change. It was a small precaution, but one she had decided worthwhile. Timing was everything now. A glance at her watch assured her that the St. Johns would be busy in the Fiesta Room, entertaining the press with early cocktails. That would give her over an hour before Lauren would be expected back in the Presidential Suite to change for the gala Christmas Eve dinner party.

Adrianne would put in a late appearance, after her dinner with her cousin. If Lauren chose to wear her rubies that night, it should make an interesting diversion.

It was a short drive north, and the evening was balmy with sunset still an hour or two away. When Adrianne pulled up in the El Grande's parking lot, she was wearing oversize sunglasses and a floppy hat as well as a long-sleeved, concealing muumuu. She would be taken, as she intended, for an American tourist of dubious taste.

Swinging the straw bag over her shoulder, she walked in the main entrance. Looking neither right nor left, she strode to the elevators. Once inside, she stopped the car between floors, stripped off the muumuu, and stuffed it and the hat and glasses into the bag. All of these were pushed into a laundry bag she'd folded and pushed down the bodice of the maid's uniform she wore.

It took less than thirty seconds before the car was gliding smoothly again toward the top floor. She wore a wig, black flecked with gray and bundled under a hairnet. She'd added a long thin scar down her cheek. If she was seen, and anyone asked questions, they would remember a middle-aged maid with a scar.

Linens were kept in a storage closet at the end of each hallway. She could have picked the lock with a hairpin if it had been necessary. Instead, she slipped a tool out of the cinch she wore around her thigh. Adrianne tossed the laundry bag into an empty cart, then took an armful of towels. She was backing the cart out of the closet when she heard the elevator sound.

With her head lowered she began to push the cart slowly up the hallway.

"*Buenas tardes,*" she murmured as a couple passed her, smelling of chlorine and suntan oil. She'd shared breakfast with them only that morning. They didn't bother to answer the greeting, but continued to argue over where to go skiing the following week.

At the door to the Presidential Suite, Adrianne knocked, then called out in broken English. "Housekeeping. Fresh towels." She waited, counting carefully to ten.

Using the same tool, Adrianne dealt with the lock. It was pitiful, she thought, how much faith the average person put in a key. Perhaps one day, after she'd retired, she'd write a series of articles on the subject. For now she pulled the maid's cart inside, blocking the door with it.

If something went wrong, the obstacle would give her a few precious moments.

Sumptuous, she thought as she gazed around the suite. The St. Johns had spared no expense for comfort. They had chosen peach and cream tones offset by glossy black, with deep carpets and a sprawling sofa. The flowers were fresh, showing Adrianne that the maid had already tidied, though Lauren's clothes were tossed over chairs and tables.

Adrianne preferred the bright orange and gold furnishing of the El Presidente. Someone should tell Charlie that people come to the island not only to relax, but to feel as though they were roughing it a bit.

She'd learned enough about the new hotel from the blueprints and her two-day stay. Lunch with Lauren at the Russian Tea Room had added the few missing details. Adrianne had picked up the tab, figuring it was the least she could do.

As a precaution, she took a quick tour of the rooms. The bath was identical to her own, as her information had promised. A heap of damp towels on the floor, and the lingering scent of Norell told her that Lauren had bathed before meeting the press.

Assured she was alone, she moved unerringly to the closet in the dressing room. The safe, that extra amenity Charlie provided in all of his hotels, was there.

Rather than a combination, it worked with a key the guest was to keep in a purse or pocket. Not only was there no alarm, but a child with determination and a screwdriver could open it in less than half an hour. Adrianne lifted her skirt up and unsnapped a key from a small pocket. It was the key from the safe in her own room one floor down.

It slid in, but didn't turn. After choosing a file, she began to make adjustments. It took patience. She could file off only a fraction at a time, replace the key, and try it again. Crouched like a catcher behind home plate, she worked second by second, minute by minute. Now and then she heard a door close or the elevator sound. She would wait, holding her breath until footsteps moved passed the suite.

As always, she felt the thud of satisfaction when the lock gave. Setting the key on top of the safe, she took out a jewelry case. Pearls, very nice, opera length. She replaced the case, then took out another. These were diamonds, rather small but fine and worked into a chain. She supposed Lauren would consider them casual wear. Adrianne replaced those as well, then found the diamond and ruby suite.

Using her loupe, she examined three of the stones in the necklace. Burmese, as Lauren had said, masculine stones of deep color with a lovely satiny texture and a minimum of silk, or flaws. The diamond accents were excellent, V.S.I. with just a trace of yellow. Stones of the second water, but well cut. She slid them and the matching bracelet and earrings into her pocket, replaced the case, then relocked the safe. A glance at her watch showed she had adequate time to return to her own hotel and change for dinner with her cousin.

It was then she heard a key turn in the lock.

"Goddammit, get this thing out of the way."

Cursing under her breath, Adrianne leapt to obey. "Excuse, señora. Fresh towels, *por favor.*"

"Give me one then. Shit." Lauren snatched a towel off the pile on the cart and began dabbing at a stain the size of a dinner plate on her skirt. "Clumsy son of a bitch spilled rum punch all over me."

Adrianne battled back a chuckle. The rubies hung heavy in her pocket. "Señora. *Agua* . . . ah, water? Cold water?"

"This is silk, you idiot." Tossing her head up, Lauren gave Adrianne a furious glare. She saw only a servant, an old and obviously stupid one. "What would you know about silk? God! There's not a decent dry cleaners on this ridiculous island. Why Charlie didn't build in Cancún, I don't know." She held the de la Renta skirt out. "Two thousand fucking dollars, and I might as well toss it out the window." Snarling, she tugged viciously at the zipper. "Haven't you got anything to do? We pay you by the hour. Get the hell out of here and earn your pesos."

"*Sí*, Señora St. John. *Gracias. Buenas tardes.*"

"And speak English." Lauren gave Adrianne a shove through the door, then slammed it.

Like Adrianne, Philip had a large supply of patience. He had pulled into the El Grande's parking lot and situated himself in a position where he could watch not only her Jeep, but the entrance as well. It was hot. The sweat rolled down the back of his cotton shirt and dampened it against the seat. He swigged from a bottle of Pepsi and promised himself he wouldn't have another cigarette until Adrianne walked back out. He'd keep his distance for a while longer. Sooner or later she would lead him to the man Philip admired for his skill and envied for Adrianne's loyalty.

He'd have to be good, damn good, Philip thought, if he was going to lift something from the hotel in broad daylight. But then, Philip already knew The Shadow was more than good. The Moreau heist had been the last of a long list of perfect robberies.

As yet, he hadn't quite figured out what part Adrianne was playing. A diversion? An informer? From her position, she would be perfect as a supplier of inside information. But why?

She was laughing when she came out again. Quietly, at some private joke. He'd find out the why, he promised himself, and everything else there was to know about her. For now he followed at a distance.

At the El Presidente, Philip waited for her to come out again. He estimated that she'd have to push it if she was going to make it back to the El Grande in time for the St. Johns' party. Whether she took the elevator or the rampway, he would be able to see her from his position in the lobby. It was sundown when she came down, looking cool and self-possessed in a billowy, backless sundress. She didn't head for the parking lot, but for the beach. From a distance he watched her walk down a pier and onto a sleek white yacht that bore the name *The Alamo*.

The woman she'd had drinks with earlier greeted her, along with a balding, ruddy-faced man and a slim young boy. He watched Adrianne offer a hand to the boy, then laugh and toss her arms around him while the setting sun shot spears of fire into her hair.

If it was a business meeting, Philip mused, then he didn't know infrared from a heat sensor. Readjusting his plans, he went up to her room.

He hadn't picked a lock in a number of years. Like riding a bike or making love, it was something that came back—and once reaccomplished, gave enormous satisfaction.

She was tidy, Philip mused as he walked through her suite. He'd wondered about that, about how she lived when she was alone. There were no clothes carelessly tossed over a chair, no shoes left in the middle of the floor. On the vanity counter her bottles and tubes were capped and aligned. In the closet her clothes were neatly hung. She'd chosen the casual and roomy, he thought, as suited the hot days and warm nights. Her scent was there, lingering.

When he caught himself daydreaming, he shook himself and began to search.

Why the second set of rooms, he wondered. Why the assumed name? Now that he was in, he didn't intend to leave until he had an answer.

The makeup case wouldn't have interested him, but he'd never seen Adrianne wear more than a few smudges of eye shadow and brushes of lipstick. In the three days she'd been in Mexico, she'd bothered to add the minimum only for evenings. So what would a woman who was very confident in her looks, and who rarely bothered to enhance them, need with a full makeup case?

There were enough grease pencils and foundations to accommodate the chorus in a Broadway show. Intrigued, he lifted off the top layer and found putty, false lashes, and adhesive beneath. It appeared Adrianne liked to play at disguises. Beneath that layer he found Lauren St. John's jewelry.

Good? Had he thought The Shadow was good? The man was a genius. Somehow, in hardly more time than it took to tell about it, he had gained entrance to the St. Johns' rooms, lifted the stones, then transferred them to Adrianne, without ever showing his face.

She'd hidden them in a hollowed-out case that had once held an array of eye shadows. Holding them now, Philip felt the old temptation, that siren's call of stones. Wars had been fought for them, lives lost, and hearts broken. They were dug out of the ground, chipped from rock, cut and polished and sold to adorn the necks, the wrists, the fingers. There were cultures that still believed they could ward off evil spirits or death.

He understood why as the blood-red rocks and the diamonds glittered in his hands and whispered to him.

He could have had them, slipped them into his pocket and walked away. He still had the contacts who could exchange them for cash and let him walk away richer and still free. It would be sweet, wonderfully sweet. And he was tempted, not so much because of the money, but because of the stones themselves. They lay hot in his hand, somehow feminine and taunting.

With a sigh he put them back. It was unfortunate that he'd developed a certain loyalty to Spencer. Still, his decision came more because of Adrianne. He would wait and watch to see what she did with them, and with whom.

He shut the case, then replaced it on the shelf at the top of the closet. After deciding it best to forgo dinner himself, he took a pillow from the sitting room, tucked it into the back of the spare closet there, then settled down to wait.

He'd dozed off, but since he habitually slept lightly, a trait of thieves as well as of heros, he roused when he heard her key turn in the lock. He stood to watch her through the thin crack between the closet doors.

She seemed relaxed. That was something else he'd begun to watch for, the shifting of her moods. The light she'd
switched on fell over her back as she moved into the bedroom. He heard the rustle of her dress and imagined, though
it did him more harm than good, the way she would look
stepping out of it. The hangers slid metallically over the
closet rail as she hung it up. When she moved past the door
she'd left open between the two rooms, she was wearing a
short robe, not yet belted. He could see the slender line of
flesh from the well of her breasts and down.

She was moving briskly, not at all like a woman who was
preparing to end an evening. Philip cursed the wall between
them as he heard her rattle bottles on the counter of the
vanity.

There were long silences, then the click of a jar being
opened or closed, the splash of water running. Then he heard
the sound of her door opening slowly, and the quick click that
followed.

He waited, five seconds, ten, before he slipped out of
the closet. At the rampway he had to hold himself back from
hurrying after her. When he reached the bottom, he thought
he'd lost her. The only woman he saw was broad-shouldered,
wide-hipped, with frizzed blond hair. Philip continued to look
for Adrianne. Then abruptly he swiveled his gaze back to the
blonde. It all had to do with the way she moved, he thought,
and nearly smiled as he watched her cross the parking lot.

It was Adrianne, but he doubted she was on her way to a
masquerade.

As she drove toward San Miguel he kept a quarter of a
mile back. The traffic was sparse, with an occasional cab
barreling from town to the hotel district. On the left the sea
was dark and calm, the bright, colorful lights of a cruise ship
draped across the sky like jewels. Soon midnight would bring
the first breath of Christmas. Children were already sleeping,
wishing for morning. Tourists were prolonging their parties.
Though the shops were closed, there was still music from the
bars and restaurants.

Adrianne parked across from the square. Her business
should be over quickly enough. She wanted it over. Tonight,
sitting on her cousin's yacht, watching Duja with her family,
sharing memories of life in Jaquir, she'd decided the rubies

were her last job. Once she'd transferred the money and the dust had settled, she would be on her way east to the home of their childhood. And to The Sun and the Moon.

There had been a festival in the square. The colored paper and wrappers had yet to be swept away along with a few plastic toys that had burst from a pinata and had been lost in the cracks. The town smelled of the water that hemmed it. The moon was clear and white, the stars holding enough fire within to shimmer red at the edges. Above her the palms whispered in the warm, moist air so typical of islands.

She went through an alleyway, and the music that echoed in the square was muffled. Another turn and she was in the stalls where by day the merchants hawked and haggled for the tourists. There were bargains to be had here, if one had a good eye and a quick wit. When the stalls were open there would be leather fashioned into belts, bags, sandals. Trinket boxes with little birds carved for handles could be had for a few thousand pesos or a pair of crisp American singles. The black coral the island was famed for could be seen in row after row of display cases. There would be hammered silver, abalone, cotton dresses festooned with embroidery.

Now it was empty, the merchandise swept back from the narrow aisles and locked away behind garage doors. There would be no bargaining on Christmas. At least not for the tourists.

Adrianne stopped, and waited.

"You're on time, señorita."

He melted out of the shadows, a short, spare man with deep marks in his face from acne or chicken pox. His lighter, with its inlay of turquoise, flared as he lit a cigarette and she saw the pucker of an old scar on the back of his hand.

"I'm always on time for business." There was a twang of Texas to her voice now. "You have the amount we agreed on?"

"You have the merchandise?"

She knew the kind of man she was dealing with. "I'll see the money first."

"As you wish." With a key he unlocked one of the stall doors. It lifted along its runners with bumps and rattles. Inside, it was crammed with cheap silver jewelry that hung on the walls and lay behind dusty glass. It smelled of overripe fruit and stale tobacco. He drew a satchel from behind him.

211

"One hundred and fifty thousand American dollars. My backer wished to pay only one hundred, but I persuaded him."

"Fortunate for both of us." Adrianne pulled on a surgical glove, then drew a pouch from her bag. "You'll want to examine the stones, though I can assure you they're genuine."

"Naturally. You'll want to count the money, though I can assure you it's all there."

"Naturally." Cautious, eyes locked, they exchanged bags. Adrianne flipped through the bills before taking out a small device and running the face of a fifty over it. "These are also genuine. It's been a pleasure doing business with you."

"The pleasure's been mine." He slipped the loupe and the pouch into his pocket. The knife he brought out glittered in the shadows. "I'll take the money back, señorita."

She looked at the knife, then raised her eyes to his. It was always best to watch the eyes. "Is this the way your backer does business?"

"It's the way I do business. He gets the necklace, I get the money, and you, pretty lady, get to keep your life."

"And if I don't want you to keep the money?"

"Then you lose your life, and I still keep the money." He took a step forward with the knife between them. "It would be a pity to die alone in the dark on Christmas Eve."

Perhaps it was simple reflex, her own instinct for survival. Or perhaps it had been his words, bringing back the horror of her mother's death. But when he reached for the satchel, Adrianne ignored the knife and brought her foot up hard between his legs. The knife clattered to the ground only seconds before he did.

"Bastard," she muttered as she sent the knife careening into the dark. "Now your pride's as small as your brain and just as useless."

"Well put," Philip said as he came up behind her. He held up a hand as Adrianne whirled. In his other was a snub-nosed .38. He doubted he would need it, as the courier was currently retching onto the concrete. "Remind me to wear reinforced shorts around you, darling. Now pick up the pouch and let's be on our way."

"What the hell are you doing here?"

"I was about to save your life, but you took care of that.

The jewels, Addy. I'd prefer not to spend Christmas in a Mexican jail."

She snatched up the pouch and strode past him. "And I'd prefer that you'd go to hell."

Philip engaged the safety before dropping the pistol back into his pocket. "At this rate I'm sure we'll meet there eventually. Personally, I'd like to put that moment off." Giving in, he grabbed her arm and whirled her around. "Are you out of your mind coming here alone, dealing with a man like that?"

"I know precisely what I'm doing and how to do it. You can attempt to arrest me here and now, but I'll make you look like a fool."

He considered her a moment. Even with the makeup he could see the woman he knew beneath. "I believe you could. We'll take my car."

"I'll drive myself."

"Don't push it."

"Where are we going?"

"First we're going back to the hotel so that you can get rid of that ridiculous wig. It makes you look like a tramp."

"Thanks so much."

"Then we're going to put those pretty rocks back where they came from."

They were halfway across the square when she stopped, jerked out of his hold, and stared. "Now *you're* out of your mind."

"We'll discuss it. If it's all the same to you, I'd like to be several kilometers away before your friend recovers."

As he gave her a shove toward his car, the clock in the square struck midnight.

Chapter Seventeen

The drive back to the El Presidente hadn't calmed her. If possible, Adrianne was only more furious when she slammed into her room. Losing her temper was a rare treat for a woman who was used to strapping down any sign of her true feelings. But there were times, and there were people, who rated exceptions.

"Goddamn you, Philip. You've given me nothing but trouble since the first time I saw you. Poking around, interfering, following me." She jerked off the wig and hurled it in the vicinity of the sofa. It fell, gaudy as a stripper's G-string, to the carpet.

"And this is the thanks I get."

"If you were trying in your own limited way to play hero, I can tell you I detest heros."

"I'll bear that in mind." He closed the door gently at his back. He'd always thought there was little more fascinating to watch than a woman in a temper.

After unclipping cheap gold loops from her ears, she hurled them against the wall. "I hate men!"

"All right."

Seething, she began to pull off fake fingernails, letting them fall, in dime store grandeur, to the floor. "And you in particular."

"I always prefer being singled out by beautiful women."

"Can't you find something more interesting to do than screw up my work?"

"Not at the moment." He watched as she shook her hair loose. The beauty mark she'd painted at the corner of her mouth didn't suit her any more than the lavender eye shadow she'd troweled on. "Adrianne darling, what have you done to your face?"

With a sound of frustration, she wheeled away into the bedroom. "Go away, will you?" she demanded as he strolled along behind her. "I've had a long day."

"So I've noticed." He sniffed at her. The perfume, Rose's—or now Lara's—perfume, definitely had to go. He only smiled when she swatted him back like an annoying fly. "Was that a cousin you had drinks with this afternoon?"

Setting her teeth, she began to rip off face putty. "You've been spying on me. I can't think of anything lower."

"Then your imagination needs work. I favor the red bikini, but there's a lot to be said for the blue one with all those tiny little stars."

"You're disgusting." Dabbing her fingers in cold cream, she removed traces of putty and spirit gum. "But that's not surprising. What did you do, sit at your window with binoculars?" When he only grinned, she began to pull out tissues, one by one. "You must love your work."

"It's had its moments lately. You're very good at that," he commented when she'd removed the last traces of Lara from her face.

"So glad you think so." Expertly, she popped out electric-blue contacts. He was surprised that the fury behind them hadn't caused them to melt. "If you'll excuse me, I'd like to change."

"Darling, as long as the St. John jewelry is in question, you're not getting out of my sight." He chose the arm of a chair and made himself comfortable. "I'd suggest something in black. Replacing jewels requires the same precautions as taking them."

"I'm not putting them back."

"No, you're not," he agreed. "I'm putting them back, and you're coming with me."

She plopped down on a chair. She was very close to sulking, a luxury she rarely indulged in. "Why should I?"

"Two reasons." There was a clutch of orange and scarlet blossoms, a little droopy, on a table. Philip drew one out and waved it under his nose. He preferred it to whatever dime-store cologne she'd doused herself with. "The first is that I could make things very uncomfortable for you if you refused to cooperate."

With an inelegant snort she scooted farther down in the chair. "Terrifying."

He gave her a cool look that made her want to straighten again. Defiantly, she stretched out her legs. "Second," he continued. "If there's a major theft here, of this style, not only will I be unable to protect you from the consequences, but it will foul up the path I've set up that leads away from you."

"What are you talking about?"

"Just this afternoon I sent my superiors on a wild goose chase to Paris."

Now she did straighten. "Why?"

He was tired of her asking that question, just as he was tired of asking it of himself. "I wanted to give you the chance to explain—to me."

She stared at him longer than either was comfortable with, then she looked down at her hands. "I don't understand you."

Small wonder. He didn't understand himself. Impatient, he tossed the blossom aside. "There's time for that later. Now, I'd appreciate it if you'd get moving. I want to finish this business."

She sat a moment longer. It would have been easier if he'd shouted back at her, hurled insults and accusations. Instead, he was calmly, logically, outlining what needed to be done. And dammit, for some reason he'd managed to put her under obligation to him.

"I didn't know you were on the island."

"You don't know me very well. Yet. I know you better than you might think. This hotel is your usual choice when you're down this way." He ignored the quick flash in her eyes. "People in our business are very good at research, Addy." Watching her, he plucked another flower to tap it against his palm. "I thought it best, under the circumstances, that I skip the festivities at the St. Johns' and keep an eye on you from a distance. Imagine my delight when I discovered you were keeping rooms here as well."

He'd discovered a great deal more than that. She could

learn to detest him for it. "I've always considered spies a lower life form. Like snakes and grubs."

"What a way to talk—after my attempt at playing Sir Galahad."

"I didn't ask you to do me any favors."

"No, you didn't."

"I'm certainly not going to thank you for it."

"I'm crushed."

Deliberately, she crossed her legs. "It's you who's been poking your nose in where it isn't wanted, needed, or appreciated. I've been plodding along just fine without you."

"When you're right, Your Highness, you're right. The common man deserves to have dust kicked in his face."

"This has nothing to do with rank, and dammit, you won't make me feel guilty."

But oh, he thought, he already had—and only smiled at her.

She drummed her fingers on the arm of the chair. "I suppose if they weren't put back, things would get sticky for you."

"Now, why would you think that? Just because I was a thief for nearly fifteen years and I sent Interpol scurrying off to Paris while a half a million dollars in stones was stolen while I was here?"

"I get the point." Rising, she pulled a black shirt and slacks from the dresser, then stared at him.

Philip drew out a cigarette. "If you're shy, change in the closet."

"A gentleman to the end," she muttered as she strode away.

"While you're at it, you can give me the layout."

Hangers rattled as she struggled out of Lara's padding. "I don't have to give you a bloody thing."

"Perhaps I should come in and give you a hand with that while we discuss it."

She snapped a plastic hanger in two. "They have a suite on the top floor. Four rooms, two baths. There's a safe in the dressing room closet. Opens with a key."

"Which you have?"

"Of course."

"Handy. And the way in?"

217

In the closet Adrianne flipped her hair out of the collar of her shirt. It wasn't the jewels that mattered, she reminded herself. It was the money. Since she already had that, she could afford to be cooperative.

"I used Plan B this evening because I wanted to have dinner with my cousin and her family. Maid's uniform, linen cart. The St. Johns were entertaining the press at a cocktail party."

She'd stolen them herself. Intrigued, Philip tossed the blossom aside and rose to pace. "Any problems?"

"Nothing I couldn't handle. Lauren did pop in just as I was finishing up, but she never looks twice at a servant."

"You're a cool one."

"Is that a compliment?" She pushed out of the closet.

"An observation. Since maids don't tidy up at this time of night, your Plan B would be a bit awkward. What's Plan A?"

With a couple of quick flicks of her wrists she had her hair bound back in a band. "Through the vents. They're narrow but adequate. There are openings in the ceilings of the bathroom." She made a brisk, disinterested study of his build. "Tight squeeze for you."

"I've always preferred them." He took out his pistol.

"What are you doing?"

He noted there wasn't any fear in her voice, though he considered the pistol a particularly nasty snub-nosed .38. Nor was there any of the revulsion that so many women felt on seeing a weapon fashioned primarily to kill. Instead, he was reminded clearly of how perfect her aim had been, and how stunning the blow, when her "business associate" had attempted to change the rules.

"I don't carry weight on a job." He opened the drawer to a table and set the gun inside.

"Smart," she said with a shrug. "Armed robbery carries a stiffer term."

"Stiffer than what? I've never had any intention of going to jail. I simply don't care to have any blood on my stones."

She studied him again, with more interest. It wasn't arrogance, she decided. He meant what he said. "If we're going to do this, I'd like to do it quickly. It goes against the grain."

He knew exactly how she felt. He took out the necklace

and let the stones glimmer and bleed over his hands. "Pretty, aren't they? I always leaned toward diamonds, but there's something elegant about colored stones. You checked these, I suppose."

"Naturally." She hesitated, then went on impulse. She knew what it was to hold pretty fortunes, and pretty desires, in her hands. "Would you like to see? I have my loupe."

It was tempting. Too tempting. "Not really worthwhile in this case." With something like regret he replaced them and got down to business. "We'll need a flashlight, extra gloves, and the key, of course."

Adrianne gathered up gear. "This isn't the way I intended to spend the night."

"Think of it as a Christmas present to the St. Johns."

"They don't deserve it. He's a fool and she's a mercenary opportunist."

Philip slipped the key into the deep pocket of his slacks. "People who live in glass houses."

Taking her arm, he led her out.

There was a doorway at the side of the El Grande. Down a short flight of concrete steps, it was built into the wall more for serviceability than for style. Paying guests would have no use for it. In this way, the housekeeping and maintenance crews could enter the hotel without passing through the elegant lobby.

The Dumpster for garbage was a few feet away. The lid was closed, but couldn't contain the smell the heat had intensified. It carried on the breeze strongly enough to make the eyes water.

"Almost as seductive as Rose's perfume," Philip commented. "You have a room here. Why not follow the vents from there?"

"I chose this time because there are a lot of pockets to be picked at the El Grande. It's entirely possible there'll be more thefts. If and when there's an investigation, I'd rather they start from here than from inside."

"An ounce of prevention?" he asked, then examined Adrianne's tools when she drew them out. "Very nice. Surgical steel?"

"Of course."

"Allow me."

He chose a pick and dealt handily with the lock. Adrianne saw just how handily from her view over his shoulder. He all but felt the lock open, ear tilted toward it, fingers moving as delicately as a virtuoso's on a violin. She'd always considered herself an excellent locksmith, but had to admit, at least to herself, that he was better.

"How long have you been out of the business?"

"Five years. Nearly." He replaced her pick before pushing the door open.

"You haven't lost your touch."

"Thanks."

Together they entered the bowels of the hotel. It was damp and smelled it, but it was a reprieve from the garbage. Adrianne played her light along the plain concrete floor and walls. Someone had tacked up a poster of what she assumed was a Mexican pop star. There were a few chairs scattered here and there, but they didn't look as though they offered much comfort. The overhead bulbs were bare.

"You'd think he could funnel a bit of his profits into dragging the working conditions into the twentieth century." She watched a lizard sidle up the wall and blink.

"We'll discuss the St. Johns' debt to society later. Which way?" When she gestured, he moved through the room into an alcove that opened up into a large utility area. Here the water heater hummed along, doing its job. The huge air conditioner whirled, making him think of the frost on the windowpanes in his home in Oxfordshire, where Christmas would feel like Christmas. Frowning, he studied the ductwork. She'd been right when she'd spoken of a tight squeeze.

"All right, give me a boost up, then I'll pull you along." He held out his hand for the light.

Adrianne was thinking about the less than grand conditions in the room beyond. The Mexican economy was a mess, and its people were struggling. She could resell the St. John jewels and funnel the profits through Catholic Charities.

"I don't suppose you'd reconsider. I could put those stones to much better use than adorning Lauren's neck. We'd split sixty-forty."

"Sixty-forty?"

"I've done all the work," she pointed out. "It's a more than fair split."

He wished she hadn't suggested it—he really did. It made it even more difficult for a man who'd been born to take to give back. It wasn't the money, but the principle. Unfortunately, he'd developed other principles over the last few years. A lowering admission. He thought of Spencer sitting behind his desk puffing on his pipe.

"The light," he repeated.

With a shrug she passed it to him. "It's a much better deal than this one, but have it your way."

"You said the top floor, which room?"

"It's the last on the west side; it takes the corner of the building."

"You have a compass?"

"No." She grinned. "Don't you know which way west is?"

There was something to be said for British dignity. "I always used a compass."

Still grinning, she made a basket out of her hands. "Alley-oop, darling. I'll get you there."

He ignored the taunt and put his foot in her hands. Almost before she felt the weight, he was up, wriggling agilely into the vent. After a few oaths he was able to shift and hold down his hands for her. She gripped them. Their fingers curled and held fast. For a moment their eyes locked just as truly. Then her feet were off the ground.

On his hands and knees, Philip swung the light back and forth. It was like being inside a metal coffin. "From the looks of it, it's fortunate I missed my Christmas pie."

"It's narrow on the turns," she told him with some pleasure. "Perhaps we should have brought some lard for you."

There wasn't room to turn and scowl at her. "With a little time, I could come up with a much more sophisticated plan."

"I've all the time in the world."

Philip merely sucked in his breath. "Stay close, we've a long way to go."

It was a long trip, and an uncomfortable one. More than once the sheet-metal tunnel narrowed so that Philip had to wiggle and squirm his way through like a snake burrowing under a rock. Foot by foot they slid, belly down, distributing weight. The journey had to be made in near silence. When they passed over openings, they heard voices, laughter, or occasionally water running out of a tap or shower.

Once Adrianne had no choice but to lay prone as the guest on the fourth floor came into the bathroom to gargle. If Number 422 had opened his eyes when he'd tilted his head back and swished peppermint mouthwash, he'd have gotten quite a surprise.

She stifled giggles as they bellied their way to the next floor. Whenever the ducts forked or spread out, she tugged on Philip's foot to give him direction. In her mind she'd made the trip a dozen times. Thirty exhausting minutes later they were over the vent, looking down at the St. Johns' pastel pink john.

"You're sure?" Philip hissed.

"Of course I'm sure."

"It would be very unprofessional to put the jewelry into someone else's safe."

"I said I'm sure," she whispered back. "Do you see that hideous peacock print robe on the back of the door?"

He had to bend his knees into his chest to get a look. "So?"

"I gave it to Lauren for her birthday."

Philip studied the robe. "You don't like her at all, do you?"

"She browbeats her servants, fires them whenever the whim strikes, and in the three years I've known her, she's never left a tip in a restaurant." She passed him a small screwdriver. "Do you want to do this?"

For a moment he simply sat. Then, as if in afterthought, he brushed some of the dust they'd accumulated on the trip off her cheek. "Why don't you go ahead?"

With a shrug she dealt quickly and quietly with the screws. Once they and the tool were safely in her pocket, he lifted off the grate. He was still mulling over her words. What difference could it make to Adrianne how Lauren St. John treated her servants? Now wasn't the time to think of it, he decided as he set the grate aside.

"Wait here," he said.

"Oh, no, I'm coming with you."

"There's no need."

Adrianne put a hand on his arm. "How do I know you're really going to put the stuff back?"

"Oh, for Christ's sake." Disgusted, he slid through the opening. Seconds later Adrianne followed, just as silently. He'd reached up automatically to nip her at the waist for the final drop. As his hands closed over her, he had a moment to think that there were other ways he'd have preferred spending the evening.

They'd both taken a step forward when a sound had them jerking back. It took a minute for it to register. All Adrianne could do was cover her face with her hands and pray she wouldn't laugh.

Apparently, the St. Johns were spending the first hours of Christmas morning in passion. The bedsprings creaked. Lauren groaned. Charlie panted.

"Let's not disturb them," Philip mumbled as he melted like a shadow into the hallway.

The sounds in the adjoining room rose and fell as they crouched beside the safe. From the intensity of it, Philip thought they could have stormed into the suite like marines, blown the safe with plastique, and stormed out again without breaking the St. Johns' rhythm. It was difficult not to admire Charlie's stamina as he heard some of Lauren's keening demands.

Inside thin surgical gloves, Philip's palms began to sweat, not from nerves, but from envy as Lauren cried out and the moaning and thrashing continued. He snatched the flashlight away as the beam bobbed and jerked from Adrianne's shaking laughter.

"Get a grip on yourself," he grated out.

"Sorry. I was just imagining Charlie naked."

"Please, not on an empty stomach." He found the jewel case Adrianne had left behind and laid the glitter of rubies and diamonds inside. It hurt, he realized, more than just a little to give them back. Then it was all he could do not to groan himself as Lauren's moan lifted to a wail and Adrianne's thigh pressed snugly to his.

Rising, he pulled her through the hall and into the bath. "Up." His voice was curt enough to make her chin rise.

"You certainly know how to take the fun out of it." She stood on the seat of the commode and hauled herself through.

Philip was half in and half out of the hole when footsteps padded outside the door. Jackknifing, he dove through just as the door opened.

"Good God." It was Charlie's voice, exhausted, as he leaned against the sink and dragged his thinning hair from his eyes. From their perch above, Adrianne and Philip could do no more than sit like stones. He poured water, then gulped it down like a dying man. Philip watched as he braced one hand on the wall and emptied his bladder. The scents of sex and urine rose up through the vents. From the bedroom, Lauren's voice came plaintively.

"Charlie, come back to bed. I've got another present for you."

Naked, paunchy, past his prime, he shook his head. "Name of God, woman. I'm not a rabbit." But he said it quietly, before he turned off the light and went back to do his best.

With her arms wrapped tight around her waist, Adrianne rocked back and forth. It was worth the loss of the jewels . . . almost.

"Try for some dignity, Your Highness," Philip told her as he replaced the grate. "Let's get out of here."

It wasn't the same exhilaration that came from taking something out of a safe, but it was close. For the first time, she'd used the moves, the thoughts, and the skills with a partner. The laughter she'd been forced to bottle up during their long trip back through the ducts bubbled out during the drive to the El Presidente. It hadn't stopped even when Philip followed her into her suite.

"Incredible, simply incredible." She dropped into a chair, sprawled out, relaxed, her face glowing. This was a side of her Philip hadn't seen. After toeing off her shoes, she smiled at him. "It was so incredible that I'm almost not mad at you anymore."

"Well then, I can sleep tonight."

"Are you always cranky after a job?"

What he was, was wired. It had been a mistake to let her lead the way out of the ducts. He'd had to crawl along, tantalized and teased by the view of her pretty, tightly clad bottom. Unable to sit, he paced to the window and back.

"I missed dinner waiting for you to move."

"Aw." There was little sympathy in the sound. "No room service at this hour, I'm afraid. I do have a chocolate bar."

"Hand it over."

Because she was feeling too good to be ungracious, Adrianne routed it out from the depths of one of her bags, then tossed it to him. "There's some wine left."

Philip ripped at the wrapper of the plain, inadequately thin Hershey bar. "No almonds."

"I don't care for nuts."

"You proved that when you slammed your foot between the legs of your friend this evening."

"Crude." She poured wine into two glasses and took one to him. "I suppose I shouldn't really be angry. I do still have the money."

He took her wrist before she could go back to her seat. "Is the money so important?"

She thought of the abuse center she'd earmarked. "Yes, it is."

He let her go to resume his pacing. "What do you get out of this, Addy? Does he toss you a few thousand now and again? Are you indebted to him, in love with him? Either the debt or the love must go a long way, because as far as I've been able to see, he takes none of the risks and you put yourself on the line over and over again."

She sipped the warm wine as she watched Philip move around the room. Like a panther, she thought. Restlessly pacing off the length and breadth of his cage. "Who," she asked slowly, "is he?"

"You tell me." He whirled back to her. Neither of them had realized how close both his patience and control had been to snapping. Jealousy, bare and ugly, was too easy to recognize in himself. And he'd be damned if he waited another hour to learn whom he was jealous of. "I want to know who he is, why you fell in with him, why you help him steal."

She watched him intently as he found his cigarettes and pulled one out before he tossed the pack on a table, then said softly, "I don't help anyone steal."

"I've had enough games for one evening."

"I told you before, I do what I do of my own choice."

225

"You also told me you do it because of a man."

"Yes, but not in the way you seem to think. There is no man blackmailing me, paying me, or sleeping with me." She sat again, lounging back. "I work alone, for myself. I have no partner and no debt to pay."

Slowly, he blew out smoke. He seemed to shrug impatience off like an annoying hand on his shoulder. In its place came interest and intensity. "Are you trying to make me believe that you and you alone are responsible for the theft of millions of pounds in gems over the last nine to ten years?"

"I'm not trying to make you believe anything. You asked for the truth, and I decided to give it to you." She frowned consideringly into her wine. "It doesn't really matter, you see, because you've no evidence you can take in. Your superiors would think you were crazy, and in any case, I had already decided that this particular job was the last in this phase of my career."

"That's ridiculous. You'd have been a child when this began."

"Sixteen when I started. Very green," she continued when he stared at her. "But a fast learner."

"Why did you start?"

The faint smile disappeared, and she set her wine aside so that the glass clicked against the table. "That's none of your business."

"We're past that, Adrianne."

"That's my private life."

"You don't have one any longer that doesn't include me."

"A very large assumption, Philip." She rose, looking across at him. She could, when necessary, be as royal as her title. "Not that it hasn't been an entertaining evening, but I really must say good night. I'm exhausted."

"Sleep late tomorrow; we haven't finished." He glanced at his watch. "I need to make a call before we go on. I have a friend in Paris who can make enough of a show to keep Interpol amused for a day or so." Without asking permission he walked through the doorway to use the phone in the bedroom.

When he came back she was asleep.

He looked at her as she lay curled on the sofa, one hand pillowing her head, the other loose at her side. Her hair

Sweet Revenge

curtained her face, and when he brushed it back, her breathing remained slow and even. She didn't look cool or regal now, but young and vulnerable. He knew he should wake her, knew he should question her now, while her defenses were down. Instead, he switched off the light and let her sleep.

It was almost dawn when he heard her. The light was a soft, quiet gray that would, with the strength of the sun, soon turn white and brilliant. Philip was stretched out on her bed with his shoes and shirt tossed carelessly on the floor. He woke quickly, immediately oriented, but had sat up in bed before he realized it hadn't been the light that had woken him, but the sobbing.

He went into the adjoining room to see her balled tight, as if in defense against an attack or in great pain. It was only when he crouched beside her, lifting a hand to her wet cheek, that he realized she was still asleep.

"Addy." He shook her, gently at first, then harder when she fought him. "Addy, wake up."

She flinched violently, as if he'd slapped her, bundling herself back against the cushions with her eyes wide and terrified. He continued to murmur to her though some instinct kept him from gathering her close. Gradually, the glazed look faded and he saw the grief.

"A bad dream," he said quietly as he took her hand. Hers trembled, but for a moment, just a moment, she gripped his fingers hard and held on. "I'll get you some water."

There was a bottle still unopened on the counter. He watched her as he pried off the top and poured. Soundlessly, she drew her knees in close to her chest and dropped her forehead on them. Nausea ground in her stomach while she took long, deep breaths and struggled for equilibrium.

"Thank you." She took the glass, steadying it with both hands. Humiliation grew sharper as grief dulled. She said nothing, only prayed he would leave and let her gather up the tatters of her pride.

But when he sat beside her she had to fight back the urge to turn into him, to rest her head on his shoulder and be comforted.

"Talk to me."

227

"It was just a dream, as you said."

"You're hurting." He touched her cheek. This time she didn't jerk away, only closed her eyes. "You talk, I'll listen."

"I don't need anyone."

"I'm not going away until you talk to me."

She stared down at the water in her glass. It was warm and tasteless and no comfort against the raw feeling in her stomach. "My mother died on Christmas. Now, please leave me alone."

Saying nothing, he took her glass and set it aside. Just as quietly he drew her into his arms. She stiffened, pulled back, but he ignored her reaction. Rather than giving the words of sympathy she would have hated, he stroked her hair. Her breath came out in a half sob, half sigh as she went limp against him.

"Why are you doing this?"

"My good deed for the day. Tell me about it."

She never spoke of it. It was too hard. But now, with her eyes closed and his shoulder cushioning her head, the words came. "I found her just before sunrise. She hadn't fallen. It was as though she'd been too weak to stand and had simply laid down. It looked as though she might have been trying to crawl out for help. She may have called to me, but I never heard." Unconsciously, she worked her hand on his shoulder. The fingers opened and closed, opened and closed. "You would have heard the stories. Suicide." There was a raw edge to the word, as though it hurt her mouth to say it. "But I know it wasn't. She'd been ill for so long, so much pain. She was only looking for a little peace, an easy night. She would never have killed herself that way, knowing that I . . . knowing that I would find her."

He continued to stroke her hair. He knew the stories, the scandal. It still surfaced from time to time, weaving itself into a mystique. "You'd have known her best."

She drew back to look at him then, to search his face before she let her head drop back to his shoulder. Nothing that had ever been said to her had eased more. "Yes, I did know her. She was kind and loving. And simple. No one really understood that the glamour belonged to the actress but not to the woman. She trusted people, the wrong people. That's what killed her in the end."

"Your father?"

He cut cleanly to the bone, so cleanly, Adrianne didn't feel the pain until after the cut bled. "He broke her." She rose then, to wrap her arms tight around her body and pace. "Bit by bit, day by day. And he enjoyed it." There was no weakness now. Her voice rang as clear as the bells in the square that had heralded Christmas, but without the joy. "He married the woman who was considered the most beautiful of her time. A Western woman. An actress men thought of as a goddess. She fell in love with him and gave up her career, her country, her culture, then he proceeded to destroy her because she was everything he wanted, and everything he despised."

She walked to the window. The sun was strengthening, shooting diamonds onto the clear water. The sweep of beach was empty.

"She didn't understand cruelty. She had none. There was so much I didn't know until years later, when it all began to pour out of her in her despair and confusion. In Jaquir she would talk to me because there was no one else she could talk to."

"Why didn't she leave him sooner?"

"You'd have to understand Jaquir, and my mother. She loved him. Even after he took another wife because she'd displeased him by giving him a female child, she loved him. He insulted and humiliated her, but she hung on. She spent her days trapped in the harem while his second wife swelled with his son, and she loved him still. He beat her, and she accepted it. She couldn't have more children, and she blamed herself. For nearly ten years she stayed, veiled and abused while he destroyed her confidence, her ego, her self-respect. The damage was great, but she held on. For me. She might have been able to get out, to escape, but she thought first of me."

She took a long breath, looking out blindly at the sun-washed sand. "Everything she did, everything she didn't do, was for my welfare."

"She loved you."

"Perhaps more than she should have, more than was good for her. She stayed with him year after year because she wouldn't leave me. He beat her. He humiliated her. He

229

raped her. God knows how many times he raped her. But once I was there, curled under the bed, with my hands over my ears trying to block it out. And hating him."

His eyes sharpened at that. The sympathy he'd been feeling changed to a dull, throbbing anger. She'd have been only a child. He started to speak, then held his tongue. There was nothing he could say to gloss over that kind of pain.

"I don't know if she ever would have found the courage to leave. Then one day when I was eight, Abdu told her he was sending me away to school. I was to be betrothed to the son of an ally."

"At eight?"

"The marriage would have waited until I turned fifteen, but the betrothal was a good political move. There must have been some of the actress in her yet. She accepted his decision, even seemed pleased by it. And she talked him into taking me along to Paris with them to teach me a little of the world. If I was to be a good wife, I should know how to behave outside of Jaquir. She convinced him that she was delighted with his interest in my welfare, that she approved of the coming marriage. It's not uncommon for a woman of my country to marry at fifteen."

"Whether they want to or not?"

She had to smile. He sounded so British. "Marriages are still arranged in Jaquir, from the farmer's daughter to the king's. Its purpose is to strengthen the tribe and legitimize sex. Love and choice have nothing to do with it."

The light was changing. She saw a young man, covered with sand, walk groggily along the edge of the beach. "When we were in Paris, she managed to contact Celeste. Celeste arranged for tickets to New York. Abdu cultivated a progressive image outside of Jaquir, so we were allowed to shop and go to museums. My mother was permitted to have her hair unbound and her face unveiled. We lost the bodyguards in the Louvre, and ran."

She pressed the heels of her hands against her eyes. They were swollen and gritty. The bright beam of sun made them ache. "She was never well again, and she never stopped loving him." She dropped her hands to her sides before she turned. "It taught me that when a woman lets herself love, she loses. It taught me that to survive, you rely on yourself, first and last."

"It should also have taught you that sometimes love has no threshold."

She felt a sudden chill race up her arms. His eyes were calm, steady. There was something in them she didn't want to see, just as she didn't want to analyze why she had told him more than she'd ever told anyone. "I want a shower," she said briskly. She moved past him to the connecting door. Something made her hesitate before she shut it firmly between them.

Chapter Eighteen

She thought he had gone. She lingered in the shower, letting the hot spray beat over her skin. The spearing headache she'd developed lessened to a dull throb she knew could be erased by a couple of aspirin. Because it soothed her, she slathered on scented cream and slipped into a loose robe with the idea of stretching out on the terrace lounge and letting her hair dry in the sun.

The beach would wait. This morning it would be better to be alone, without the roving cocktail waiters to see to her thirst, or vacationers splashing, shouting, or baking nearby. She always spent Christmas morning alone, avoiding well-meaning friends and social obligations. Memories of her mother's last Christmas weren't as sharp or as painful as they once had been, but she couldn't bear the sight of holly or shiny colored balls.

Phoebe had always put a white angel on top of the tree. Every year from the first they'd spent in America. Except for the last, when she had been caught so deep in that dark tunnel she had been sucked into.

Adrianne looked at her mother's illness that way, like a tunnel, dark, deep, with hundreds of blind corners and dead ends. It was better to have that tangible vision than the cold comfort of all the technical terms in the dozens of books on abnormal behavior Adrianne had pored over. Better still than all the diagnoses and prognoses she'd received in quiet leather-scented rooms from respected doctors.

It had been the tunnel that had pulled her mother deeper as time went by. Somehow over the years, Phoebe had been able to find her way out again. Until she'd been too tired, or until the dark seemed easier than the light.

Perhaps time did heal, but it didn't make you forget.

She felt better for having put her feelings into words, though she was already regretting having given Philip so much. She told herself it didn't matter, that soon they would be going their separate ways and whatever she'd said, whatever she'd shared, would mean little as time went on. If he'd been kind where kindness hadn't been expected, it couldn't matter. If she'd wanted where desire could never exist, she could overcome it. She'd taken care of herself too long, guarded her emotions too carefully, to let him make a difference.

From now on every thought, every feeling, had to be focused on Jaquir—and revenge.

But when she opened the door between the rooms he was still there, shirtless, barefoot, talking in surprisingly fluid Spanish to a white-suited smooth-faced waiter. She watched Philip pass bills over—enough, apparently, to make the young man glad he was working, holiday or not.

"*Buenas días,* señora. Merry Christmas."

She didn't bother to correct his assumption of her relationship with Philip, or the fact that Christmas hadn't been merry for her in quite a long time. Instead, she smiled, pleasing him almost as much as the pesos already in his pocket.

"*Buenas días. Felices Navidad.*" Adrianne folded her hands and waited for the sound of the door closing. "Why are you still here?" she asked when they were alone.

"Because I'm hungry." He walked outside onto the terrace and sat. Obviously settled and comfortable, he poured coffee. There were ways and ways to gain trust, he thought. With a bird with a broken wing, it took patience, care, and a gentle touch. With a high-strung horse that had been whipped, it took diligence and the risk of being kicked. With a woman, it took a certain amount of charm. He was willing to combine all three.

She came out, frowning. "I might not have wanted breakfast."

"Fine. I can eat yours too."

"Or company."

"You can always go down to the beach. Cream?"

She might have resisted the smell of coffee, or the golden light of the sun. She told herself she could certainly have resisted him. But she couldn't, wouldn't, resist the scent of hot food.

"Yes." She took her seat as if granting an audience. Philip's mouth twitched.

"Sugar? Your Highness."

Her eyes narrowed, heated. A storm brewing. Then just as quickly they cleared with her smile. "I use my title only on formal occasions, or with idiots."

"I'm flattered."

"Don't be. I'm still debating whether you're an idiot or not."

"I'd like to give you the day to make up your mind." He cut into his omelette. Spicy odors steamed out. He had an idea Adrianne was like that, smooth and elegant outside, and, once opened up, full of heat and surprises. "Since I've been busy watching you, I haven't had much time to take advantage of the water or the sun."

"Pity."

"Exactly. The least you could do is take advantage of it with me." He spread strawberry jam on a piece of toast and handed it to her. "Unless you're afraid to spend time with me."

"Why should I be?"

"Because you know I want to make love with you and you're worried that you'd enjoy it."

She bit into the toast, making the effort to keep her eyes steady. "I've already told you, I've no intention of sleeping with you."

"Then a few hours in the sun won't make any difference." As if it were settled, he continued to eat. "Did you mean what you said last night?"

The omelette was taking the edge off. As the sun baked away the last of the aches, she glanced over. "About what?"

"About this being your last job."

She poked at her eggs with her fork. Rarely did she have a problem with lying, and didn't care to discover it was difficult with him. "I said it was the last job of this phase of my career."

"Meaning?"

"Just that."

"Adrianne." This was a time, he thought, for patience and a firm hand. "I have an obligation to my superiors. I also have a need to help you." He saw the wariness in her eyes, but she didn't pull away when he laid a hand over hers. "If you're honest with me, there might be a way I could accomplish both. If you're not, I could be in as much trouble as you."

"You won't be in trouble if you leave me to it. I can tell you it's a private matter, Philip, and nothing to concern Interpol or you."

"It has to concern me."

"Why?"

"Because I care for you." He tightened his grip when her hand moved restlessly under his. "Very much."

She'd have preferred it if he'd used a line, one of the standard and easily ignored lines men doled out to women they were attracted to. This was too simple, too direct, and too sincere. "I'd rather you didn't."

"So do I, but we're both stuck with it." He let her hand go, then went back, as calmly as he could, to his meal. "I'll make it easy for you. Start by telling me why you got into second-story work."

"You won't give me any peace until I do?"

"No. More coffee?"

She nodded. It hardly mattered now, she decided. Besides, they had this in common, they knew the same sensations, the same emotions, the same triumphs. "I told you my mother had been ill for some time."

"Yes."

"There were doctors and medicines and treatments. Often she had to be hospitalized for long periods."

He knew that, of course. Anyone who had read a magazine in the last decade knew the tragedy of Phoebe Spring. Still, he thought it best if he heard it in Adrianne's words, and with her feelings. "What was wrong with her?"

This was the hardest, she knew. If she said it quickly, it would be done. "She was diagnosed as a manic-depressive. There were times she would talk and talk and make outrageous plans. She wouldn't be able to sit or sleep or eat because the energy, it was almost like a poison, was burning through her system. Then she'd swing down so low that she couldn't talk at all. She'd just sit and stare. She wouldn't know anyone, not even me."

She cleared her throat and deliberately took a sip of coffee. That was the most difficult memory of all—thinking back to the way it had felt to sit, holding her mother's hand, talking to her, even pleading, and receiving only a blank stare. At those times Phoebe had been lost in the tunnel and tempted by the dark and the silence.

"That must have been hell for you."

She didn't look at him, couldn't. Instead, she looked out to the water, calm and impossibly blue under a mirror sky. "It was hell for her. Over the years she developed a problem with alcohol and with drugs. That had begun in Jaquir—though God knows how she managed it—and had spiraled out of control when she tried to pick up the pieces in Hollywood. I don't honestly know whether the mental illness fed the alcoholism or if the alcoholism fed the illness. I know only that she fought both for as long as she could, but when we got to California, the scripts weren't there with the parts she'd been used to playing, and she couldn't handle the failure. She had bad advice which she swallowed like a starving woman. Her agent was slime."

Her voice tightened there, stretched but didn't waver. There was enough of a change, however subtle, to make him narrow his eyes and focus on hers. "What did he do? To you?"

Her head jerked up at that. For an instant her eyes were clear as glass. Just as quickly, the shutter lowered.

"How old were you?" he asked very carefully while his fingers bit into the metal of his fork.

"Fourteen. It wasn't as bad as you think. Mama came in before he could—while I was fighting him. I'd never seen her like that. She was incredible, like the cliché about the tigress defending her cub." Because it made her uncomfortable, she set the matter, and the memory, aside. "What matters is that he dragged her down, used her, exploited her, and she was too battered from those years in Jaquir to pull herself back up."

He let it pass, only because when you needed to win trust, you could only push so much so fast. "You didn't stay in California?"

"We came back to New York right after the incident with her agent. She seemed better, really better. She was talking about trying theater work again. Stage. She was thrilled, talking about all the offers she was getting. There weren't any, or no important ones, but I didn't know it then, because I believed, wanted to believe, everything was all right. Then one day, just after I turned sixteen, I came home from school to find her sitting in the dark. She didn't answer me when I spoke to her. I shook her and shouted. Nothing. I can't tell you what that was like—it was as if she were dead inside."

He said nothing, just linked his fingers with hers. Adrianne stared down at their joined hands. Such a simple thing, she thought, one of the most basic forms of human contact. She'd never known it could be so comforting.

"I had to put her into a sanitarium. That was the first time. A month there, and there was no money left. But she pulled out of it for a while. I quit school and got a job. She never knew."

She should have been in school, leading cheers and dating skinny young boys. "Wasn't there anyone, any family you could have gone to?"

"Her parents were dead. She'd been raised by her grandparents, and they both died while I was a baby. There'd been a little insurance money, but that had been sent to Jaquir and it remained there." She brushed that off as if it hardly mattered. "I didn't mind working, in fact I enjoyed it a great deal more than school. But the little I could earn wasn't enough for the rent and food, much less medicine and nursing care. So I began to steal. I was good at it."

"Didn't she wonder where the money came from?"

"No. Those last years she was in a dream half the time. She often thought she was still making films." A smile began to form. She watched a gull swoop down over the sound and wheel, screaming, out to sea. "Eventually, I told Celeste; she went wild. She would have paid for everything, but I couldn't let her. My mother was my responsibility. In any case, I never stole from anyone who didn't deserve it."

"How do you figure?"

"I've always been selective about my targets. I've always stolen from the very rich."

"That's always wise," Philip said ironically.

"And very close-fisted. Take Lady Caroline."

"Yes, the diamond." Tilting his chair back, Philip took out a cigarette. "Twenty-two carats, nearly flawless. I've always envied you that one."

"It was a fabulous job." She braced her elbows on the table, resting her chin on her open hands. "She kept it in a vault, top-notch security. Heat sensors. Motion detectors. Infrared. It took me six months to plan it out."

"How did you?"

"I was invited for the weekend. That way I didn't have to worry about the outside security. I used magnets and a minicomputer. They had sensor beams on the first floor, but it was simple enough to crawl under them. The vault itself was a time lock, but I fooled the computer into thinking it was six hours later. I'd rigged a device out of an alarm clock and some microchips. Once inside the vault, I had to bypass two backup alarms and jam the cameras, then I was home free. Once I was snug in my room, I tripped the alarms with a remote control."

"You tripped the alarms while you were still in the house?"

"What better way?" Her appetite came back, so she spread more jam on toast. "I'd pushed the diamond into my face cream, though, of course, they never searched my belongings."

"Of course."

"I was there to be awakened at four A.M. by the alarms, and to be horrified with Lady Caroline."

Philip watched her nip into the bread and jam. "One might call that cold."

"She didn't rate my sympathy. She has forty million pounds in real assets, and gives less than one half of one percent to charity."

He tilted his head to study her. "Is that your gauge for a deserving mark?"

"Yes. I know what it is to be poor, to need, to hate being in need. I promised myself that I wouldn't forget." She moved her shoulders as if soothing an old ache. "When my mother died, I continued to steal."

"Why?"

"Two reasons. The first is that it gave me the opportunity

to spread the wealth of people who would have kept it locked in both hands, or buried in dark vaults. Madeline Moreau's sapphire was liquidated into a hefty contribution to the Widows' and Orphans' Fund."

Philip pitched his cigarette over the terrace, then took a long drink of cooling coffee. "Are you trying to tell me you've been playing Robin Hood?"

Adrianne thought that one out. It was an interesting and appealing comparison. "In a manner of speaking, but it's more honest to say it's a business. I do take a commission. Not only is stealing expensive when you consider the overhead in equipment and time, but it pays to keep up appearances. Besides, I don't like being poor."

"I never had much use for it myself." He plucked a flower out of the centerpiece and twirled it. "How much commission?"

"That would vary, generally between fifteen and twenty percent, depending on the initial outlay for the job. For example, the St. Johns' jewelry." She ticked off on her fingers. "I had my airfare, my hotel bill—this one. I wouldn't count the bill at the El Grande."

"Naturally not."

"Then there's food, the maid's uniform and wig—oh, and a few long distance calls. Any shopping or excursions are, of course, my own expense."

"Of course."

She met his eyes with a level look. "You're in a difficult position to judge, Philip, since you spent a great deal of your life being a thief."

"I'm not judging, I'm amazed. First you're telling me that you did all of these jobs, all of these years, on your own."

"That's right. Didn't you?"

"Yes, but . . ." He held up a hand. "All right. Now you're telling me that for the past few years you've been giving away all except a fifteen to twenty percent commission?"

"More or less."

"An eighty percent contribution to charity."

"In my way, I'm a philanthropist." Then she grinned. "And I do enjoy my work. You know how it feels to hold millions in your hands. To watch diamonds glitter in your palms and know they're yours because you're clever."

"Yes." He understood all too well. "I know how it feels."

"And when the night's cold and the wind's in your face as you scale a building. Your hands are steady as rocks and your mind is so sharp it's like the edge of a knife. The anticipation is so great—it's like the instant before you open a bottle of Dom Pérignon, just that instant before the cork flies off and all the excitement bubbles out."

He drew another cigarette out of the pack. It was more than that, he thought. It was a bit like the instant before your seed and the passion with it burst out of you and into a woman. "I know how addictive it can be. I also know there comes a time to quit while you're on top."

"Like you did?"

"That's right. A smart gambler knows when the odds are stacking up too high and when it comes time to change games." He blew out smoke. "You've given me one reason, Addy. What's the other?"

She didn't answer immediately, but instead rose and moved to the railing overlooking the beach. She couldn't say she trusted him. Indeed, why should she? But like recognized like. He'd been a thief, and perhaps was enough of one still to appreciate what she planned to do without understanding her great need to do it.

"I'll need some assurance first." She turned so that the warm breeze caught at her hair to blow it, rich, black, and fragrant, away from her face.

"Of what sort?" Though even as he asked he saw something in her eyes, something in the way she stood that made him realize he would have promised her anything. A realization like that numbed a man.

"That what I tell you stays between us. That it won't be something you take back to your superiors."

His eyes were hooded against the sun, but he watched her. "Haven't we gone beyond that?"

"I don't know." She fenced a moment longer, trying to measure him. She could give him a lie, or could try to, but wondered if the truth would be safer. As long as he was dogging her heels, she would never get to Jaquir to take back what was hers. "I know what you were, Philip, and haven't asked your reasons."

"Would you like them?"

The surprise came clearly before she turned her head. She hadn't expected to find him so willing to give them. "Someday perhaps. I told you more this morning than anyone else knows. Even Celeste has heard only bits and pieces. I don't like anyone involved in my private life."

"It's too late to take back what was said, and a waste of time to regret it."

"Yes." She turned back. "I like that about you. Romantic or not, you're a practical man. The best thieves are a combination of the practical and the visionary. How much vision have you?"

He rose as well, and though he stood at the rail, the width of the table remained between them. "Enough to see our paths crossing again and again—no matter how uncomfortable it might be for both of us."

Even under the strong sun she shivered. Destiny was the one thing she knew couldn't be stolen. "That may be, but it isn't the issue. You asked why I continued to work, and I'll tell you. It was practice, training you could say, for the biggest job of my life. Perhaps of anyone's."

He felt the muscles of his stomach tighten. In fear, he realized, in simple, sharp-edged fear. For her. "What do you mean?"

"You've heard of The Sun and the Moon?"

Now the fear raced out of his stomach and into his throat like something vile. "Jesus Christ. You must be out of your mind."

She only smiled. "Then you have heard of it."

"There's no one in the business who hasn't heard of that necklace, or of what happened in 1935 when someone had the bad sense to try to steal it. The thief's throat was slit after both of his hands were severed."

"And his blood washed over The Sun and the Moon." She moved her shoulders. "Such things legends are made of."

"It's not a game." He moved on her, grabbed her by the shoulders and yanked so quickly that she nearly lost her balance. "They don't lock thieves nicely in jail in that country. For God's sake, Adrianne, you should know better than anyone how rough your father's justice would be."

"It's justice I want, and I'll have." She jerked out of his grasp. "Since the first time I stole to keep my mother out of a

ward, I swore I'd have justice. The necklace was hers, given
to her as a marriage gift. The bride price. In the laws of
Jaquir what a woman is given in marriage she keeps after
death or divorce. Whatever a woman possesses becomes her
husband's, whatever she is, is his to do with precisely as he
chooses. But the bride price remains the bride's, so The Sun
and the Moon was my mother's. He refused to give her what
was hers, so I'll take it."

"What good will it do her now?" He knew he was rough,
too rough, but could find no other way. "No matter how
much it hurts, she's gone."

"You think I don't know she's gone?" It wasn't grief that
came into her eyes, but anger driven by passion. "A fraction
of the necklace's worth would have kept her for years, the
best doctors, the finest treatment. He knew how desperate
we were. He knew because I buried my pride and wrote,
begging him for help. He wrote back, telling me that the
marriage was ended, and with it, his responsibility. Because
she was ill, and I was a child, there was no way to go back to
Jaquir and demand, through the law, that the necklace be
returned."

"Whatever he did to you, to your mother, is over now.
It's too late for the necklace to make any difference now."

"Oh, no, Philip." Her voice changed. The passion hadn't
gone, but it had iced over and was all the more deadly. "For
revenge, it's never too late. When I take it, the pride of
Jaquir, my father will suffer. Not as she did, never as she did,
but enough. And when he knows who has it, who took it from
him, it will be only sweeter."

He didn't understand true hate. Not once had he stolen
for any purpose other than to survive, or to survive in more
comfort. But he recognized true hate, and believed it was the
most volatile of human fuels. "Do you have any idea what will
happen to you if you're caught?"

Her eyes were steady and very dark as they met his.
"Better than you. I know my title and my American citizenship won't protect me. If I pay, then I pay. Some gambles are
worth the risk."

He looked at her, at the way her skin glowed gold in the
sunlight. "Yes," he agreed. "Some are."

"I know how to do it, Philip. I've had ten years to plan."

And he had weeks, perhaps only days, to change her mind. "I'd like to hear about it."

"Maybe. Some other time."

In an abrupt change of mood, he smiled. "We'll make it soon, but I'd say that's enough shop talk for now. How about that swim?"

No, she didn't trust him, Adrianne thought again. There was something a bit too charming about that smile. It might be best all around if, while he was watching her, she was watching him. "I'd love it. I'll meet you on the beach in fifteen minutes."

Adrianne had traveled alone for so long she'd forgotten what it was like to have someone to share small pleasures with. The water was cool and clear, liquid glass through which she could skim and watch the life around her. Like a forest in autumn, coral glowed gold, orange, scarlet, with wispy fans of lacy purple that waved in the current. Velvet-tailed fish darted, their lavish colors gleaming as they nibbled on sponges.

Hampered only with a mask and snorkel, she could dive down to be nipped at by a tiny and pugnacious damselfish or to be watched by the sergeant majors who loitered, waiting for a handout. They swam out where the depth changed, sliding from the reef to fifty mirror-clear feet. Signals between them were a touch of the hand on the arm and gestures. It seemed to be enough that they understood each other, and that the afternoon was theirs.

Adrianne didn't want to question why she felt so at ease with him—relaxed as she had been on the evening they'd spent at a country inn outside London. She wasn't a woman who had legions of friends, but, rather, acquaintances, people who came and went in her life. Where she gave friendship, she gave herself with it completely, with no limitations, and therefore she gave it carefully. Though trust wasn't fully in place, she felt friendship for him, and despite her reservations was pleased to have him with her.

She wasn't a princess now, or a master thief, but a woman enjoying the sun and the magic of the sea.

She surfaced, laughing, and balanced one flipper precariously on a stump of coral. Water poured off her hair and

skin, gleaming jewellike. She pushed her mask back on her
head as Philip rose with her.

"What's funny?" He shook his hair back before pushing
back his own mask.

"That fish with the big bulging eye. All I could think of
was Lord Fume."

He lifted a brow and steadied himself. "Do you always
make fun of your victims?"

"Only when it's apt. Oh, the sun's wonderful." With her
eyes closed she lifted her face to it and made him think of
mermaids and sirens. "But you shouldn't stay out in it long
with that pale British skin."

"Worried about me?"

When she opened her eyes there was amusement in
them rather than caution. Progress, he thought. However
small. "I'd hate to be responsible for you being sunburned."

"I imagine it's snowing in London now, and families are
sitting down to the Christmas goose."

"And in New York the goose isn't cooked yet." She
cupped a handful of water, then let it pour through her
fingers. "We always had turkey. Mama loved the smell of it
roasting." She shook off the feeling and managed a smile.
"One year she decided to cook it herself, the way her
grandmother had in Nebraska. She pushed so much stuffing
in the bird that when it expanded with the heat, it burst. The
poor turkey was a mess." Shielding her eyes, she looked
toward the horizon. "Look, a ship's coming in."

She shifted for better purchase and slid off the rock into
his arms. Water lapped over her shoulders, then to her
breasts as he lifted her up and to him. She drew back, but
was held firm with her feet unable to reach the sandy floor
and her hands gripping his shoulders for support.

She saw his eyes darken, like the fog when the moon
slipped behind a cloud. His breath feathered over her lips as
his hands slid through the water and over her skin. When he
leaned toward her, she turned her head so that his mouth
brushed her cheek gently, patiently. Need rolled inside of
her, with a pang that came as much from fear as from desire.

"You taste of the sea," he said. "Cool and unconquered."
He skimmed his lips to her ear and her fingers dug into his

muscles; he heard her breath catch and felt her body shudder. "Adrianne."

She made herself look at him. Facing what couldn't be escaped had always been her way. The sun was bright on his hair, almost blinding as it hit the water and refracted. From somewhere behind them a woman was scolding a child. But the sound came dimly as her heart hammered in her ears.

And he smiled. "Relax," he told her as his fingers moved up her spine. "I won't let you go under."

But he did. As his lips took hers she went down, farther and faster than safety allowed. Though her head remained in the air and the sun, she fell fathoms deep, heart racing, breath trapped. She could taste sun and salt as his lips coaxed hers open. Coaxed. There should have been a comfort in that, in the lack of demand, in the absence of pressure. Instead, she trembled from the pressure cooker of needs inside her own body.

He strapped his needs down. If there were chains around his passions now, he promised himself there would come a time when he would unshackle them. She needed something more than desire. He needed to give something more. Testing, he nipped into her full lower lip and heard her moan of response. Knowing control could be stretched only so far, he drew her away. Her eyes were clouded, heavy. Her lips were ripe. And his nerves were scraped raw.

"How about a drink?"

She blinked at him. "What?"

He kissed the tip of her nose and struggled to keep his hands light. "I said let's have a drink so I can get my pale British skin out of the sun."

"Oh." It was like being released from the effect of a drug, she thought. An addictive one. "Yes."

"Good. Last one to the bar buys." With this he let her go. Unprepared, Adrianne sank under the water. When she'd surfaced, he was halfway to shore. Even as she pulled down her mask to barrel after him, she was laughing.

They drank tart, icy margaritas and listened to the trio of marimba players chime out Christmas carols. With appetites sharpened by sun and water, they dug into enchiladas smothered in cheese and spicy sauce. Later, with the afternoon winding lazily ahead of them, they drove around the island, taking a narrow dirt road on a whim. They passed small stone monuments that made Adrianne think of old worship and older gods.

He was determined to fill her day, to make her forget the grief that had come with dawn. He no longer questioned the need to protect and comfort. When a man had spent most of his life with women, he recognized the right one.

Deliberately, he took the Jeep over a pothole so that it bucked and shimmied. Adrianne only laughed and pointed out another one. The road took them to the north point and a lighthouse. There was a family living at the base with pens holding scruffy hens. A bony cat stretched out on the dirt by a cooler which the enterprising family stocked with cold drinks to sell to tourists for twice what they would pay in the village. Armed with two bottles, they sat on humps of dried sea grass and watched the spray spume. The water was very rough here so that the waves slapped the shore and geysered where time and tide had cut channels.

"Tell me about your home."

"In London?"

"No." Adrianne slipped off her sandals. "The one in the country."

"You'd say it was very British." It was another measure of their progress that she didn't shift away when he touched her hair. "The house is Edwardian, brick, very tidy with three floors. There's a portrait gallery, but as I'm not acquainted with my ancestors, I've borrowed some."

"From where?"

"Antique shops. There's Uncle Sylvester—a very dour Victorian type and his wife, Aunt Agatha. Pudding-faced."

"Pudding-faced." Giggling, Adrianne settled back. "That is British."

"We are what we are. There are assorted cousins, of course, some of them very grand, and a few sinister types. Then, there's Great-Grandmama; she was a bit of a strumpet who married into the family despite heated objections, then proceeded to rule with an iron hand."

"You missed having a big family."

"Perhaps I did. In any case, they fill out the gallery nicely. The parlor opens up into the garden. Since it suited the house, I went with very formal, very neat arrangements.

Roses, rhododendron, lilacs, lilies. There are hedges of yews and a grove of ash to the west, where a little stream runs. There's wild thyme there, and wood violets that get as big around as my thumb."

She could almost smell it. "Why did you buy it? You don't seem like the sort of man to go in for quiet evenings by the fire or walks through the woods."

"There's a time for everything. I bought it so I'd be ready when I decided to settle down and become a pillar of the community."

"Is that your goal?"

"My goal's always been comfort." He shrugged and drained his bottle. "I learned young that to find comfort on the streets of London, you had to take what you could take, and be quicker about it than the next." He settled the bottle on the sand beside him. "I was quicker."

"You were a legend. No, don't grin at me, you were. Every time something spectacular was stolen, the rumors started that it was a P.C. job. The de Marco collection, for instance."

He grinned, watching the spray rise up at her back. "Are you fishing?"

"Did you take it?" She straightened when he only smiled and reached for a cigarette. "Well, did you?"

"The de Marco collection," he mused. "One of the finest examples of diamonds and precious stones in Milan, or anywhere, for that matter."

"I know what it was! Did you take it?"

He settled back as a storyteller might in front of a roaring fire. "The museum had the best security available on that exhibit. Light sensors, heat sensors, a weight-sensitive alarm. The floor was wired for twenty feet around the exhibit. The exhibit itself was in a glass dome that was considered virtually impenetrable."

"I know all that." Spray flew up and dashed her hair. "How did you do it? I heard dozens of conflicting reports."

"Did you ever see *Royal Wedding*, the one where Astaire dances on the ceiling?"

"Yes, but that was movie magic through trick camera work. I'll concede that you're clever, but not that clever."

"Getting in was just a matter of having the right uniform

247

and forging the right identification. Once in, I had two hours before the guard made rounds. It took me a quarter of that just to crawl up the wall and over the ceiling."

"If you don't want to tell me how you did it, just say so."

"I am telling you. You finished with that?" He took the bottle from her and drank. "Suction cups. Not quite the hardware store variety, but the same concept. It gives you insight into how a fly feels."

"You stuck yourself to the ceiling?"

"More or less. They wouldn't hold, of course, for the whole job. I rigged a trapeze into the ceiling with toggle bolts. I remember hanging by my knees over all those shiny rocks. I couldn't even afford to sweat. I had a carbide bit drill packed in Styrofoam to muffle the noise. When I got through the glass, the real work started. I had stones in my pouch the exact weight of the various pieces in the collection. Piece by piece, I switched. You had to be fast and very sure. More than a fraction of a second without the right weight, and the alarm would go. It took almost an hour, with the blood rushing to my head and my fingers going numb. Then I swung out on the trapeze and landed outside the alarm field. I remember that it felt as though someone were shooting arrows into my legs when I landed. I could barely crawl. That was the worst part and one I'd failed to calculate." He could laugh now, looking back. "I sat there in a heap, beating on my legs to get the circulation going again and visualizing myself caught, not because I wasn't good enough, but because my bloody legs had gone to sleep."

With her head pillowed on sea grass, Adrianne laughed with him. "What did you do?"

"I pictured myself in a cell, then made a very fast and very inelegant exit, mostly on my hands and knees. By the time the alarm was given, I was soaking in the tub at my hotel."

When he brought himself back and glanced at her, she was smiling. "You miss it."

"Only in rare moments." He flipped his cigarette into the spray. "I'm a businessman first, Addy. It was time to get out of the business. Spencer, he's my superior, had come too close too often."

"They knew about you, yet they let you in."

"Better a wolf in the fold than loose, I suppose. Sooner or later you get sloppy. It takes only one mistake."

She looked back at the sea with its turbulent water. "I have only one more job, and I've no intention of being sloppy."

He said nothing. With a little time, a little care, he was certain he could persuade her to let it go. If talk didn't work, there were roadblocks he could construct. "What do you say to a siesta, then Christmas dinner?"

"All right." She rose, carrying her sandals by the straps. "But I get to drive back."

Perhaps it was foolish to fuss, but she couldn't resist. It felt good to linger in a scented bath and dust on clouds of fragrant powder. These were peculiarly women's habits, a seed of which had been sown in her in the harem. She enjoyed taking a long, leisurely time preparing, though her evening with Philip could hardly be called a date. She knew that a good part of the reason he was making himself so available as an escort was to watch her. She might have told him she had no other business on the island, but there was no reason he should believe her. In any case, being with him served her purpose. Or so she told herself as she chose a thin white dress with yards of skirt and no back. She would be as free with her time with him as he was with her. In that way, he wouldn't be on guard when she slipped out of the country . . . tomorrow.

There were plans to be finalized, plans she'd begun to make a decade ago. Soon after the new year she would go back to Jaquir. She clipped stones on her ears that were as cold as her thoughts and as false as the image she would present to her father.

But for tonight she would enjoy the lingering light of a tropical sunset and the whisper of calm seas.

When Philip knocked on her door she was ready. He, too, wore white, with his shirt a splash of blue against his jacket.

"There's something to be said for spending winters in hot climates." He ran his hands down her bare shoulders. "Did you rest?"

"Yes." She didn't tell him she'd made a quick trip to the

El Grande to pack her things there and check out. At his touch she felt the frustrated confusion of a horse who's spurred and curbed at the same time. "And like a tourist, my thoughts rarely go beyond the next meal."

"Good. Before we go I have something for you." He drew a small velvet box from his pocket. This time she did step back as though she'd been pinched.

"No." Her voice was cooler than she wanted it to be, but he took her hand and placed the box in it.

"It's not only rude to refuse a Christmas gift, it's bad luck." He didn't add that he'd had to pave his way with bribes and tips until he'd found a jeweler who would open his shop on the holiday.

"It wasn't necessary."

"Should it have been?" he countered. "Come now, Adrianne, a woman like you should know how to accept a present graciously."

He was right, of course, and she was being a fool. She flipped open the box and studied the pin resting on white satin. Not resting, she thought, stalking, like the panther it was, richly black, sharply carved with its ruby eyes on fire.

"It's beautiful."

"It made me think of you. Something we have in common." He pinned it on her dress with the ease of a man accustomed to doing such things.

She needed to take it lightly, and smiled. "From one cat burglar to another?" But her fingers strayed up to stroke it.

"From one restless soul to another," he corrected her, and slipping the box back into his pocket, took her hand.

They dined on delicately grilled lobster and sharp, fruity wine while mariachis strolled singing songs of love and longing. From their table by the window they could watch people walk along the seawall and small boys, always eager for a coin, loiter by the row of cabs waiting to open a door.

While they ate, the sun went down in a blaze of color, and the moon, less rushed, rose majestically.

She asked him about his childhood and was surprised when he didn't evade or pass it off with a joke.

"My mother sold tickets at the cinema. That came as a plus for me, as I could always go in and watch whatever was showing, sometimes for a whole afternoon. Other than that, it didn't go much further than paying the rent on a miserable two-room flat in Chelsea. My father had breezed into her life long enough to make me, then breezed out again when he learned I was on the way."

She felt a pang, and would have reached for his hand, but he lifted his wine. The moment passed. "It must have been difficult for her. Being alone."

"I'm sure it was hell, but you'd never know it. She's a born optimist, the kind of woman who can be content with whatever she has no matter how little or how much. She's a great fan of your mother's, by the way. When she found out I'd taken Phoebe Spring's daughter to dinner, she lectured me for an hour for not bringing you to see her."

"Mama had a way of endearing herself to people."

"Didn't you ever think of following in her footsteps as an actress?"

It was easy to smile as she lifted her glass. "Didn't I?"

"How much is an act, I wonder."

"An act?" She gestured with her hands. "Whatever's necessary. Does your mother know about your—vocation?"

"You mean sex?"

He hadn't been sure she would laugh, but she did, then leaned forward so that the candlelight caught in her eyes. "Not avocation, Philip, vocation."

"Ah. Well, it's nothing we discuss. Suffice it to say that Mum's no fool. More wine?"

"Just a little. Philip, do you ever think about going back, about one last, incredible job? Something that would keep you warm in your old age."

"The Sun and the Moon?"

"That's mine," she said rather primly.

"The Sun and the Moon," he repeated, amused as he watched her. "Two fascinating jewels in one necklace. The Sun, a two-hundred-eighty-carat diamond of the first water, absolutely pure, brilliantly white, and according to legend a stone with a checkered past. It was found in the Deccan region of India in the sixteenth century, the rough cut being over eight hundred carats. The stone was found by two brothers, and like Cain and Abel, one murdered the other to have it. Rather than being banished to the Land of Nod, the surviving brother found misery in his homeland. His wife and children drowned, leaving him with the rather cold comfort of the stone."

Philip sipped, and when Adrianne made no comment, topped off his wine, then hers. "Legend has it he went mad, and offered the stone to the devil. Whether he was taken up on it or not, he was murdered and the stone began its travels. Istanbul, Siam, Crete, and dozens of other exotic places, always leaving a trail of betrayal and murder in its wake. Until, having satisfied the gods, it found a home in Jaquir around 1876."

"My great-great-grandfather bought it for his favorite wife." She ran a finger around and around the rim of her wineglass. "For the equivalent of one and a half million American dollars. It would have cost him more, but the stone had developed a nasty reputation." Her finger stilled. "There were people starving in Jaquir at that time."

"He wouldn't be the first ruler to ignore such things, or the last." He waited, watching her as the waiter cleared their plates. "It was cut by a Venetian, who either from nerves or lack of skill lost more of the rough stone than he should have. His hands were severed and hung around his neck before he was left in the desert. But the stone survived to be paired with a pearl, just as ancient, that had been plucked out of the Persian Gulf, perfectly spherical, with an orient that defies description. Lustrous, glowing, like two hundred fifty carats of moonlight. While the diamond flashes, the pearl glows, and legend has it the pearl's magic fights against the diamond's. Together they're like peace and war, snow and fire." He lifted his glass. "Or sun and moon."

Adrianne took a sip of wine to ease her throat. Talk of the necklace excited as much as it upset. She knew just how it had looked, draped around her mother's neck, and she could imagine, only imagine the way it would feel in her hands. Magic or not, legend or not, she would take it.

"You've done your homework."

"I know about The Sun and the Moon the same way I know about the Kohinoor or the Pitt, as stones I may admire, even lust after, but not as stones to risk my life for."

"When the motive is only money or acquisition, even diamonds can be resisted." She started to rise, but he caught her hand. His grip was firmer than it should have been, and his eyes were no longer amused.

"When the motive is revenge, it should be resisted." Her hand flexed once in his, then lay passive. Control, he thought, could be both blessing and curse. "Revenge clouds the mind so that you can't think coolly. Passions of any kind lead to mistakes."

"I have only one passion." The candlelight flickered over her face, deepening the hollows of her cheeks. "I've had twenty years to cultivate it, channel it. Not all passions are hot and dangerous, Philip. Some are ice cold."

When she rose he said nothing, but promised himself he would prove her wrong before the evening was over.

Chapter Nineteen

He was a difficult man to measure, Adrianne thought. He could be intense one moment and frivolous the next. As they drove to the hotel, he spoke lightly, amusingly, of mutual acquaintances. That moment might not have passed in the restaurant when he'd taken her hand, looking into her eyes as if he could bend her to his will by the look alone. Now it was all tropical breezes and moonlight. Talk of the necklace and the blood that had been spilled for it were blown away.

It was easy to see how he had slipped into the circle of the rich and the pampered. You didn't see a fatherless street thief from Chelsea when you looked at him. Nor did you see a calculating, sure-footed cat burglar. Instead, you saw the cultured, the faintly bored, and the charmingly aimless. While he was none of those things.

Even knowing it, she relaxed. Part of his power was the way he had of making a woman tremble one moment and laugh and put up her feet the next. She found herself regretting when the car was parked and the evening had whittled down to the walk to her door.

"I was annoyed to find you here," she told him as she dipped into her bag for her key.

"You were furious to find me here." Taking the key from her, he slid it into the lock himself.

"All right." She was amused and relaxed. Both showed in her smile. "I don't often change my mind, but it's been nice having your company today."

"I'm glad to hear that, as I intend to stay with you." As

he spoke, he cupped her elbow and moved through the door with her.

"If you think I might nip back to take the St. Johns' jewels, you needn't worry."

He tossed the key on her dresser, then took her evening bag and sent it in the same direction. "My being here at the moment has nothing to do with jewels." Before she could step back, he laid his hands on her shoulders, then ran them with terrifying gentleness down her arms. Quite naturally, his fingers linked with hers.

"No."

He lifted one hand, kissed it, then lifted the other. "No what?"

Like a rocket the heat tore down her fingertips. It was one thing to ignore what you'd never needed, and another to resist what you suddenly did. "I want you to go."

Keeping one of her hands caught in his, he brushed her hair back from her shoulder, his fingertips just skimming her bare flesh. He felt the jolt of reaction, but wasn't certain if it was hers or his. "I would, if I believed you. Do you know they call you unattainable?"

She knew it very well. "Is that why you want me? Because I'm unattainable?"

"It might have been enough." He toyed with her hair. "Once."

"I'm not interested, Philip. I thought I'd made that clear."

"Your talent for lying is one of the things I most admire about you."

He was closer, already closer than he should have been. "I'm not sure what else I can do to convince you you're wasting your time."

"It doesn't take much, when it's true. You have a way of looking at a man, Addy, that turns the hottest blood to ice. You aren't looking at me that way now." He cupped the back of her neck. Even as she went rigid he watched her mouth, ripe, full, soft, tremble open. If a man were sated, he'd still hunger for it.

She felt her heart spring up to her throat to beat wildly when his lips whispered over hers. She started to lift a hand to push him away. That was self-preservation. But she curled her fingers into his shirt and held on. That was need.

Then with need, surprisingly, came regret.

"I can't give you what you want. I'm not like other women."

"No, you're not." Instinctively, he ran his fingers along her neck, soothing, reassuring even while his lips played havoc with her nerves. "And I don't want any more than you're able to give."

When he deepened the kiss, she moaned. There was something both of despair and of wonder in the sound. For an instant, only an instant, she gave in to it. Her body pressed against his, her lips parted, her heart opened. He had a glimpse of beauty, of generosity so overwhelming it left him shaken.

Then she was drawing back, turning away. "Philip, I know what my image is, but it's only an image. This kind of thing isn't for me." She clasped her hands together to hold them steady.

"Maybe it hasn't been." Again, he put his hands on her shoulders. "Until now."

She had pride. It had gotten her through the unstable and confusing years. Because it was strong, she was able to speak without shame. "I've never been with a man. Never wanted to."

"I know." She turned back, as he'd hoped she would. "I understood that this morning when you told me about your father, what you'd seen happen between him and your mother. There's nothing I can say to erase that or ease your feelings about it—except that it doesn't have to be that way, should never be that way."

He touched her again, a hand to her cheek. It was as much a test for himself as for her. She closed her eyes, allowing herself to absorb the feel of his fingers on her skin and the jangle of nerves and needs it brought to her. She'd always been a woman who'd known her own mind, and her own destiny. Tonight, it seemed, he would become a part of both.

"I'm afraid."

He slipped the twin ivory combs out of her hair. "So am I."

She opened her eyes at that. "I don't believe you. Why should you be?"

"Because you're important." He set the combs aside to let his fingers tunnel through her hair. "Because this is important." He drew her close again, struggling to remain gentle, to remember her fragility rather than her strength. Both were there, both had snagged him from the first instant. "We can analyze this all night, Addy. Or you can let me love you."

There wasn't a choice, nor had there ever been. Adrianne believed in fate. She'd been destined to leave Jaquir, as she was destined to return. And she was destined to spend this night, if only this one night, with Philip, and learn what it was that made women give their hearts, and their freedom, to men.

She expected passion. She understood it. That was the wild frenzy that made men search for a form of release. She knew of sex from the frank talk of the harem to the wistful romantic chatter at tea parties. Women were as hungry as men, if not always as able to sate the hunger. The impression of sex that had remained with her since childhood was a tangle of limbs, a torrent of sound and movement best done in the dark.

When his lips came to hers again, she was prepared to give herself over to it.

But it was only a whisper of a kiss, the brush, retreat, brush of mouth against mouth. Her eyes blinked open in surprise to find him watching her.

He saw the confusion, and the desire growing moment by moment as he toyed with her mouth. There was no urge to devour or possess. Not this time. Not with her. Whatever skill he had, whatever patience he'd developed, he would use tonight. He let his hands lose themselves in her hair, giving them both time to adjust to the unexpected.

So when he touched her, she didn't stiffen. Her body seemed ready to be stroked and discovered. He shrugged out of his jacket and she no longer hesitated to run her hands over his shoulders, down his back. Impatient to know the same freedom he was experiencing, she tugged at his shirt until it was free and she could feel the flesh beneath.

She heard him suck in his breath at her touch. His mouth

257

became more urgent on hers, his heartbeat less steady. She heard him murmur, but didn't understand his request to go slowly. She couldn't know how much it cost him to undress her carefully, to keep his hands easy when he wanted to grasp greedily. Naked, she shivered once. The sound of her dress falling to a pool at her feet echoed like thunder in his head.

Her skin glowed in the vague moonlight that silvered the ends of her hair as it fell over her breasts. He'd known what it was to want, but he hadn't known that the edge of desire could be so jagged—so jagged his hands shook as he tugged off his shirt, so jagged his throat ached as he lay her on the bed.

She, too, had known want. But her desires had always had a clear route and a definite end. Security, reputation, restitution. Now she learned that some desires had a morass of paths leading to many destinations. She was still afraid, but no longer of him. She feared herself now, and what price she might be willing to pay to go on feeling as she felt tonight.

He showed her what it was to burn, slowly, while still craving the heat. She heard her own shuddering sigh as her body, so long restricted from this one pleasure, strained, shivered, and accepted. Here was passion that liquefied, tenderness that excited, and knowledge that broke down long-held beliefs.

He took, as she had known he would, but there was giving as well. And no pain. She'd been so certain there would be pain. Yet his hands moved over her like water. Even when his mouth fit over her breast and her body arched in reaction, there was only pleasure. Waves of it.

She smelled of smoke and silk and secrets. Enough to drive a man mad. She touched, but cautiously. Though her response was everything a man could wish for, he sensed a knot of tension remaining. She was building to a peak he knew she couldn't understand. Part of her mind was holding back, perhaps wary of the price. Where there was intense pleasure, there was intense vulnerability. Murmuring, he covered her mouth with his. Hers opened, so that her tongue moved in an experimental dance with his.

The tastes were new to her, and yet . . . familiar. The feel of his body moving against, fitting itself to, sliding over hers wasn't foreign or frightening as she'd expected. She didn't experience the violation she'd been prepared for when he touched what no man had touched.

Then there was more, more than pleasant sensations, more than easy discovery. Her breath grew shallow and she struggled for air. Her skin, so sensitized by each stroke, heated until even the breeze flitting through the open windows couldn't relieve it. Helplessness. It was something she'd sworn never to feel, not at the hands of a man. She struggled against it, against him, as the heat gathered, knotted, then expanded in her center.

Here was the pain, but nothing like any pain she'd known. She fought against it while she fought for it. She clawed at the sheets in a desperate attempt to find her balance.

Slowly, he skimmed his hand up her thigh, feeling the tremor of each separate muscle. And he found her, hot and moist. There was an instant of resistance, a strangle of breath as sensation intensified. Her body contracted, then on a moan of astonished release went lax.

From that moment she was trapped, greedy for whatever she could feel, desperate for all he could teach. Her blood pumped hot, fast, and close to the surface as she wrapped herself around him. There was a freedom here she embraced, as she embraced him. There was trust. She opened herself to it as she opened to him.

When he slid into her there was shock, there was pleasure, one for the other. He couldn't have told her that at that moment, with her body cupped around him, he was more vulnerable than he'd ever been and more willing to risk.

Later, she lay quiet beside him. It shouldn't have meant so much. It couldn't change anything. She knew it was foolish to feel differently. In her country a woman of her age would have been long married, and if God were kind, would have borne children. What had happened tonight was simply a natural function. A woman was born to give a man pleasure and sons.

She was thinking like a woman of Jaquir! The shock of realization left a bitter taste in her mouth, one that overpowered the lingering flavor of the man beside her. She started to shift away, perhaps to run. Then his arm draped over her.

Braced on his elbow, he studied her face. There were still secrets there, and, beneath the glow of quenched passions, reservations he couldn't guess at.

"Did I hurt you?" It wasn't his first thought, but he was no more ready to share his secrets than she.

"No, of course not."

He touched her face. Though she didn't shift away, neither did she return the touch. Because her skin had cooled, he drew the sheet up, waiting for her to say something, to give him any sign of how she felt, or what she needed. The silence stretched out and drew into knots.

"You won't forget me, you know," he murmured. "One never forgets the first lover."

There was just enough bite in the words to let her see he was holding his temper, but not enough for her to recognize hurt. "No, I won't forget you."

He rolled her until she lay across him, her hair curtaining both of them. Their eyes met. There was a challenge, acknowledged and accepted. "Let's make sure of it," he told her before he brought her mouth to his.

The sun was high and white when she woke. There was an ache, dull and somehow sweet, through her body to remind her of the night. She wanted to smile, to snuggle back in bed and hug it to herself like an accomplishment, like a bag full of the finest diamonds. But there was still a part of her, a part dug deep, that believed a woman's submission in bed meant submission everywhere.

He was sleeping beside her. She hadn't thought he would stay the night, or hold her throughout it. Nor had she known how comforting it could be to lie awake in the dark and listen to his steady breathing. She knew now how good it felt to study his face in the morning sunlight.

Tenderness. She felt it, fought against it. Her fingers itched to run along his cheek, to comb through his hair. It would be so satisfying to touch him now, as if what had happened in the night had been real and important.

Cautious, she uncurled her fingers from her palm and started to reach out. Her fingertips just brushed his skin when his eyes blinked open. Adrianne snatched her hand away.

Even in sleep his reflexes were quick. Philip wrapped his fingers around her wrist and brought her hand to his lips. "Morning."

"Good morning." Awkward. She felt foolishly, miserably awkward. "We slept later than I intended."

"That's what vacations are for." In one smooth move he rolled on top of her to nuzzle at her neck. "And other things."

She closed her eyes. It was harder, much harder than she ever had believed to fight the need to give. If possible, she wanted him more now than she had during the night. Love, like any indulgence, was craved more after the first taste.

"Like breakfast?" she said, willing her voice to be light.

After nibbling on her lips, he drew back. "Hungry?"

"Starved."

"Shall I ring up room service?"

"Yes—no," she said, and already hated herself for the deception. "I'd really like to shower and change, then I'd been toying with the idea of diving, going out to Palancar."

"Have you hired a boat?"

"Not yet."

When he sat up she shifted, just slightly, so their bodies no longer touched. "Why don't I see to it? I'll go have a shower myself, then meet you in the dining room in an hour. We can take off after we eat."

"Perfect." She managed a smile. "I might be a bit longer than that; I need to call Celeste."

"Not too much longer." He kissed her, and because she was already regretting, she poured herself into it. With a murmur of approval he drew her closer. "A person can go for days without food."

Her laugh was only a little strained. "Not this person."

She waited until she was alone to bring her knees up and drop her head on them. It shouldn't hurt. Doing what was necessary shouldn't hurt. Oh, but it did. Tossing the sheets aside, she rose quickly and began to move.

He gave her an extra quarter of an hour as he sat by the window in the dining room and watched the sun worshipers oil up. He knew there were women who did not value time.

261

But, finally, he reminded himself that Adrianne wasn't one of them. Holding back impatience, he lingered over a second cup of coffee. A man was in bad shape when he started counting the minutes. Philip picked up the rose he'd set beside her plate. He was in very bad shape.

More had happened to him the night before than passion and release. Things had clicked inside him, and settled unalterably into place. He hadn't been looking, hadn't even wanted to look for someone who fit him so perfectly. But there was no going back. For her either, he thought as he lit a cigarette. She might think she could pick up her life where she'd left it off before him, but he was going to prove her wrong.

He'd made his decision, perhaps the first in his life that hadn't been self-serving or with an eye to profit, but he'd made it. And dammit, he wasn't going to waste the rest of the morning waiting to start convincing her it was the right one.

He crushed his cigarette, leaving it smoldering and his coffee cooling as he strode out of the dining room. He was feeling uneasy by the time he got to her door. Lovesick fool, he called himself, with not a little disgust. He rapped, harder than was necessary, then tried the door when she didn't answer. It was locked, but he had his door key in his pocket, along with a credit card and a thin coin. He didn't bother to glance around as he went to work.

When he opened the door, he knew. He was already swearing when he went to the closet to pull it open. It was empty, but for her scent. There was a trace of powder on the vanity counter, but the bottles and tubes were gone.

He let the closet door slam, then jammed his hands into his pockets. For a moment there was only rage and impotence. Never a violent man, he knew then what it was to anticipate murder with relish. Subduing his emotion, he walked to the phone and dialed the front desk.

"How long ago did Lara O'Conner check out?" He waited, fantasizing violence and retribution. "Forty minutes? Thank you."

She could run, he thought as he replaced the receiver. But she'd never run fast enough.

*   *   *

As Philip vowed his own revenge, Adrianne buckled her seat belt. Her eyes were hidden behind dark glasses. They weren't red-rimmed. She hadn't allowed herself tears. But there was regret in them. He would be angry, she thought. Then he would go on—as she would, as she had to. Emotions, the kind he could pull out of her, had no place in her life. Until The Sun and the Moon was in her hands, there was no room for anything but revenge.

Chapter Twenty

It had snowed in London. The streets were gray with slush. Along the curbside it was piled high, blackened like coal and every bit as ugly. But on the rooftops it lay as pristine as in an untouched meadow and glittered even in the sluggish sun. A stiff wind tore at the coats and hats of pedestrians who hurried along, hunched over, hanging on to whatever threatened to whip away. It was the kind of cold that penetrated bone and begged for spiced ale. Hours before, Philip had been under the streaming Mexican sun.

"Here's the tea, dear." Moving quickly from the long habit of trying to catch up, Mary Chamberlain came in to her own cozy parlor. Turning from the window, Philip took the loaded tray from her. All of his boyhood favorites were on it. As dark as his mood was he had to smile. Mary had always tried to spoil him when she'd had the means, and when she hadn't.

"You've made enough for an army."

"You should offer your guest something when he comes." She took a seat by the tea table, then lifted the pot to pour. It was a fine Meissen tea set, with pale pink roses and gold leaf. She always felt very grand using it. "Before he does, I thought we could have a cup together and a little chat."

She added a dollop of cream to his tea and remembered he hadn't used sugar since he'd been twelve. The fact that he was past thirty still amazed her. She hardly felt more than that herself. Like any mother, she considered her son too thin and set two white frosted cakes on a plate for him.

"There now." Pleased, she stirred a healthy dose of sugar

in her own cup. There was nothing quite like hot sweet tea on a winter afternoon. "Isn't this cozy?"

"Hmmm?"

"Drink your tea, dear. It's always a shock to the system to travel from one climate to another." And whatever was really troubling him would come out sooner or later.

He obeyed automatically, studying her over the rim. She'd put on weight in the last few years. Flattering weight, Philip thought. She'd always been too thin when he'd been a child. Her face was comfortably round, and if her skin lacked the dewiness of a girl's, it had the glow of a mature woman's. A few lines, certainly, but they came as much from laughing as from age. Mary had always been one for laughing. Her eyes were a clear, blameless blue.

He'd inherited his looks not from her, but from the man who had swung in, then out of her life. As a child it had bothered him a great deal, so much so that he'd watched every man, from the postman to the prince regent, looking for a resemblance. To this day he wasn't sure what he'd intended to do if he'd found one.

"You've changed your hair."

Mary fluffed it. The gesture was flirtatious and totally innate. "Yes. What do you think?"

"That you're beautiful."

She laughed, full and rich and delighted. "I've a new hairdresser. His name's Mr. Mark. Mr. Mark, can you imagine?" She rolled her eyes and licked a dab of frosting from her finger. "He flirts so nicely, you just have to give him an extra tip. All the girls are wild about him, but I think he might be of another persuasion."

"Episcopalian?"

Humor danced in her eyes. Her Phil had always been a devil. "Yes. Now..." Settling back with her tea, she smiled. "Tell me all about your vacation. I hope you didn't drink the water. You hear such foul things about it. Did you have a good time?"

He thought of crawling through ducts, hiding in closets, and of making love, leisurely love with Adrianne. "It had its moments."

"Nothing quite like a winter vacation in the tropics. I

still remember when you flew me down to Jamaica in the middle of February. I felt decadent."

That had been a side benefit of the de Marco heist. "And kept the natives restless."

"I thought I behaved like a very proper British matron." Then she giggled. If there was one thing Mary would never be, it was matronly. "I'm thinking of taking a cruise myself. Perhaps the Bahamas." She spotted Chauncy, the fat slug of a cat she'd adopted years before. Before he could leap on the tray she poured cream into a saucer for him. "That lovely Mr. Paddington's invited me."

"What?" Brought back with a thud, Philip stared at her. Beside them, the cat lapped greedily. "Run that through again?"

"I said I was thinking of going to the Bahamas with Mr. Paddington. Chauncy, you're such a pig." Soft-hearted, she dropped half a cake on the saucer. He took it in one pounce.

"Go on a cruise with that oily old lecher? That's ridiculous."

Mary debated having another cake herself. "Mr. Paddington's a very respected member of the community. Don't be a noodle, Phil."

"I've no intention of seeing my mother ravished on the high seas."

"Oh, my—what a lovely thought." Laughing, she leaned over and patted his hand. "In any case, dear, you wouldn't see. Now, why don't you tell me what's bothering you? I hope it's a woman."

He rose, impatient with tea and cakes, to stalk the room. As always, Mary had loaded a Christmas tree with whatever ornaments struck her fancy. There was no theme to it, no harmony of color. She had everything from plastic reindeer to porcelain angels. Philip pulled off a bit of tinsel to run it through his hands.

"It's just business."

"I've never seen you walk the floor over business. Could it be that sweet girl I spoke with on the phone? Phoebe Spring's daughter?" When he snapped the string of tinsel in two, Mary all but rubbed her hands together. "Oh, that's wonderful."

"There's nothing wonderful about it, so you can stop

smelling orange blossoms." He came back to slump in the chair. "What are you smiling at?"

"I think you're in love. Finally. How does it feel?"

He scowled down at his feet, more than a little tempted to kick the cat. "Rotten."

"Good, good. That's just how it should feel."

Unable to do otherwise, he laughed. "You're always a comfort to me, Mum."

"When can I meet her?"

"I don't know. There's a problem."

"Of course there is. So there should be. Real love requires problems."

He doubted if love of any kind had a two-hundred-and-eighty-carat diamond and a pearl beyond price to deal with. "Tell me what you know about Phoebe Spring."

"Oh. She was glorious. There's no one today who can compare with her, the glamour, the—presence." Just remembering made her sigh. She'd had dreams of her own about being an actress, a star. Then there'd been Philip, and she'd settled for selling tickets to films rather than being in them. It never occurred to her to regret. "You know, most cinema stars now look like ordinary people—a bit prettier perhaps, a bit sleeker, but so could anyone with a bit of fuss. Phoebe Spring was never ordinary. Wait, I'll show you."

She was up and moving quickly into another room. Philip heard her rummaging, shifting boxes. Something thudded. He only shook his head. His mother was an obsessive collector, a saver. There had always been bits of colored glass, old swatches of material, shelves of salt shakers, a drawer of old movie stubs.

In Chelsea the windowsills had been lined with little plaster animals. Pets hadn't been allowed, so in her usual way Mary had compensated. He could still remember her laboriously clipping and pasting pictures of everyone from the royal family to the latest film god. They'd replaced the traditional family album for a woman who had had no one but herself and a small boy.

She came back blowing dust from a large red scrapbook. "You know how I kept books on my favorite celebrities."

"Your star books."

"Yes." Unashamed, Mary sat down and opened it. When

Chauncy jumped on it, she tut-tutted and patiently set him back on the floor. "This is Phoebe Spring. Look here, this picture would have been taken at the premiere of her first movie. She couldn't have been more than twenty."

He moved over to sit on the arm of her chair. The woman in the picture had her hand on the arm of a man, but you didn't notice him. Only her. Her dress was some fantasy of sequins and sparkles with her hair dark and full around the shoulders. Even in black and white her luster shone through. Her eyes were all innocent excitement, her body all promise.

"It made her a star," Mary mused, flipping through the pages. There were other pictures, some studio-posed, others candid. She was never less than beautiful. Through the pictures, some curling at the edges with age, she exuded sex. Taped with them were snippets of gossip Mary had clipped from movie magazines and tabloids. Rumors of Phoebe's affairs with her leading men, with producers, directors, politicians.

"Here, this one was at the Oscars when she was nominated for *Tomorrow's Child*. Pity she didn't win, but she was escorted by Cary Grant, and that counts for something."

"I saw that movie. She fell in love with the wrong man, bore his child, then had to fight against him and his wealthy parents for custody."

"I cried buckets—every time I watched it. She was so valiant and mistreated." Mary sighed again and turned the page.

There was a picture of Phoebe in some stiff, pale satin, curtsying gracefully to the queen, then one of her dancing with a dark, sharp-featured man in a tuxedo. Philip didn't have to be told it was Adrianne's father. The eyes, the bone structure, the coloring, said everything.

"This?"

"That's her husband. King Abdu something or other. She married only once, you know. Oh, the papers and magazines were full of it. How they met right here in London while she was filming *White Roses*. How they fell in love the minute they clapped eyes on each other. He sent her two dozen white roses every day until her hotel suite was like a greenhouse. He booked a whole restaurant so they could have dinner alone. Him being a king and all made it ever so romantic."

From her position as an onlooker, even after more than a quarter century, Mary's eyes still misted. "People started remembering Grace Kelly and Rita Hayworth, and sure enough she ended up leaving the movies and marrying him. Going off to that tiny little country over there." She indicated it with a wave of her hand.

"Jaquir."

"Yes, that's it. Like a fairy tale it was. Here's a picture of her on her wedding day. Looks like a queen."

The dress was breathtaking with layers of lace and miles of silk. Even under the tulle, Phoebe's hair had shone like a beacon. She'd looked radiantly happy, achingly young. In her arms she had carried white roses, dozens of them. And around her neck, glittering, glowing, all but burning through the photograph was The Sun and the Moon.

Both diamond and pearl dropped, one resting tight beneath the other, from a heavy double-braided chain of gold. The settings were like starbursts, ornate, old-fashioned, and glorious.

He may have been retired, but the tips of his fingers itched, and his pulse increased. To hold that, to own that for even a moment, would be like owning the world.

"After they were married there wasn't much news, and hardly ever pictures. There's some custom over there against pictures. You heard she was having a baby, then that she'd had a little girl. That would be your Adrianne."

"Yes."

"People talked for a while, then you read less and less until she showed up in New York with her daughter a few years later. It seems the marriage wasn't a happy one, and she ended up leaving him to go back home and pick up her career. There's an interview here soon after, but she didn't say much other than she'd missed acting."

She turned the page and there was another picture. This Phoebe was still beautiful, but the lushness, the glory, was gone. In its place were strain and nerves. Beside her was Adrianne. She couldn't have been more than eight, and small for her age. She stood straight, staring at the camera, but her eyes were carefully guarded. She clung to her mother's hand—or Phoebe clung to hers.

"Such a sad thing. Phoebe never made another really good film. Just ones where she took her clothes off and such." She turned the pages to a different Phoebe, one with lines around the eyes and dresses cut to show off still-smooth breasts. There was a vacant look to her face and a desperation to her smile. Replacing innocence was a hard edge. "She did one of those layouts for a men's magazine." Mary wrinkled her nose. She was anything but a prude, but there were limits. "Had an affair with her agent, among others. There were hints, though, that he had an eye for her daughter. Filthy stuff for a man of his age."

Something curled in the pit of Philip's stomach. "What was his name?"

"Oh, Lord, I don't remember, if I ever knew. It might be in here somewhere."

"Can I take this along with me?"

"Of course. Does it matter, Phil?" She laid a hand on his as he closed the book. "Whoever her parents were, whatever they were, doesn't change who she is."

"I know that." He touched his lips to her cheek. "She needs to."

"She's lucky to have you."

"Yes." He grinned and kissed her again. "I know."

When the buzzer sounded, Philip checked his watch. "That'll be Stuart, prompt as always."

"Shall I heat up the tea?"

"It's warm enough," he told her as he walked to the door. "Stuart."

With his nose and cheeks reddened by the wind, Spencer stepped inside. "Miserably cold. We'll have snow again after nightfall. Mrs. Chamberlain." He took her offered hand and patted it. "Good to see you."

"You'll warm up with a nice cup of tea, Mr. Spencer. Phil will pour. I'm afraid I have a few errands to run." She slipped into the black mink her son had given her for Christmas. "More cakes in the pantry if you want them."

"Thanks, Mum." He drew her collar together. "You look like a movie star."

Nothing could have pleased her more. After giving his cheek a pinch she went out.

"Lovely woman, your mother."

"Yes. She's thinking of going on a cruise with some greengrocer named Paddington."

"Greengrocer? Well." Spencer folded his coat, laying it neatly over a chair before turning toward the tea tray. "Sure she'll be sensible about it." He helped himself to the tea. "I thought you were taking the holidays off."

"I am."

Spencer lifted a brow. It rose a fraction higher when Philip drew out a cigarette. "I thought you'd given those up."

"I did."

Spencer added a squirt of lemon. "Seemed time that I filled you in on Paris."

Though he already knew precisely what had happened, he took a seat and prepared to listen.

"As you suspected, the countess was marked. We had an agent inside undercover as kitchen help, and two more in the field. Our man must have sensed it, because he moved a little too fast. Set off an alarm. That's a first for him."

Philip poured a second cup of tea, then sent Chauncy a warning look. "Indeed."

"The outside men caught a glimpse of him, another first, though the description's vague at best. Both of them claim he must be as native to Paris as a sewer rat, but that may be because they lost him."

"The countess' jewels?"

"Safe." Spencer heaved a pleased sigh. "We fouled up the works for him there."

"Perhaps more than that." Philip offered the cakes. Spencer resisted a moment, then broke off a bite. "I've heard some rumors."

"Such as?"

"They might be nothing more than that, but I've had my ear to the ground. Did you know our man has a woman accomplice?"

"A woman?" Spencer forgot the cake and reached for his notebook. "We've had nothing on a woman."

Philip flicked the ash of his cigarette. "That's why you need me, Captain. I don't have a name, but she's a redhead,

271

a bit of a tart, and only bright enough to carry out his orders."
He had to smile at that, thinking how furious the description
would make Adrianne. "In any case, she talked to a contact of
mine." He held up a hand, anticipating. "You know I can't tell
you, Stuart. That's been part of the deal from the beginning."

"One I regret making. When I think of all the lowlifes
and petty thieves I could brush off the streets . . . never
mind. What did she have to say?"

"That The Shadow, you know they call him The Shadow?"

"They will romanticize."

"The Shadow's getting along in years apparently, and has
a touch of arthritis." Philip flexed his fingers. "That's one of
the greatest fears of artists of all kinds. Musicians, painters,
thieves. Dexterity is an invaluable tool."

"I have a difficult time sympathizing."

"Have another cake, Captain. Rumor is, The Shadow's
going into retirement."

Spencer paused with the cake halfway to his lips. His
eyes widened and glazed. Philip was reminded of a bulldog
who'd just discovered the juicy bone he'd been about to sink
his teeth into was nothing but plastic. "What do you mean,
retire? I'm damned if he can retire. We almost had our hands
on him in Paris two days ago."

"It's only a rumor."

"Bloody hell." Spencer let the cake drop and sucked on
his fingers.

"Maybe he'll only take a vacation."

"And you suggest?"

"Until he moves again, if he does, we wait."

Spencer worried the information like a bit between his
teeth. "It may pay to focus on the woman."

"It may." With a shrug Philip discounted it. "If you've
time to corral all the redheaded tarts on two continents."
Leaning forward, he picked up his cup. "I know it's frustrat-
ing, Stuart, but the close call in Paris might have been the
last straw for him." He'd have to remember to send a check, a
generous one, to his old friend André, who'd made certain
the Paris agents had had something to report. "I have some
business, personal business, to see to over the next few
weeks. If I hear anything that can be of use to you, I'll pass it
along."

"I want this man, Philip."

A ghost of a smile touched Philip's mouth. "No more than I, I promise you."

It was after two A.M. when Adrianne let herself into her apartment. The New Year's Eve party she'd slipped out of would probably last until dawn. She'd left Celeste flirting with an old flame and bottles of champagne unopened. Adrianne's escort had certainly noticed her absence by now, but she was sure he could find something, or someone, to entertain him.

It had been difficult not to look at the jewelry with an eye toward a job. For so many years she'd admired a necklace, studied a bracelet while calculating its return in dollars and cents. That was a habit she was trying to break. There was only one more job for her, and those jewels she could envision anytime of the day or night. She could see them in the portrait she'd had painted of her mother from an old photograph. She could feel them, ice and fire, in her hands.

When she returned from Jaquir, she would be the woman everyone already believed she was. Her life would be parties, and benefits and trips to the spots a woman of her means was supposed to frequent. She would learn to enjoy it the way a woman enjoyed success when her life's work was done. And she would enjoy it alone.

She wouldn't regret that. Success had a price; no matter how steep, it had to be paid. She'd burned her bridges when she'd boarded that plane out of Cozumel. Perhaps she'd lit the match years before.

He'd forget her. In all likelihood he'd already begun to. She was just another woman, after all. She hadn't been his first, nor did she have any illusions that she would be his last. He was both for her, and that she accepted.

She draped her coat over her arm as she climbed the stairs that curved to the second floor. She couldn't afford to think about Philip. She certainly couldn't afford to regret having loved him, or having closed the door on what that love might have led to. Dead ends, she thought. When a woman loved a man, it always led to a dead end.

What she wanted now was sleep, a long, deep sleep. She

would need all her energy, all her skill and wit over the days to come. Her flight to Jaquir was already booked.

She didn't turn on the light in the bedroom, but tossed her coat over a chair, then began to unbraid her hair in the dark. Outside, the noise of traffic rose in waves, reminding her of the sea. She could almost smell it—that and the edge of tobacco, the tang of soap that brought Philip so clearly to mind.

She froze, her arms lifted, her hands caught in her hair when the light by the bed flashed on.

She looked like something carved out of alabaster and amber, with her skin glowing gold against a white beaded gown. It fell like a tube down her body, straight and snug and glittering. But as Philip lifted a glass to his lips, he watched her eyes. It pleased him to see shock, pleasure, then control flash in them.

"Happy New Year, darling." He toasted her with his champagne glass, then put it down and lifted the bottle to pour the wine into the second glass he had waiting.

He was all in black, a turtleneck, snug jeans, supple leather boots. While he'd waited for her to return, he'd made himself at home, propped against the heaps of pillows Adrianne grouped on her bed.

She felt everything at once—need, annoyance, delight, and guilt. Because of it, her voice was as cool as the wine he offered. Slowly, she let her arms fall back to her sides.

"I didn't expect to see you again."

"You should have. No toast to the new year, Addy?"

To prove her disinterest to herself, and to him, she walked over to take the glass. Her gown shivered like water. "To beginnings then, and the payment of old debts." Crystal rang against crystal. "You've come a long way for a drink."

Her scent clung, to her skin, to the air, to his senses. He could have strangled her for it. "But you stock an excellent vintage."

It tasted like sand. "If you like, I'll apologize for leaving so abruptly."

"Don't bother." He checked himself. Anger was closer to the surface than he'd intended. "I should have understood you were a coward."

"I'm not a coward." She set her drink, almost untasted, beside his.

"You are," he began slowly, "a pitiful, quivering, self-serving coward."

She slapped him before she'd realized she intended to, before he'd read the intent on her face. The sound of flesh meeting flesh cracked, then echoed. Philip's eyes went dark with answering violence before he calmly lifted his glass again. But his knuckles went white on the stem.

"That doesn't change anything."

"You've no right to judge me, no right to insult me. I left because I chose to leave, because I thought it best and because I won't be an amusement to you."

"I can assure you, there's very little about you that amuses me, Adrianne." After setting his glass aside again, he steepled his fingers and watched her over them. "Did you think all I was interested in was a few tropical fucks?"

Her color faded at that, then came back fast and hot enough to sting her cheeks. "It's more to the point that I'm not interested in an affair."

"Use whatever term you like. You're the one who lowered what happened between us to a cheap one-night stand."

"What does it matter?" The fury leapt in her voice chased by the shame of hearing the truth. "One night, two, or a dozen?"

"Damn you." He caught her wrist and yanked her to the bed. Even as she fought back, he covered her body with his and pinned her arms. Flames licked. "It was more than that and you know it. It wasn't just sex, it wasn't rape, and I'm not your father." She went still at that. The angry color drained out of her face, leaving it bone-white. "That's it, isn't it? Every time a man got close, every time you were tempted, you'd think of him. Not with me, Adrianne. Never with me."

"You don't know what you're talking about."

"Don't I?" His face was only inches from hers. He could almost see the life pump back into it, the color, the anger, the denial. "Hate him if you like, you have the right, but I'll be damned if you'll measure me by him or anyone else."

His mouth came down on hers not with the tenderness he'd shown her before, not with care or coaxing, but with an angry demand edged with hunger. She didn't struggle, but the hands he pinned curled into fists even as her blood began to heat and swim.

"What happened between us happened because you wanted as much as I did, you needed as much as I did. Look at me," he demanded when she kept her eyes shut. He waited until she opened them, and the light beside them slanted across her face. "Can you deny it?"

She wanted to. The lie formed on her lips, then died into the truth. "No. But what happened is over."

"A long way from over. Do you think it's just temper that has your pulse pounding? Do you think two people can come together the way we did, then walk away and forget?" He released her hands, only to drag his own through her hair. "I showed you one way that night. Now, by God, I'll show you another."

His mouth was hot and hard and hungry. When it closed over hers, she lay limp, determined to give him nothing, and take nothing for herself. But her breath began to quicken, and her lips warmed and opened. He invaded, letting his tongue tempt and his teeth excite.

This was seduction, more so than soft words and soft light. This was challenge, a gauntlet thrown. This was the answer to questions she'd never dared ask.

All at once she was clinging, giving back, but nothing seemed to satisfy him.

He moved down her body, raced, dragging her gown to her waist to free more flesh. No exploration now, but exploitation. He filled his hands with her breasts, then tugged and sucked and teased until her nipples were hard and hot and aching, until her body writhed and arched and shuddered. Reaching for him, she accepted.

She called to him, mindless, with incoherent words that sent the blood racing to his loins to throb with every beat of his heart. So the seducer was seduced.

This was a lock he would open, once and for all. He had the skill, the experience, and the need. The treasures here were richer and more tempting than any he'd ever taken from the deepest vaults, the darkest safes. With his hands and mouth alone he drove her up, dragging her over the edge.

There was a darkness here, like velvet, and the air was

as thick and heavy. She fought to pull it into her lungs only to have it catch and lose it again in moans. She should have understood from the hints he'd given her before that pleasure could rack the body, turn it into a mass of sensations and needs. The choice to give and take, to offer and receive, was out of her hands.

She tore at his clothes, all sense of denial and self-preservation winked out like the tip of a candle. There had been pleasure before, with its twin face of pain. But not like this. To want like this was to forget all other wants. Never had she been so aware of her body so that she could feel every pulse beat, hundreds of them pounding wherever he touched, wherever she wanted to be touched.

Sweat sprang out on her skin. And his. She could taste the salt as they rolled over the bed. The scent of passion rose, sharp, pungent, arousing. She could hear his breath come ragged and strained as he pinned her beneath him again. Their eyes locked. His head pounded as air tore in and out of his chest. He could feel the bite of her nails in his back, and the give of her breasts beneath him.

"I'm going to watch you go up," he told her, and the words hurt his throat. "You're going to know I'm the only one who can take you there."

He plunged into her, pounding, thrusting so that her eyes went wide and glazed. The gasp of pleasure strangled in her throat.

He could feel each separate muscle in his body bunching, straining. Then her hips were moving like lightning, meeting him thrust for thrust. Sensations sharpened. He could see the light falling over her face, hear the rustle of sheets, almost feel the pores of his body open. Her scent, like her arms, like her legs, like her hair, wrapped around him. Reality focused to the point of a pin. He thought it must be like dying. Then even his vision dimmed. Her cry of release was like an echo as he poured into her.

She waited for the shame to come, and the self-disgust. But there was only the soft, lingering glow of pleasure. He'd done things to her that she'd never known she could enjoy. And she had welcomed them. Wallowed in them. Even now, with passion spent, she knew she would welcome them again. She kept her eyes closed, knowing he watched her.

She couldn't know how she looked, Philip thought. Naked, her long, lean legs still spread in abandon, her skin warmed with that afterglow of good sex, her hair spread wildly over white lace pillows. She wore nothing but diamond drops at her ears. They winked erotically in the light of the lamp.

"These are real," he said as he toyed with them.

"Yes."

"Who gave them to you?"

"Celeste. For my eighteenth birthday."

"That's good. If they'd come from a man, I'd have had to be jealous. I don't have much energy for it at the moment."

She opened her eyes and nearly smiled. "I don't know what I'm supposed to say."

"You could say something about this being an excellent way to start the new year."

She wanted to touch his hair. It was almost gold in the light and mussed around his face. Her hands had done that in passion, but she kept them lowered now. "Philip, you have to understand this can't change anything. It would be best for you to go back to London."

"Umm-hmm. Do you know you have a mole just here." He skimmed his fingers down her hip. "I could find it in the dark."

"I have to be practical." Even as she said it, meant it, she moved against him. "I need you to be practical."

"An excellent idea. Let's drink to it." Reaching over her, he picked up their glasses.

"Philip, I want you to listen to me. It may have been wrong of me to leave the way I did in Mexico, but I thought it would be easier. I wanted to avoid saying things that have to be said."

"The problem with you, Addy, is that you try to think more than feel. But go ahead, say what's on your mind."

"I can't afford to be involved with you, with anyone. What I have to do requires all my concentration. You know as well as I how vital it is not to let outside problems interfere with work."

"Is that what I am?" He was sated enough to be amused rather than angry. "An outside problem?"

She was silent for a moment. "You have no part in my plans in Jaquir. Even after I've finished, I intend to stay alone. I won't ever allow myself to build my life around a man, to make decisions based on my feelings for one. If that sounds selfish, I'm sorry. But I know how easy it is to lose who and what you are."

He listened to her, his eyes very clear, his mouth very sober. "That would be all well and good except for one slight problem. I love you, Adrianne."

Her lips parted. In shock, he realized wryly. Then she pushed herself up and was nearly out of bed before he caught her.

"No, you won't turn away from me." He pulled her back, ignoring the glass she'd dropped over the side of the bed and the wine that was soaking into the carpet. "And I won't let you turn away from yourself."

"Don't do this."

"Already done."

"Philip, you're just letting your imagination run away with you. You've romanticized what's been happening between us, added violins and moonlight."

"Does it make you feel safer to think so?"

"It's not a matter of being safe, it's a matter of common sense." But that wasn't true, not when she could feel the fear dancing inside her stomach. "Let's not complicate this any more than it already is."

"Fine. We'll keep it simple." He took her face in his hands, gently this time. "I'm in love with you, Addy. You'll have to get used to it because you won't shake me loose. Now relax." He skimmed a hand down to cup her breast. "And I'll show you what I mean."

Chapter Twenty-One

Adrianne snuggled into the pillow, blinked against the intrusion of light, then stretched. Philip's arm rose with hers. Metal rang. In speechless shock she stared at the handcuffs that bound her wrist to his while he grumbled.

"You bastard."

"We've already established that." With one jerk he had her tumbling against his chest. She was smoothly, warmly naked. "Morning, darling."

She pushed off, then fell against him again. "What the hell is this?" Adrianne yanked her arm hard enough to make him wince.

"A simple precaution—to keep you from slipping under the door." Using his free hand, he caught her hair to pull her face down to his. He was already hard, just remembering. "I love you, Addy, but I don't trust you."

"Take these off immediately."

He rolled so that his legs tangled with hers. "I was hoping you'd let me prove that I can make love to you with one hand tied behind my back. So to speak."

She swallowed a chuckle. "Some other time."

"Suit yourself." He settled back on the pillow and closed his eyes.

"Philip, I said to take these off."

"I will, when it's time to get up."

She gave their joined arms another jerk. "I refuse to be shackled like some sort of body slave—"

"Lovely idea."

"And I am getting up."

He opened one eye. "At this hour?"

"It's after noon." Disgusted, she lifted the cuffs so that she could study the lock. She supposed she could drag him to her tools. "I was an early riser before I met you."

That made him open both eyes. "Whatever for?"

On a hiss of frustration she climbed over him. "Where's the damn key?"

"All right, don't get testy."

Planting her feet, Adrianne pulled. She had to drop to her knees, but it was satisfying enough to watch Philip hit the floor.

"Christ." Forgetting dignity, he rubbed the part that hit the floor first. "What's the hurry?"

Fighting back laughter, she scooped her hair out of her eyes. "If you must know I want—no, I need the loo."

"Oh. Why didn't you say so?"

Air whistled out between her teeth as she clamped them together. "I didn't realize I'd need to announce it until I found myself shackled to you."

"Nice feeling, isn't it?" he said as he bent over to kiss her.

"Philip."

"Yes, the key." He glanced around, then spotted his jeans heaped at the foot of the bed. "Come along." With Adrianne in tow and swearing at him, he reached his jeans. "It's in the pocket." He dipped into one, found nothing, then tried another. "I don't suppose you want company."

"Philip!" She wouldn't laugh. At this moment laughter could be a disaster.

"No? Well then." He tossed the jeans back into a heap. "Got a hairpin?"

When he started downstairs a short while later, he was hoping for coffee. The last thing he'd expected was to find Adrianne, dressed in baggy sweats, grilling bacon. The scent was enough to make him fall in love.

"What are you doing?"

"Fixing breakfast. Coffee's hot."

He walked to the stove to stare at the meat grilling in the skillet. "You cook?"

"Of course I cook." She lifted bacon out and set it to

281

drain. "Mama and I spent a lot of years without servants. I still prefer to see to myself."

"And you're fixing me breakfast."

Embarrassed, she snatched up a carton of eggs. "For heaven's sake, it's not as though I'm laying down my life."

"You're fixing me breakfast," he said again, and brushed the hair from the nape of her neck so he could kiss it. "You do love me, Addy. You just don't realize it yet."

He bided his time through the meal, letting her relax. What he didn't know was that she was doing precisely the same thing. Lounging by her window that opened up to a view of Central Park, they lingered over coffee. They were there, looking out, when the first flakes of snow began to fall.

"The city's lovely in the snow. The first time I saw it I cried because I thought it wouldn't stop until we were all buried in it. Then Mama took me out and showed me how to build a snowman." She pushed away her coffee, knowing the caffeine would make her jumpy if she indulged in any more. "I wish I could take the next few days and show you around New York, but I have a lot of business to see to."

"I don't mind tagging along."

She cleared her throat and tried again. "If you could come back in a few weeks, I'd be free to take you to some museums, a few shows, a gallery or two."

He tapped his cigarette on the table before lighting it. "I didn't come here to be entertained, Addy, but to be with you."

"Philip, I leave for Jaquir at the end of the week."

He took a long, soothing drag. "That's something we need to discuss."

"No, that's something I'm going to do. I'm sorry you don't understand or approve, but it doesn't—it can't—make any difference."

He continued to look out at the snow. A young boy was heading into the park walking a fleet of dogs. A pretty scene, he thought. He could be content spending a portion of his life on this continent, in this city, in this room. When he spoke, it wasn't in anger, it wasn't meant as a threat. It was said with the calm simplicity of fact.

"There are things I can do, Addy, that would make it

difficult if not impossible for you to leave the country, much less go to an area as unstable as the Middle East."

Her head came up just a fraction, but it was enough to lend her the air of royalty. "I am Princess Adrianne of Jaquir. If I choose to visit the country of my birth, neither you nor anyone can stop me."

"You do that well," he said. Well enough that the picture of her father's face flashed in his mind. "And if it were only a visit you planned, you'd have a point. As it is, I can stop you, Adrianne, and I will."

"This isn't something for you to decide."

"Keeping you alive has become a matter of some interest to me."

"Then you should understand that if I don't go and do what I have to do, I may as well be dead."

"You're dramatizing." Leaning over the table, he grabbed her hands, forcing her to look at him. "I know a bit more now. I've spent a great deal of time over the last few days reading about your mother, digging up what scraps I could about your father, your early life."

"You had no right—"

"It has nothing to do with rights. I know it was difficult, even horrible in many ways, but it's over." He tightened his grip. "You're clinging to something you should have let go a long time ago."

"I'm taking back what's mine by right, by the law, and by my birth. I'm taking back what dignity was stolen from my mother and from me."

"We both know that stones don't bring dignity to anyone."

"You don't understand. You can't." Her fingers tightened on his a moment, then relaxed. "Come with me a minute."

She led him out of the breakfast nook, through the hall, into a sitting room. She'd decorated it in white on white with a few passionate slashes of red and royal blue. Over a marble fireplace scrubbed clean as glass was the portrait.

More than the clipped photographs, more than any film he'd ever seen, it showed Phoebe Spring in her glory. Her hair, that furious trademark red, fell wave upon wave to her shoulders. Her skin was like new milk against an emerald gown that dipped to her breasts and left her arms and shoulders bare. She was smiling, on the edge of a laugh, so that her wide, luxurious mouth seemed all the fuller. Her eyes, a striking Viking blue, were lit with promise and unmistakable innocence. A man couldn't look at it and not be drawn, not want, not wonder.

Around her neck, as he'd seen before, was The Sun and the Moon.

"She was magnificent, Addy. The most beautiful woman I've ever seen."

"Yes. But she was more than her looks. She was kind, Philip. Truly kind. Her heart would break over a stranger's trouble. She was easily hurt, a sharp word, an angry look. All she ever wanted to do was make people happy. She didn't look like this when she died."

"Addy—"

"No, I want you to see. I had this painted from a picture that was taken of her just before she married. She was so young, younger than I am now. And so much in love. You can see just by looking that at that moment she was a woman secure in herself, happy with life."

"Yes, I can see that. Time passes, Addy, things change."

"It wasn't a matter of time for her, or of natural change. That necklace—she told me once how she'd felt the first time she'd put that necklace on. She'd felt a queen. It hadn't mattered to her that she'd be giving up everything she'd known, going to another country to live under different rules. She'd been in love and she'd felt like a queen."

He touched a hand to her cheek. "She was."

"No." She lifted her hand and laid it on his wrist. "She was only a woman, naive, big-hearted, afraid of the dark side of life. She'd made something of herself, become something. Then she let it go because he asked. The necklace was a symbol, a promise that he was as committed to her as she was to him. When he took it back, he was making a statement that he renounced her, and me. He took it back because divorce wasn't enough. He wiped away the marriage, as if it had never been. When he did that, he took the last of her dignity, and he stole my birthright."

"Addy, sit down a minute. Please." He lowered to the sofa with her, keeping her hands in his. "I understand how it feels. There was a time I looked for my father in every stranger's face. In every teacher I ever had, every cop I avoided, even in the marks I chose. I spent my childhood hating him for turning his back on my mother and refusing to acknowledge me. But I still looked. I don't know what I would have done if I'd found him, but I do know that there comes a time when you have to be enough for yourself."

"You have your mother, Philip. What happened didn't destroy her. You didn't have to watch her die bit by bit. I loved her so much. I owe her so much."

"What's between a parent and child doesn't require payment."

"She risked her life for me. It was no less than that. It was for me she left Jaquir much more than for herself. If she'd been caught, taken back, her life would have been over. No, he wouldn't have killed her," she said when Philip's eyes narrowed. "He wouldn't have dared, but she would have wished herself dead. She'd have been better off dead."

"Addy, however much you loved her, whatever you feel you owe her isn't worth risking your life. Ask yourself if she'd want you to."

She shook her head. "It's down to what I want. The necklace is mine."

"Even if you managed to get out of Jaquir with the necklace, you'd never be able to claim it publicly, you'd never be able to wear it."

"But I don't take it to own it, to wear it." A fire came back into her eyes, a dangerous one. "I take it so he knows, he finally knows how much I detest him."

"Do you think it would matter to him?"

"That his daughter hates him? No. A daughter means less than nothing to a man like him. A commodity to be traded, as he's already traded his others for political security." She looked back at the portrait. "But The Sun and the Moon means everything. There's nothing worth more in Jaquir, not for its monetary value. It's beyond price. It's a matter of pride and of strength. If it passes out of the hands of the royal family, there'll be revolution and bloodshed and the crumbling of power. The unrest that borders Jaquir will cross over and sweep it away."

"Do you want revenge on your father or on Jaquir?"

She brought herself back. Her eyes were blurred as if

she'd been dreaming. "I could have both, but that's up to him. Abdu will never risk Jaquir or his position. His pride. In the end it will be his pride that makes restitution."

"His pride could as easily strike back at you."

"Yes. It's a risk I'm willing to take." She stood then, her back toward the portrait, her hand offered to him. "Don't say anything more yet. There's something else I want to show you. Will you come with me?"

"Where?"

"You'll need your coat. I'll take you."

The snow fell in sheets, whipped by the wind that tunneled through the buildings. With her mink tossed over her sweats, Adrianne tried to relax in the warmth of the limo. She hadn't told anyone so much, not even Celeste. She hadn't shown anyone what she intended to show Philip.

It mattered. Though she'd tried hard to deny it, it mattered what he thought. For the first time in more years than she could count, she needed someone else's support and approval.

The east side neighborhood was far less affluent than her Central Park address. The covering of snow helped, but the crude graffiti spray-painted on the sides of buildings stood out. Here and there windows were boarded up, and more than one car parked along the curb was as hot as a five-dollar watch. A knock on the right door could get you a nickel bag of heroin, first class stereo components that still sizzled, or a knife in the back. Philip hadn't been there before, but he recognized it.

"An odd place to pay New Year's calls."

She tucked her hair under a mink hat. "We won't be long," she told the driver. He nodded and fervently hoped so.

There were a few choice pieces of garbage in the gutter. An empty crack vial, a used condom, broken glass. Philip steered her around it as his anger grew.

"What in the hell are we doing in a place like this? You can get your throat slit for your shoes alone, and you wear mink."

"It's warm." She reached in her bag for keys. "Don't worry, I know most of the people who live on this block."

"There's good news." He took her arm as she started up

a set of crumbling, slippery steps. "Let's hope they don't have any cousins visiting from out of town. What the hell is this place?"

She opened three locks. When she pushed in the door, her voice flowed in, then back to him. "It's mine."

He shut the door behind him, but it did nothing to keep out the cold. "You never mentioned you were a slumlord."

"I don't rent it." They walked into a huge empty room. The floor gapped in places, making him think uncomfortably of rats. Two of the windows were boarded, and the others were covered with a thick scum of grime and dust. What light fought through was weak and as dirty as the walls. A few boxes and rickety tables were pushed into corners. Some local artist had drawn pictures of couples in various sexual positions, then had added unnecessary captions.

"This used to be a rather seedy hotel." Her footsteps echoed as she moved around the room. "I'd take you upstairs and show you the rooms, but the staircase fell in a couple of months ago."

"Just my luck."

"There are twelve rooms on each floor. The plumbing is, well, unreliable at best, and the wiring has to be completely updated. Naturally, a new furnace is in order."

"In order for what? Shit." He tugged spiderwebs out of his face. "Addy, if you're thinking about going into the hotel business, think again. This place would take close to a million just to shovel out the dirt and kill the vermin."

"I estimate one and a half million to renovate, another million to adequately stock and staff. I want the best."

"The best is several miles away at the Waldorf." Something began to gnaw cozily behind the wall. "I hate mice."

"Probably rats, anyway."

"That's all right, then. Addy, I love you." He dragged more cobwebs out of his hair. "And if you've got some notion about retiring and giving the St. Johns a run for their money in the hotel trade, fine. But I think we can do a bit better than this."

"It's not going to be a hotel. It's going to be a clinic, The Phoebe Spring Abuse Clinic, staffed with the best therapists I can draw in. When it's finished, it will be able to house thirty women and children who have no place else to go."

"Addy—"

She shook her head to hold him off. Her eyes were lit now with a new kind of passion. "Can you understand what it's like to have no place to go? To stay with someone because you don't know what else to do, because over the years you've grown almost used to the beatings, the humiliation? So used to it that you've started to feel as if you deserve it?"

He had no glib remark for her now, no soothing comment. "No, I can't."

"I've seen women like that, and children. Battered, more than bruises, Philip, scars on the mind, on the heart. They're not always poor, not always uneducated, but they have something in common. The hopelessness, the helplessness." She turned away for a moment. Her emotions always took over here, but she wanted him to see the practical side. "We should be able to handle at least thirty more on an outpatient basis. Double that if and when we expand. The staff will be made up of both professionals and volunteers. Fees will be on a sliding scale, based on ability to pay. No one will be turned away."

Wind whistled through cracks in the windows and crept through the floorboards. It was a miserable place in a miserable neighborhood. He wished he could leave it at that, but like Adrianne, he had vision. "How long have you been planning this?"

"I bought the building about six months ago, but I've had the idea for quite a bit longer." Her footsteps echoed again as she crossed the floor. Above her head the ceiling was sagging and waterstained. "Taking the necklace is something I have to do, for myself. The motive is completely selfish."

"Is it?"

"Oh, yes." She turned back. "Don't attach any nobility to it, Philip, or to me. It's revenge, pure and simple. But after it's done, it's done. I don't want it, I have no need for it. Abdu can have it back—for a price." In the dull light, her eyes were very dark. Swathed in dark mink, she looked every bit the princess. "Five million American dollars. It's only a fraction of what the necklace is worth, both monetarily and emotionally, but it's enough. Enough to set this place up, to give my mother back her dignity, and to allow me to retire a very wealthy woman. I need to do all three of those things.

I've spent the last ten years of my life preparing for it. There's nothing you can say, nothing you can do to stop me."

He dug his hands into his pockets. "What makes you think he'll pay? Even if you get it, and manage to get out of Jaquir alive, he has only to notify the authorities."

"And admit publicly that he broke the law by keeping it from my mother?" Her lips curved. "Admit publicly that he was bested by a woman and bring shame on the House of Jaquir? He'll want *me* shamed, he may even want me dead, but he'll want his pride, and The Sun and the Moon even more."

"There's a chance he'll find a way to have all three."

Under the fur she shivered. "It's cold. Let's go back."

He said nothing as they drove. He could still see the way she looked surrounded by those filthy walls. It was easy enough to understand why she'd taken him there, why she'd told him of her plans. She'd made it clear in the way words never could that she was committed. He couldn't stop her. But there was something else he could do. Every decision he'd made in the past had been with an eye toward his own gain. He didn't regret it, and never would. He could only hope that this decision, one made selflessly, wouldn't bring regret.

The moment he closed the door of her apartment, he became businesslike. "You have blueprints of the palace?"

"Of course."

"Specs of security, timetables, alternate routes?"

She shrugged out of the mink. Her sweatshirt bagged at her hips. "I know my job."

"Show them to me."

After removing the hat, she shook out her hair. "What for? I don't need a consultant."

"I don't go into a job until I know all there is to know. We'll use the dining room table."

"What are you talking about?"

"That should be obvious." He brushed melting snow from his coat. "I'm going with you."

"No." She grabbed his arm before he could walk into the next room. Her fingers, long and delicate, dug in like spokes. "No, you're not."

"I assure you, you can afford my fee."

"This isn't a joke. I work alone. I always work alone."

He removed her hand from his arm and brushed it with his lips. "Your ego's showing, darling."

"Stop it." Swinging away, she hurtled up the steps. When he reached her, she was pacing the bedroom. "I've spent half of my life planning this. I know the country, the culture, and the risks. This is *my* vision, Philip, *my* life on the line. I won't have you there, I won't have your blood on my hands."

He stretched out on the bed, much as he had the night before. "My dear girl, I was picking locks while you were still playing with dolls. I'd stolen my first million before you were out of a training bra. You may be good, Addy, you may be very good, but you'll never be half the thief I am."

"You conceited, self-centered son of a bitch." She whirled on him, to his delight. "I'm as good as you ever were, and probably better. And I haven't spent the last five years on my duff pruning roses."

He only smiled. "I was never caught."

"Neither was I." When his smile widened, she swore and swung away again. "That was entirely different. You only suspected until I decided to tell you."

"You were sloppy when you broke into my room to get your necklace back—because you were angry. Because you let your emotions take over. Revenge might be your purpose now, but revenge is among the strongest of emotions. You're not going to Jaquir alone."

"You're retired."

He picked up a small jar of hand cream from her nightstand, unscrewed the lid, and sniffed. "I'm temporarily back in the game. You asked me once if I didn't long to do one last job, one last, incredible job." After replacing the jar, he tucked his hands behind his head. "I've decided this is it."

"This is my job. Find your own."

"You go to Jaquir with me or not at all. I have only to pick up the phone. There's a man in London who'd be very pleased to make your acquaintance."

"You'd do that?" Torn between fury and betrayal, she sat at the foot of the bed. "After everything I've told you?"

"I'll do whatever I have to do." He was quick. She'd almost forgotten how quick. His arms snaked out and pulled her against him. "I'm in love with you. That's a first for me. I have no intention of losing you. I've got a home in the country that might have been built with you in mind. Whatever it takes, you'll be there with me in the spring."

"Then I'll come in the spring." Too desperate to think clearly, she grabbed his sweater. "I'll give you my word, but I couldn't stand it if anything happened to you."

His eyes narrowed. His grip tightened. "Why?"

She shook her head and started to move away.

He started to demand, then forced himself to settle back. "All right, that can wait. Just listen. I'm not giving you a choice, not in this. With me or not at all. I'm trying to understand why this is so important to you, why you can't turn away from it. You'll have to understand why that makes it just as important to me."

When he released her, she sat back. He looked so much as he had that first night she'd seen him in the fog—dressed in black, his hair dragged back from his face, his eyes intense. She reached out, for the first time without his urging, to touch his face.

"You are a romantic, Philip."

"Apparently."

"I'll get the plans."

They spread all of Adrianne's research on the dining room table. She'd chosen the traditional here, Chippendale, Waterford, Irish linen. On one salmon-colored wall was a Maxfield Parrish sea nymph. Noting it, Philip had affirmed that Adrianne was more of a romantic than she wanted to admit.

Philip questioned her, point by point, moving forward, backtracking, overlapping while the snow fell steadily outside. When dusk came early, they switched on the lights and reheated coffee. The files and ledgers, the occasional click of a calculator gave their plotting the atmosphere of a business meeting. He made his own notes while they picked at an evening meal of cold sandwiches.

"How can you be sure the security system hasn't been updated?"

"I still have contacts inside." Adrianne wrinkled her

nose. The dregs of the coffee were bitter. "Cousins, aunts. When Abdu's son—"

"Your brother?"

"Abdu's son," she repeated. She wanted no emotion there. It would hurt too much to think of the little boy and how terribly she had loved him. "When he attended college in California, we spent a little time together. I was able to finesse some information. Like most members of the House of Jaquir who travel abroad, Fahid considered himself very Americanized, very progressive. At least while he was wearing Levis and driving a Porsche. He wanted to see Abdu make some changes politically and culturally. One of his complaints was that the palace remains much the same as it has for centuries. The guards still carry arms, when a modern electronic security system would make it unnecessary."

"That's outside."

"Yes. The guards and the palace's position are enough to insure security. Particularly since no one in Jaquir would consider challenging it. There are ramparts and battlements on this side, the sea on that, making a clandestine approach from the outside difficult. Which is why I will exercise my right to be housed inside."

"Give me the rundown on the vault one more time." He touched a finger to the blueprints.

"The vault is more than a hundred years old. It's twenty feet square, airtight, soundproof. Shortly after the turn of the century, an adulterous wife was locked inside so that she could die slowly, and alone, among a mountain of jewels. It was once called the treasure room, but since then has been known as Berina's Tomb." She rubbed eyes gritty with strain. "Sometime after World War Two the door of the vault was modernized. It has three locks, two combinations, and one key. The key is traditional. The ruler of Jaquir carries it on his person as a symbol of his power to open, or to close."

"And the alarms?"

She sighed and pushed her empty cup aside. "Installed in the seventies, when the oil boom brought so many infidels to Jaquir and the Middle East."

"Infidels?"

She ignored the amusement in his tone. "American businessmen in particular. As in most Arab countries, they were both used and despised. Their technology was needed, and needed desperately to allow Jaquir to profit from its oil. Money flowed, progress in certain areas was made. Electricity, modern roads, an upswing in education and health care. But foreigners were never trusted. In order to insure that none of them entered the palace without supervision, or that no one in the palace left to fraternize, the alarms were installed. Again, they are mainly to guard against break-in. There was, however, a system installed on the vault." She pushed the specs toward him. "Very basic, really. The wires can be clamped and deactivated, here and here at the source." She indicated the points. "I prefer that to cutting in this case, as it may be some time after the theft before I can leave the country."

"That takes care of the alarm when you unlock the door, not when it's opened."

"I've had to rig a remote control for the secondary alarm. It's very similar to the device used to control stereo components or a television from across the room. It's taken me nearly a year to perfect it."

"And you're quite sure you've succeeded?"

"I used it on the Barnsworth job last fall." She gave him a bland smile. "Electronics are rather a speciality of mine."

"I've noticed."

"With it, I'll be able to shut off the alarm from a distance of one hundred and twenty feet. The tricky part comes from a more human element. Guards patrol the palace inside as well. Until I'm in, I won't be able to learn the timetable."

"Security cameras?"

"None. Abdu abhors cameras."

"What's this?"

"The old tunnel into the harem from the king's rooms. A woman could be sent for and leave the harem without risking showing herself.'"

"Is it still used?"

"Possibly. Probably, why?"

"Just looking for escape routes. What's the drop from this window?"

"Sixty, perhaps seventy feet. Into the rocks and the sea."

"I prefer the harem."

"Yes, you'd only be castrated for being caught in there."

She said it briskly as she handed him a book. "This is an excellent work on the customs and the country. You'd do well to read up before you find yourself in a dark cell for touching a woman's arm in the marketplace or asking the wrong question."

"Thanks a lot."

"It isn't a place you'll understand, Philip. You'll be on your own while I'm inside. I still have no idea how I'll be able to contact you and let you know it's done."

"If you have the idea that I'll be kicking my heels in some hot, miserable hotel while you play princess in the palace, you're mistaken. I'm going in with you."

Sitting back, she waved a finger at the book. "You really are going to have to read that. Once I'm in Jaquir, you won't even be able to speak to me, much less go into the palace with me. That's a matter of law. As a woman, I'll be forbidden contact with any man outside of my family. If I were married, I could also see men in my husband's family."

"We'll have to find a way around that." He flipped through the book. "And you'll have to wrangle me an invitation to the palace."

"I'm hardly in the position to ask Abdu any favors. He has to let me come back or shame himself, but he doesn't have to grant me any requests."

"Then you'll have to marry me."

"Don't be ridiculous." She was up and grabbing the coffeepot, striding into the kitchen.

"We could postpone that, I suppose." He followed her into the kitchen, then began to rout in the refrigerator for something more interesting than sandwiches. "I would like you to meet my mother first."

"I'm never getting married." She dumped grounds into the trash.

"All right, we'll live in sin until the first child comes along, but back to the business at hand." He found a pint of ice cream in the freezer and, locating a spoon, ate out of the carton. "What if we were engaged—as far as Abdu was concerned," he finished before she could object again.

"We're not getting engaged as far as anyone's concerned."

"Think about it a minute. It makes sense. After all these years you're going back to Jaquir to make peace with your father before you marry. Just to fit in a bit better, the trip could have been at my insistence. I'm happy to play the arrogant chauvinist."

"You'd do it well." But she was thinking. Taking the carton from him, she sampled. "I suppose it could work. It might even be an advantage. He'd want you to stay at the palace so that he could look you over. He'd expect his approval to carry weight. If you're going to be there in any case, you might as well be of some use."

"Thank you very much." He pushed her nose into the carton. "Now, why don't you practice playing the quiet, subservient wife-to-be while I make some calls?"

"I'd rather swallow a roach."

"Be that as it may, it wouldn't hurt you to brush up on how to nod agreeably and walk two paces behind."

"I don't intend to be there more than two weeks." She wiped ice cream from her nose. "So don't get used to it."

"I'll do my best."

"Who are you calling?"

"I have to pull a few strings to get a visa for Jaquir. And then I'm going to insure that news of our engagement spreads quickly. All the better for cover, Your Highness."

"I'm not going to marry you, Philip."

"Right." He started out, then turned back. "One question. If I'm caught making love with you in Jaquir, what can I expect?"

"Being camel-whipped, at the very least. A beheading's more likely—for both of us."

"Hmmm. Gives a man something to think about."

Adrianne shook her head when the door swung shut behind him. Glancing down at the coffeepot, she set it aside. What she wanted now was a drink. A stiff one.

Part III

THE SWEET

Soon or late love is his own avenger.
— LORD BYRON

The bitter past, more welcome is the sweet.
— SHAKESPEARE

Chapter Twenty-Two

Seventeen years was a long time to wonder. It was a long time to plan. It was a long time to hate. The deep sapphire blue of the Mediterranean spread like a carpet below, disturbed by a few wispy clouds and a dot of land that was Cyprus. Jaquir was almost in reach. The waiting was over.

Adrianne settled back. Beside her in the cushy seat of the private jet, Philip dozed. His suit jacket, his tie, even his shoes were on the seat behind them so that he could stretch out unencumbered and take advantage of the last stage of their journey. Adrianne was fully dressed, fully awake, and fully aware of each minute that passed.

They'd made desperate love after their takeoff from Paris. Or perhaps it had been only she who had been desperate. She'd needed that wild, mindless intimacy of flesh against flesh as much as she'd needed the comfort and serenity that followed.

Most of her life had been devoted to this homecoming. Now the years had whittled down to minutes, and she was afraid. It wasn't a fear she could explain to herself or to Philip. The emotion didn't make the hands clammy or leave a taste of copper in the mouth. It rolled unsteadily in the stomach and beat, a dull ache, behind the eyes.

She still had the image of her father that had formed in a child's mind, with the intense love and fear that accompanied it. She could see him as he had been then, an athletically trim man with an unsmiling mouth and strong, beautiful hands.

For two decades she had lived under Western law, Western tradition, Western beliefs. Never once had she allowed herself to doubt that she was, in every way, a Western woman. But the truth, long buried, was that she had bedouin blood, and that blood might respond in a way no American woman would understand.

Who would she become once she was back in Jaquir, living in her father's house, bound by the laws of the Koran and the traditions decreed and enforced by men? Much sharper than the fear of being caught, of being imprisoned or executed, was the fear of losing the woman she had worked so hard to become.

That fear kept her from making promises to Philip. It kept her from saying the words that came so easily to the lips of other women. She did love him, but love wasn't the soft, silky words the poets spoke of. Love, with its twin edges, was the one factor that weakened so many women, that pushed them to compromise their own wants, their own needs and wants of another.

The plane dipped. The sea seemed to rise up toward them. Nerves taut, Adrianne laid a hand on Philip's shoulder. "I have to get ready. We'll be landing soon."

He came awake instantly, recognizing the tension in her voice. "You can still change your mind."

"No. I can't." Rising, she moved across the aisle to open a flight bag. "Remember, after we deplane we'll be taken to the terminal in separate cars. There's customs to deal with." While she spoke, she bound her hair in a black scarf until no wisp showed. "That can be a humiliating process, but Abdu's influence should take the edge off. I won't see you again until we're inside the palace, and I can't say when that will be allowed. Outside, there can be no contact at all. Inside, because I am not full-blooded, and am believed to be marrying a Westerner, the rules will be somewhat more relaxed. Don't come to me under any circumstances. If and when possible, I will come to you."

"Forty-eight hours." While he knotted his tie he watched her cloak herself in the black *abaaya*. It covered her from neck to foot, as drab as sackcloth. More than her eyes or the color of her skin, it made her a woman of Islam. "If you haven't found a way to contact me by then, I'll find you."

"And be deported at the very least." It was the veil that bothered her the most. Rather than attach it, Adrianne let it dangle from her fingers. With his suit jacket smoothed over his shoulders, Philip looked very British and suddenly foreign. She ignored the ache in her throat where her heart had begun to pound. The gulf was widening. "You have to trust my judgment in this, Philip. I intend to spend no more than two weeks in Jaquir, and I intend to leave with the necklace."

"I'd rather you made that we."

"We, then." With a hint of a smile she waited until he'd stepped into his shoes. "Just make sure you convince Abdu that you'll make me a proper husband. Oh, and haggle over the bride price."

He stepped closer to take both of her hands. They were steady against his, but cold. "How much do you figure you're worth?"

"A million would be a good starting point."

"A million what?"

It was a relief that she could still laugh as she took her seat and strapped in. "Pounds sterling. Anything less, with the background you've invented for yourself, would be an insult."

"In that case we'd better start with this." He took a box out of his pocket. The ring inside it made Adrianne pull her hand back. Philip merely took it in his and slipped the diamond on her third finger. Her reaction was precisely the reason he'd waited until the last minute. This way she'd have little chance to argue. "You can consider it part of the cover if you like."

It was more than five carats, and from its icy white fire, Adrianne thought it would be Russian, of the finest water. Like the best diamonds, it was both passionate and aloof. Against the stark black of her *abaaya* it shot flame—and made her want more than she should have. "A costly deception."

"The jeweler assured me he'd be more than happy to buy it back."

She looked up quickly at that, and saw his grin just before his mouth covered hers. There was fire here, too, climbing higher even as the plane bumped to earth. For a moment she wanted to forget everything but this, the promise on her finger, the seduction of the kiss.

"I'll go first." After taking a long breath, she unhooked

her belt. "Be careful, Philip. I don't want your blood on The Sun and the Moon."

"In two weeks we have a date in Paris with a bottle of champagne."

"Make it a magnum," she told him, then veiled her face.

It had changed. Even knowing that the oil boom had swept through Jaquir in the seventies, knowing that the West had pushed its way through hadn't prepared her for the huddle of buildings, some shiny with steel and glass, or the roads smoothly paved to accommodate the now heavy traffic. When she had left, the tallest building in Karfia, the capital of Jaquir, had been the water tower. Now it was dwarfed by office buildings and hotels. Still, despite the modern highways and glittering glass, it seemed as though the city could, if Allah decreed, slip back into the desert.

There were huge Mercedes trucks barreling down the highway. Freighters crammed the port while shipments waiting for clearance lined the docks. She knew that Jaquir straddled the political fence, managing through skill, guile, and money to placate its neighbors in the East and its nervous backers in the West. War raged close by the borders, but Jaquir, at least on the surface, clung to neutrality.

It had stayed so much the same. As they drove into town, Adrianne saw that in spite of the buildings, the modern roads, and the stubborn struggle of Western expatriates, Jaquir was as Jaquir wished to be. She had seen that at the airport, as women, loaded down with baggage, bedding, and strollers were herded into separate buses and ushered through a door marked WOMEN AND FAMILIES, always policed by men barking orders. She saw it now as the minarets on the mosque pierced through the pristine blue sky.

Noon prayer call was over, so the shops and markets were open. Though she kept her window up, she could almost hear the hum of activity, the cadence of Arabic, the click of prayer beads. Women wandered the stalls, in groups or accompanied by a male relation. Policing the streets, jealously guarding the religious laws were the *matawain* with their straggly henna-tipped beards and camel whips. Through the tinted window of her limo Adrianne watched one advance on a Western woman who'd had the bad sense to push up her sleeves and reveal her arms.

No, it may have been the last years of the twentieth century, but Jaquir had changed little.

Date palms lined the road. So did Mercedes, Rolls Royces, and limos. The House of Dior boasted two doors, one for males, one for females. She caught the glint of precious stones beaming in the midday sun in a shop window. There was a donkey, laden with dust, being led by a man in a white *throbe* and broken sandals.

Here much of the housing was made of mud, and no more permanent than the desert sand. Yet flowers climbed the walls. Windows were latticed, always latticed, to hide the women within—not because they were prized and revered, Adrianne thought, but because they were considered foolish creatures, victims of their own uncontrollable sexual drive.

Men, robed and turbaned, sat on red carpets eating sandwiches. *Shwarma.* Odd that the taste of the spiced lamb on flat bread came back to her, she mused.

The limo passed through the market and climbed. Here the houses were more elegant, shaded by trees. One or two even boasted the luxury of grass. She thought she remembered visiting in one of them, drinking green tea in a dim parlor with the sound of silk rustling and the smell of incense clogging the air.

They drove through the gates to the palace, past the dark, blank eyes of the guards. This, too, had changed little, though her child's mind had lent it more grandeur than it deserved. In the harsh afternoon sun its stucco walls were brilliantly white. The green tile roof was an arrogant slash of color. Its windows, most curtained against the glare, glinted. Its minarets rose, but in deference to Allah rose no higher than those of the mosque. Parapets circled so that in times of civil strife or foreign attack it could be defended. The sea hammered at its back. Its gardens were lush, shielding it from prying eyes, and, more, shielding the women of the house from temptation when they chose to wander through them.

Though there was a door for women as well as one for men, it was to the garden rather than the main entrance the limo drove. Adrianne's brow rose only slightly. So, she was to be delivered to the harem before seeing Abdu. That was perhaps for the best.

She waited until the driver opened her door. Though she was certain he must have been a relation, however distant, he didn't offer a hand to assist her out. His eyes remained carefully averted. Gathering up her skirts, she stepped out into the blast of heat and scent. Without a backward glance she let herself in through the garden gate.

There was a trickle of water from the fountain, the fountain she knew her father had had built for her mother during their first year of marriage. It fed a small pond where carp grew as long as a man's arm. Around it flowers bent, drawn to the moisture.

Before she reached the hidden door, it was opened. Adrianne stepped through, beyond the black-clad servant, and smelled the women's scents that brought her back to childhood. As the door shut, closing her in, she did what she had longed to do throughout the long drive from the airport. She pulled off her veil.

"Adrianne." A woman stepped into the shadowed light. She smelled strongly of musk and wore a red-sequined gown suited to a nineteenth-century ball. "Welcome home." As she spoke, the woman gave the traditional greeting, a kiss on both cheeks. "You were only a child when I last saw you. I am your aunt, Latifa, wife of Fahir, brother of your father."

Adrianne returned the greeting. "I remember you, Aunt Latifa. I've seen Duja. She's well and happy. She sends love to you and honor to her father."

Latifa nodded. Though Adrianne outranked her, she had given birth to five strong sons and held a place of honor and envy in the harem. "Come, there is refreshment. The others want to welcome you."

Here, too, little had changed. There was the scent of spiced coffee and the heavy seduction of perfume mingling with the bite of incense. A long table had been spread with a white cloth edged in gold and was laden with food no less colorful than the gowns of the women. There were silks and satins, and even though the temperature soared, the sheen of velvet. Beads and spangles glistened. There was the warmth of gold, the ice of silver, and always the sparkle of jewels.

Bracelets clanged and lace whispered as traditional greetings were exchanged.

She brushed her lips over the cheeks of Abdu's second wife, the woman who so many years before had caused Phoebe such unhappiness. Adrianne could find no resentment. A woman did as a woman was bid. That was confirmed as Leiha, already the mother of seven, and more than forty, was obviously pregnant again.

There were cousins she remembered and a score of minor princesses. Some had cropped or crimped their hair. This was, like the vivid gowns, something they did for their own pleasure, and like children with a new toy, to show off among themselves.

There was Sara, Abdu's latest wife, a small, big-eyed girl of about sixteen who was already swollen with child. From the looks of it, both she and Leiha had conceived at about the same time. Adrianne noticed that the stones on her fingers and at her ears were no less brilliant than those worn by Leiha. Such was the law. A man could take four wives, but only if he could treat each equally.

Phoebe had never been an equal here, but Adrianne couldn't find it in her heart to despise a young girl because of it. "You are welcome here," Sara said in a whispery, musical voice that stumbled over the English phrase.

"This is Princess Yasmin." Adrianne's aunt put a hand on the shoulder of a girl of about twelve with dusky cheeks and thick gold hoops through her ears. "Your sister."

She hadn't expected this. She'd known she would meet Abdu's other children, but she hadn't expected to look into eyes the same shape and color as her own. She wasn't prepared for the spark of kinship or recognition. Because of it, her greeting was stilted when she bent to kiss Yasmin's cheeks.

"Welcome to my father's house."

"Your English is good."

Yasmin lifted her brows in a gesture that told Adrianne though she was months away from the veil, she was a woman. "I attend school so that I will not be ignorant when I go to my husband."

"I see." The acknowledgment was equal to equal as Adrianne removed her *abaaya*. Gesturing a servant aside, she

305

folded it herself, and carefully. Sewn into the lining were the tools of her trade. "You'll have to tell me what you've learned."

Yasmin studied Adrianne's simple white skirt and blouse with the eyes of a fashion critic. Once Duja had smuggled in newspaper pictures of Adrianne, so Yasmin knew her sister was beautiful. She thought it a pity Adrianne hadn't worn something red that glittered.

"First I will take you to my grandmother."

Behind them women were already dipping into the buffet. Food, the richer the better, was a favored recreation. Talk was already centering around babies and shopping.

The old woman seated in a brocade chair was resplendent in emerald green. The wrinkles and folds of her face had fallen into jowls, but her hair was stubbornly hennaed. Fingers, curled a bit with arthritis, were studded with rings that flashed as she cuddled a boy of two or three on her lap. Two servants flanked her, waving fans so that the smoke from a brass incense jar would scent her hair.

It had been nearly twenty years, and Adrianne had been only eight when she'd left, but she remembered. The tears started so abruptly, so stunningly, she could do nothing to stop them. Instead of the greeting expected, she went to her knees and laid her head in her grandmother's lap. The mother of her father.

Her bones were thin and brittle. Adrianne could feel them beneath the stiff satin. Her scent was the same, incredibly the same, a mixture of poppies and spice. As she felt the hand stroke her hair, she leaned into it. The sweetest, the kindest memories she had of Jaquir were of this woman brushing her hair and telling her stories of pirates and princes.

"I knew I would see you again." Jiddah, a frail seventy, the mother of twelve, the only wife King Ahmend had ever taken, sat stroking the hair of her much-loved grandchild and cuddling her newest against her breast. "I wept when you left us, and weep when you come back."

Like a child, Adrianne dried her cheeks with the backs of her hands. She rose up for the kiss. "Grandmother. You're more beautiful than I remembered. I've missed you."

"You come back to me a grown woman, with the look of your father."

She stiffened, but managed to smile. "Perhaps I have the look of my grandmother."

Jiddah smiled back, showing teeth too white and straight to be her own. The dentures were new, and she was as proud of them as she was of the emerald collar at her throat. "Perhaps." She accepted tea from a servant. "Chocolate for my granddaughter. You still have a taste for it?"

"Yes." Adrianne settled on a cushion by Jiddah's feet. "I remember that you used to give me a handful all wrapped in red and silver paper. I'd take so much time unwrapping them that they'd melt. But you never scolded me." She noticed then that Yasmin was still standing beside her, her young face impassive but for a glint in her eyes that might have been jealousy. Without thinking, Adrianne lifted a hand and drew her down to the cushion. "Does Grandmother still tell stories?"

"Yes." After a brief hesitation, Yasmin unbent. "Will you tell me about America and the man you will marry?"

With her head against her grandmother's knee, and a cup of green tea in her hand, Adrianne began. It wasn't until later that she realized she'd been speaking in Arabic.

As far as palaces went, Philip decided he preferred the European style. Something in stone with mullioned windows and old, dark wood. This one was dim, as blinds and shades and lattices closed out the power of the sun. It was rich, certainly, with wall hangings spun from silk, and Ming vases tucked into wall niches. It was modern. The bath in the suite he'd been given had water that steamed hot out of gold faucets. He supposed he was too British to appreciate the Eastern flavor of prayer rugs and gauzy mosquito netting.

His rooms overlooked the garden, which he could approve of. In spite of the sun, he threw open a window and let the hot scent of jasmine blow in.

Where was Adrianne?

Her brother, Crown Prince Fahid, had met him at the airport. The young man, barely into his twenties, had worn a burnoose over an impeccably tailored suit. Philip had found him a perfect example of East meets West with his excellent English and his inscrutable manners. His only reference to

Adrianne had been to tell Philip that she would be taken to the women's quarters.

Closing his eyes, he imagined the blueprints. She would be two floors down and in the east wing. The vault was in the opposite end of the palace. Tonight he would take a tour on his own. But for now—he flipped open his suitcase—he would play the perfect guest and prospective bridegroom.

He'd taken advantage of the huge sunken tub and had finished his unpacking when he heard the prayer call. The deep throated voice of the muezzin came through the open window. *Allahu Akbar.* God is great.

With a glance at his watch Philip calculated that this would be the third call of the day. There would be another at sundown, then the last at an hour past.

The markets and suqs would close, and men would kneel to touch their faces to the ground. Inside the palace, as everywhere else, all business would stop in submission to the will of Allah.

Moving quietly, Philip opened his door. It was as good a time as any to take stock.

He thought it best to check out his neighbors first. The room next to his was empty, the drapes drawn, the bed made with military precision. The room across was the same. He edged down the hall and pushed open another door. Here there was a man, no, a boy, bent in supplication, his body facing south toward Mecca. His prayer rug was threaded with gold and the hangings over the bed were royal blue. Philip pulled the door to before making his way to the second floor.

Abdu's offices would be there, along with the council rooms. There was time enough to look if warranted. He walked down to the main floor, where the rooms were quiet as a tomb. Conscious of the time elapsing, he made his way through the winding corridors to the vault room.

The door was locked. He had only to take a nail file out of his pocket to open it. With a quick glance right, then left, he slipped inside and shut the door behind him.

Where other rooms had been dim, this was dark. There were no windows here. Wishing he'd risked bringing a flashlight, he groped his way in the direction of the vault. Its door was smooth steel and cool to the touch. Using his fingertips as his eyes, Philip measured its length, its width, the position of the locks.

As Adrianne had told him, there were two combinations. He was careful not to touch the dials. He used his nail file to measure and found the keyhole oversize and old-fashioned. The picks he carried wouldn't work on a lock that old, but there were always other ways. Satisfied, he stepped back. He'd need to come back with a light, but that was for later.

His hand was nearly on the doorknob when he heard footsteps outside. There wasn't time to swear as he plastered himself against the wall behind the door.

There were two men speaking Arabic. One of them, if tone was any indication, was angry, the other tense. Philip willed them to pass by. Then he heard Adrianne's name. He could only curse the fact that he didn't speak Arabic.

They were arguing about her. He was sure of it. There was enough venom in one of the voices to have his muscles tense and his hands ball into fists. There was a sharp command answered by silence, then the impatient click of heels on tile as one man strode off. With his ear at the door Philip heard the one remaining mutter a curse in plain English. Prince Fahid, Philip mused. Then it was certain the angry voice had come from Abdu. Why were Adrianne's father and brother arguing about her? Over her?

He waited until Fahid walked away, then let himself out. The hall was deserted again, the door locked. With his hands in his pockets Philip strolled in the direction of the gardens. If found there, he could make a plausible enough excuse about his interest in flora. The truth was, he wanted out, and he wanted to think.

Adrianne hadn't realized it would be so hard to do what she had come to do. Not technically—she was confident in her skill, and in Philip's. What she hadn't known was that there would be so many memories. Like ghosts, they whispered to her, brushed against her. There was something comforting about the harem with its women's talk, its women's scents, its women's secrets. It was possible to forget its confines for a short time and bask in its security. No matter what happened now, she'd never be able to fully turn her back again.

Talk went on, still focusing on sex and shopping and

fertility, but there were new things. A cousin who'd become a doctor, another who'd earned her teaching degree. There was a young aunt who worked in construction as an administrator, though all contact with the men she worked with was done by letter or phone. Education had opened up to women, and they were taking it with both hands. Male instructors taught over closed circuit television, but they taught. And the women learned.

If there was a way to juggle the old with the new, they were going to find it.

She didn't notice the servant slip in and lean close to her grandmother's ear. When Jiddah touched a hand to her hair, Adrianne turned and smiled.

"Your father wishes to see you."

Adrianne felt her pleasure dry up as if it had been a pool struck by the desert sun. She rose. Though she slipped the *abaaya* over her shoulders, she refused the veil. He would see her face, and he would remember.

Chapter Twenty-Three

Like Jaquir, its ruler had changed yet had remained, essentially, the same. He'd aged. It was the first thing that struck Adrianne when she saw him. Her memory, enhanced by the old newspaper prints her mother had hoarded, was of a man hardly older than she herself was now, with a hawklike, unlined face and rich black hair. The hawk was still there in features carved sharp and hard, but there were lines that time and sun had dug deeply. They were chiseled beside a mouth that smiled rarely, etched around eyes that watched and measured. His hair was still rich, still brushed back like a mane, as full as in his youth and part of his vanity. Silver glinted in it. Over the years he'd put on very little flesh so that his body remained one of a soldier.

His white *throbe* was embroidered with gold, his sandals studded with jewels. If possible, age had made him only more handsome in the way it does with men. It was a face women would be drawn to even though, or perhaps because, there was so little compassion in it.

Adrianne's stomach clenched as she approached. She moved slowly, not from uncertainty, not even from respect, but from the desire to bring this moment, so long awaited, so long imagined, into clear focus. Nothing had been forgotten. Nothing would be forgotten.

As with that one stunning moment of memory in the harem, there were scents here—polish, flowers, a trace of incense. She continued, moving closer to a past she had never fully released. She had walked toward him before, or cowered away. Until that moment she hadn't realized she couldn't recall one instance when he had come to her.

He hadn't brought her to one of his private rooms, but to the large, brightly lit area where he would give his weekly *majlis*, or audiences. The drapes on the windows were heavy, the royal blue he had always preferred. The rug was old, one his father, his grandfather, and the kings before them had all walked over. It had a dense pattern of blue and black worked through with gold in a sinuous design, like a snake. There were urns as tall as a man on either side of the door. Legend had it that they had been brought from Persia to another Abdu two centuries before. Inside each had been a virgin.

A lion fashioned from gold with sapphire eyes guarded the chair of blue silk, where Abdu would sit and grant his time to his people.

Though this room was closed to women on such occasions, it showed Adrianne that he still thought of her as a subject, not as a daughter. Like the virgins of Persia, she would be expected to submit to the will of the king.

She stopped in front of him. Though he wasn't a tall man, she had to tilt her chin to keep her eyes directly on his. Whatever he felt, if he felt, was carefully masked. He bent and gave her the traditional greeting. He barely touched his lips to her cheeks, and with less emotion than he might have given a stranger. It hurt. She hadn't expected it, hadn't been prepared for it, and it hurt.

"You are welcome here."

"I'm grateful for your permission to return."

He sat, and after a long, silent moment, gestured to a chair. "Are you a child of Allah?"

This she had expected. Religion was breath in Jaquir. "I am not a Muslim," she said steadily, "but God is One."

Apparently it satisfied him, because he signaled for a servant to pour tea. It was a concession of sorts that two cups were waiting. "It pleases me that you will marry. A woman requires a man's protection, his guidance."

"I'm not marrying Philip for his protection or his guidance." She sipped at the tea. "Nor does he marry me to increase his tribe."

She had spoken flatly, as a man might speak to another man, not as a woman to a king. He could have struck her; it was his right. Instead, he sat back, cupping the tea in both hands. The cup was delicate, of fragile French porcelain. His hands were broad and studded with rings. "You've become a woman of the West."

"My life is there, as my mother's was."

"We will not speak of your mother." He set his cup down, then held up a hand as a servant sprang forward to refill it.

"She spoke of you. Often."

Something came into his eyes. Adrianne couldn't prevent a part of her from hoping it would be regret. But it was anger. "As my daughter you are welcome here, and with the honor that is your right as a member of the House of Jaquir. While you are here, you will abide by the rules and traditions. You will cover your hair and cast down your eyes. Your dress and speech will be modest. If you bring me shame, you will be punished as I would punish any woman of my family."

Because her fingers weren't steady, she dug them into the teacup. After all these years, she thought, so many years, and he could speak only in orders and threats. Her plan to be the woman he would expect was overrun with her need to be what she was.

"I bring you no shame, but I feel shame. My mother suffered and died miserably while you did nothing to help." When he rose, she stood as well, so quickly that the cup fell from her hand and shattered on the tiles. "How could you do nothing?"

"She was nothing to me."

"Nothing but your wife," Adrianne tossed back. "It would have taken so little, but you gave nothing. You abandoned her, and me. The shame is yours."

He struck her then, with a backhanded blow that snapped her head back and made her eyes water. It wasn't the careless slap an angry parent might give an ill-mannered child, but the deliberate, full-fledged hit a man deals an enemy. If she hadn't crashed into the heavy chair and gripped for support, she would have fallen. Though she staggered, she managed to stay on her feet.

Her breath came quickly as she fought for control, fought to keep the stinging tears back. Slowly, she lifted a hand to wipe at the blood where a jewel from his ring had nicked her. Their eyes held, so similar in shape, so alike in expression. It hadn't been her he had struck, and they both knew it. It had been Phoebe. It was still Phoebe.

"Years ago," she managed, "I might have been grateful for that much attention from you."

"I will say this, then it will not be spoken of again." Carelessly, he signaled for the broken china to be cleared. The rage she incited in him was rage unbecoming a king. "Your mother left Jaquir and forfeited all rights, all loyalty, and all honor. By doing so, she also forfeited yours. She was weak, as women are, but she was also sly and corrupt."

"Corrupt?" Though it might have earned her another blow, Adrianne couldn't bite back the words. "How can you speak of her so? She was the kindest, most pure-hearted woman I've ever known."

"She was an actress." He said it as though a word could taste vile. "She flaunted herself before men. My only shame is that I allowed myself to be blinded by her, to bring her to my country, to lie with her as a man lies with any whore."

"You called her that before." This time Adrianne's voice shook. "How does a man speak so about the woman he married, about the woman he shared a child with?"

"A man can marry a woman, can plant his seed within her, but cannot change her nature. She would not embrace Islam. When I brought her here and my eyes were cleared, she would not accept her place, her duties."

"She was ill and unhappy."

"She was weak and sinful." He held up his hand, a man used to doing no more to be obeyed. "You are the result of my early blindness and are here only because my blood runs through you and because Fahid interceded on your behalf. This is a matter of honor, my honor. You remain only so long as you respect that."

She wanted to toss it back in his face, to shout, to scream that he had no honor. The part of her that had still yearned for love closed off. Not even the most clever of thieves could have broken the lock now. Adrianne folded her hands. She lowered her eyes. Gestures of submission. He could have struck her again, and she would have accepted it. He could have maligned her mother, insulted her, and she would have accepted it. Such was the power of revenge.

"I'm in my father's house and respect my father's wishes."

He nodded, expecting no less from a woman of his family. His kingship sat on him comfortably. When he had returned to Jaquir so many years before with a queen, a Western queen, he had been bewitched. He had forgotten his roots, his duties, his laws because of a woman.

His punishment had been that his first child had been a female, and his queen unable to give him more children. Now the daughter of that shameful marriage stood before him, her head bowed, her hands folded. Since Allah had willed that she would spring from his first seed, he would give her her due, but no more.

With one sharp word and a gesture a servant hurried over to give him a box. "A gift, for your betrothal."

Her control was back, making it easy for her to reach out. Adrianne lifted the lid. The rich purple of amethyst glinted up at her, set in heavy, intricately worked gold. The center stone was square cut, as wide as her thumb. A necklace suitable for a princess. The price of it, had it come from him years before, might have changed both their destinies.

Now it was just a colored rock. She'd always stolen better ones.

"You're very generous. I'll think of my father whenever I wear it." That was a promise.

He signaled again before he spoke. "I will meet your betrothed. Then, while we discuss the terms of the marriage, you will go back to your quarters or walk in the garden."

She tucked the box into the folds of her *abaaya* so that he wouldn't see her fingers tighten on it. "As you wish."

When Philip followed the servant into the room, he wasn't expecting to see Adrianne at all, much less to see her still dressed in black with her head bowed and her shoulders braced as if for a blow. Beside her, Abdu's white *throbe* was a striking contrast. They stood close, so close the materials nearly touched, but there was no sense of reunion or kinship. Abdu looked over her head as if she didn't exist.

"With your permission," she murmured.

"Yes." Abdu gave it without glancing at her.

"King Abdu ibn Faisal Rahman al-Jaquir, head of the House of Jaquir, sheikh of sheikhs, may I present Philip Chamberlain, the man, if you consent, I will marry."

"Mr. Chamberlain." With a hand extended, Abdu stepped forward. He could behave in Western fashion when it suited him. "Welcome to Jaquir, and to my house."

315

"Thank you." Philip clasped hands. Abdu's was smooth and strong.

"Your rooms are suitable?"

"More than. I'm in your debt."

"You are my guest." He flicked a glance toward Adrianne. "You may go."

It was the tone one used to dismiss a servant. Philip caught it, resented it, had nearly decided to be amused by it. Then she lifted her face. The look was brief, but long enough for Philip to see the mark along her cheekbone that was already darkening to a bruise. She bowed her head again, and with her long skirts whispering around her, she left them.

He had to take a breath, a long, slow breath. For her sake, he wouldn't do or say anything rash. Perhaps he'd been mistaken. Surely at their first meeting Abdu couldn't have struck the daughter he hadn't seen in almost twenty years.

"Will you sit?"

Pulling himself back, Philip turned to Abdu. The eyes that met his were very sharp, very measuring. "Thank you." The moment he had, fresh cups were hurried over and tea was poured.

"You are British."

"Yes, I was born in England and have spent most of my life there, though I travel frequently."

"In your business." Ignoring the tea, Abdu folded his many-ringed hands. "You deal in the buying and selling of gems."

He'd worked with that cover for years. With Interpol's assistance, it was solid. "Yes. It requires a good eye and a flair for bargaining. I enjoy handling stones."

"Arabs are natural bargainers, and we have always understood the value of stones."

"Of course. The ruby on your third finger. May I?"

With a lift of brow, Abdu held out his hand.

"Seven to eight carats, Burmese at a guess—excellent color, what they call a pigeon-blood red with the vitreous luster you expect from a quality stone." Sitting back, Philip picked up his cup. "I recognize, and respect, gems of great value, Your Highness. Which is why I want your daughter."

"You're frank, but there is more involved in a marriage of this nature than your wants." Abdu said nothing more for a moment. He'd given Adrianne's marriage some thought, as he would any minor social or political matter. If she had been of pure blood, he would never have sanctioned her marriage to a European, and certainly not some pale-skinned British gem merchant. However, her blood was tainted. She was of much less value to him than a good horse. In a small way, she could be a link between Jaquir and Europe. More important, he had no desire to have her in Jaquir.

"I've had little time to explore your background, Mr. Chamberlain, but what I have learned is satisfying enough." And perhaps unlike her mother she would bear sons. Grandsons in England could be of some use in the future. "If Adrianne had remained in my house, a different marriage would have been arranged for her, one that suited her position. However, since that is not the case, I'm inclined to approve—if terms can be agreed upon."

"I don't claim to be an expert on your culture, but I understand that a settlement is customary."

"The bride price, a gift which you will offer to my daughter. This gift will be hers, and remain hers." He didn't think of The Sun and the Moon, but Philip did. "It is also expected that you will make a gift to her family, in recompense for our loss of her."

"I see. And what gift would recompense you for Adrianne?"

He considered toying with Philip. The reports had indicated the Englishman was wealthy, but there were things more important to Abdu than money. The first of these was pride. "Six camels."

Though his brow shot up, Philip managed, barely, to conceal amusement. Thoughtfully, he tapped a finger on the arm of his chair. "Two."

Abdu was more pleased than he would have been with an easy agreement. "Four."

Though he wasn't sure where he was going to get his hands on one camel, much less four, Philip nodded. "Agreed."

"So it shall be written." Still watching Philip, Abdu barked an order to a servant. "My secretary will draft the contracts, in both Arabic and English. This is satisfactory?"

"I'm in your country, Your Highness. We'll do things your way." He set aside his cup and longed for a cigarette. The tea was laced with some spice his British palate found mildly objectionable. "As Adrianne's father you would be concerned that she will be well provided for."

Abdu's face remained impassive. There may have been a trace of sarcasm in Philip's voice, or it may have been the British accent. "Of course."

"Of course. I had a million pounds in mind for her settlement."

It was rare for Abdu to be taken by surprise, rarer still for that surprise to show on his face. The Englishman was either mad or besotted. Perhaps Adrianne, like her mother, had the power to blind a man. But the Englishman's fate was no more concern to him than that of the daughter who reminded him, just by existing, of a mistake. He wouldn't give her the honor of bargaining.

"It shall be written. We will have a meal this evening to introduce you to my family, and to announce the betrothal." He rose in dismissal.

"It will be my pleasure." He'd been prepared to find Abdu cold, but the reality was more rigid, more dispassionate than any speculation. "Will you attend the wedding in the spring?"

"The spring?" Abdu's lips curved for the first time in what might have been a smile. "If you wish to have a ceremony in your own country, it is no concern of mine. However, the marriage will take place here, next week, as is fitting under the laws and traditions of Jaquir. You will wish to rest until this evening. A servant will show you the way."

Philip stood where he was as Abdu left him. He might have laughed, but he doubted Adrianne would find the news amusing.

The evening was to be a mixture of the old ways and the new. Adrianne bound her hair but ignored the veil. She dressed modestly, adhering to *aurat,* things that cannot be shown, by choosing a gown with long sleeves and skirt and a high neck. But the label was Saint Laurent. Word had spread through the women's quarters that Philip would be introduced. That alone told her that he had pulled it off. Now that Philip and the engagement had been accepted, the first stage of the plan was behind her.

It was too late to turn back. It had always been too late. The diamond on her finger winked in the mirror as she concealed the bruise on her cheek with makeup. Symbols, she thought, of the two men who had changed her life.

Stepping back, she took a last inventory. She'd chosen black deliberately, knowing the other women would be arrayed in peacock colors. In black she would appear only more modest and obedient. Reluctantly, she fastened the amethyst around her neck. Abdu would expect it. Until she left Jaquir she intended to go on giving him what he expected.

Philip had been right about one thing. When she allowed her emotions to surface, she became reckless. However true her words to Abdu had been that afternoon, they had been rashly said. She had the bruise to remind her that he was not now, nor had he ever been, a man to listen to a woman's heart.

She touched a finger to it again. She wasn't angry about the blow, or even resentful. The pain had been brief, and the mark itself served to remind her that no matter how many new buildings, new roads, new freedoms existed in Jaquir, men still ruled however they saw fit. She was less of a daughter to Abdu than she was a thing to be married off and shuttled out of the country, where whatever mistakes she made wouldn't reflect on his honor.

She wasn't sorry for that, but she was sorry that she had harbored a place in her heart for the hope that there might have been love and regret and reunion.

Hope was dead. Adrianne turned at the knock on the door. Now there was only purpose.

"*Yellah.*" Yasmin, dressed in bright striped satin, grabbed her hand. "Come on. Hurry," she repeated in English. "My father has sent for us. Why do you wear black when red would be more flattering?" Even as Adrianne's lips twitched, Yasmin was pulling her toward the other women.

The men were already in the salon. Abdu, three of his brothers, his two sons, a smattering of cousins. Adrianne flicked a glance at the boy who was her younger brother. He'd only be fourteen, but he was already ranged with the men. In a matter of seconds they studied one another. She saw a mirror of the curiosity she was feeling, the same grudging kinship. This time she didn't try to prevent the smile, and was rewarded by the brief curving of his lips. In his smile she saw her grandmother.

319

Then there was Philip, looking wonderfully, coolly European. Like an oasis, she thought, refreshing and comforting. She wanted to reach out, if only for a moment, and link hands. Make a connection. Instead, she kept her hands folded in front of her.

He wanted five minutes alone with her. There had been no opportunity for a single word since they'd stepped off the jet. He'd have preferred to tell Adrianne about the monkey wrench Abdu had tossed in the works. Five minutes, he thought, fretting against the customs that were both cover and restraint. There was a volcano in her. He'd seen it flare briefly in her eyes that afternoon. There was no telling if Abdu's announcement would cause it to erupt.

One by one, with a formality suited to Buckingham Palace, the women were introduced to him. In their opulent party wear they were a rainbow of dark women with dark eyes and soft voices. Some gowns were elegant, some gaudy, some chic, some foolish, but the women were all identical in attitude. Heads were lowered, eyes downcast, pretty ringed hands were folded at the ends of concealing sleeves.

He watched Adrianne step forward, at her father's gesture, to greet her brothers. Fahid kissed her cheeks, then gave her arms a quick squeeze. "I'm happy for you, Adrianne. Welcome home."

He meant it, she realized. While it was impossible for Jaquir to be home she felt a comfort. *I love Adrianne.* He had often said it to her, simply, honestly, in the way of children. Those children were gone, but there was something of them left in the way their eyes met, held. How could she have known, after doing without for so long, that family would mean something?

"I'm glad to see you again." And she, too, meant it.

"Our brother Rahman."

She waited, as was proper, for him to kiss her. It wasn't restraint she felt from him when his lips brushed her cheeks, but shyness.

"Welcome, sister. We praise Allah for bringing you back to us."

Rahman. He had the eyes of a poet and the name of their great-grandfather, the warrior. Adrianne wanted to speak with him, forge some link. But Abdu was looking at her.

Philip continued to watch as she was presented to the rest of her family. Her younger brother he recognized as the boy who had been praying in the room close to his own. How would it feel, he wondered, to face a brother you'd never seen before? Strange, but until now he'd never considered the fact that he might have siblings. He thought of the gulf between Adrianne and the other children of her father. Perhaps it was best never to know.

She was speaking Arabic smoothly, musically. That more than anything made the entire scene like a dream. Though he willed her to, she didn't even glance in his direction, but moved, as directed, to Abdu's side.

"Tonight we rejoice." In deference to Philip, Abdu spoke in clear, precise English. "I give this woman of my family to this man. Under the will of Allah, and for His honor, they shall be married." Taking Adrianne's hand, he placed it in Philip's. "May she be a fruitful and modest wife."

Adrianne might have smiled at that, but she saw her grandmother, supported by younger women, wipe a tear from her eye.

"The documents have been signed," Abdu continued. "The price set. The ceremony will take place one week from today. *Inshallah.*"

Philip felt her fingers jerk in his. Her head came up, and for two heartbeats the volcano was there, smoldering. Then she was lowering her eyes again and accepting wishes for happiness and children.

They still had exchanged no words when she, along with the other women, filed out to where they could celebrate out of sight of the men.

Adrianne's dreams were disturbing enough to make her toss in bed. They weren't clear. One bled formlessly into the next, leaving her with a feeling of unease and grief. She'd hoped to exhaust herself, then escape into sleep. After all the chattering about wedding dresses and wedding nights, she *had* been exhausted. But a sleep chased by dreams wasn't escape.

When a hand covered her mouth, she shot up in bed, one hand grabbing a wrist, the other groping for purchase.

"Easy." Philip said the word in a whisper directly into

321

her ear. "You start yelling and your relatives are going to cut vital little pieces off my body."

"Philip." The first wave of relief was so intense, she threw her arms around him. He slid easily to the bed with her, then cut off even her murmur with his mouth. That was it, the taste he'd needed, craved, all evening. He hadn't known need could build so high in a matter of hours, or that worry could press like an anvil's weight on the back of the neck.

"I've been going crazy," he muttered against her throat. "Wondering when I could talk to you, touch you. I want you, Addy." He nipped lightly at her ear. "Now."

On a murmured agreement she combed her fingers through his hair. The next instant she was shoving him aside and sitting up. "Goddammit, what are you doing in here? Do you know what will happen if they find you?"

"I missed you too."

"This isn't a joke. They still have public beheadings near the suqs."

"I don't intend to lose my head over you." He took her hand and brought it to his lips. "Any more than I already have."

"You're a fool." And her pulse was thready.

"A romantic."

"Same thing." Tossing the sheet aside, she scrambled out of bed. "We have to get you out of here, and quickly."

"Not until we talk. Adrianne, it's three in the morning. Everyone's in bed loaded down with lamb and pomegranates."

She dropped back on the bed. Five minutes longer wouldn't hurt, she told herself. And it was so good to have him there. "How did you get into the women's quarters?"

"The tunnel." He'd been right. He could find a mole in the dark.

"Good God, Philip, if you'd been seen—"

"Wasn't."

"Will you listen to me?"

"I'm all ears."

"And hands." She batted them away. "It's a foolish enough risk for you to be out of your own wing, but here . . ." She paused long enough to pull his light and clever fingers away from the buttons on her nightshirt. "How did you find my room?"

"I have my ways."

"Philip."

"A little tracking device on your makeup case."

With a sound of disgust she rose to pace. "You've been with Interpol too long. If you keep treating this like something out of a spy novel, you are going to lose your head."

"I needed to see you. I needed to see that you were all right."

"I appreciate that, but you were supposed to wait until I contacted you."

"I didn't. Would you like to waste time arguing about it?"

"No." She didn't think it was wise to risk the lamp, but lighted two candles instead. "I suppose it's best if we do talk after Abdu's little bombshell."

"I'm sorry it was sprung on you that way. It was impossible to warn you."

"More to the point, what are we going to do about it?"

"What can we do?" The trace of smugness in his voice wasn't lost on her. "I've signed on the dotted line. I seriously doubt if we can manage to steal the necklace and work out an alternate way of leaving the country in less than a week."

"No." She sat again, trying as she had all evening to think it through. "I've wondered if he suspects something, and that's why he's rushing the marriage."

"Suspects that his daughter's one of the top thieves of the decade?"

She lifted a brow. "One of?"

"I'm still around, darling." He picked up her veil and ran it through his hands. "I find it difficult to imagine that Abdu suspects your intent when you've had Interpol chasing down blind alleys all these years. Isn't it more likely that he wants to have a hand in the arrangements?"

"Out of fatherly sentimentality? Hardly."

"You're not thinking, Addy." He said it quietly because the edge to her voice worried him. "I suspect it's more a matter of pride and image."

She sat a moment, fighting past the bitterness. "Yes, that rings true. Both are enormously important to him." She twisted the diamond around on her finger. "How do we handle it?"

"You tell me." He tossed the veil aside. "It's your game."

"It's going to put you in a very awkward position, Philip."

"A position I'd already decided to put myself in, if you recall. I intend to marry you anyway. Here or in London hardly matters."

In all her career she'd never felt more neatly cornered. "You know how I feel about that."

"I know very well. So?"

She continued to sit on the bed, worrying the ring, working through the stages. "It's only a ceremony, after all. Neither of us is Muslim, so we don't have to take it seriously."

"A wedding's a wedding."

She'd said the same thing to herself. "All right, then, we can go through with it. A Muslim wedding can be ended by Muslim customs. Once we're home again you can divorce me."

Amused, Philip sat beside her. "On what grounds?"

"You're a man, you don't need any to speak of. All you have to do is say 'I divorce you' three times and it's over."

"Handy." He reached for a cigarette, then stopped himself. "And I'll only be out the price of four camels."

"Is that what he asked for me? Four camels?" With what might have been a laugh, she wrapped her arms around her chest.

"I haggled, as you suggested, but I didn't know if I was being taken or not."

"Oh, no, it's quite a bargain. You'd pay more for a lame third wife."

"Adrianne—"

"The insult is to me, not to you." She shrugged off his hand. "It doesn't matter, or it won't once I have The Sun and the Moon. Four camels or four hundred, I'm still being bought and sold."

"We have to play by his rules only while we're here." Gently, he tucked her hair behind her ear. "In a couple of weeks we'll—" The candlelight flickered over her face so that the bruise stood out. "How did you come by this?"

"Honesty." She started to smile when she saw his expression. The look in his eyes had her mouth drying up. "Philip—"

"He did this to you?" He spoke as if each word might break if not handled with care. "He struck you?"

"It's nothing." Panic had her grabbing for him as he rose from the bed. "Philip, it is nothing. He has the right—"

"No." He pulled away from her hands. "No, by God, he doesn't."

"Here he does." She was speaking quickly, blocking his way to the door. Passion threaded through the voice she didn't dare raise. "His rules, remember? It's just as you said yourself."

"Not when they include putting marks on you."

"Bruises fade, Philip, but if you walk out that door and do what I see in your eyes you intend to do, it's over for both of us. There are better ways to avenge your honor, and mine. Please." She lifted a hand to touch his face, but he turned away.

"Give me a minute." She was right. He knew she was right. He'd always been able to think of the game logically, but he'd never experienced this surge of violence. He hadn't known until this moment that he had the capacity to kill. Or that he might enjoy it.

He turned to see her standing in a pool of candlelight, her hands clenched together, her eyes wide and dark. "He won't hurt you again."

The air she'd been holding tumbled out between her lips. He was Philip again. "He can't. Not where it matters."

He crossed to her to run a thumb lightly over the bruise. "Not in any way." He brushed a kiss over her forehead, then one on her lips. "I love you, Addy."

"Philip." She held on to him, her cheek pressed against his shoulder. "You mean more to me than anyone ever has."

He ran a hand down her hair and tried to take it lightly. It was the closest she'd come to giving him the three small words he'd discovered he needed. "I've been into the vault room." When she started to pull back, he just held her tighter. "Don't harangue me, Addy. It's boring. The setup's precisely as we discussed, but I think we'd be better off if we both could take a close look. As to the key—"

"The dummy key I had made up will have to do. It can be filed and adjusted once we need it."

"I'd feel better if we took care of that ahead of time." He

stepped back, knowing that with Adrianne, this would be tricky ground. "If you'll let me have it, I can take it in, say tomorrow night, and deal with that end."

She thought about it. *"We'll* go in tomorrow night and deal with that end."

"There's no need for both of us to be there."

"Fine. I'll take care of it."

"You're being hardheaded, Addy."

"Yes. There's no part of this job I intend to be excluded from. Adjusting the key ahead of time makes sense. At least the preliminary adjustments. We do it together, or I do it alone."

"Your way, then." He touched a fingertip to the mark on her cheek again. "There'll come a time when you won't always have things your way."

"Maybe. In the meantime, I've given some thought to our wedding night."

"Have you?" With a grin he hooked a finger in the top of her nightshirt and pulled her to him.

"There's that, too, but I have my priorities."

"Which are?"

"As it works out, there couldn't be a more perfect night to take the necklace."

"Business before pleasure? You trample my ego, Addy."

"You have no idea how long, how tiring, or how boring wedding ceremonies are here. It'll take hours, and everyone will eat themselves into a stupor. Then we'll be given total privacy. No one would think of disturbing us. Within a day, two at the most, we can leave without anyone being offended."

"I'd say it's a pity you're not more romantic, but it makes sense. And I suppose it's fitting that two thieves spend their first night of marriage stealing."

"Not just stealing, Philip. Stealing a legend." She kissed him quickly, then started for the door. "Now, you've got to go. It's dangerous for you here. If everything goes well, I'll meet you in the vault room at three-thirty tomorrow morning."

"Shall we synchronize our watches?"

"I don't think that's necessary."

"This is." Before she could open the door to check the hallways, he swept her into his arms. "If I'm going to risk my head, it's going to be for more than talk." He carried her back to the bed.

Chapter Twenty-Four

"You will be a beautiful bride." Dagmar, the couturiere who had been flown in from Paris, draped white satin over Adrianne's shoulders. "Few women can wear pure white well. More lace here." She pinned, hunching down, as she was a half foot taller than Adrianne. Her hands were ugly, but quick and clever. She smelled of the fragrance that bore her name and which she had just begun to market. "So that it flows down the throat to the bodice."

Adrianne stared at the reflection in the mirror. Her father worked quickly. It would cost a great deal to have a dress by one of Paris' top designers put together in a week. Again a matter of honor, she thought. King Abdu could hardly send his daughter to her husband in less than the best.

Her fingers began to ache. Slowly, deliberately, she relaxed them. "I prefer it simple."

Dagmar tightened the long sleeves. "Trust me. It will be simple but not plain, elegant but not opulent. Too much this, too much that makes people notice only the gown and not the woman." She glanced up as two assistants entered carrying more dresses. "For the bridal party. We were given a list." She pulled a pin out of the pincushion at her wrist and tucked in the waist.

"I see. And how many will there be in the bridal party?"

Dagmar glanced up for only a moment, surprised the bride-to-be would have to ask. "Twelve. The teal is an excellent color. Very rich." She gestured for an assistant to hold up a gown. It had a festive off-the-shoulder neckline and a full tea-length skirt overlaid with lace. "The choice was left to me. I hope you approve."

327

"I'm sure all the dresses will be fine."

"Turn, please." It was rare to meet a bride so solemn, or so indifferent. Dagmar knew of Princess Adrianne, had hoped to have an opportunity to dress her, but she'd never expected to do so in Jaquir for a wedding so hastily put together. If the bride was pregnant, Adrianne's narrow waist and flat stomach gave no sign. In any case, Dagmar was too discreet to gossip about her clients—particularly when a job could lead to others. She was French; she was practical.

"The train will be attached here." She indicated a spot beneath Adrianne's shoulders. "It will pour out of the dress like a river. Sweep down." With her narrow, ugly hands she gestured. "Very royal. *N'est-ce pas?*"

For the first time, Adrianne smiled. The woman was doing her best. "It sounds lovely."

Encouraged, Dagmar walked back around to fuss with the line. Over the years she had dressed the wealthy and the celebrated, cleverly camouflaging flaws and bulges. The princess had a lovely body, small and beautifully formed. Whatever she designed for a body like this would be noticed and envied. She thought it was a pity a trousseau hadn't been commissioned.

"Your hair. How do you wear it? Up, down?"

"I don't know. I hadn't thought."

"You must think. It must flatter my dress." After patting Adrianne's hair she stepped back. She was a stringy woman with thin, homely features and beautiful green eyes. "In a braid I think. Very French, very subtle, like the dress. But not severe. Soft here." Satisfied, she turned her critical eye on the dress. "You will wear jewelry, something special?"

She thought of The Sun and the Moon gleaming against her mother's wedding gown. "No, nothing on the dress." They both heard the laughter and noise outside the door.

"The wedding party." Dagmar rolled her beautiful eyes. "We will be crazy in a week, but everything will be perfect."

"Madame, how much do you charge for this dress?"

"Your Highness—"

"I prefer to know the price of what's mine."

Dagmar shrugged and twitched at the skirt of the dress. "Perhaps two hundred and fifty thousand francs."

With a nod Adrianne touched the lace at her throat.

She'd earned more than that on her commission from the St. John job. It seemed fitting, if ironic, that it be put to use here. "You will bill me, not the king."

"But, Your Highness—"

"You will bill me," Adrianne repeated. She wouldn't wear something he had paid for.

"As you wish."

"The wedding's in Jaquir, Madame." Adrianne smiled again. "But I'm an American. Old habits are hard to break." In dismissal she turned as the door opened. There was more than the wedding party, but at least another dozen women who had come to watch, to drink tea, to talk of weddings and fashion. Adrianne estimated that Dagmar would have commissions for at least another six gowns before the afternoon fittings were done.

Women stripped down to their underwear. Since lingerie was as much a passion for them as jewelry, it ranged from the gorgeous to the embarrassing. Red garter belts and black lace, white satin and transparent silk. Over the babble of voices gowns were tried on and exclaimed over. There were questions about flowers, about gifts, about the honeymoon. It might have been amusing, even touching, Adrianne thought, except for the headache that was drumming behind her eyes. Perhaps the wedding would be a farce, a temporary measure, even a convenience, but the preparation was very real.

She watched her young sister being basted into a dress suitable for a woman twice her age. "No." Adrianne waved a hand at the woman who was pinning the hem. "That won't do for her."

Yasmin took a handful of the wide skirt. "I like it. Keri and the others are wearing it."

"It makes you look like a child playing grown-up." At Yasmin's rebellious expression, Adrianne gestured to Dagmar. "I want something special for my sister, something more suitable."

"Your father instructed that the wedding party have identical dresses."

Adrianne's eyes met the dressmaker's in the long mirror. "I'm telling you that my sister won't wear this. I want something softer, more—" She caught herself before she said youthful. "More contemporary. In rose perhaps, so she'll stand out among the others."

Yasmin's eyes lit up. "In red."

"Rose," Adrianne repeated.

Because she agreed, and because she was more likely to receive further business from Adrianne than from the king, Dagmar decided to cooperate. "There is perhaps something in the salon I could send for."

"Then do so. Bill this to me as well." She touched a hand to Yasmin's cheek. "You'll look beautiful. Special. Like a rose among ferns."

"I look beautiful in this."

Adrianne turned so that they both faced the mirrors. "More beautiful. It's a tradition for one member of the wedding party, the maid of honor, to wear a gown of a different style or a different color than the rest, so she'll be noticed."

Yasmin considered and approved. She would accept the veil happily when the time came, but whenever possible, she preferred to be noticed. "In silk?"

She had once been a young girl who had yearned for a silk dress. "In silk, then."

Satisfied, Yasmin studied their reflections. "When I marry I will wear a dress like yours."

"You may wear this one if you like."

Yasmin's brows shot up. "Wear a dress already worn?"

"It's another tradition to wear the wedding dress of your mother, or your sister or your friend."

While she considered, Yasmin ran a finger down the satin of Adrianne's skirt. It was an odd custom, she thought, but one—if the dress was right—worth thinking about. "I wouldn't wear my mother's dress. It could not be as beautiful as this. She was a second wife. Why don't you wear your mother's dress?"

"I don't have it. I have a picture. Sometime you will visit me in America and I'll show you."

"Visit you?" She waved away impatiently, and imperiously, Adrianne thought, a cup of tea offered by a servant. "When?"

"When it's permitted."

"We will eat in a restaurant?"

"If you like."

For a moment Yasmin looked like any young girl being offered a treat. "Some women in Jaquir eat in restaurants, but my father does not permit it for the family."

Adrianne took her hand. "We'll eat in restaurants every night."

Philip saw little of the king, but he was treated well. Like a visiting diplomat, he thought, after his thorough guided tour of the palace. He was taken into every room, excluding the women's quarters, while the crown prince gave him a long, often tedious history of Jaquir. While he listened, Philip took mental notes on windows, doorways, entrances, and exits. He watched guards and servants come and go with an eye to the timing and routine.

He asked questions. The book Adrianne had given him had briefed him well enough to know what comments or inquiries would be taken as criticism. So he didn't ask about the women hidden behind garden walls and latticed windows— for their own good. He didn't ask about the slave markets that were still in effect, though conducted in secret. Or the beheadings, which were not.

They lunched on caviar and quail eggs in a room that boasted its own rippling pool. Bright-feathered birds trilled in cages hung from the ceiling. Art and literature were discussed. The camel whippings in the suqs were not. Rahman joined them briefly. Once he'd battled back his shyness, he bombarded Philip with questions about London. His mind was like a sponge.

"There is a large Muslim population in London."

Philip sipped the coffee and longed for good British tea. "I believe so."

"I would like to see it, the buildings and museums, but in the winter when there is snow. I should like to see snow."

He remembered how Adrianne had spoken of her first glimpse of snow. "Then you should come next year and stay with Adrianne and me."

Rahman thought it would be wonderful, to see the great city, to spend time with his sister with the lovely eyes and smile. There would be so much to learn in London, and he wanted badly to learn. He shot a quick look at his brother. They both knew their father's mind.

"You are very kind. One day I will come to London, if Allah wills. You will excuse me, I must go back to my studies."

Later, in an air-conditioned limo, they drove through the city. Fahid pointed out the ships in port as he talked of the excellent trade agreements between Jaquir and Western countries.

There was great beauty here; Philip saw it in the dark distant hills, in the harsh blue of the sea. Despite the traffic and mad rush of taxis there was a sense of antiquity, and, more, of a stubborn resistance to change.

They passed a courtyard where less than five years before a minor princess and her lover had been executed for adultery. In the distance Philip could see the silver column of an office building topped with a satellite dish.

"We are a country of contrasts." Fahid watched a member of the Committee for the Protection of Virtue and the Prevention of Vice grab an unescorted woman by the arm. "There has been much change in Jaquir in the last twenty-five years, yet we are, and will always be, a country of Islam."

Since the opening had been given, Philip pried it a bit further. "Is it awkward for you, having been educated in the West?"

Fahid studied the *matawain* who shouted at the lone woman and shoved her roughly out of the suq. He disapproved of such things, but he was not yet king. "It is sometimes difficult to find the balance between what is best in your world and what is best in my own. If Jaquir is to survive more progress, more compromise will be necessary. The laws of Islam cannot change, the traditions of men must."

Philip, too, had seen the exchange in the suq. "Traditions such as manhandling women?"

Fahid gave brief instructions to the driver, then settled back. "The religious police are dedicated, and it is religion which governs in Jaquir."

"I'm not one to criticize another's religion, Fahid. But it's difficult for a man to sit by and watch a woman mistreated." He was thinking beyond the woman in the suq to Adrianne, and to Phoebe. Fahid had no trouble following the trail.

"On some points you and I will never agree."

"What will you change when you rule?"

"It is not so much what I will change, but what the people will allow to be changed. Like many Europeans, you believe it is the government that makes the people what they are. That oppresses or that frees. In many ways, perhaps in most, it is the people themselves who hold off change. They struggle against progress even as they rush to embrace it." Fahid smiled. There was a jug of chilled juice which he poured into crystal goblets for both of them. "Would it surprise you that many women enjoy their veils? It is not the law. They became popularized by the elite many centuries ago. What became fashionable during Mohammed's time has become tradition."

When Philip drew out a cigarette, Fahid took a gold lighter and flicked on the flame. "You see that no woman is permitted to drive in Jaquir. This is not a law, but a tradition. It is not written that it is unseemly for a woman to operate a car, but it is . . . discouraged, because if she were to have a flat, no man could assist her. If she were to drive recklessly, the police could not detain her. So it is tradition that becomes more solid than the law itself."

"Are your women content?"

"Who knows the mind of a woman?"

Philip grinned. "On that East and West can agree."

"This is what I wanted to show you." As the limo stopped, Fahid gestured out the window. "Ahmand Memorial University. The woman's college."

The single building was constructed out of good American brick. The windows were latticed as much for protection against the sun as to discourage prying eyes. Philip saw three women dressed in traditional garb hurry up the steps and through the door. He also noted that beneath the *abaaya* the women wore Nikes and Reeboks.

"Families are encouraged to have their women educated here in Jaquir. Traditions can be flexible, you see. Jaquir needs women doctors, women teachers, women bankers. For now, this is to make it less complicated for our women to receive medical treatment, to be educated, and to handle their money. It will not always be so."

Philip turned back from his study of the building. "You understand that."

"Very well. I work closely with the Minister of Labor. It

is an ambition of mine to see the people of my country, men and women, strengthen Jaquir with knowledge and skill. With education comes knowledge, but discontent comes as well, and a need to know more, to see more, to have more. Jaquir will be forced to adjust—and yet blood does not change. Women will wear the veil because they choose to wear it. They will cling to the harem because they find comfort there."

"You believe that?"

"I know that." After signaling to the driver, he folded his hands on his lap. He was a poised, erudite man not yet twenty-three. He would be king. Not from the moment of birth had he been allowed to forget it. "I was educated in America, loved an American woman, enjoyed many American things. But I have bedouin blood. Adrianne had an American mother and was raised in the West. But she has bedouin blood. It will course through her veins until the day she dies."

"That makes her what she is. It doesn't change her."

"Adrianne's life has not been a simple one. How much does she hate my father?"

"Hate's a strong word."

"But apt." Fahid lifted a hand, palm up. It was an important question, and the main reason he'd insisted on having this private time with Philip. "Passions of love and hate are never simple. If you love her, take her away after the marriage. While my father lives, keep her out of Jaquir. He, too, does not forgive."

The prayer call sounded, a deep-throated song. With little confusion and no questions doors closed and men knelt to lower their faces to the cracked ground. Fahid stepped out of the car. His robes were silk, but he blended with the other men who submitted themselves to Allah.

Restless, Philip stepped out into the afternoon heat. He could see the muezzin on the steps to the mosque calling the faithful. It was a strong scene, almost humbling, with the baking sun and the hot smells of sweat and spice from the suqs, the robed men with foreheads lowered to the ground. Women stood back huddled in what shade could be found. They might pray in silence, but were not permitted to answer the call. A few Western businessmen waited with the patience of the resigned.

As he watched, Philip began to understand Fahid. The people didn't merely adhere or submit to tradition. They embraced it, they perpetuated it. This way of life revolved around religion and male honor. Buildings could spring up, education could be offered, but nothing would change the blood.

He turned away from Mecca and looked toward the palace. Its gardens were a mist of color in the distance. Its green-tiled roofs shone in the sun. Somewhere within its walls was Adrianne. Would the prayer call draw her to the window?

The device Adrianne carried was very sensitive. For this brief rendezvous she left the rest of her tools hidden in her room and took only the small amplifier, the brass key, and a file. For caution's sake her black slacks and shirt were also left behind. If she were stopped tonight, it would be best if she were found in long skirts.

She used the tunnel, making her way as women had for generations from their quarters to the main palace. Some would have gone gladly, others resignedly. Always with purpose, Adrianne thought, as she did tonight. Her sandals were silent on the worn floor. The way, as it had been from the beginning, was lit with torches rather than with electric light. Their low, sputtering flames added shadows, and romance.

A man might pass there, a king or a prince. But at this hour the palace slept and she walked alone.

She worried about Philip. It was always possible his rooms were watched. If he were caught in the wrong place at the wrong time, he would be deported before they could exchange a word. She might be beaten or confined to the women's quarters, but that was a small price to pay for the ultimate goal.

She came out of the tunnel into the king's apartment. He would be asleep in the bedroom beyond. Alone—whichever wife he had chosen for the night sent back to her own bed after her duty was done.

She could smell him here faintly, in the sandalwood incense he preferred. And she wondered how many times

335

her mother had been summoned to these rooms like a bitch singled out for breeding.

For a moment, just a moment, she was tempted to fling open the door to his bedroom, to wake him out of smug sleep and tell him everything she felt, everything that had sprouted and grown out of those early bitter seeds. But that satisfaction would last only as long as the words did. She wanted more than that, much more.

The guards didn't change until an hour before dawn. Adrianne glanced at the luminous dial of her watch and gauged the time she had. Enough, she thought. More than enough.

The hallway was deserted, dark, silent. From the blueprint in her mind she turned down it and made her way to the adjoining wing. She moved to the door of the vault room and, crouching, began to pick the lock. Her hands were steady enough, but they were sweating. Annoyed, she wiped them on her skirt before she finished the job. With a quick look right and left she slipped inside, then shut and locked the door behind her.

When a hand clamped over her mouth, her heart stopped. When it started again, she swore at Philip. Jerking away, she switched the narrow beam of her flashlight in his face.

"You do that again, you're going to lose that hand."

"Glad to see you too." He bent to kiss her. "Had a little trouble with the lock, did you?"

"No." She started to brush by him, then turned and threw her arms around his neck. "Philip, I didn't know I'd miss you so much."

He nuzzled into her hair, into the scent, into the texture. "Well. It gets better and better. What were you doing all day while I was getting a tour of the city?"

"Drinking endless cups of tea, listening to a recital on fertility and childbirth, and being fitted for my wedding dress."

"You don't sound as if you enjoyed any of it."

"It's difficult, I didn't know how difficult to deceive my grandmother. And I don't like being pinned into white satin for a wedding that's only a show."

"Then we'll make it more."

He said it lightly, but she couldn't find any amusement

in his eyes. "You know how I feel about that, and this isn't the time to discuss it. Have you looked at the vault?"

"Top to bottom." He shone his light on the steel door. "From the specs, there's an alarm wired to each lock. Time-consuming, but fairly straightforward. We'll clamp those as you suggested. I've a good feel for combinations, so it shouldn't take long."

"This should help." She handed him a dial as thick as his thumb and half again as wide as a quarter. "It's an amplifier. I've been working on it for a while. Put it against the door there and it should pick up a sneeze three rooms away."

Thoughtful, Philip played his light over it. "You designed this?"

"Redesigned, really. I wanted something compact as well as sensitive."

"For someone who didn't finish school, you do have an amazing knack for electronics."

"Natural talent. I estimate an hour to open the vault."

"Forty minutes, fifty on the outside."

"Let's give it sixty." She smiled and touched his cheek. "No reflection on your talent, darling."

"A thousand pounds says I do it in forty."

"Done. Now then, you won't be able to start safely until three. At two-thirty I'll start on the alarms. It'll work more smoothly if you come directly here. Don't touch anything until three. I'll join you as soon as I can."

"I don't like the idea of your handling that part alone."

"I'd be handling the entire job alone if I had my way. Start with the top dial and work down."

"We've been over this, Addy. I know how to open a vault."

She walked past him, drawing out the key. "Don't let your ego get in the way."

"I won't, I'm too busy dodging yours. How can I be sure you've cut the alarms?"

"Faith." At his expression she lifted her chin. "I've worked too hard, planned too carefully to make a mistake now. Trust me, or leave me to it."

He watched her run the file delicately over the key. "I'm not used to working with a partner."

"Neither am I."

337

"Then it's fortunate that we're both retiring after this. Addy, I'd feel better if you weren't so tense."

"I'd feel better if you were in London." She held up a hand before he could speak. "We may not have a chance to talk this through again. If anything goes wrong, if it looks like something's going wrong, I want you to bail out. Promise me."

"You won't."

"Can't. There's a difference."

"You still don't understand, do you?" He caught her chin in his hand, fingers tense. "It still isn't getting through. You can make noises all you want about not believing in love, not being able to feel it or accept it, but that doesn't change the way I feel about you. There's going to come a time, Addy, when this is behind us and it'll be just you and me. You're going to have to deal with that."

"This is a job, it has nothing to do with love."

"Doesn't it? You're in this as much because you loved your mother as because you hate your father. Maybe more. I'm here because everything you are and feel is important to me."

"Philip." She put a hand lightly to his wrist. "I never know what to say to you."

"It'll come to you." Always one to take advantage of the moment, he drew her closer. "Are you going to invite me back to your room?"

"I'd like to." She closed her eyes and enjoyed the kiss. "But I can't. How about a raincheck?"

"As long as it's soon."

She turned away to fit the key into the lock again. Her ears were tuned to hear the slight grate of metal on metal where it didn't slide true. "I can't risk unlocking it now. The more detailed filing has to wait until the alarms are off. But I think . . ." She slipped the key in, then out again. "It's going to be close." She stopped, and with the key still warm in her hand stared at the door. "It's just beyond there, only a few feet away. I'm surprised we can't feel the heat."

"Have you ever considered keeping it?"

"When I was young. I'd imagine it—imagine putting it around my mother's neck and watching the life come back into her face. I imagined putting it around my own and feeling..."

"Feeling what?"

She smiled a little. "Like a princess." She dropped the key back into its pouch. "No, it's not for me, but for all the tragedy that's followed it over the years, this time there'll be some good." She shrugged, feeling foolish. "I suppose that sounds idealistic and stupid."

"Yes." He brought her hand to his lips. "But you see I only lusted after you before I knew you were idealistic and stupid." He kept her hand in his as they walked to the door. "Addy, be careful. I mean with your father."

"I rarely make the same mistake twice, Philip." She put the listening device against the door and waited until she was greeted with only silence. "Don't worry about me, I've been playing princess for years."

He caught her before she could slip out of the door. "Adrianne, you don't have to play at what you are."

Chapter Twenty-Five

She wasn't convinced he was right. Over the next few days Adrianne had to call on all her poise, all her control. Part of the ability may have been a matter of her royal blood. As far as Adrianne was concerned, the bulk of the talent had been inherited from a Nebraska girl who had once taken Hollywood by storm.

She attended parties—countless luncheons and buffets hosted by various female relatives, where the talk was invariably the same. She listened to advice and answered questions any bride-to-be might expect. She saw Philip in snatches, and never alone. Hours were spent in fittings, more still shopping with aunts and cousins.

Gifts were already pouring in from all over the world. That was one aspect of the deception she hadn't anticipated, but which she'd turned to her own advantage. Gold plates, silver urns, Sung vases from heads of state and royal allies. Revenge that had once been intensely personal had spread to encompass friends as well as strangers. Though they were unaware, princes and presidents had become part of the game.

As was expected, she acknowledged the gifts herself. Time was eaten up writing letters and receiving guests who were flown in for the ceremony.

But there was one, one very important gift that had been sent from New York. It had been Philip's job to call Celeste and request it. Now it sat among the others, a beautifully lacquered Chinese box. A puzzle box with a delightfully complex pattern of sliding doors and springs. In a matter of days, Adrianne would nest The Sun and the Moon in the secret drawer and ship it, as she would ship the vases and platters, home.

The brazen and potentially dangerous plan of smuggling the necklace out on her person could be rejected. Abdu, through his own pride, had given her the perfect route to revenge.

She saw him only once more before her wedding day, and then it was she who was obliged to approach him. Written permission from a male relation was still necessary for a woman's outing, princess or not.

Adrianne stood, hands folded at the ends of her long sleeves. She wore only the diamond Philip had given her, and the earrings which had been a gift from Celeste. The amethyst was already put away. It would be liquidated for the plumbing in the clinic.

"Thank you for seeing me."

Her father's offices were a symphony of royal red and blue. A sword with a jeweled hilt hung on the wall at his back. He sat behind an ebony desk with his ringed fingers drumming impatiently on the surface.

"I have only a short time to give you. You should be preparing for tomorrow."

The pride she'd inherited from him flared. The skill she'd inherited from her mother banked it so that her voice was quiet. "Everything's ready."

"Then your time should be spent contemplating marriage and your duties."

Before she spoke, she forced her hands to relax. "I've thought of little else. I must thank you for arranging everything." They both knew that the cost of a daughter's wedding was another way a man was judged.

"Is that all?"

"I've also come to ask your permission to take Yasmin and my other sisters to the beach for a few hours today. I've had very little time to get to know them."

"The time was there; you chose to live it elsewhere."

"They are still my sisters."

"They are women of Jaquir, daughters of Allah; you are not and have never been."

Keeping her head lowered and her voice quiet was one

of the most difficult things she'd ever done. "Neither you nor I can deny blood, however much we might wish to."

"I can deny my daughters the corruption of your influence." He spread his hands on the desk. "Tomorrow you will be married in a ceremony as is fitting your rank. Then you will leave Jaquir and I will no longer think of you. *Inshallah*. To me you have been dead since you left Jaquir. There is no need to deny what doesn't exist."

She stepped forward not caring whether she was struck for it, or worse. "There will come a time," she said softly, "when you will think of me. I swear it."

That night, alone in her room, she didn't dream. But she wept.

The prayer call woke her on her wedding day. Adrianne pushed the windows open, welcoming the heat and the light. This day would be the longest and perhaps the most difficult of her life. She had only a little time before women and servants would invade her privacy and begin the ordeal of dressing her.

Letting her mind go blank, she filled the huge sunken tub with hot water and laced it with bath oil.

If the wedding were real, real in her heart, would there be excitement, joy, anxiety? All she felt now was the dull throb of grief for what couldn't be. The ceremony would be a lie, as the promises made in such ceremonies from one end of the world to another were so often lies.

What was marriage but bondage for a woman? She took a man's name and forfeited her own, and with it her rights to be other than a wife. His will, his desires, his honor, never hers.

In Jaquir it was called *sharaf*, the personal honor of men. Laws were built around it, traditions grew from it. If it was lost, it could never be recovered. So women of the family were guarded fanatically—or their chastity was, for a man was responsible for his daughter's behavior as long as she lived. In place of freedom they were given servants, an absence of physical labor, and empty lives. This gilt-edged slavery went on and on as women allowed themselves to be sold into marriage, just as she, for the price of revenge, was allowing herself to be.

Sweet Revenge

But what her father had said had been true. She wasn't a woman of Jaquir, and Philip had no bedouin blood. It was all pretense, all masquerade. On this, the most important day of her life, the day she had waited for since childhood, she had to remember that. She might have had the blood of Abdu in her veins, but she was not his daughter.

When it was over, when the long fanfare of celebration had ended, she would do what she had come to do. What she had sworn to do. Revenge, still hot after so many years, would be both wild and sweet.

When it was done, all ties to family would be irrevocably severed. She would suffer for that, ache for that. Adrianne knew it already. There was a price for everything.

The women of the house joined her while she was still damp from her bath. They came to scent her skin, to scent her hair, to darken her eyes with kohl, and redden her lips. It became like a dream, the incessant music of the drums, the feel of fingertips on her skin, the sound of women's voices murmuring. Her grandmother sat in a gilded chair instructing, approving, dabbing her eyes.

"Do you remember your wedding day, Grandmother?"

The sigh came, as thin and fragile as her bones. "A woman does not forget the day she truly became a woman."

They slipped silk over Adrianne's body, sheer, embroidered white on white. "How did you feel?"

Jiddah smiled, remembering. She was old for a woman of her culture, but she remembered being a girl. "He was handsome and straight, and so young. You have the look of him, as does your father. We were cousins, but he was much older, as is fitting. I was honored to be chosen for him, afraid I would not please him." Then she laughed, and her sexuality, undimmed, flashed in her eyes. "But that night I was no longer afraid."

Jokes were made about the wedding night to come, some with amusement, some with envy. Hands were in Adrianne's hair, braiding, crimping, curling while smoke from incense was fanned into it. Adrianne couldn't find it in her heart to object.

Most of the women were shooed out when the couturiere arrived with the wedding gown. With tongue clicking and muttered instructions, Dagmar helped Adrianne into the

343

dress. She had had enough of paradise and wanted Paris, where the worst a woman could expect on an afternoon stroll were a few whistles and propositions. There were oohs and aahs as she fastened an array of two dozen covered buttons.

"You make a magnificent bride, Your Highness. Wait." Dagmar gestured impatiently for the headdress. "I want you to see the full effect when you look."

Filmy tulle was draped in front of her eyes. A veil, even now. Only more of a dream, Adrianne thought as she looked out in the misty light. The mirror was turned and she saw herself draped in icy white satin and stiff lace with a luxurious train that gleamed in the light as it poured to the far end of the room. Seamstresses had worked more than a hundred combined hours sewing on the pearls that adorned it. The headdress glittered, a small crown of pearls and diamonds circling before it fell into yards of thin tulle.

"You look stunning. The dress is everything I promised."

"Yes, and more. Thank you."

"It's been a pleasure." And a relief to be done with it. "I'd like to wish you happiness, Your Highness. May today be everything you want."

She thought of The Sun and the Moon. "It will be."

She accepted the bouquet of orchids and white roses.

She was a bride, but there would be no wedding march, no shoes tied to a bumper, no rice thrown. It made it easier somehow to pretend it was only a show, one more part of the game.

With her hands cool and steady, her heartbeat easy, she followed her attendants into the room where she would be presented to her husband and the men of her family.

She took his breath away. There was no other way for him to describe it. One moment he was breathing, thinking like any man, and the next, the moment he saw her, everything stopped. Even his fingers went numb. The nerves he thought he didn't have reached up and grabbed him by the throat.

She was kissed by each male relative in turn, sometimes solemnly, sometimes joyfully. Then stiffly by her father. Abdu took her hand and placed it in Philip's. And he was finished with her.

They were blessed. Words from the Koran were read,

but in Arabic, so Philip understood nothing except her hand was cold in his and just beginning to tremble.

She hadn't known he would wear the white *throbe* and headdress of Islam. It should have made it only more unreal, but somehow it struck her that no matter how much she pretended or denied, the marriage was fact. It would be temporary and easily dissolved, but today it was real.

It was more than an hour before the procession began. It was heralded by a shout, then the traditional clicking of tongues of the bedouin women waiting in the wedding hall. He could hear the drums and the music as they began the long walk.

Tonight they would walk through these halls again, in secret.

"Is that it?"

She nearly jolted at Philip's whisper, then told herself it was time to see the humor of it. "Not by a long chalk. The wedding guests need to be entertained. Musicians and dancers go down first. You aren't allowed to see them." She gave him a quick smile. "It shouldn't take more than twenty minutes."

"And then?"

"The bridal party. We'll walk down between the chairs. There'll be a podium of some kind set up. Lots of flowers. We'll sit up there for the ceremony, then to receive congratulations for the next two hours."

"Two—lovely," he muttered. "Do they feed us?"

She wanted to kiss him for that, if only that. Instead, she laughed. "After, at the wedding feast. Why are you dressed like that?"

Because her father had requested it, but he thought it best not to say so. "When in Rome," he said easily. Then there was no more time for talk.

She hadn't exaggerated about the flowers. There were walls of them reaching from floor to ceiling. The only thing more stunning were the jewels draped over the women privileged to have been invited. Nor had she exaggerated about the time. They sat under a bower and shook hands and exchanged kisses and good wishes for more than two hours while the scent of roses and heavy perfume had a headache pounding behind his eyes.

But there was still more to come. They were ushered, herded, Philip thought, into a huge room with one narrow doorway. In it were table after table loaded with food, sugared fruits, glossy desserts, spiced meats. In the center was a cake that towered twenty layers high.

Someone had smuggled in a Polaroid camera, and women were gleefully posing then secreting away the pictures. Philip begged one of himself and Adrianne, then tucked it away.

Eight hours after she had put on her wedding gown, she and Philip were ushered to the rooms where they would spend their first night as husband and wife.

"Well," she managed when the door was closed and the last giggle had died away. "That was quite a show."

"It was missing only one thing."

"Mud wrestlers?"

"Such a cynic." He took her hands before she could remove her headdress. "I haven't kissed the bride."

She relaxed enough to smile. "There's still time."

She leaned to him, leaned on him. Just this once. That's what she told herself. Just this once she'd let herself believe in happily ever after. The scent of flowers still lingered. Her dress rustled as he wrapped his arms around her. His kiss was warm, solid, and more than anything what she needed.

"You're so beautiful, Addy. I almost swallowed my tongue when you walked into that room."

"I wasn't nervous until I saw you." She rested her head against his shoulder. "I'll never be able to pay you back for what you're doing for me."

"When things are done for selfish purposes, there's no reason to pay back. We're leaving tomorrow."

"But—"

"I've already told your father." After unpinning her headdress, he set it aside. His fingers were already itching to work their way into her hair. "He has no problem with me wanting to take my wife on a honeymoon right away. I made sure he understood we would be in Paris for two weeks, then in New York."

"You're right, it's best. The less I see of my brothers and sisters, the easier it will be not to see them again."

"You can't be sure that will happen."

"He won't permit them to contact me after this. I know that, and I accept it. I just didn't know it would be difficult to give up something I've had for such a short time." She reached her hands to the back of her neck to begin undoing buttons. "We should rest, Philip. It's going to be a long night."

He replaced her hands with his. "Some things come before rest." He brushed kisses over her face as he worked his way down the buttons. "I've missed you, Addy. I've missed the taste of you."

She pushed the robe from his shoulders. "Just this once, you can taste all you want."

The dedicated French seamstresses would have winced when the satin slid to a heap on the floor.

He awoke in the dark and lay still, feeling the weight of Adrianne's body pressed against his. She was sleeping, but lightly, so that he knew if he moved, or spoke her name in a whisper, she would come alert. There was time for that yet.

It was rare for him to sleep at all before a job. The problem with some professions was that they never became routine or ordinary or boring enough to be taken for granted.

The Sun and the Moon. There would have been a time, in the not so distant past, when the idea of holding it, of taking it, would have satisfied him for weeks. Now he wished the damn thing were over, that he had Adrianne tucked up in Oxfordshire before a cozy fire with a couple of wolfhounds at his feet.

Must be getting old.

Must be, God forbid, becoming conventional.

The truth was he was in love, and it still wasn't easy to swallow.

He ran a fingertip over the ring she wore, the diamond circle he'd slipped onto her finger during the circus that had passed for a wedding. It meant something, more than he'd ever expected, or wanted, such an ordinary symbol to mean. She was his wife, the woman he wanted to take home, to show off to his mother, to plan the future with.

Plan the future. He lifted his free hand to drag his hair back from his eyes. He'd taken a big leap in a short time from planning the next evening's entertainment to thinking of children and family dinners. But he'd taken leaps before and always, until now, had landed on the balls of his feet. A good cat burglar needed balance as well as dexterity. He'd need both tonight.

A pity it couldn't have been a simple wedding night. Champagne, music, and madness until dawn. Though he'd had to admit there'd been madness enough before they'd slept. She'd been like a volcano, smoking, dangerous, and the ultimate eruption had left him trembling like a teenager in the backseat of a car. The hesitations and fears she'd brought to their first bed had been swallowed up by the passions he'd seen smoldering in her eyes. The tensions they'd both lived with since coming to Jaquir had been forgotten, if only for a few hours.

They were partners in bed, and now, for better or worse, they'd be partners in revenge. He touched a hand to her cheek, murmured her name. She woke instantly.

"What's the time?"

"Just after one."

With a nod she was up and dressing.

They'd worn white that afternoon. Tonight it would be black. There was no need for words as they checked tools, secured belts. Adrianne slung a thin pouch crossways over her breasts. In it were wire clamps, a remote control, a padded box, her files, and a brass key.

"Give me thirty minutes." She checked her watch, then punched in the stopwatch mode. "Don't leave the suite before two-thirty or you'll risk running into the guard in the east wing."

"We wouldn't have to separate if we moved quickly enough."

Like him, she snapped on surgical gloves. "Philip, we've been over and over this. You know I'm right."

"That doesn't mean I have to like it."

"Just concentrate on the combinations." She rose on her toes to kiss him. "Luck."

Yanking her back, he kissed her harder. "Only the best."

Like a shadow, she was out of the room and gone.

She had to think of it as she did any job, coolly. She'd planned it that way. She'd waited that way. Now that the night she'd waited for all her life was here, she was jittery as a first-time shoplifter at Macy's on a slow day. She moved fast, keeping close to the walls and listening, listening, listening.

Her eyes adjusted quickly to the dark, and here and there were patches of moonlight where a window hadn't been latticed. There were fortunes in the hallways and small parlors—Indian ivory, Chinese jade, French porcelain. They interested her no more than trinkets at a flea market. The guards interested her. Adrianne hurried down the staircase to the first floor.

Here was silence. She listened to her own pulse. Flowers that had been shipped in from Europe for her wedding added a sweet scent. A pair of white doves slept in a gold cage in the midst of a thousand petals. Adrianne slipped past them, past the salons, the great hall, the offices. The door to the security room was built unobtrusively into a corner. Guests should be protected without being bothered with mundane matters such as alarms and weapons. Holding her breath, Adrianne slid the hidden door aside.

She waited five beats, ten—but the darkness and silence remained constant. Her rubber-soled shoes were noiseless as she stepped inside and closed the door at her back. Here the stairway was steep and open. If her timing was off and she was caught, there would be no place to hide and no excuses to be made. Without a light, with no banister to guide her, she couldn't go quickly and risk a fall. Cautious, too slow for her peace of mind, she descended.

Because her heart was hammering when she reached the bottom, she forced herself to take long, deep breaths. A glance at her watch showed her she had twenty minutes to deal with the alarms before Philip touched the first dial. Time enough. Taking out a small, wide-beamed flashlight, she scanned the room.

There were packing crates stacked as high as two men. The layer of dust told her they weren't new. Taking up one wall was a glass cabinet, double locked. In it rifles were stacked like soldiers. Oil gleamed on the barrels. On the opposite wall was the alarm. Trying to ignore the guns at her back, Adrianne went to work.

The system for outside security she left alone. It took her five sweaty minutes to unscrew the plate on the alarm and identify and clamp the first wire. There would be twelve in all, four for each lock. Precisely, with the specs of the alarm focused in her mind, she wove through, going through the color codes in order. First white, then blue, then black, then red.

She glanced up at the ceiling, wondering if Philip was in position yet. Two alarms were disengaged, but the tension remained a solid knot at the base of her skull. The slightest error now, and a lifetime of planning would be dust.

She'd located the last wire and was reaching for a clamp when she heard the footsteps. With no time to panic, she pressed the shield back into place and finger-turned a single screw to hold it before she dove behind the crates.

There were two of them, each armed with a pistol snug in a shoulder holster worn over a *throbe*. Their voices, pitched at a normal range, sounded like gunshots in her head. Adrianne rolled herself into a ball and held her breath.

One was complaining about the extra night work required because of the wedding and guests. The other was more philosophical and bragged about a recent trip to Turkey where he had sampled the whores brought in from Budapest. His wife now had the syphilis he'd passed on to her.

The lights came on before they stopped less than a foot away from where Adrianne tried to meld with the crates. With a laugh the second man drew out a magazine from under his robes. On the cover was a woman, naked, legs spread, with her hand at work between them. Palace guards or not, if the *matawain* had discovered the book, they could lose a hand or an eye. Sweat dripped down Adrianne's neck as the minutes ticked away from her.

A Turkish cigarette was produced and lit while both men pored over the pictures. The smoke drifted over Adrianne and made her head spin with whatever it was laced with. One man reached down to stroke himself before passing the cigarette back to his companion.

She listened to the grunts and the remarks that might have made a long-time prostitute blush. One man shifted so that the hem of his *throbe* almost brushed her foot. She could smell the sweat on him. Bargaining ensued, good-natured at first, then more intense. She didn't dare shift, even enough to look at her watch. Philip would be overhead now, perhaps with his fingers on the first dial. At any moment the alarm could scream. Everything would be lost.

Money changed hands. The magazine disappeared. The cigarette was extinguished and the butt secreted away. Through the pounding in her ears she heard their laughter. They moved on and she waited in torment for the light to go out.

The moment it did, she was up. There was no time for caution now. The dial on her watch showed her she had only ninety seconds to clamp the last wire.

Her mouth was dry. Both that and the nausea were a new experience. When she pulled off the shield it nearly slid through her numb fingers. Forty-five seconds. She braced the shield between her knees and picked through for the wire. Her hand was steady, so steady it seemed to belong to someone else, not the woman whose skin was soaked with sweat. With the delicacy of a surgeon she looped it. Twenty seconds. She slid the clamp over the loop, turned, fastened.

Adrianne rubbed the back of her hand over her mouth before she looked at her watch again. Two seconds. She waited, counting them off. Then she stood, patient, counting off another full minute. No alarm broke the silence. She stopped praying long enough to reattach the shield.

Philip's fingers were nimble, and his ear was keen. He worked with the patience of a master jewel cutter. Or thief. Part of his brain asked the same question over and over as he listened for the click of tumblers. Where was she?

It was fifteen minutes beyond the optimum time they'd calculated for her passage through the halls to the vault room.

Through her amplifier he heard the satisfying clatter that meant the first lock was freed. She'd dealt with the alarm. It was some small comfort. He caressed the second dial, tilted his head, and kept his eye on the door. Five minutes more, he promised himself. If she didn't show in five minutes, he'd go find her and the hell with the necklace. He flexed his fingers like a pianist about to arpeggio. The first tumbler fell just before he heard the doorknob turn. He was behind the door and pressed flat when Adrianne stepped in.

"You're late."

The giggle escaped and told her how close her nerves were to snapping. "Sorry, I couldn't get a cab." She reached for him, held on, and that was enough to steady her.

"Trouble?"

"No, not really. Just a couple of guards with a dirty magazine and some Turkish dope. It was quite a party."

He tilted her head up to his. Her eyes were clear and steady but she was pale. "I'll have to remind you you're a married woman now. Next time you don't go to a party unless I'm invited."

"It's a deal." She pulled back, amazed at how quickly the fear had drained. "Any luck?"

"What a thing to ask. Better start working on the key, darling. I'm almost through."

"My hero."

"Keep that in mind."

They worked side by side, Philip on the last combination, Adrianne on the unwieldy key. Twice he stopped her because her filing distracted him.

"That's that." He stepped back. "I'd almost forgotten what a delightful sound tumblers make." With a quick check of his watch, he grinned. "Thirty-nine minutes, forty seconds."

"Congratulations."

"You owe me a thousand pounds, darling."

She swiped sweat from her brow as she glanced up. "Put it on my tab."

"Should have known you'd welch." Sighing, he bent over her shoulder. "Nearly done?"

"I gave you the easy part," she muttered. "It's a very complicated design. If I take too much off at once, I won't be able to make it work."

"I could try my hand at picking it. Might eat up an hour."

"No, I'm getting closer." She put the key in, turned it gently left, then right. She could feel the resistance in her fingertips. With her eyes closed she could almost see the brass rubbing against the fittings. Pulling it out again, she filed a fraction here, a fraction there, adding drops of oil, then switching to sandpaper for the more intricate work. Her fingers cramped like a surgeon's during a long, tedious operation.

It took thirty more long minutes. At last she slid the key in, turned, and felt the lock give. For a moment she could only kneel where she was, the key still in her hand. All of her life she'd been driven toward this moment. Now that it was here, she couldn't move.

"Addy?"

"It's a little like dying, you know? To finally accomplish the most important goal in your life. To know that when it's done, it's done, and nothing else you ever do will have the same impact." She drew the key out, then placed it back in her pouch. "Still, it's not done yet." Taking out the remote control, she punched in the code. The light blinked red. The diamond on her finger flashed as she set the bypass. The red light winked out and its mate lit in a steady green.

"That should do it."

"Should?"

She turned to smile at Philip. "It didn't come with a warranty."

Because he understood, he stepped back and let her pull open the vault door herself. There was a rush of hot air. Adrianne could almost hear it. Perhaps it was the long-dead queen weeping. She swept her light into the vault, where it glinted on gold and silver and precious stones.

"Aladdin's cave," Philip said. "Every thief's ultimate fantasy. My God. I thought I'd seen everything."

Gold bars were stacked in a waist-high pyramid, silver ingots beside them. There were cups and urns and platters made out of the same precious metals, some crusted with jewels. A woman's headdress with rubies dripping like blood was set beside a crown starred with diamonds. In a chest which Adrianne opened were uncut stones deep enough so that a man could reach in and bury his arm to the elbow.

There was art as well, works by Rubens, Monet, Picasso. The kind of paintings Abdu would never display in the palace but that he would be wise enough to invest in. They caught Philip's eye, taking his attention away from the flash of jewels. He stooped, playing his light over canvases and thinking.

"The king's treasure." Adrianne's voice echoed dully. "Some bought with oil, some with blood, some with love, some with treachery. All this, and my mother died with nothing but what I could steal for her." He straightened and turned to her. "And the worst, the worst is that she died still loving him."

Gently, Philip ran his thumbs over her cheeks to dry the tears. "He isn't worth it, Addy."

"No." With a sigh she rid herself of the rest of the grief. "I'll take what's mine."

She turned her light on the opposite wall, skimming slowly. When she found it, The Sun and the Moon seemed to explode with life.

"There."

She moved toward it. Or perhaps it pulled her. Now her hands did tremble, but not from fear, not from grief. From excitement. It was enclosed in glass, but the glass couldn't dim the fire. Love and hate. Peace and war. Promise and betrayal. One had only to look at it to feel the passions and the pleasures.

All jewels were personal, but none would ever be so personal as these.

Philip played his light over the necklace, crossing and merging the beam of his with hers. "God, it's more than I imagined. Nothing I've ever fantasized about taking compares to it. It's yours." He laid a hand on her shoulder. "Take it."

She lifted it out and held it. It was heavy. Somehow the weight surprised her. It looked like an illusion, as if it might pass through the hands of anyone who tried to claim it. But it hung heavy in hers, pulsing with life, glowing with promise. As the light ran over it, she could almost see the flow of blood that had washed it so many years before.

"It might have been made for her."

"Perhaps it was."

That made her smile because she knew he understood. "I always wondered what it would be like to hold my destiny in my hands."

"And?"

She turned to him, the necklace draped over her hands like a promise. "I can only remember how it sounded when she laughed. My one regret is that I can't give it back to her."

"You're doing more than that." He thought of the rat-infested building in Manhattan that Adrianne was going to turn into an abuse clinic. "She'd be proud of you, Addy."

With a nod she took the roll of velvet out of her pouch and laid the necklace inside. "He'll come for it." She covered the diamond, covered the pearl. Her eyes were as passionate as the necklace. "You understand that."

"I understand that life with you won't be boring."

She took a last sweep with her light. Some carving on the wall behind the empty case caught her eye. Moving over, she studied it. It was old but still clear enough. It might have been carved into the wall with a diamond.

"What does it say?"

"It's a message from Berina. It says 'I die for love not shame. *Allahu Akbar*.'" She reached for Philip's hand. "Maybe now she can rest in peace as well."

Chapter Twenty-Six

It was going to hurt. Adrianne continued to pack as Yasmin wandered the room, stopping here to sniff at a bottle of perfume, pausing there to toy with the petals of a wilting flower. The sunlight streamed through the window and fell over the bright stripes on Yasmin's dress, glinted on the gold she wore on her wrists, her fingers, and at her ears. Adrianne wished it had been the sun that made her eyes ache and tend to water. It had hurt when she'd left Jaquir before, but she'd survived it.

This time she was taking the necklace with her. But she was leaving more behind than she'd ever thought possible.

"You could stay longer, another day." Yasmin watched Adrianne fold a long skirt into a suitcase. It didn't seem fair that she should be given such a beautiful and fascinating sister only to lose her again so quickly. Her other sisters were boring, if for no other reason than she'd known them all of her life.

"I'm sorry. I can't." It would have been easier if she hadn't discovered how simple it could be to love. She tucked away a box that held a wide double bracelet of hammered gold, a gift from Rahman. He wanted to be an engineer—for the glory of Allah. Was it odd, or was it fate, that he shared the goal of her childhood? Adrianne took the box out again, then slipped the bracelet onto her arm. On the lapel of her suit she fastened the jeweled panther. "Philip has business. He's already stayed away too long." And so had she if she had time to regret. She closed the top of the case. It would have given her great pleasure to throw it and its contents of long, concealing skirts and high-necked blouses out of the plane and into the sea. "When you're allowed to come to America, you will stay with me."

"To see the place you told me of—Radio City?"

Adrianne had to laugh even as she cloaked herself in the *abaaya*. "That and more."

"Bloomerdale's."

"Bloom*ing*dale's." Adrianne covered her hair with the scarf.

"It's truly bigger than the suq?"

It hadn't taken much time to know where Yasmin's heart lay. "All the clothes you can imagine in one place, under one roof. Counters and counters of perfumes and creams."

"And I can have whatever I like if I have the plastic card."

With a shake of her head Adrianne picked up her veil. "The salesforce is going to love you." It would happen one day. She needed to believe it.

"I want very much to come and see these places like the subway and the Trump Tower."

"The Trumps will be delighted to see you too."

"It's good to have it to think about while you are gone. But you'll come back to Jaquir."

She could have lied. She'd learned to smoothly enough. Turning, she looked at her sister sitting among the mounded cushions on a chaise. "No, Yasmin, I won't come back to Jacquir."

"Your husband will not permit it?"

"Philip would, if it was what I wanted."

Yasmin pushed away from the cushions. "You don't wish to see me again."

Weary, Adrianne sat, drawing Yasmin down beside her. "When I came to Jaquir, I didn't know you, or Rahman; Fahid was still a little boy in my memories. I didn't think it would matter that I could stay only a short time. Now it breaks my heart to leave you."

"Then why don't you stay? I've heard America is an evil place, with godless men and women without honor." She conveniently forgot Bloomingdale's and Radio City. "Better that you stay here, where my father is wise and generous."

May he always be with you, Adrianne thought. "America is no more evil and perhaps no more good than other places.

357

The people there are like people everywhere, some good, some bad. But it's my home, as Jaquir is yours. My heart's there, Yasmin, but I leave a little piece of it here with you." She took off a ring, a simple aquamarine, square cut and set in thin gold. "This belonged to my mother's mother. Now it's a gift to you, so you'll remember me."

Yasmin turned the stone so that it caught the light. Her experienced eye told her it had little real value. But she found it pretty and was woman enough to be sentimental. On impulse she pulled off the thick gold hoops in her ears. "So you'll remember me. You will write?"

"Yes." The letters might be seized, but she thought she could count on her grandmother to get them through. To please them both, Adrianne took out her pearl studs and replaced them with the hoops. "One day I'll show you all the places I'll write to you about."

Yasmin accepted the embrace. She was still a child and "one days" were only as far away as her imagination. "You were right about the dress," she said. "It made me look special."

Adrianne kissed her again. She wondered if Yasmin's life would always be as simple as the right dress. Chances were she wouldn't see her sister again until Yasmin was a grown woman with daughters of her own. "I'll remember how you looked in it. Come, I must say good-bye to Jiddah."

She didn't want to cry. She didn't want to feel this wrenching sense of loss. But as she knelt at her grandmother's feet, the tears came. This was a part of her childhood that had been returned to her briefly, and after today would be gone forever.

"A new bride should shed no tears."

"I shall miss you, Grandmother, but I shall never forget you."

Jiddah curled her fingers into Adrianne's palms as she kissed her cheeks. She knew her son as well as she knew herself. His heart would never open wide enough to include Adrianne. "I love you as I love all the children of my children. I will see you again. Not in this life, but there is another."

"If I have children, I will tell them all the stories you told me."

Sweet Revenge

"You will have children. *Inshallah*. Go to your husband."

There were other good-byes to be said before she stepped through the garden door. More than one woman envied her the freedom to go. More than one woman pitied her for losing the protection of the harem. She kissed Leiha, then Sara. Both of them carried lives that tied her to Jaquir. She would never see them again, nor the children they would bear. As Adrianne turned her back on them, she wondered if she would ever feel that fierce kind of unity again.

Then the harem, with all its scents, all its symbols, was behind her. She heard the waters of the fountains ringing as she walked through the garden and beyond. The palace, and the memories it held, were behind her.

The car was already waiting. Beside it she saw Philip, and both of her brothers.

"I wish you happiness." Fahid kissed her cheeks. "And a long, fruitful life. I have always loved you."

"I know." She laid a palm against his face. "If you come to America, my home is open to you. To both of you." She stepped quickly into the car.

She didn't speak on the way to the airport. Philip left her to her thoughts, knowing they weren't on the necklace in the box strapped in the cargo hold of a plane already heading west, but of the people she was leaving behind. She looked neither right nor left as they drove through the city, nor did she turn even once to look back at the palace as it shrunk with distance.

"Are you all right?"

She continued to stare straight ahead, but laid a hand on his. "I will be."

At the airport he managed to discourage the wild-tongued Turkish porters who grabbed at bags to carry them to cabs or gates whether the owners wished it or not. With threats and gestures he held them back so that between himself and the driver they carried the bags to the waiting plane. The pilot stood ready, his hand out to assist Adrianne up the ramp.

"Afternoon, sir, ma'am. Hope you had a nice trip."

Philip had an urge to kiss the pilot hard on the mouth for

no other reason than his cheerful British voice. "How's the weather in London, Harry?"

"Miserable, sir, plain miserable."

"Thank God."

"Your room's booked in Paris, sir. And may I congratulate you on your marriage."

"Thanks." He took a last look over his shoulder at Jaquir. "Get us out of here, will you?"

Adrianne had already shed her *abaaya* when Philip boarded. Under it she wore a tailored suit the color of raspberries. Her hair, uncovered now, was in a sleek French twist. He wondered if she knew the style made her seem more exotic than ever.

"Feel better now?"

She glanced as he did at the symbols she'd shed, the *abaaya*, the scarf, and the veil. "Some. How soon before we take off?"

"As soon as we get clearance. Would you like a drink?"

Because she'd already seen the bucket of champagne, she managed to smile. "I'd love one." She started to sit, then knowing she was too restless, paced the small cabin. "Why should I be more nervous now than when we arrived?"

"Natural enough, Addy."

"Is it?" She fiddled with the pin on her lapel. "You're not."

"I'm not leaving anything behind."

She dropped her hand, then linked her fingers. It was difficult to say whether she appreciated or resented the fact that he read her so well. "We've got a lot to work out, Philip, not the least of which is what we're going to do with those truckloads of wedding gifts."

If she didn't want to think about the real reason for her emotional turmoil, he could wait. He eased the cork out with a muffled pop. Champagne raced toward the lip, then retreated. "I thought they were being shipped to New York as camouflage for the necklace."

"They are. We can't keep them."

He sent her a mild look as he poured the wine. "For a thief, you have an unusual conscience."

"Stealing's entirely different from accepting gifts under

false pretenses." She took the glass. He touched his rim to hers, watching her carefully.

"Wasn't the ceremony legal?"

"Yes, I suppose it would be considered so, but it's more a matter of intent, isn't it?"

He knew exactly what his intent was, so he smiled. "I'd say we'd do better to concentrate on The Sun and the Moon than on a few sets of sheets and towels." He watched her brows lift at his dismissal of a small fortune in gifts. "One step at a time, Addy."

"All right. The secret drawer in the puzzle box will hold the necklace safely enough."

"Particularly since it's lined with lead."

"Not as satisfying as strolling out with it around my neck, but more practical." She managed a smile. "It's highly unlikely customs will dig too deeply into Princess Adrianne's wedding gifts. Since I put the alarm back in operating order, it might be weeks before Abdu notes the loss."

"Does that bother you?"

"What?" She fought to shake off the past. "No. No, I might have preferred having a showdown with him then and there, but it would be remarkably stupid to incite an altercation on his ground." The focus now was on the future. "He'll come to me."

"Then we'll worry about that when it happens."

The intercom clicked. "We've been cleared for takeoff, sir. Please be seated and fasten your safety belts."

The little plane sped down the runway. Adrianne felt the moment the wheels left ground. Left Jaquir. The tilt of the plane pushed her back in the seat where she closed her eyes. She thought of her mother and another time.

"The last time I left Jaquir it was for Paris too. I was so excited, so nervous. It was the first time I'd been out of the country. I kept thinking of the new dresses my mother promised I'd have and being allowed to eat in a restaurant." Because that made her think of Yasmin, she shook her head. "Mama had already decided to escape and must have been terrified. But she laughed as we flew over the sea and showed me a book with pictures of the Eiffel Tower and Notre Dame. We never got to the top of the Eiffel Tower."

"We'll go if you like."

Nora Roberts

"Yes, I would." Weary, she rubbed her hands over her eyes. With them closed she could see the necklace as it had looked when she had secreted it away at dawn. Sunlight had struck it. Ice had warred with fire in a combat that had never, would never be resolved. "She left it behind. She left everything behind but me. It wasn't until we were safe in New York that I realized she'd risked her life to get me away."

"Then I'm in her debt as much as you are." He took both her hands and brought them to his lips. He felt the pulse and the power that stirred inside her. "She was an extraordinary woman," he said. "As extraordinary as her daughter and the necklace you've taken back for her. I won't forget the way you looked when you held it in your hands. You were wrong, you know. It is for you."

She remembered the weight. She remembered the glory. And she felt the grief. "Make love with me, Philip."

He unhooked his belt, then hers. Taking her hand, he drew her to her feet. As they stood in the narrow aisle he slipped her jacket from her shoulders and let it fall. When he lowered his mouth to hers he felt the nerves she'd been steadily battling back. Her lips were soft, and parted, and vulnerable. Her fingers, always so sure, fumbled with the buttons of his shirt.

"Silly," she said, and let her hands fall away. "It feels like the first time."

"In a way it is. There are all kinds of turning points in life, Addy." He slipped the blouse from her, then let her skirt slide from her hips. She wore only a filmy chemise and the rings he'd given her.

Slowly, needing to prolong the moment, he unpinned her hair so that it flowed over her breasts. She stepped closer, fitting her body against his.

He took his time, as much for himself as for her. Slow kisses, soft caresses. A murmur. A sigh. As the plane cruised over the sea they lowered to the narrow sofa, wrapped around each other.

There was such strength in him, a strength she had discovered layer by layer. He was much more than a man who offered a woman roses and sparkling wine in the moonlight. More than a thief who climbed through windows in the

362

dark. He was a man who would keep his word, who would stand by her if only she allowed it. A man who would offer both surprises and, oddly, stability.

She couldn't have said when she'd gone beyond her own borders and fallen in love with him. She couldn't have said why it had happened despite her determination to prevent it. Perhaps it had been that very first night when they'd been strangers passing in the fog. But she did know the moment when she finally admitted it to herself. Now.

He felt the change but couldn't describe it. Her body seemed warmer, softer, so that her skin flowed like wine under his hands. Her heart beat like thunder. She pulled him closer, her mouth open on his. The flavor of passion was there, but spiked with something darker, deeper. Her skin was damp, heating degree by degree as he stroked a hand down her—breast, waist, thigh. Yet she trembled. When he lifted his head, he saw her eyes, too, were damp.

"Addy—"

"No." She touched her fingers to his lips. "Just love me. I need you."

His eyes darkened at that, went to smoke in a warning of either temper or desire. But his mouth came to hers gently as he restrained the urge to savage what was offered. "Tell me again."

Before she could speak, he drove her up so that her fingers clutched at his shoulders, then slid off, damp flesh against damp flesh. Her passion poured, a flood into his hand, leaving her gasping but far from empty. He watched her eyes widen and glaze over as her body contracted then went lax under his. Her breath caught as she began the next rise. Now her thoughts were only of him, and her body was like water, flowing, undulating, cresting. Light washed the cabin and beat against her closed lids in a red haze.

She shifted, desperate to give him the same mindless pleasures. His body was a delight, hard and lean, his skin shades and shades paler than her own. She cruised over it now, leaving moist kisses and lines of heat. Through her lips she felt the beat of his heart; with fingertips she sent it racing faster. Some was instinct, some he had taught her. Combined, her knowledge was everything he could have asked for.

She felt his fingers trail down her arms, glide. Their palms met. Opening her eyes, she saw he was watching her. Their fingers laced, gripped firm, like a promise.

She shuddered when he filled her. Then moved to him, moved with him, beat to beat.

The plane rocked through clouds. Locked together, they felt only the turbulence of one to one. Paris was a haze in the distance. It was his name she called out, telling him everything he wanted to know.

"We're leaving for New York tomorrow." Philip carried the phone to the window and looked out at Paris. The city was slick with sleet, the sky gray as pewter. Not for the first time he wished that Adrianne weren't out alone.

"It's big of you to check in."

Philip let Spencer's sarcasm roll over him. "A man's entitled to privacy during his honeymoon."

"As to that . . ." Spencer grumbled and bit down on the stem of his pipe. "Congratulations."

"Thanks."

"You might have let me know."

"It was—ah—a whirlwind romance. That doesn't mean you can slip out of sending a present, old boy. Something tastefully expensive."

"Not putting a reprimand in your file's present enough. Bypassing channels for clearance then sneaking off behind my back to some godforsaken country while we're hip-deep in a case."

"Love does strange things to a man, Stuart, I'm sure you remember. As to the case," he added while Spencer harrumphed. "I haven't neglected it completely. Word from my former associates is that our man has retired. Dropped off the continent for the moment."

"Bloody hell."

"Yes, exactly. I may be able to make it up to you."

"How?"

"You recall a Rubens that was stolen from the Van Wyes collection about four years ago."

"Three and a half—there was a Rubens along with two Corots, a Wyeth, and a Beardsley pen and ink."

"Phenomenal memory you have, Captain. It's the Rubens I may help you with."

"In what way?"

"I've a lead on it." He smiled a little, remembering the way his light had passed over it inside Abdu's vault. Yes, there were all sorts of paths to revenge. "It's possible that the Rubens could lead you to the others."

"I want you in London tomorrow, Philip, for a full report."

"I'm afraid I have a previous commitment. But," he continued before Spencer could shout at him. "I'll be more than willing to tell you everything I know, which is considerable, in a few days. Providing we can come to an agreement."

"What kind of a bloody agreement? If you have information on a stolen painting, it's your duty to tell me."

Philip heard the door open. His smile widened as Adrianne stepped in. Her hair was damp with sleet. At the moment he felt enormous pleasure from watching her do no more than peel off her gloves.

"Captain, I know exactly where my duty lies. Exactly." He wrapped an arm around Adrianne's waist and kissed the top of her head. "We'll have a nice long chat. See if you can get to New York. I'd like you to meet my wife."

He hung up so that he could kiss Adrianne more satisfactorily. "You're cold." He rubbed his hands over hers.

"That was your Captain Spencer?"

"He sends his congratulations."

"I'll bet." She set aside a shopping bag. "How annoyed is he?"

"Very. But I have something that should perk him up. Buy me anything?"

"Actually, I did. I picked up a Hermès scarf for Celeste, and I saw this." She pulled out a cashmere sweater the same color as his eyes. "You didn't pack for winter in Paris. I imagine you have dozens at home."

Perhaps it was foolish to be moved, but he was. "I don't have one from you. Is this why you wouldn't let me come with you?"

"No." She fussed with the hem of the sweater when he pulled it over his head. "I needed to be alone for a while, to think. I checked in with Celeste. Everything's been delivered to my apartment. She unpacked the Chinese box."

"And the necklace?"

"Is exactly where I put it. I told her to leave it there. I prefer to handle it myself when we get back."

"You seem to have it all under control." He tilted up her chin with a finger. "Now, why don't you tell me what's really on your mind?"

She drew a long breath. "Philip, I sent a letter to my father. I told him I have The Sun and the Moon."

Chapter Twenty-Seven

"I have to tell you I'm terribly hurt you got married without me."

"Celeste, I've already explained to you that it was only a ruse."

"Ruse or not, I should have been there." Celeste arranged the new scarf around her neck and studied the results in the mirror. "Besides the fact that if I'm any judge, you'll have to run long and hard to get away from a man like Philip Chamberlain." She grinned, running her fingers down the scarf. "Twenty years ago I'd have raced you for him."

"Be that as it may, as soon as this is over, we'll be going our separate ways."

"My dear." She turned away from the mirror to face Adrianne. "You're not nearly the actress your mother was."

"I don't know what you're talking about."

"You're in love with him, terminally I'd guess. And I'm thrilled for you."

"Feelings don't change facts." She worried the ring on her finger. "Philip and I have an agreement."

"My darling." She kissed Adrianne's cheek. "Feelings change everything. Would you like to talk about it?"

"No." She sighed, annoyed that the sound was plaintive. "Actually, I don't even want to think about it quite yet. I've enough on my mind."

It took only that for Celeste's smile to fade. "I'm worried about you, worried about what he'll do now that he knows you have it."

"What can he do?" In dismissal, Adrianne picked up her coat. "He might want to murder me, but that wouldn't get him back the necklace." She faced herself in the mirror again as she secured the hooks. "Believe me, I know how much he'll want it, how much he'll compromise to get it."

"How can you talk about all of this so calmly?"

"Because I'm bedouin enough to accept my own destiny. This is what I've been waiting for all my life. Don't worry, Celeste, he won't kill me, and he'll pay." In the glass she saw her own eyes harden. "Once he does, maybe I'll be able to see the rest of my life more clearly."

"Addy." Celeste took her hand, holding her back. "Has it been worth it?"

She thought of the roads she'd taken, all of which had led her to an airless vault in an ancient palace. Involuntarily, she reached up to touch the hoops in her ears. "It has to be. It will be."

She left, deciding to walk the few blocks to her own apartment rather than take a cab. The street was quiet. It was almost February now and too cold for casual strolls. There would be a few diehards jogging their frigid way around the park, breath pumping out in clouds. Doormen stood wrapped in wool, ears tingling. With her hands deep in her pockets, Adrianne walked without hurry.

She knew she was being followed. She'd spotted the tail the day before. Her father's handiwork, she was certain, though she hadn't mentioned it to Philip. The necklace was her insurance.

Philip would be at his meeting with Spencer by now. There was some secret there, she mused. He'd been distracted when they'd gone their separate ways that afternoon. Actually, he'd been distracted from the moment Spencer had called to say he'd arrived.

Not her business, she reminded herself. Hadn't she just finished telling Celeste that she and Philip had an agreement? If he had secrets, or problems with his superior, he was entitled to his privacy. But she wished—couldn't help but wish—that he had confided in her.

She saw the long black limo outside her building. It wasn't an unusual sight, but her heart began to hammer. Somehow she knew even before the door opened who would step out.

Abdu had exchanged his *throbe* for a business suit, his

368

sandals for good Italian leather, but he still wore the headdress of his country. They stood watching each other in silence.

"Come with me."

She eyed the man beside him, knowing he would be armed, knowing he would obey without question any command from his king. Fury might make Abdu want to have her shot on the street, but he wasn't a fool.

"I think it best you come with me." She turned her back on him and held her breath as she walked into the building. "Leave your man outside," she said as she felt him behind her. "This is between the two of us."

They stepped onto the elevator. If anyone had looked, they would have seen a handsome, distinguished man in a dark chesterfield and a young woman, obviously his daughter, in mink. Some might have noted what a stunning picture they made before the elevator doors closed them in.

She was hot. It had nothing to do with the heat of the building or the warmth of her fur. It wasn't fear, though she was well aware his hands were strong enough to choke her before they'd reached the top floor. It wasn't even triumph, not yet, but merely anticipation of the moment she'd waited for so long.

"You got my letter." Though he didn't answer, she tilted her head to look at him. "I sent you another years ago. You didn't come then. Apparently the necklace is worth more than my mother's life."

"I could have you taken back to Jaquir. You would be grateful to have only your hands severed."

"You have no hold over me." She stepped out as the doors opened. "Not anymore. I loved you once, and feared you more. Now even the fear's gone."

She opened the door of her apartment and saw that his men had already been there. Cushions were slashed, tables upturned, drawers tossed out. It was more than a search, more personal, more vindictive. Fury leapt out and into her eyes.

"Did you think I would keep it here?" She moved into the room, skirting the rubble. "I've waited much too long to make it simple for you." She was expecting the blow and managed to step back enough so that it glanced off her cheek. "Touch me again," she said evenly, "and you'll never see it. I swear to you."

369

He clenched his hands at his sides. "You will return what belongs to me."

She took off her coat to toss it aside. The Chinese box lay broken at her feet, but it had done its work. The necklace was once more in a vault. This time in a New York bank. "I have nothing that belongs to you. What I have belonged to my mother, and now to me. That is the law of Islam, the law of Jaquir, the law of the king." Her eyes were a mirror of his. "Do you defy the law?"

"I am the law. The Sun and the Moon belongs to Jaquir and to me, not to the daughter of a whore."

Adrianne walked over to the portrait of her mother that had been ripped from the wall and thrown aside. Carefully, she righted it so that the glorious face was turned toward him. She waited until he looked, and saw, and remembered.

"It belonged to the wife of a king, before God and before the law." She crossed back to him. "It was you who stole—her necklace, her honor, and in the end, her life. I swore I would take it back, and I have. I swore you would pay, and you will."

"It is like a woman to lust after stones." He gripped her arm, fingers digging. "You have no knowledge of their true value, their true meaning."

"As well as you," she said, and managed to pry free. "Perhaps better than you. Do you think I care about the diamond, about the pearl?" With a sound of disgust she whirled away from him. "It was the gift of it that mattered to her, and the betrayal when you took it away and usurped her. She didn't care about the necklace, about the cut, the color, the carats. It mattered only that you'd given it in love and taken it in hate."

He hated having the portrait there, staring at him, reminding him. "I was mad when I gave it, sane when I took it back. If you want to live, you will bring it to me."

"Another death on your hands?" She moved her shoulders as if it mattered no more to her than to him. "If I die, it dies with me." She waited until she was certain he believed her. "Yes, you see I mean what I say. I've been prepared to die for this. If I do, I'll still have revenge. But I'd prefer to avoid that. You can take it back to Jaquir, but not without a price."

"I will take it back, and the price will be yours to pay."

She turned to him. This was her father, yet she felt nothing. Thank God this time she felt nothing. "I've spent most of my life hating you." She said it calmly, flatly, her voice a mirror of her emotions. "You know how she suffered, how she died." She waited, watching his eyes. "Yes, you would know. Pain, torment, grief, confusion. I watched her die a little year by year. Knowing that you should understand there's nothing you can do to me that could matter."

"Perhaps not, but you are not alone."

She went pale, pleasing him. "If you harm Philip, I'll see you dead. I swear it, and The Sun and the Moon's only home will be in the bottom of the sea."

"So he matters to you."

"More than you're capable of understanding." With her throat tight, she played her final card. "But even he doesn't know where the necklace is. Only I know. You deal with me, and only me, Abdu. I promise you the value I put on your honor will be far below the value of my mother's life."

He raised his fist this time. Adrianne braced just as the door slammed shut. "You lay a hand on her again, and I'll kill you." Even as Adrianne stumbled back, Philip had Abdu by the lapels.

"No, don't." Panicked, she grabbed Philip's arm and pulled. "Don't. He didn't hit me."

He spared her a brief glance. "There's blood on your lip."

"It's nothing. I—"

"Not this time, Addy." He said it very calmly an instant before he rammed his fist into Abdu's jaw. The king went down, taking a Queen Anne table with him. The sting in Philip's knuckles gave him more satisfaction than holding a hundred rare stones. "That was for the bruise you put on her face." He waited until Abdu had pulled himself onto the torn couch. "For the rest you owe her, I'd have to kill you, but she doesn't want you dead. So I'll say this, there are ways to maim a man. I'm sure you're aware. Think of them and think of them carefully before you raise your hand to her again."

Abdu wiped the blood from his mouth. He was breathing heavily, not from pain but from humiliation. Not since the day he'd become king had he been struck, or touched unless he had granted permission. "You are a dead man."

"I think not. Your two goons outside are already answering

371

a few questions of my associate as to why they're carrying concealed weapons. That's Captain Stuart Spencer of Interpol. I neglected to mention I worked for Interpol, didn't I?" He glanced around. "We'd better fire that housekeeper, Adrianne. I could do with a brandy. Would you mind hunting some up?"

She'd never seen him look like this. She'd never heard his voice carry this edge. She hadn't been afraid of Abdu, but she was afraid of Philip at this moment. And afraid for him. "Philip—"

"Please." He touched a hand to her cheek. "Do this for me."

"All right. I'll just be a minute."

He waited until she was out of the room, then sat on the arm of a chair.

"In Jaquir you would not live to see the sun set, and you would praise God when you died."

"You're a bastard, Abdu. The fact that your blood's blue doesn't make you less of one." He let out a long breath. "Now that the pleasantries are over, I want to start off saying that I don't give a damn about your ways, not here. What I feel for or about you at the moment doesn't matter either. This is business. Before we get down to it, I'd like to explain the rules to you."

"I have no business with you, Chamberlain."

"Whatever else you are, you're not a stupid man. I don't have to detail the reasons for Addy taking the necklace. You should know that the plan was hers. I came in on it only during the last stages, and though it bruises the pride to admit it, she could have carried it off alone. She slipped it out from under your nose, and it's to her you'll make payment." He paused a moment. "But it's to me you'll answer if any harm comes to her. I should add that if you've any thought of making a deal, then having our throats quietly slit, Interpol already has the details of the entire transaction. Our deaths, accidental or otherwise, will trigger an investigation of you and your country which I believe you'd prefer to avoid. She's bested you, Abdu. My advice is to take it like a man."

"What would you know of being a man? You're nothing but a woman's lapdog."

Philip only smiled, but even the amusement was deadly.

"Would you prefer to go outside and settle this in an alley? I assure you I'm agreeable." He glanced over as Adrianne walked back into the room. "Thank you, darling." After accepting the brandy he gestured to Abdu. "I think we'd better get on with business. Abdu's a busy man."

Her hands were steady again. She deliberately chose a chair between Philip and Abdu. "As I said, the necklace is my property. This is the law, one which would be held up even in Jaquir if the situation were made public. I'd prefer to avoid publicity, but will go to the press here, in Europe, and in the East if it becomes necessary. The scandal would be of little consequence to me."

"The story of the theft and your treachery would ruin you."

"On the contrary." Now she smiled. "I could dine off the story for the rest of my life. But that's hardly the issue. I'll return the necklace to you and forfeit all claim to it. I'll keep silent about your treatment of my mother, and of your dishonor. You can return to Jaquir with The Sun and the Moon and your secrets—for five million dollars."

"You put a high price on your honor."

Hard, unwavering, her eyes met his again. "Not on mine, on my mother's."

He could have them dead. Abdu weighed the satisfaction of seeing them blown apart by a car bomb, assassinated by a silenced bullet, poisoned at some decadent American party. He had the means and the power to arrange it. The satisfaction would be great. But so would the consequences.

If their deaths were traced back to him, he could not hold off the outcries. If it became known that The Sun and the Moon had been taken from him, his people might riot and he would be shamed. He wanted the necklace back and couldn't, as yet, afford to avenge himself.

His ties with the West were hateful but necessary. Money was pumped out of the desert every day. Five million dollars would scarcely lighten his purse.

"You will have your money if money is what you require."

"It's all I require from you." Rising, she opened her purse and took out a business card. "My attorneys," she said as she handed it to Abdu. "The transaction will be made through them. The moment I'm assured the deposit has been made in my Swiss account, I'll give The Sun and the Moon to you or your representative."

"You will not return to Jaquir or have contact with any members of my family."

Her price, and it was heavier than she'd ever imagined. "I will not, as long as you live."

He spoke to her in Arabic softly, so that she paled. Then he turned away and left her standing in the rubble of her home.

"What did he say to you?"

Because it was important not to care, even now, she shrugged. "He said that he would live a very long time, but that to him, and to all members of the House of Jaquir, I was already dead. He will pray to Allah that I will die in pain and despair, like my mother."

Philip rose and tilted her chin up with his hand. "You could hardly expect a blessing."

She forced a smile. "No. It's done, and I expected to feel a fabulous wave of joy, if not satisfaction."

"What do you feel?"

"Nothing. After all this, after everything, I can't seem to feel anything at all."

"Then maybe we should go down and look at your building."

Now the smile came easily. Then she laughed and dragged her hands through her hair. "That might do it. I need to know it was right." When she looked over at her mother's portrait her stomach muscles unclenched. "The money meant nothing to him, but I want to be sure he understood, and he remembers."

"He understood, Addy. And he'll remember."

"Philip." She touched his hand, then drew back. "We have to talk."

"Am I going to need more brandy?"

"I want you to know how grateful I am for everything you've done."

"Mmm-hmm." He decided it best to sit again.

"Don't take it lightly. You helped me turn the most important corner in my life. Without you I might have accomplished it, but it wouldn't have meant the same thing."

"Oh, I doubt it. Doubt that you could have pulled it off

374

without me," he explained. "But if it makes you feel better to think so, go ahead."

"I knew exactly what—" She caught herself. "Never mind. The point is that I want to thank you for everything."

"Before you walk me to the door?"

"Before we each get back to our own lives," she corrected him. "Are you trying to annoy me?"

"Not at all. I'm only trying to be certain I know exactly what you want. Have you finished thanking me yet?"

"Yes." She turned to kick at a broken vase. "Quite finished."

"Well, you might have gushed a bit more, but I'll have to settle. Now, if I have this right, you'd like me to stroll out the door and out of your life."

"I'd like you to do what's best for both of us."

"In that case." When his hands came to her shoulders she pulled away.

"It's over, Philip. I've got plans I've got to start in motion. The clinic, my retirement, my—social life."

He decided he could wait a day or two to tell her she would be working for Interpol. When the time was right, he'd add the fact that Abdu was going to have to answer some tricky questions about possession of a stolen painting. But they had other business, personal business, first.

"And you don't have room for a husband."

"The wedding was part of the act." She turned back. This was supposed to be easy, she thought. Something they should have been able to laugh over before they went their separate ways. "It may be a bit awkward dealing with the press and well-meaning friends, but between us, the entire thing can be dissolved very simply. There's no reason why either of us should be bound by a—"

"Promise?" he finished. "There were a few promises tossed about in there, I believe."

"Don't make this difficult."

"All right, then. We've played it your way until now. We'll finish it your way. How do I go about it again?"

Her mouth was dry. Adrianne picked up his brandy and took a gulp. "It's easy. You only have to say 'I divorce you' three times."

"Just like that? I don't have to stand on one foot and say it under the light of a full moon?"

She set the snifter down with a click. "That's not funny."

"No, it's ridiculous." He took her hand, curling his fingers tight around hers when she would have pulled away. He knew how to figure the odds, had always known. This time he couldn't be sure they were in his favor. "I divorce you," he said, then leaned down to touch his mouth to hers. Her lips trembled. Her own fingers tightened. "I divorce you." With his free arm he pulled her closer and deepened the kiss. "I—"

"No." Swearing, Adrianne threw her arms around him and clung. "No, dammit."

Relief made his knees weak. For a moment, just a moment, he buried his face in her hair. "You've interrupted me, Addy. Now I'll have to start all over again. In about fifty years."

"Philip—"

"My way now." He drew her back so that he could look at her face. She was pale again. Good. He hoped he'd scared the life out of her. "We're married, for better or worse. If necessary we'll have another ceremony here or in London. The kind that requires solicitors, a great deal of money, and a great deal of trouble to dissolve."

"I never said I'd—"

"Too late." He nipped at her lower lip. "You blew your chance."

She closed her eyes. "I don't know why."

"Yes, you do. Say it out loud, Addy. Your tongue won't fall out." When she pulled back he tightened his grip. "Come now, darling, you've never been a coward."

That had her eyes opening. He watched them spit at him and grinned. "Maybe I love you."

"Maybe?"

She let out a huff of breath. "I think I love you."

"Try one more time. You'll get it right."

"I love you." Now her breath came out in a rush. "There. Satisfied?"

"No, but I intend to be." He dragged her down to the ruined couch.

Look for another Nora Roberts favorite,
available now from Bantam Books

PUBLIC SECRETS

Please turn the page for a riveting preview of

Public Secrets

The first time Emma met her father, she was nearly three years old. She knew what he looked like because her mother kept pictures of him, meticulously cut from newspapers and glossy magazines, on every surface in their cramped three-room flat. Jane Palmer had a habit of carrying her daughter, Emma, from picture to picture hanging on the water-stained walls and sitting on the dusty scarred furniture and telling her of the glorious love affair that had bloomed between herself and Brian McAvoy, lead singer for the hot rock group Devastation. The more Jane drank, the greater that love became.

Emma understood only parts of what she was told. She knew that the man in the pictures was important, that he and his band had played for the queen. She had learned to recognize his voice when his songs came on the radio, or when her mother put one of the 45's she collected on the record player.

Emma liked his voice, and what she would learn later was called its faint Irish lilt.

Some of the neighbors tut-tutted about the poor little girl upstairs with a mother who had a fondness for the gin bottle and a vicious temper. There were times they heard Jane's shrill curses and Emma's sobbing wails. Their lips would firm and knowing looks would pass between the ladies as they shook out their rugs or hung up the weekly wash.

In the early days of the summer of 1967, the summer of love, they shook their heads when they heard the little girl's cries through the open window of the Palmer flat. Most agreed that young Jane Palmer didn't deserve such a sweet-faced child, but they murmured only among themselves. No one in that part of

London would dream of reporting such a matter to the authorities.

Of course, Emma didn't understand terms like alcoholism or emotional illness, but even though she was only three she was an expert on gauging her mother's moods. She knew the days her mother would laugh and cuddle, the days she would scold and slap. When the atmosphere in the flat was particularly heavy, Emma would take her stuffed black dog, Charlie, crawl under the cabinet beneath the kitchen sink, and in the dark and damp, wait out her mother's temper.

On some days, she wasn't quick enough.

"Hold still, do, Emma." Jane dragged the brush through Emma's pale blond hair. With her teeth gritted, she resisted the urge to whack the back of it across her daughter's rump. She wasn't going to lose her temper today, not today. "I'm going to make you pretty. You want to be especially pretty today, don't you?"

Emma didn't care very much about looking pretty, not when her mother's brush strokes were hurting her scalp and the new pink dress was scratchy with starch. She continued to wriggle on the stool as Jane tried to tie her flyaway curls back with a ribbon.

"I said hold still." Emma squealed when Jane dug hard fingers into the nape of her neck. "Nobody loves a dirty, nasty girl." After two long breaths, Jane relaxed her grip. She didn't want to put bruises on the child. She loved her, really. And bruises would look bad, very bad, to Brian if he noticed them.

After dragging her from the stool, Jane kept a firm hand on Emma's shoulder. "Take that sulky look off your face, my girl." But she was pleased with the results. Emma, with her wispy blond curls and big blue eyes, looked like a pampered little princess. "Look here." Jane's hands were gentle again as she turned Emma to the mirror. "Don't you look nice?"

Emma's mouth moved stubbornly into a pout as she studied herself in the spotted glass. Her voice mirrored her mother's Cockney and had a trace of a childish lisp. "Itchy."

"A lady has to be uncomfortable if she wants a man to think she's beautiful." Jane's own slimming black corset was biting into her flesh.

"Why?"

"Because that's part of a woman's job." She turned, examining first one side, then the other in the mirror. The dark blue dress was flattering to her full curves, making the most of her generous breasts. Brian had always liked her breasts, she thought, and felt a quick, sexual pull.

God, no one ever before or since had matched him in bed. There was a hunger in him, a wild hunger he hid so well under his cool and cocky exterior. She had known him since childhood, had been his on-again, off-again lover for more than ten years. No one knew better what Brian was capable of when fully aroused.

She allowed herself to fantasize, just for a moment, what it would be like when he peeled the dress away, when his eyes roamed over her, when his slender, musician's fingers unhooked the frilly corset.

They'd been good together, she remembered as she felt herself go damp. They would be good together again.

Bringing herself back, she picked up the brush and smoothed her hair. She had spent the last of the grocery money at the hairdresser's getting her shoulder-length straight hair colored to match Emma's. Turning her head, she watched it sway from side to side. After today, she wouldn't have to worry about money ever again.

Her lips were carefully painted a pale, pale pink—the same shade she had seen on supermodel Jane Asher's recent *Vogue* cover. Nervous, she picked up her black liner and added more definition near the corner of each eye.

Fascinated, Emma watched her mother. Today she smelled of Tigress cologne instead of gin. Tentatively, Emma reached out for the lipstick tube. Her hand was slapped away.

"Keep your hands off my things." She gave Emma's finger an extra slap. "Haven't I told you never to touch my things?"

Emma nodded. Her eyes had already filmed over.

"And don't start that bawling. I don't want him seeing you for the first time with your eyes all red and your face puffy. He should have been here already." There was an edge to Jane's voice now, one that had Emma moving cautiously out of range. "If he doesn't come soon . . ." She trailed off, going over her options as she studied herself in the glass.

She had always been a big girl, but had never run to fat. True, the dress was a little snug, but she strained against it in interesting places. Skinny might be in fashion, but she knew men preferred round, curvy women when the lights went out. She'd been making her living off her body long enough to be sure of it.

Her confidence built as she looked herself over and she fancied she resembled the pale, sulky-faced models who were the rage in London. She wasn't wise enough to note that the new color job was unflattering or that the arrow-straight hair made the angles of her face boxy and harsh. She wanted to be in tune. She always had.

"He probably didn't believe me. Didn't want to. Men never want their children." She shrugged. Her father had never wanted her—not until her breasts had begun to develop. "You remember that, Emma girl." She cast a considering eye over Emma. "Men don't want babies. They only want a woman for one thing, and you'll find out what that is soon enough. When they're done, they're done, and you're left with a big stomach and a broken heart."

She picked up a cigarette and began to smoke it in quick, jerky puffs as she paced. She wished it was grass, sweet, calming grass, but she'd spent her drug money on Emma's new dress. The sacrifices a mother made.

"Well, he may not want you, but after one look he won't be able to deny you're his." Eyes narrowed against the smoke, she studied her daughter. There was another tug, almost maternal. The little tyke was certainly pretty as a picture when she was cleaned up. "You're the goddamn image of him, Emma luv. The papers say he's going to marry that Wilson slut—old money and fancy manners—but we'll see, we'll just see about that. He'll come back to me. I always knew he'd come back." She stubbed the cigarette in a chipped ashtray and left it smoldering. She needed a drink—just one taste of gin to calm her nerves. "You sit on the bed," she ordered. "Sit right there and keep quiet. Mess with any of my stuff, and you'll be sorry."

She had two drinks before she heard the knock on the door. Her heart began to pound. Like most drunks, she felt more attractive, more in control, once she'd had the liquor. She smoothed down her hair, fixed what she thought was a sultry smile on her face, and opened the door.

He was beautiful. For a moment in the streaming summer sunlight, she saw only him, tall and slender, his waving blond hair and full, serious mouth giving him the look of a poet or an apostle. As nearly as she was able, she loved.

"Brian. So nice of you to drop by." Her smile faded immediately when she saw the two men behind him. "Traveling in a pack these days, Bri?"

He wasn't in the mood. He was carrying around a simmering rage at being trapped into seeing Jane again and put the bulk of the blame on his manager and his fiancée. Now that he was here, he intended to get out again as quickly as possible.

"You remember, Johnno." Brian stepped inside. The smell, gin, sweat, and grease from yesterday's dinner, reminded him uncomfortably of his own childhood.

"Sure." Jane nodded briefly to the tall, gangly bass player. He was wearing a diamond on his pinky and sported a dark, fluffy beard. "Come up in the world, haven't we, Johnno?"

He glanced around the dingy flat. "Some of us."

"This is Pete Page, our manager."

"Miss Palmer." Smooth, thirtyish, Pete offered a white-toothed smile and a manicured hand.

"I've heard all about you." She laid her hand in his, back up, an invitation to lift it to his lips. He released it. "You made our boys stars."

"I opened a few doors."

"Performing for the queen, playing on the telly. Got a new album on the charts and a big American tour coming up." She looked back at Brian. His hair fell nearly to his shoulders. His face was thin and pale and sensitive. Reproductions of it were gracing teenagers' walls on both sides of the Atlantic as his second album, *Complete Devastation,* bulleted up the charts. "Got everything you wanted."

Damned if he'd let her make him feel guilty because he'd made something of himsel. "That's right."

"Some of us get more than they want." She tossed her long hair back. The paint on the swingy gold balls she wore at her ears was chipped and peeling. She smiled again, posing a moment. At twenty-four she was a year older than Brian, and considered herself much more savvy. "I'd offer tea, but I wasn't expecting a party."

"We didn't come for tea." Brian stuck his hands in the wide pockets of his low-riding jeans. The sulky look he'd worn throughout the drive over had hardened. True, he was young, but he'd grown up tough. He had no intention of letting this old, gin-soaked loner make trouble for him. "I didn't call the law this time, Jane. That's for old time's sake. If you keep ringing, keep writing with all your threats and blackmail, believe me I will."

Her heavily lined eyes narrowed. "You want to put the bobbies on me, you go right ahead, my lad. We'll see how all your little fans and their stick-in-the-mud parents like reading about how you got me pregnant. About how you deserted me and your poor little baby girl while you're rolling in money and living high. How would that go over, Mr. Page? Think you could get Bri and the boys another royal command performance?"

"Miss Palmer." Pete's voice was smooth and calm. He'd already spent hours considering the ins and outs of the situation. One glance told him he'd wasted his time. The answer here would be money. "I'm sure you don't want to air your personal business in the press. Nor do I think you should imply desertion when there was none."

"Ooh. Is he your manager, Brian, or your blinking solicitor?"

"You weren't pregnant when I left you."

"Didn't know I was pregnant!" she shouted and gripped Brian's black leather vest. "It was two months later when I found out for sure. You were gone by then. I didn't know where to find you. I could have gotten rid of it." She clung harder when Brian started to pry her hands off. "I knew people who could have fixed it for me, but I was scared, more scared of that than of having it."

"So she had a kid." Johnno sat on the arm of a chair and pulled out a Gauloise, which he lit with a heavy gold lighter. In the past two years he'd gotten very comfortable with expensive habits. "That don't mean it was yours, Bri."

"It's his, you freaking fag."

"My, my." Unperturbed, Johnno drew on the cigarette, then blew the smoke lightly but directly into her face. "Quite the lady, aren't we?"

"Back off, Johnno." Pete's voice remained low and calm. "Miss Palmer, we're here to settle this whole matter quietly."

And that, she thought, was her ace in the hole. "I'll just bet you'd like to keep it quiet. You know I wasn't with anybody else back then, Brian." She leaned into him, letting her breasts press and flatten against his chest. "You remember that Christmas, the last Christmas we were together. We got high and a little crazy. We never used anything. Emma, she'll be three next September."

He remembered, though he wished he didn't. He'd been nineteen and full of music and rage. Someone had brought cocaine and after he'd snorted for the first time he'd felt like a thoroughbred stud. Quivering to fuck.

"So you had a baby and you think she's mine. Why did you wait until now to tell me about her?"

"I told you I couldn't find you at first." Jane moistened her lips and wished she'd had just one more drink. She didn't think it would be wise to tell him she'd enjoyed playing the martyr for a while, the poor, unwed mother, all alone. And there'd been a man or two along the way to ease the road.

"I went on this program, they have them for girls who get in trouble. I thought maybe I'd give her away, you know, for adoption. After I had her, I couldn't, because she looked just like you. I thought if I gave her up, you'd find out about it and get mad at me. I was afraid you wouldn't give me another chance."

She started to cry, big fat tears that smeared her heavy makeup. They were uglier, and more disturbing, because they were sincere. "I always knew you'd come back, Brian. I started hearing your songs on the radio, seeing posters of you in the record store. You were on your way. I always knew you'd make it, but, Jesus, I never knew you'd be so big. I started thinking—"

"I'll bet you did," Johnno murmured.

"I started thinking," she said between her teeth. "That you'd want to know about the kid. I went back to your old place, but you'd moved and nobody would tell me where. But I thought about you every day. Look."

Taking his arm she pointed to the pictures she'd crowded on the walls of the flat. "I cut out everything I could find about you and saved it."

He looked at himself reproduced a dozen times. His stomach turned. "Jesus."

"I called your record company, and I even went there, but they treated me like I was nobody. I told them I was the mother of Brian McAvoy's baby daughter, and they had me tossed out." She didn't add that she'd been drunk and had attacked the receptionist. "I started reading about you and Beverly Wilson, and I got desperate. I knew she couldn't mean anything to you, not after what we had. But I had to talk to you somehow."

"Calling Bev's flat and raving like a maniac wasn't the best way to go about it."

"I had to talk to you, to make you listen. You don't know what it's like, Bri, worrying about how to pay the rent, whether you've got enough for food. I can't buy pretty dresses anymore or go out at night."

"Is money what you want?"

She hesitated just an instant too long. "I want you, Bri, I always have."

Johnno tapped out his cigarette in the base of a plastic plant. "You know, Bri, there's been a lot of talk about this kid, but I don't see any sign of her." He rose, and in a habitual gesture, shook back his gleaming mop of dark hair. "Ready to split?"

Jane sent him a vicious look. "Emma's in the bedroom. And I'm not having all of your troop in there. This is between Brian and me."

Johnno grinned at her. "You always did your best work in the bedroom, didn't you, luv?" Their eyes held for a moment, the disgust they had always felt for each other clear. "Bri, she was a first-rate whore once upon a time, but she's second-rate now. Can we get on?"

"You bloody queer." Jane leaped at him before Brian caught her around the waist. "You wouldn't know what to do with a real woman if she bit you on the dick."

He continued to grin, but his eyes frosted over. "Care to give it a shot, dearie?"

"Always could count on you to keep things running smoothly, Johnno," Brian muttered as he twisted Jane around in his arms. "You said this business was with me, then keep it with me. I'll have a look at the girl."

"Not them two." She snarled at Johnno as he shrugged and pulled out another cigarette. "Just you. I want to keep it private."

"Fine. Wait here." He kept his hand on Jane's arm as she walked to the bedroom. It was empty. "I'm tired of the game, Jane."

"She's hiding. All these people put her off, that's all. Emma! Come here to your mam right now." Jane dropped to her knees beside the bed, then scrambled up to search through the narrow closet. "She's probably in the loo." Rushing out, she pulled open a door off the hallway.

"Brian." Johnno signaled from the kitchen doorway. "Something here you might want to see." He held up a glass, toasting Jane, "You don't mind if I have a drink, do you, luv? The bottle was open." He jerked the thumb of his free hand toward the cabinet under the sink.

The stale scent was stronger there, old liquor, ripening garbage, molding rags. Brian's shoes stuck to the linoleum as he crossed to the cupboard, then crouched. He pulled open the door and peered inside.

He couldn't see the girl clearly, only that she was hunched back in the corner, her blond hair in her eyes and something black hugged in her arms. He felt his stomach turn over, but tried to smile.

"Hello there."

Emma buried her face in the furry black bundle she held.

"Nasty little brat. I'll teach you to hide from me." Jane started to make a grab, but a look from Brian stopped her. He held out a hand and smiled again.

"I don't think I can fit in there with you. Would you mind coming out a minute?" He saw her peep up over her folded arms. "No one's going to hurt you."

He had such a nice voice, Emma thought, soft and pretty like music. He was smiling at her. The light through the kitchen window was on his hair, making the deep, rich blond shine. Like an angel's hair. She giggled, then crawled out.

Her new dress was smeared and spotted. Her wispy baby hair was damp from a leak under the sink. She smiled, showing little white teeth with a crooked inciser. Brian ran his tongue over a similar one in his own mouth. When her lips curved, a dimple winked at the left corner of her mouth, a twin of his. Eyes as deep and blue as his own stared back at him.

"I fixed her up real nice." There was a whine in Jane's voice now. The smell of the gin was making her mouth water, but she was afraid to pour a glass. "And I told her it was important to stay tidy. Didn't I tell you to stay tidy, Emma? I'll wash her up." She grabbed Emma's arm hard enough to make the girl jump.

"Let her be."

"I was only going to—"

"Let her be," Brian repeated, his voice flat and dull and threatening. If he hadn't been staring at her still, Emma might have dashed under the sink again. His child. For a moment he could only continue to stare at her, his head light and his stomach fisted. "Hello, Emma." There was a sweetness in his tone now, one women fell in love with. "What have you got there?"

"Charlie. My doggie." She held the stuffed toy out for Brian to examine.

"And a very nice one." He had an urge to touch her, to brush his hand over her skin, but held back. "Do you know who I am?"

"From the pictures." Too young to resist impulses, she reached out to touch his face. "Pretty."

Johnno laughed and swallowed some gin. "Leave it to a female."

Ignoring him, Brian tugged on Emma's damp curls. "You're pretty, too."

He talked nonsense to her, watching her closely. His knees were like jelly, and his stomach tightened and loosened like fingers snapping to a beat. Her dimple deepened as she laughed. It was like watching himself. It would have been easier to deny it, and a great deal more convenient, but impossible. Whether he had meant to or not, he had made her. But guidance didn't come along with acceptance.

He rose and turned to Pete. "We'd better get to rehearsal."

"You're leaving?" Jane dashed forward to block his path. "Just like that? You only have to look at her to see."

"I know what I see." He felt a pang of guilt as Emma inched back toward the cupboard. "I need time to think."

"No, no! You'll walk out like before. You're only thinking

of yourself, like always. What's best for Brian, what's best for Brian's career. I won't be left back anymore." He had nearly reached the door when she snatched up Emma and raced after him. "If you go, I'll kill myself."

He paused long enough to look back. It was a familiar refrain. He could have set it to music. "That stopped working a long time ago."

"And her." Desperate, she flung out the threat, then let it hang as they both considered it. The arm she had banded around Emma's waist tightened until the girl began to scream.

He felt a bubble of panic as the child's, his child's, screams bounced off the walls. "Let her go, Jane. You're hurting her."

"What do you care?" Jane was sobbing now, her voice rising higher and higher to drown out her daughter's. "You're walking out."

"No I'm not. I need a little time to think this through."

"Time so your fancy manager can make up a story, you mean." She was breathing fast, gripping the struggling Emma with both arms. "You're going to do right by me, Brian."

His hands had balled into fists at his sides. "Put her down."

"I'll kill her." She said it more calmly this time, having centered on it. "I'll slit her throat, I swear it, and then my own. Can you live with that, Brian?"

"She's bluffing," Johnno muttered, but his palms were sweating.

"I've got nothing to lose. Do you think I want to live like this? Raising a brat all on my own, having the neighbors gossip about me? Never being able to go out and have fun anymore. You think about it, Bri, think about what the papers will do when I call in the story. I'll tell them everything right before I kill us both."

"Miss Palmer." Peter held up a soothing hand. "I give you my word we'll come to an arrangement that suits everyone."

"Let Johnno take Emma into the kitchen, Jane. We'll talk." Brian took a careful step toward her. "We'll find a way to do what's best for everyone."

"I only want you to come back."

"I'm not going anywhere." Braced, he watched her grip relax. "We'll talk." He signaled Johnno with a slight nod of the head. "We'll talk it all through. Why don't we sit down?"

Reluctantly, Johnno pried the girl from her mother. A fastidious man, he wrinkled his nose a little at the grime she'd accumulated under the sink, but carried her into the kitchen. When she continued to cry, he sat down with Emma on his lap and patted her head.

"Come on now, cutie, give over. Johnno won't let anything bad happen to you." He jiggled her, trying to think what his mother might have done. "Want a biscuit?"

Damp-eyed, hiccuping, she nodded.

He jiggled some more. Under the tears and dirt, he decided, she was a taking little thing. And a McAvoy, he admitted with a sigh. A McAvoy through and through. "Got any we can pinch?"

She smiled then, and pointed to a high cupboard.

Thirty minutes later, they were finishing up a plate of biscuits and the sweet tea he'd brewed. Brian watched them from the kitchen doorway as Johnno made faces so that Emma giggled. When the chips were down, Brian thought, you could always depend on Johnno.

Going in, Brian ran a hand down his daughter's hair. "Emma, would you like to ride in my car?"

She licked crumbs from her lips. "With Johnno?"

"Yeah, with Johnno."

"I'm a hit." Johnno popped the last biscuit into his mouth.

"I'd like you to stay with me, Emma, in my new house."

"Bri—"

He cut Johnno off, lifting a hand palm up. "It's a nice house, and you could have your own room."

"I have to?"

"I'm your da, Emma, and I'd like you to live with me. You could try it, and if you're not happy, we'll think of something else."

Emma studied him, her full bottom lip pushed out in a pout. She was used to his face, but it was different somehow from the pictures. She didn't know or care why. His voice made her feel good, safe.

"Is my mam coming?"

"No."

Her eyes filled, but she picked up her battered black dog and hugged it close. "Is Charlie?"

"Sure." Brian held out his arms, and lifted her.

"Hope you know what you're doing, son."

Brian sent him a look over Emma's head. "So do I."